# THE LAST SÉANCE

COLLINS 💀 CHILLERS

# · THE LAST ·
# · SÉANCE ·

## TALES OF THE SUPERNATURAL BY
## AGATHA CHRISTIE

HarperCollins*Publishers*

HarperCollins*Publishers*
1 London Bridge Street,
London SE1 9GF
www.harpercollins.co.uk

HarperCollins*Publishers*
1st Floor, Watemarque Building, Ringsend Road
Dublin 4, Ireland

This edition 2019

8

A catalogue record for this book is available from the British Library

ISBN 978-0-00-833673-8

Typeset by Palimpsest Book Production Ltd,
Falkirk, Stirlingshire

Printed and Bound in the UK using 100% Renewable Electricity at
CPI Group (UK) Ltd

MIX
Paper from
responsible sources
FSC™ C007454

This book is produced from independently certified FSC™ paper
to ensure responsible forest management.

For more information visit: www.harpercollins.co.uk/green

# CONTENTS

# THE LAST SÉANCE

Raoul Daubreuil crossed the Seine humming a little tune to himself. He was a good-looking young Frenchman of about thirty-two, with a fresh-coloured face and a little black moustache. By profession he was an engineer. In due course he reached the Cardonet and turned in at the door of No. 17. The concierge looked out from her lair and gave him a grudging 'Good morning,' to which he replied cheerfully. Then he mounted the stairs to the apartment on the third floor. As he stood there waiting for his ring at the bell to be answered he hummed once more his little tune. Raoul Daubreuil was feeling particularly cheerful this morning. The door was opened by an elderly Frenchwoman whose wrinkled face broke into smiles when she saw who the visitor was.

'Good morning, Monsieur.'

'Good morning, Elise,' said Raoul.

He passed into the vestibule, pulling off his gloves as he did so.

'Madame expects me, does she not?' he asked over his shoulder.

'Ah, yes, indeed, Monsieur.'

Elise shut the front door and turned towards him.

'If Monsieur will pass into the little *salon* Madame will be with him in a few minutes. At the moment she reposes herself.'

Raoul looked up sharply.

'Is she not well?'

'*Well!*'

Elise gave a snort. She passed in front of Raoul and opened the door of the little *salon* for him. He went in and she followed him.

'*Well!*' she continued. 'How could she be well, poor lamb? *Séances, séances*, and always *séances*! It is not right—not natural, not what the good God intended for us. For me, I say straight out, it is trafficking with the devil.'

Raoul patted her on the shoulder reassuringly.

'There, there, Elise,' he said soothingly, 'do not excite yourself, and do not be too ready to see the devil in everything you do not understand.'

Elise shook her head doubtingly.

'Ah, well,' she grumbled under her breath, 'Monsieur may say what he pleases, I don't like it. Look at Madame, every day she gets whiter and thinner, and the headaches!'

She held up her hands.

'Ah, no, it is not good, all this spirit business. Spirits indeed! All the good spirits are in Paradise, and the others are in Purgatory.'

'Your view of the life after death is refreshingly simple, Elise,' said Raoul as he dropped into the chair.

The old woman drew herself up.

'I am a good Catholic, Monsieur.'

She crossed herself, went towards the door, then paused, her hand on the handle.

'Afterwards when you are married, Monsieur,' she said pleadingly, 'it will not continue—all this?'

Raoul smiled at her affectionately.

'You are a good faithful creature, Elise,' he said, 'and devoted to your mistress. Have no fear, once she is my wife, all this "spirit business" as you call it, will cease. For Madame Daubreuil there will be no more *séances*.'

Elise's face broke into smiles.

'Is it true what you say?' she asked eagerly.

The other nodded gravely.

'Yes,' he said, speaking almost more to himself than to her. 'Yes, all this must end. Simone has a wonderful gift and she has used it freely, but now she has done her part. As you have justly observed, Elise, day by day she gets whiter and thinner. The life of a medium is a particularly trying and arduous one, involving a terrible nervous strain. All the same, Elise, your mistress is the most wonderful medium in Paris—more, in France. People from all over the world come to her because they know that with her there is no trickery, no deceit.'

Elise gave a snort of contempt.

'Deceit! Ah, no, indeed. Madame could not deceive a new-born babe if she tried.'

'She is an angel,' said the young Frenchman with fervour. 'And I—I shall do everything a man can to make her happy. You believe that?'

Elise drew herself up, and spoke with a certain simple dignity.

'I have served Madame for many years, Monsieur. With all respect I may say that I love her. If I did not believe that you adored her as she deserves to be adored—*eh bien*, Monsieur! I should be willing to tear you limb from limb.'

Raoul laughed.

'Bravo, Elise! you are a faithful friend, and you must approve of me now that I have told you Madame is going to give up the spirits.'

He expected the old woman to receive this pleasantry with a laugh, but somewhat to his surprise she remained grave.

'Supposing, Monsieur,' she said hesitatingly, 'the spirits will not give *her* up?'

Raoul stared at her.

'Eh! What do you mean?'

'I said,' repeated Elise, 'supposing the spirits will not give *her* up?'

'I thought you didn't believe in the spirits, Elise?'

'No more I do,' said Elise stubbornly. 'It is foolish to believe in them. All the same—'

'Well?'

'It is difficult for me to explain, Monsieur. You see, me, I always thought that these mediums, as they call themselves, were just clever cheats who imposed on the poor souls who had lost their dear ones. But Madame is not like that. Madame is good. Madame is honest and—'

She lowered her voice and spoke in a tone of awe.

'*Things happen*. It is not trickery, things happen, and that is why I am afraid. For I am sure of this, Monsieur, it is not right. It is against nature and le bon Dieu, and *somebody will have to pay*.'

Raoul got up from his chair and came and patted her on the shoulder.

'Calm yourself, my good Elise,' he said, smiling. 'See, I will give you some good news. Today is the last of these *séances*; after today there will be no more.'

'There *is* one today then?' asked the old woman suspiciously.

'The last, Elise, the last.'

Elise shook her head disconsolately.

'Madame is not fit—' she began.

But her words were interrupted, the door opened and a tall, fair woman came in. She was slender and graceful, with the face of a Botticelli Madonna. Raoul's face lighted up, and Elise withdrew quickly and discreetly.

'Simone!'

He took both her long, white hands in his and kissed each in turn. She murmured his name very softly.

'Raoul, my dear one.'

Again he kissed her hands and then looked intently into her face.

'Simone, how pale you are! Elise told me you were resting; you are not ill, my well-beloved?'

'No, not ill—' she hesitated.

He led her over to the sofa and sat down on it beside her.

'But tell me then.'

The medium smiled faintly.

'You will think me foolish,' she murmured.

'I? Think you foolish? Never.'

Simone withdrew her hand from his grasp. She sat perfectly still for a moment or two gazing down at the carpet. Then she spoke in a low, hurried voice.

'I am afraid, Raoul.'

He waited for a minute or two expecting her to go on, but as she did not he said encouragingly:

'Yes, afraid of what?'

'Just afraid—that is all.'

'But—'

He looked at her in perplexity, and she answered the look quickly.

'Yes, it is absurd, isn't it, and yet I feel just that. Afraid, nothing more. I don't know what of, or why, but all the time I am possessed with the idea that something terrible— terrible, is going to happen to me . . .'

She stared out in front of her. Raoul put an arm gently round her.

'My dearest,' he said, 'come, you must not give way. I know what it is, the strain, Simone, the strain of a medium's life. All you need is rest—rest and quiet.'

She looked at him gratefully.

'Yes, Raoul, you are right. That is what I need, rest and quiet.'

She closed her eyes and leant back a little against his arm.

'And happiness,' murmured Raoul in her ear.

His arm drew her closer. Simone, her eyes still closed, drew a deep breath.

'Yes,' she murmured, 'yes. When your arms are round me I feel safe. I forget my life—the terrible life—of a medium. You know much, Raoul, but even you do not know all it means.'

He felt her body grow rigid in his embrace. Her eyes opened again, staring in front of her.

'One sits in the cabinet in the darkness, waiting, and the darkness is terrible, Raoul, for it is the darkness of emptiness, of nothingness. Deliberately one gives oneself up to be lost in it. After that one knows nothing, one feels nothing, but at last there comes the slow, painful return, the awakening out of sleep, but so tired—so terribly tired.'

'I know,' murmured Raoul, 'I know.'

'So tired,' murmured Simone again.

Her whole body seemed to droop as she repeated the words.

'But you are wonderful, Simone.'

He took her hands in his, trying to rouse her to share his enthusiasm.

'You are unique—the greatest medium the world has ever known.'

She shook her head, smiling a little at that.

'Yes, yes,' Raoul insisted.

He drew two letters from his pocket.

'See here, from Professor Roche of the *Salpêtrière*, and this one from Dr Genir at Nancy, both imploring that you will continue to sit for them occasionally.'

'Ah, no!'

Simone sprang suddenly to her feet.

'I will not, I will not. It is to be all finished—all done with. You promised me, Raoul.'

Raoul stared at her in astonishment as she stood wavering, facing him almost like a creature at bay. He got up and took her hand.

'Yes, yes,' he said. 'Certainly it is finished, that is understood. But I am so proud of you, Simone, that is why I mentioned those letters.'

She threw him a swift sideways glance of suspicion.

'It is not that you will ever want me to sit again?'

'No, no,' said Raoul, 'unless perhaps you yourself would care to, just occasionally for these old friends—'

But she interrupted him, speaking excitedly.

'No, no, never again. There is danger. I tell you. I can feel it, great danger.'

She clasped her hands on her forehead a minute, then walked across to the window.

'Promise me never again,' she said in a quieter voice over her shoulder.

Raoul followed her and put his arms round her shoulders.

'My dear one,' he said tenderly, 'I promise you after today you shall never sit again.'

He felt the sudden start she gave.

'Today,' she murmured. 'Ah, yes—I had forgotten Madame Exe.'

Raoul looked at his watch.

'She is due any minute now; but perhaps, Simone, if you do not feel well—'

Simone hardly seemed to be listening to him; she was following out her own train of thought.

'She is—a strange woman, Raoul, a very strange woman. Do you know I—I have almost a horror of her.'

'Simone!'

There was reproach in his voice, and she was quick to feel it.

'Yes, yes, I know, you are like all Frenchmen, Raoul. To you a mother is sacred and it is unkind of me to feel like that about her when she grieves so for her lost child. But—I cannot explain it, she is so big and black, and her hands—have you ever noticed her hands, Raoul? Great big strong hands, as strong as a man's. Ah!'

She gave a little shiver and closed her eyes. Raoul withdrew his arm and spoke almost coldly.

'I really cannot understand you, Simone. Surely you, a woman, should have nothing but sympathy for another woman, a mother bereft of her only child.'

Simone made a gesture of impatience.

'Ah, it is you who do not understand, my friend! One cannot help these things. The first moment I saw her I felt—'

She flung her hands out.

'Fear! You remember, it was a long time before I would consent to sit for her? I felt sure in some way she would bring me misfortune.'

Raoul shrugged his shoulders.

'Whereas, in actual fact, she brought you the exact opposite,' he said drily. 'All the sittings have been attended with
marked success. The spirit of the little Amelie was able to
control you at once, and the materializations have really
been striking. Professor Roche ought really to have been
present at the last one.'

'Materializations,' said Simone in a low voice. 'Tell me,
Raoul (you know that I know nothing of what takes place
while I am in the trance), are the materializations really so
wonderful?'

He nodded enthusiastically.

'At the first few sittings the figure of the child was visible
in a kind of nebulous haze,' he explained, 'but at the last
séance—'

'Yes?'

He spoke very softly.

'Simone, the child that stood there was an actual living
child of flesh and blood. I even touched her—but seeing that
the touch was acutely painful to you, I would not permit
Madame Exe to do the same. I was afraid that her self-control
might break down, and that some harm to you might result.'

Simone turned away again towards the window.

'I was terribly exhausted when I woke,' she murmured.
'Raoul, are you sure—are you really sure that all this is *right*?
You know what dear old Elise thinks, that I am trafficking
with the devil?'

She laughed rather uncertainly.

'You know what I believe,' said Raoul gravely. 'In the
handling of the unknown there must always be danger, but
the cause is a noble one, for it is the cause of Science. All
over the world there have been martyrs to Science, pioneers
who have paid the price so that others may follow safely in
their footsteps. For ten years now you have worked for
Science at the cost of a terrific nervous strain. Now your
part is done, from today onward you are free to be happy.'

She smiled at him affectionately, her calm restored. Then
she glanced quickly up at the clock.

'Madame Exe is late,' she murmured. 'She may not come.'

'I think she will,' said Raoul. 'Your clock is a little fast, Simone.'

Simone moved about the room, rearranging an ornament here and there.

'I wonder who she is, this Madame Exe?' she observed. 'Where she comes from, who her people are? It is strange that we know nothing about her.'

Raoul shrugged his shoulders.

'Most people remain incognito if possible when they come to a medium,' he observed. 'It is an elementary precaution.'

'I suppose so,' agreed Simone listlessly.

A little china vase she was holding slipped from her fingers and broke to pieces on the tiles of the fireplace. She turned sharply on Raoul.

'You see,' she murmured, 'I am not myself. Raoul, would you think me very—very cowardly if I told Madame Exe I could not sit today?'

His look of pained astonishment made her redden.

'You promised, Simone—' he began gently.

She backed against the wall.

'I won't do it, Raoul. I won't do it.'

And again that glance of his, tenderly reproachful, made her wince.

'It is not of the money I am thinking, Simone, though you must realize that the money this woman has offered you for the last sitting is enormous—simply enormous.'

She interrupted him defiantly.

'There are things that matter more than money.'

'Certainly there are,' he agreed warmly. 'That is just what I am saying. Consider—this woman is a mother, a mother who has lost her only child. If you are not really ill, if it is only a whim on your part—you can deny a rich woman a caprice, can you deny a mother one last sight of her child?'

The medium flung her hands out despairingly in front of her.

'Oh, you torture me,' she murmured. 'All the same you are right. I will do as you wish, but I know now what I am afraid of—it is the word "mother".'

'Simone!'

'There are certain primitive elementary forces, Raoul. Most of them have been destroyed by civilization, but motherhood stands where it stood at the beginning. Animals—human beings, they are all the same. A mother's love for her child is like nothing else in the world. It knows no law, no pity, it dares all things and crushes down remorselessly all that stands in its path.'

She stopped, panting a little, then turned to him with a quick, disarming smile.

'I am foolish today, Raoul. I know it.'

He took her hand in his.

'Lie down for a minute or two,' he urged. 'Rest till she comes.'

'Very well.' She smiled at him and left the room.

Raoul remained for a minute or two lost in thought, then he strode to the door, opened it, and crossed the little hall. He went into a room the other side of it, a sitting room very much like the one he had left, but at one end was an alcove with a big armchair set in it. Heavy black velvet curtains were arranged so as to pull across the alcove. Elise was busy arranging the room. Close to the alcove she had set two chairs and a small round table. On the table was a tambourine, a horn, and some paper and pencils.

'The last time,' murmured Elise with grim satisfaction. 'Ah, Monsieur, I wish it were over and done with.'

The sharp ting of an electric bell sounded.

'There she is, that great gendarme of a woman,' continued the old servant. 'Why can't she go and pray decently for her little one's soul in a church, and burn a candle to Our Blessed Lady? Does not the good God know what is best for us?'

'Answer the bell, Elise,' said Raoul peremptorily.

She threw him a look, but obeyed. In a minute or two she returned ushering in the visitor.

'I will tell my mistress you are here, Madame.'

Raoul came forward to shake hands with Madame Exe. Simone's words floated back to his memory.

'So big and so black.'

She *was* a big woman, and the heavy black of French mourning seemed almost exaggerated in her case. Her voice when she spoke was very deep.

'I fear I am a little late, Monsieur.'

'A few moments only,' said Raoul, smiling. 'Madame Simone is lying down. I am sorry to say she is far from well, very nervous and overwrought.'

Her hand, which she was just withdrawing, closed on his suddenly like a vice.

'But she will sit?' she demanded sharply.

'Oh, yes, Madame.'

Madame Exe gave a sigh of relief, and sank into a chair, loosening one of the heavy black veils that floated round her.

'Ah, Monsieur!' she murmured, 'you cannot imagine, you cannot conceive the wonder and the joy of these *séances* to me! My little one! My Amelie! To see her, to hear her, even—perhaps—yes, perhaps to be even able to—stretch out my hand and touch her.'

Raoul spoke quickly and peremptorily.

'Madame Exe—how can I explain?—on no account must you do anything except under my express directions, otherwise there is the gravest danger.'

'Danger to me?'

'No, Madame,' said Raoul, 'to the medium. You must understand that the phenomena that occur are explained by Science in a certain way. I will put the matter very simply, using no technical terms. A spirit, to manifest itself, has to use the actual physical substance of the medium. You have seen the vapour of fluid issuing from the lips of the medium. This finally condenses and is built up into the physical semblance of the spirit's dead body. But this ectoplasm we believe to be the actual substance of the medium. We hope

to prove this some day by careful weighing and testing—but
the great difficulty is the danger and pain which attends the
medium on any handling of the phenomena. Were anyone
to seize hold of the materialization roughly the death of the
medium might result.'

Madame Exe had listened to him with close attention.

'That is very interesting, Monsieur. Tell me, shall not a
time come when the materialization shall advance so far
that it shall be capable of detachment from its parent, the
medium?'

'That is a fantastic speculation, Madame.'

She persisted.

'But, on the facts, not impossible?'

'Quite impossible today.'

'But perhaps in the future?'

He was saved from answering, for at that moment Simone
entered. She looked languid and pale, but had evidently
regained entire control of herself. She came forward and
shook hands with Madame Exe, though Raoul noticed the
faint shiver that passed through her as she did so.

'I regret, Madame, to hear that you are indisposed,' said
Madame Exe.

'It is nothing,' said Simone rather brusquely. 'Shall we
begin?'

She went to the alcove and sat down in the armchair.
Suddenly Raoul in his turn felt a wave of fear pass over
him.

'You are not strong enough,' he exclaimed. 'We had better
cancel the *séance*. Madame Exe will understand.'

'Monsieur!'

Madame Exe rose indignantly.

'Yes, yes, it is better not, I am sure of it.'

'Madame Simone promised me one last sitting.'

'That is so,' agreed Simone quietly, 'and I am prepared to
carry out my promise.'

'I hold you to it, Madame,' said the other woman.

'I do not break my word,' said Simone coldly. 'Do not

fear, Raoul,' she added gently, 'after all, it is for the last time—the last time, thank God.'

At a sign from her Raoul drew the heavy black curtains across the alcove. He also pulled the curtains of the window so that the room was in semi-obscurity. He indicated one of the chairs to Madame Exe and prepared himself to take the other. Madame Exe, however, hesitated.

'You will pardon me, Monsieur, but—you understand I believe absolutely in your integrity and in that of Madame Simone. All the same, so that my testimony may be the more valuable, I took the liberty of bringing this with me.'

From her handbag she drew a length of fine cord.

'Madame!' cried Raoul. 'This is an insult!'

'A precaution.'

'I repeat it is an insult.'

'I don't understand your objection, Monsieur,' said Madame Exe coldly. 'If there is no trickery you have nothing to fear.'

Raoul laughed scornfully.

'I can assure you that I have nothing to fear, Madame. Bind me hand and foot if you will.'

His speech did not produce the effect he hoped for, for Madame Exe merely murmured unemotionally:

'Thank you, Monsieur,' and advanced upon him with her roll of cord.

Suddenly Simone from behind the curtain gave a cry.

'No, no, Raoul, don't let her do it.'

Madame Exe laughed derisively.

'Madame is afraid,' she observed sarcastically.

'Yes, I am afraid.'

'Remember what you are saying, Simone,' cried Raoul. 'Madame Exe is apparently under the impression that we are charlatans.'

'I must make sure,' said Madame Exe grimly.

She went methodically about her task, binding Raoul securely to his chair.

'I must congratulate you on your knots, Madame,' he

observed ironically when she had finished. 'Are you satisfied now?'

Madame Exe did not reply. She walked round the room examining the panelling of the walls closely. Then she locked the door leading into the hall, and, removing the key, returned to her chair.

'Now,' she said in an indescribable voice, 'I am ready.'

The minutes passed. From behind the curtain the sound of Simone's breathing became heavier and more stertorous. Then it died away altogether, to be succeeded by a series of moans. Then again there was silence for a little while, broken by the sudden clattering of the tambourine. The horn was caught up from the table and dashed to the ground. Ironic laughter was heard. The curtains of the alcove seemed to have been pulled back a little, the medium's figure was just visible through the opening, her head fallen forward on her breast. Suddenly Madame Exe drew in her breath sharply. A ribbon-like stream of mist was issuing from the medium's mouth. It condensed and began gradually to assume a shape, the shape of a little child.

'Amelie! My little Amelie!'

The hoarse whisper came from Madame Exe. The hazy figure condensed still further. Raoul stared almost incredulously. Never had there been a more successful materialization. Now, surely it was a real child, a real flesh and blood child standing there.

'*Maman!*'

The soft childish voice spoke.

'My child!' cried Madame Exe. 'My child!'

She half-rose from her seat.

'Be careful, Madame,' cried Raoul warningly.

The materialization came hesitatingly through the curtains. It was a child. She stood there, her arms held out.

'*Maman!*'

'Ah!' cried Madame Exe.

Again she half-rose from her seat.

'Madame,' cried Raoul, alarmed, 'the medium—'

'I must touch her,' cried Madame Exe hoarsely.

She moved a step forward.

'For God's sake, Madame, control yourself,' cried Raoul.

He was really alarmed now.

'Sit down at once.'

'My little one, I must touch her.'

'Madame, I command you, sit down!'

He was writhing desperately in his bonds, but Madame Exe had done her work well; he was helpless. A terrible sense of impending disaster swept over him.

'In the name of God, Madame, sit down!' he shouted. 'Remember the medium.'

Madame Exe paid no attention to him. She was like a woman transformed. Ecstasy and delight showed plainly in her face. Her outstretched hand touched the little figure that stood in the opening of the curtains. A terrible moan came from the medium.

'My God!' cried Raoul. 'My God! This is terrible. The medium—'

Madame Exe turned on him with a harsh laugh.

'What do I care for your medium?' she cried. 'I want my child.'

'You are mad!'

'My child, I tell you. Mine! My own! My own flesh and blood! My little one come back to me from the dead, alive and breathing.'

Raoul opened his lips, but no words would come. She was terrible, this woman! Remorseless, savage, absorbed by her own passion. The baby lips parted, and for the third time the same word echoed:

'*Maman!*'

'Come then, my little one,' cried Madame Exe.

With a sharp gesture she caught up the child in her arms. From behind the curtains came a long-drawn scream of utter anguish.

'Simone!' cried Raoul. 'Simone!'

He was aware vaguely of Madame Exe rushing past him,

of the unlocking of the door, of the retreating footsteps down the stairs.

From behind the curtains there still sounded the terrible high long-drawn scream—such a scream as Raoul had never heard. It died away in a horrible kind of gurgle. Then there came the thud of a body falling . . .

Raoul was working like a maniac to free himself from his bonds. In his frenzy he accomplished the impossible, snapping the rope by sheer strength. As he struggled to his feet, Elise rushed in crying, 'Madame!'

'Simone!' cried Raoul.

Together they rushed forward and pulled the curtain.

Raoul staggered back.

'My God!' he murmured. 'Red—all red . . .'

Elise's voice came beside him harsh and shaking.

'So Madame is dead. It is ended. But tell me, Monsieur, what has happened. *Why is Madame all shrunken away—why is she half her usual size*? *What has been happening here*?'

'I do not know,' said Raoul.

His voice rose to a scream.

'I do not know. I do not know. But I think—I am going mad . . . Simone! Simone!'

# IN A GLASS DARKLY

I've no explanation of this story. I've no theories about the why and wherefore of it. It's just a thing—that happened.

All the same, I sometimes wonder how things would have gone if I'd noticed at the time just that one essential detail that I never appreciated until so many years afterwards. If I *had* noticed it—well, I suppose the course of three lives would have been entirely altered. Somehow—that's a very frightening thought.

For the beginning of it all, I've got to go back to the summer of 1914—just before the war—when I went down to Badgeworthy with Neil Carslake. Neil was, I suppose, about my best friend. I'd known his brother Alan too, but not so well. Sylvia, their sister, I'd never met. She was two years younger than Alan and three years younger than Neil. Twice, while we were at school together, I'd been going to spend part of the holidays with Neil at Badgeworthy and twice something had intervened. So it came about that I was twenty-three when I first saw Neil and Alan's home.

We were to be quite a big party there. Neil's sister Sylvia had just got engaged to a fellow called Charles Crawley. He was, so Neil said, a good deal older than she was, but a thoroughly decent chap and quite reasonably well-off.

We arrived, I remember, about seven o'clock in the evening. Everyone had gone to his room to dress for dinner. Neil took me to mine. Badgeworthy was an attractive, rambling old house. It had been added to freely in the last three centuries and was full of little steps up and down, and unexpected staircases. It was the sort of house in which it's not easy to find your way about. I remember Neil promised to come and fetch me on his way down to dinner. I was feeling a little shy at the prospect of meeting his people for the first time. I remember saying with a laugh that it was the kind of house one expected to meet ghosts in the passages, and he said carelessly that he believed the place was said to be haunted but that none of them had ever seen anything, and he didn't even know what form the ghost was supposed to take.

Then he hurried away and I set to work to dive into my suitcases for my evening clothes. The Carslakes weren't well-off; they clung on to their old home, but there were no menservants to unpack for you or valet you.

Well, I'd just got to the stage of tying my tie. I was standing in front of the glass. I could see my own face and shoulders and behind them the wall of the room—a plain stretch of wall just broken in the middle by a door—and just as I finally settled my tie I noticed that the door was opening.

I don't know why I didn't turn around—I think that would have been the natural thing to do; anyway, I didn't. I just watched the door swing slowly open—and as it swung I saw into the room beyond.

It was a bedroom—a larger room than mine—with two bedsteads in it, and suddenly I caught my breath.

For at the foot of one of those beds was a girl and round her neck were a pair of man's hands and the man was slowly forcing her backwards and squeezing her throat as he did so, so that the girl was being slowly suffocated.

There wasn't the least possibility of a mistake. What I saw was perfectly clear. What was being done was murder.

I could see the girl's face clearly, her vivid golden hair, the agonized terror of her beautiful face, slowly suffusing with blood. Of the man I could see his back, his hands, and a scar that ran down the left side of his face towards his neck.

It's taken some time to tell, but in reality only a moment or two passed while I stared dumbfounded. Then I wheeled round to the rescue . . .

And on the wall behind me, the wall reflected in the glass, there was only a Victorian mahogany wardrobe. No door open—no scene of violence. I swung back to the mirror. The mirror reflected only the wardrobe . . .

I passed my hands across my eyes. Then I sprang across the room and tried to pull forward the wardrobe and at that moment Neil entered by the other door from the passage and asked me what the hell I was trying to do.

He must have thought me slightly barmy as I turned on him and demanded whether there was a door behind the wardrobe. He said, yes, there was a door, it led into the next room. I asked him who was occupying the next room and he said people called Oldam—a Major Oldam and his wife. I asked him then if Mrs Oldam had very fair hair and when he replied drily that she was dark I began to realize that I was probably making a fool of myself. I pulled myself together, made some lame explanation and we went downstairs together. I told myself that I must have had some kind of hallucination—and felt generally rather ashamed and a bit of an ass.

And then—and then—Neil said, 'My sister Sylvia,' and I was looking into the lovely face of the girl I had just seen being suffocated to death . . . and I was introduced to her fiancé, a tall dark man *with a scar down the left side of his face.*

Well—that's that. I'd like you to think and say what you'd have done in my place. Here was the girl—the identical girl—and here was the man I'd seen throttling her—and they were to be married in about a month's time . . .

Had I—or had I not—had a prophetic vision of the future? Would Sylvia and her husband come down here to stay some time in the future, and be given that room (the best spare room) and would that scene I'd witnessed take place in grim reality?

What was I to do about it? *Could* I do anything? Would anyone—Neil—or the girl herself—would they believe me?

I turned the whole business over and over in my mind the week I was down there. To speak or not to speak? And almost at once another complication set in. You see, I fell in love with Sylvia Carslake the first moment I saw here . . . I wanted her more than anything on earth . . . And in a way that tied my hands.

And yet, if I didn't say anything, Sylvia would marry Charles Crawley and Crawley would kill her . . .

And so, the day before I left, I blurted it all out to her. I said I expect she'd think me touched in the intellect or something, but I swore solemnly that I'd seen the thing just as I told it to her and that I felt if she was determined to marry Crawley, I ought to tell her my strange experience.

She listened very quietly. There was something in her eyes I didn't understand. She wasn't angry at all. When I'd finished, she just thanked me gravely. I kept repeating like an idiot, 'I *did* see it. I really did see it,' and she said, 'I'm sure you did if you say so. I believe you.'

Well, the upshot was that I went off not knowing whether I'd done right or been a fool, and a week later Sylvia broke off her engagement to Charles Crawley.

After that the war happened, and there wasn't much leisure for thinking of anything else. Once or twice when I was on leave, I came across Sylvia, but as far as possible I avoided her.

I loved her and wanted her just as badly as ever, but I felt somehow that it wouldn't be playing the game. It was owing to me that she'd broken off her engagement to Crawley, and I kept saying to myself that I could only justify the action I had taken by making my attitude a purely disinterested one.

Then, in 1916, Neil was killed and it fell to me to tell Sylvia about his last moments. We couldn't remain on formal footing after that. Sylvia had adored Neil and he had been my best friend. She was sweet—adorably sweet in her grief.

I just managed to hold my tongue and went out again praying that a bullet might end the whole miserable business. Life without Sylvia wasn't worth living.

But there was no bullet with my name on it. One nearly got me below the right ear and one was deflected by a cigarette case in my pocket, but I came through unscathed. Charles Crawley was killed in action at the beginning of 1918.

Somehow that made a difference. I came home in the autumn of 1918 just before the Armistice and I went straight to Sylvia and told her that I loved her. I hadn't much hope that she'd care for me straight away, and you could have knocked me down with a feather when she asked me why I hadn't told her sooner. I stammered out something about Crawley and she said, 'But why did you think I broke it off with him?' and then she told me that she'd fallen in love with me just as I'd done with her—from the very first minute.

I said I thought she'd broken off her engagement because of the story I told her and she laughed scornfully and said that if you loved a man you wouldn't be as cowardly as that, and we went over that old vision of mine again and agreed that it was queer, but nothing more.

Well, there's nothing much to tell for some time after that. Sylvia and I were married and we were very happy. But I realized, as soon as she was really mine, that I wasn't cut out for the best kind of husband. I loved Sylvia devotedly, but I was jealous, absurdly jealous of anyone she so much as smiled at. It amused her at first, I think she even rather liked it. It proved, at least, how devoted I was.

As for me, I realized quite fully and unmistakably that I was not only making a fool of myself, but that I was endangering all the peace and happiness of our life together. I knew, I say, but I couldn't change. Every time Sylvia got a letter she didn't show to me I wondered who it was from. If she laughed and talked with any man, I found myself getting sulky and watchful.

At first, as I say, Sylvia laughed at me. She thought it a

huge joke. Then she didn't think the joke so funny. Finally she didn't think it a joke at all—

And slowly, she began to draw away from me. Not in any physical sense, but she withdrew her secret mind from me. I no longer knew what her thoughts were. She was kind— but sadly, as thought from a long distance.

Little by little I realized that she no longer loved me. Her love had died and it was I who had killed it . . .

The next step was inevitable, I found myself waiting for it—dreading it . . .

Then Derek Wainwright came into our lives. He had everything that I hadn't. He had brains and a witty tongue. He was good-looking, too, and—I'm forced to admit it—a thoroughly good chap. As soon as I saw him I said to myself, 'This is just the man for Sylvia . . .'

She fought against it. I know she struggled . . . but I gave her no help. I couldn't. I was entrenched in my gloomy, sullen reserve. I was suffering like hell—and I couldn't stretch out a finger to save myself. I didn't help her. I made things worse. I let loose at her one day—a string of savage, unwarranted abuse. I was nearly mad with jealousy and misery. The things I said were cruel and untrue and I knew while I was saying them how cruel and how untrue they were. And yet I took a savage pleasure in saying them . . .

I remember how Sylvia flushed and shrank . . .

I drove her to the edge of endurance.

I remember she said, 'This can't go on . . .'

When I came home that night the house was empty— empty. There was a note—quite in the traditional fashion.

In it she said that she was leaving me—for good. She was going down to Badgeworthy for a day or two. After that she was going to the one person who loved her and needed her. I was to take that as final.

I suppose that up to then I hadn't really believed my own suspicions. This confirmation in black and white of my worst fears sent me raving mad. I went down to Badgeworthy after her as fast as the car would take me.

She had just changed her frock for dinner, I remember, when I burst into the room. I can see her face—startled—beautiful—afraid.

I said, 'No one but me shall ever have you. No one.'

And I caught her throat in my hands and gripped it and bent her backwards.

And suddenly I saw our reflection in the mirror. Sylvia choking and myself strangling her, and the scar on my cheek where the bullet grazed it under the right ear.

No—I didn't kill her. That sudden revelation paralysed me and I loosened my grasp and let her slip on to the floor . . .

And then I broke down—and she comforted me . . . Yes, she comforted me.

I told her everything and she told me that by the phrase 'the one person who loved and needed her' she had meant her brother Alan . . . We saw into each other's hearts that night, and I don't think, from that moment, that we ever drifted away from each other again . . .

It's a sobering thought to go through life with—that, but for the grace of God and a mirror, one might be a murderer . . .

One thing did die that night—the devil of jealousy that had possessed me so long . . .

But I wonder sometimes—suppose I hadn't made that initial mistake—the scar on the *left* cheek—when really it was the *right*—reversed by the mirror . . . Should I have been so sure the man was Charles Crawley? Would I have warned Sylvia? Would she be married to me—or to him?

Or are the past and the future all one?

I'm a simple fellow—and I can't pretend to understand these things—but I saw what I saw—and because of what I saw, Sylvia and I are together in the old-fashioned words—till death do us part. And perhaps beyond . . .

# S.O.S.

'Ah!' said Mr Dinsmead appreciatively.

He stepped back and surveyed the round table with approval. The firelight gleamed on the coarse white table-cloth, the knives and forks, and the other table appointments.

'Is—is everything ready?' asked Mrs Dinsmead hesitatingly. She was a little faded woman, with colourless face, meagre hair scraped back from her forehead, and a perpetually nervous manner.

'Everything's ready,' said her husband with a kind of ferocious geniality.

He was a big man, with stooping shoulders, and a broad red face. He had little pig's eyes that twinkled under his bushy brows, and a big jowl devoid of hair.

'Lemonade?' suggested Mrs Dinsmead, almost in a whisper.

Her husband shook his head.

'Tea. Much better in every way. Look at the weather, streaming and blowing. A nice cup of hot tea is what's needed for supper on an evening like this.'

He winked facetiously, then fell to surveying the table again.

'A good dish of eggs, cold corned beef, and bread and cheese. That's my order for supper. So come along and get it ready, Mother. Charlotte's in the kitchen waiting to give you a hand.'

Mrs Dinsmead rose, carefully winding up the ball of her knitting.

'She's grown a very good-looking girl,' she murmured. 'Sweetly pretty, I say.'

'Ah!' said Mr Dinsmead. 'The mortal image of her Ma! So go along with you, and don't let's waste any more time.'

He strolled about the room humming to himself for a minute or two. Once he approached the window and looked out.

'Wild weather,' he murmured to himself. 'Not much likelihood of our having visitors tonight.'

Then he too left the room.

About ten minutes later Mrs Dinsmead entered bearing a dish of fried eggs. Her two daughters followed, bringing in the rest of the provisions. Mr Dinsmead and his son Johnnie brought up the rear. The former seated himself at the head of the table.

'And for what we are to receive, etcetera,' he remarked humorously. 'And blessings on the man who first thought of tinned foods. What would we do, I should like to know, miles from anywhere, if we hadn't a tin now and then to fall back upon when the butcher forgets his weekly call?'

He proceeded to carve corned beef dexterously.

'I wonder who ever thought of building a house like this, miles from anywhere,' said his daughter Magdalen pettishly. 'We never see a soul.'

'No,' said her father. 'Never a soul.'

'I can't think what made you take it, Father,' said Charlotte.

'Can't you, my girl? Well, I had my reasons—I had my reasons.'

His eyes sought his wife's furtively, but she frowned.

'And haunted too,' said Charlotte. 'I wouldn't sleep alone here for anything.'

'Pack of nonsense,' said her father. 'Never seen anything, have you? Come now.'

'Not *seen* anything perhaps, but—'

'But what?'

Charlotte did not reply, but she shivered a little. A great surge of rain came driving against the window-pane, and Mrs Dinsmead dropped a spoon with a tinkle on the tray.

'Not nervous are you, Mother?' said Mr Dinsmead. 'It's a wild night, that's all. Don't you worry, we're safe here by our fireside, and not a soul from outside likely to disturb us. Why, it would be a miracle if anyone did. And miracles don't happen. No,' he added as though to himself, with a kind of peculiar satisfaction. 'Miracles don't happen.'

As the words left his lips there came a sudden knocking at the door. Mr Dinsmead stayed as though petrified.

'Whatever's that?' he muttered. His jaw fell.

Mrs Dinsmead gave a little whimpering cry and pulled her shawl up round her. The colour came into Magdalen's face and she leant forward and spoke to her father.

'The miracle has happened,' she said. 'You'd better go and let whoever it is in.'

Twenty minutes earlier Mortimer Cleveland had stood in the driving rain and mist surveying his car. It was really cursed bad luck. Two punctures within ten minutes of each other, and here he was, stranded miles from anywhere, in the midst of these bare Wiltshire downs with night coming on, and no prospect of shelter. Serve him right for trying to take a shortcut. If only he had stuck to the main road! Now he was lost on what seemed a mere cart-track, and no idea if there were even a village anywhere near.

He looked round him perplexedly, and his eye was caught by a gleam of light on the hillside above him. A second later the mist obscured it once more, but, waiting patiently, he presently got a second glimpse of it. After a moment's cogitation, he left the car and struck up the side of the hill.

Soon he was out of the mist, and he recognized the light as shining from the lighted window of a small cottage. Here, at any rate, was shelter. Mortimer Cleveland quickened his pace, bending his head to meet the furious onslaught of wind and rain which seemed to be trying its best to drive him back.

Cleveland was in his own way something of a celebrity though doubtless the majority of folks would have displayed complete ignorance of his name and achievements. He was an authority on mental science and had written two excellent text books on the subconscious. He was also a member of the Psychical Research Society and a student of the occult in so far as it affected his own conclusions and line of research.

He was by nature peculiarly susceptible to atmosphere, and by deliberate training he had increased his own natural gift. When he had at last reached the cottage and rapped at the door, he was conscious of an excitement, a quickening of interest, as though all his faculties had suddenly been sharpened.

The murmur of voices within had been plainly audible to him. Upon his knock there came a sudden silence, then the sound of a chair being pushed back along the floor. In another minute the door was flung open by a boy of about fifteen. Cleveland could look straight over his shoulder upon the scene within.

It reminded him of an interior by some Dutch Master. A round table spread for a meal, a family party sitting round it, one or two flickering candles and the firelight's glow over all. The father, a big man, sat one side of the table, a little grey woman with a frightened face sat opposite him. Facing the door, looking straight at Cleveland, was a girl. Her startled eyes looked straight into his, her hand with a cup in it was arrested halfway to her lips.

She was, Cleveland saw at once, a beautiful girl of an extremely uncommon type. Her hair, red gold, stood out round her face like a mist, her eyes, very far apart, were a pure grey. She had the mouth and chin of an early Italian Madonna.

There was a moment's dead silence. Then Cleveland stepped into the room and explained his predicament. He brought his trite story to a close, and there was another pause harder to understand. At last, as though with an effort, the father rose.

'Come in, sir—Mr Cleveland, did you say?'

'That is my name,' said Mortimer, smiling.

'Ah! yes. Come in, Mr Cleveland. Not weather for a dog outside, is it? Come in by the fire. Shut the door, can't you, Johnnie? Don't stand there half the night.'

Cleveland came forward and sat on a wooden stool by the fire. The boy Johnnie shut the door.

'Dinsmead, that's my name,' said the other man. He was all geniality now. 'This is the Missus, and these are my two daughters, Charlotte and Magdalen.'

For the first time, Cleveland saw the face of the girl who had been sitting with her back to him, and saw that, in a totally different way, she was quite as beautiful as her sister. Very dark, with a face of marble pallor, a delicate aquiline nose, and a grave mouth. It was a kind of frozen beauty, austere and almost forbidding. She acknowledged her father's introduction by bending her head, and she looked at him with an intent gaze that was searching in character. It was as though she were summing him up, weighing him in the balance of her young judgement.

'A drop of something to drink, eh, Mr Cleveland?'

'Thank you,' said Mortimer. 'A cup of tea will meet the case admirably.'

Mr Dinsmead hesitated a minute, then he picked up the five cups, one after another, from the table and emptied them into the slop bowl.

'This tea's cold,' he said brusquely. 'Make us some more, will you, Mother?'

Mrs Dinsmead got up quickly and hurried off with the teapot. Mortimer had an idea that she was glad to get out of the room.

The fresh tea soon came, and the unexpected guest was plied with viands.

Mr Dinsmead talked and talked. He was expansive, genial,

loquacious. He told the stranger all about himself. He'd lately
retired from the building trade—yes, made quite a good thing
of it. He and the Missus thought they'd like a bit of country
air—never lived in the country before. Wrong time of year
to choose, of course, October and November, but they didn't
want to wait. 'Life's uncertain, you know, sir.' So they had
taken this cottage. Eight miles from anywhere, and nineteen
miles from anything you could call a town. No, they didn't
complain. The girls found it a bit dull, but he and mother
enjoyed the quiet.

So he talked on, leaving Mortimer almost hypnotized by
the easy flow. Nothing here, surely, but rather commonplace
domesticity. And yet, at that first glimpse of the interior, he
had diagnosed something else, some tension, some strain,
emanating from one of those five people—he didn't know
which. Mere foolishness, his nerves were all awry! They
were all startled by his sudden appearance—that was all.

He broached the question of a night's lodging, and was
met with a ready response.

'You'll have to stop with us, Mr Cleveland. Nothing else
for miles around. We can give you a bedroom, and though
my pyjamas may be a bit roomy, why, they're better than
nothing, and your own clothes will be dry by morning.'

'It's very good of you.'

'Not at all,' said the other genially. 'As I said just now,
one couldn't turn away a dog on a night like this. Magdalen,
Charlotte, go up and see to the room.'

The two girls left the room. Presently Mortimer heard
them moving about overhead.

'I can quite understand that two attractive young ladies
like your daughters might find it dull here,' said Cleveland.

'Good lookers, aren't they?' said Mr Dinsmead with
fatherly pride. 'Not much like their mother or myself. We're
a homely pair, but much attached to each other. I'll tell you
that, Mr Cleveland. Eh, Maggie, isn't that so?'

Mrs Dinsmead smiled primly. She had started knitting
again. The needles clicked busily. She was a fast knitter.

Presently the room was announced ready, and Mortimer, expressing thanks once more, declared his intention of turning in.

'Did you put a hot-water bottle in the bed?' demanded Mrs Dinsmead, suddenly mindful of her house pride.

'Yes, Mother, two.'

'That's right,' said Dinsmead. 'Go up with him, girls, and see that there's nothing else he wants.'

Magdalen preceded him up the staircase, her candle held aloft. Charlotte came behind.

The room was quite a pleasant one, small and with a sloping roof, but the bed looked comfortable, and the few pieces of somewhat dusty furniture were of old mahogany. A large can of hot water stood in the basin, a pair of pink pyjamas of ample proportions were laid over a chair, and the bed was made and turned down.

Magdalen went over to the window and saw that the fastenings were secure. Charlotte cast a final eye over the washstand appointments. Then they both lingered by the door.

'Good night, Mr Cleveland. You are sure there is everything?'

'Yes, thank you, Miss Magdalen. I am ashamed to have given you both so much trouble. Good night.'

'Good night.'

They went out, shutting the door behind them. Mortimer Cleveland was alone. He undressed slowly and thoughtfully. When he had donned Mr Dinsmead's pink pyjamas he gathered up his own wet clothes and put them outside the door as his host had bade him. From downstairs he could hear the rumble of Dinsmead's voice.

What a talker the man was! Altogether an odd personality—but indeed there was something odd about the whole family, or was it his imagination?

He went slowly back into his room and shut the door. He stood by the bed lost in thought. And then he started—

The mahogany table by the bed was smothered in dust. Written in the dust were three letters, clearly visible, *S.O.S.*

Mortimer stared as if he could hardly believe his eyes. It was confirmation of all his vague surmises and forebodings. He was right, then. Something was wrong in this house.

S.O.S. A call for help. But whose finger had written it in the dust? Magdalen's or Charlotte's? They had both stood there, he remembered, for a moment or two, before going out of the room. Whose hand had secretly dropped to the table and traced out those three letters?

The faces of the two girls came up before him. Magdalen's, dark and aloof, and Charlotte's, as he had seen it first, wide-eyed, startled, with an unfathomable something in her glance . . .

He went again to the door and opened it. The boom of Mr Dinsmead's voice was no longer to be heard. The house was silent.

He thought to himself.

'I can do nothing tonight. Tomorrow—well. We shall see.'


Cleveland woke early. He went down through the living-room, and out into the garden. The morning was fresh and beautiful after the rain. Someone else was up early, too. At the bottom of the garden, Charlotte was leaning on the fence staring out over the Downs. His pulse quickened a little as he went down to join her. All along he had been secretly convinced that it was Charlotte who had written the message. As he came up to her, she turned and wished him 'Good morning'. Her eyes were direct and childlike, with no hint of a secret understanding in them.

'A very good morning,' said Mortimer, smiling. 'The weather this morning is a contrast to last night.'

'It is indeed.'

Mortimer broke off a twig from a tree near by. With it he began idly to draw on the smooth, sandy patch at his feet. He traced an S, then an O, then an S, watching the girl narrowly as he did so. But again he could detect no gleam of comprehension.

'Do you know what these letters represent?' he said abruptly.

Charlotte frowned a little. 'Aren't they what boats—liners—send out when they are in distress?' she asked.

Mortimer nodded. 'Someone wrote that on the table by my bed last night,' he said quietly. 'I thought perhaps *you* might have done so.'

She looked at him in wide-eyed astonishment.

'I? Oh, no.'

He was wrong then. A sharp pang of disappointment shot through him. He had been so sure—so sure. It was not often that his intuitions led him astray.

'You are quite certain?' he persisted.

'Oh, yes.'

They turned and went slowly together toward the house. Charlotte seemed preoccupied about something. She replied at random to the few observations he made. Suddenly she burst out in a low, hurried voice:

'It—it's odd your asking about those letters, S.O.S.; I didn't write them, of course, but—I so easily might have done.'

He stopped and looked at her, and she went on quickly:

'It sounds silly, I know, but I have been so frightened, so dreadfully frightened, and when you came in last night, it seemed like an—an answer to something.'

'What are you frightened of?' he asked quickly.

'I don't know.'

'You don't know.'

'I think—it's the house. Ever since we came here it has been growing and growing. Everyone seems different somehow. Father, Mother, and Magdalen, they all seem different.'

Mortimer did not speak at once, and before he could do so, Charlotte went on again.

'You know this house is supposed to be haunted?'

'What?' All his interest was quickened.

'Yes, a man murdered his wife in it, oh, some years ago now. We only found out about it after we got here. Father says ghosts are all nonsense, but I—don't know.'

Mortimer was thinking rapidly.

'Tell me,' he said in a businesslike tone, 'was this murder committed in the room I had last night?'

'I don't know anything about that,' said Charlotte.

'I wonder now,' said Mortimer half to himself, 'yes, that may be it.'

Charlotte looked at him uncomprehendingly.

'Miss Dinsmead,' said Mortimer, gently, 'have you ever had any reason to believe that you are mediumistic?'

She stared at him.

'I think you know that you *did* write S.O.S. last night,' he said quietly. 'Oh! quite unconsciously, of course. A crime stains the atmosphere, so to speak. A sensitive mind such as yours might be acted upon in such a manner. You have been reproducing the sensations and impressions of the victim. Many years ago *she* may have written S.O.S. on that table, and you unconsciously reproduced her act last night.'

Charlotte's face brightened.

'I see,' she said. 'You think that is the explanation?'

A voice called her from the house, and she went in, leaving Mortimer to pace up and down the garden path. Was he satisfied with his own explanation? Did it cover the facts as he knew them? Did it account for the tension he had felt on entering the house last night?

Perhaps, and yet he still had the odd feeling that his sudden appearance had produced something very like consternation, he thought to himself:

'I must not be carried away by the psychic explanation, it might account for Charlotte—but not for the others. My coming has upset them horribly, all except Johnnie. Whatever it is that's the matter, Johnnie is out of it.'

He was quite sure of that, strange that he should be so positive, but there it was.

At that minute, Johnnie himself came out of the cottage and approached the guest.

'Breakfast's ready,' he said awkwardly. 'Will you come in?'

Mortimer noticed that the lad's fingers were much stained. Johnnie felt his glance and laughed ruefully.

'I'm always messing about with chemicals, you know,' he said. 'It makes Dad awfully wild sometimes. He wants me to go into building, but I want to do chemistry and research work.'

Mr Dinsmead appeared at the window ahead of them, broad, jovial, smiling, and at the sight of him all Mortimer's distrust and antagonism re-awakened. Mrs Dinsmead was already seated at the table. She wished him 'Good morning' in her colourless voice, and he had again the impression that for some reason or other, she was afraid of him.

Magdalen came in last. She gave him a brief nod and took her seat opposite him.

'Did you sleep well?' she asked abruptly. 'Was your bed comfortable?'

She looked at him very earnestly, and when he replied courteously in the affirmative he noticed something very like a flicker of disappointment pass over her face. What had she expected him to say, he wondered?

He turned to his host.

'This lad of yours is interested in chemistry, it seems!' he said pleasantly.

There was a crash. Mrs Dinsmead had dropped her tea cup.

'Now then, Maggie, now then,' said her husband.

It seemed to Mortimer that there was admonition, warning, in his voice. He turned to his guest and spoke fluently of the advantages of the building trade, and of not letting young boys get above themselves.

After breakfast, he went out in the garden by himself, and smoked. The time was clearly at hand when he must leave the cottage. A night's shelter was one thing, to prolong it was difficult without an excuse, and what possible excuse could he offer? And yet he was singularly loath to depart.

Turning the thing over and over in his mind, he took a path that led round the other side of the house. His shoes were soled with crepe rubber, and made little or no noise. He was passing the kitchen window, when he heard Dinsmead's words from within, and the words attracted his attention immediately.

'It's a fair lump of money, it is.'

Mrs Dinsmead's voice answered. It was too faint in tone for Mortimer to hear the words, but Dinsmead replied:

'Nigh on £60,000, the lawyer said.'

Mortimer had no intention of eavesdropping, but he retraced his steps very thoughtfully. The mention of money seemed to crystallize the situation. Somewhere or other there was a question of £60,000—it made the thing clearer—and uglier.

Magdalen came out of the house, but her father's voice called her almost immediately, and she went in again. Presently Dinsmead himself joined his guest.

'Rare good morning,' he said genially. 'I hope your car will be none the worse.'

'Wants to find out when I'm going,' thought Mortimer to himself.

Aloud he thanked Mr Dinsmead once more for his timely hospitality.

'Not at all, not at all,' said the other.

Magdalen and Charlotte came together out of the house, and strolled arm in arm to a rustic seat some little distance away. The dark head and the golden one made a pleasant contrast together, and on an impulse Mortimer said:

'Your daughters are very unalike, Mr Dinsmead.'

The other who was just lighting his pipe gave a sharp jerk of the wrist, and dropped the match.

'Do you think so?' he asked. 'Yes, well, I suppose they are.'

Mortimer had a flash of intuition.

'But of course they are not both your daughters,' he said smoothly.

He saw Dinsmead look at him, hesitate for a moment, and then make up his mind.

'That's very clever of you, sir,' he said. 'No, one of them is a foundling, we took her in as a baby and we have brought her up as our own. She herself has not the least idea of the truth, but she'll have to know soon.' He sighed.

'A question of inheritance?' suggested Mortimer quietly.

The other flashed a suspicious look at him.

Then he seemed to decide that frankness was best; his manner became almost aggressively frank and open.

'It's odd that you should say that, sir.'

'A case of telepathy, eh?' said Mortimer, and smiled.

'It is like this, sir. We took her in to oblige the mother— for a consideration, as at the time I was just starting in the building trade. A few months ago I noticed an advertisement in the papers, and it seemed to me that the child in question must be our Magdalen. I went to see the lawyers, and there has been a lot of talk one way and another. They were suspicious—naturally, as you might say, but everything is cleared up now. I am taking the girl herself to London next week, she doesn't know anything about it so far. Her father, it seems, was one of these rich Jewish gentlemen. He only learnt of the child's existence a few months before his death. He set agents on to try and trace her, and left all his money to her when she should be found.'

Mortimer listened with close attention. He had no reason to doubt Mr Dinsmead's story. It explained Magdalen's dark beauty; explained too, perhaps, her aloof manner. Nevertheless, though the story itself might be true, something lay behind it undivulged.

But Mortimer had no intention of rousing the other's suspicions. Instead, he must go out of his way to allay them.

'A very interesting story, Mr Dinsmead,' he said. 'I congratulate Miss Magdalen. An heiress and a beauty, she has a great time ahead of her.'

'She has that,' agreed her father warmly, 'and she's a rare good girl too, Mr Cleveland.'

There was every evidence of hearty warmth in his manner.

'Well,' said Mortimer, 'I must be pushing along now, I suppose. I have got to thank you once more, Mr Dinsmead, for your singularly well-timed hospitality.'

Accompanied by his host, he went into the house to bid farewell to Mrs Dinsmead. She was standing by the window with her back to them, and did not hear them enter. At her husband's jovial: 'Here's Mr Cleveland come to say goodbye,' she started nervously and swung round, dropping something which she held in her hand. Mortimer picked it up for her. It was a miniature of Charlotte done in the style of some twenty-five years ago. Mortimer repeated to her the thanks he had already proffered to her husband. He noticed again her look of fear and the furtive glances that she shot at him from beneath her eyelids.

The two girls were not in evidence, but it was not part of Mortimer's policy to seem anxious to see them; also he had his own idea, which was shortly to prove correct.

He had gone about half a mile from the house on his way down to where he had left the car the night before, when the bushes on the side of the path were thrust aside, and Magdalen came out on the track ahead of him.

'I had to see you,' she said.

'I expected you,' said Mortimer. 'It was you who wrote S.O.S. on the table in my room last night, wasn't it?'

Magdalen nodded.

'Why?' asked Mortimer gently.

The girl turned aside and began pulling off leaves from a bush.

'I don't know,' she said, 'honestly, I don't know.'

'Tell me,' said Mortimer.

Magdalen drew a deep breath.

'I am a practical person,' she said, 'not the kind of person who imagines things or fancies them. You, I know, believe in ghosts and spirits. I don't, and when I tell you that there is something very wrong in that house,' she pointed up the hill, 'I mean that there is something tangibly wrong; it's not just an echo of the past. It has been coming on ever since we've been there. Every day it grows worse, Father is different, Mother is different, Charlotte is different.'

Mortimer interposed. 'Is Johnnie different?' he asked.

Magdalen looked at him, a dawning appreciation in her eyes. 'No,' she said, 'now I come to think of it, Johnnie is not different. He is the only one who's—who's untouched by it all. He was untouched last night at tea.'

'And you?' asked Mortimer.

'I was afraid—horribly afraid, just like a child—without knowing what it was I was afraid of. And father was—queer, there's no other word for it, queer. He talked about miracles and then I prayed—actually prayed for a miracle, and *you* knocked on the door.'

She stopped abruptly, staring at him.

'I seem mad to you, I suppose,' she said defiantly.

'No,' said Mortimer, 'on the contrary you seem extremely sane. All sane people have a premonition of danger if it is near them.'

'You don't understand,' said Magdalen. 'I was not afraid—for myself.'

'For whom, then?'

But again Magdalen shook her head in a puzzled fashion. 'I don't know.'

She went on:

'I wrote S.O.S. on an impulse. I had an idea—absurd, no doubt, that they would not let me speak to you—the rest of them, I mean. I don't know what it was I meant to ask you to do. I don't know now.'

'Never mind,' said Mortimer. 'I shall do it.'

'What can you do?'

Mortimer smiled a little.

'I can think.'

She looked at him doubtfully.

'Yes,' said Mortimer, 'a lot can be done that way, more than you would ever believe. Tell me, was there any chance word or phrase that attracted your attention just before the meal last evening?'

Magdalen frowned. 'I don't think so,' she said. 'At least I heard Father say something to Mother about Charlotte being the living image of her, and he laughed in a very queer way, but—there's nothing odd in that, is there?'

'No,' said Mortimer slowly, 'except that Charlotte is not like your mother.'

He remained lost in thought for a minute or two, then looked up to find Magdalen watching him uncertainly.

'Go home, child,' he said, 'and don't worry; leave it in my hands.'

She went obediently up the path towards the cottage. Mortimer strolled on a little further, then threw himself down on the green turf. He closed his eyes, detached himself from conscious thought or effort, and let a series of pictures flit at will across his mind.

Johnnie! He always came back to Johnnie. Johnnie, completely innocent, utterly free from all the network of suspicion and intrigue, but nevertheless the pivot round which everything turned. He remembered the crash of Mrs Dinsmead's cup on her saucer at breakfast that morning. What had caused her agitation? A chance reference on his part to the lad's fondness for chemicals? At the moment he had not been conscious of Mr Dinsmead, but he saw him now clearly, as he sat, his teacup poised halfway to his lips.

That took him back to Charlotte, as he had seen her when the door opened last night. She had sat staring at him over the rim of her teacup. And swiftly on that followed another memory. Mr Dinsmead emptying teacups one after the other, and saying 'this tea is cold'.

He remembered the steam that went up. Surely the tea had not been so very cold after all?

Something began to stir in his brain. A memory of something read not so very long ago, within a month perhaps. Some account of a whole family poisoned by a lad's carelessness. A packet of arsenic left in the larder had all dripped through on the bread below. He had read it in the paper. Probably Mr Dinsmead had read it too.

Things began to grow clearer . . .

Half an hour later, Mortimer Cleveland rose briskly to his feet.

It was evening once more in the cottage. The eggs were poached tonight and there was a tin of brawn. Presently Mrs Dinsmead came in from the kitchen bearing the big teapot. The family took their places round the table.

'A contrast to last night's weather,' said Mrs Dinsmead, glancing towards the window.

'Yes,' said Mr Dinsmead, 'it's so still tonight that you could hear a pin drop. Now then, Mother, pour out, will you?'

Mrs Dinsmead filled the cups and handed them round the table. Then, as she put the teapot down, she gave a sudden little cry and pressed her hand to her heart. Mr Dinsmead swung round his chair, following the direction of her terrified eyes. Mortimer Cleveland was standing in the doorway.

He came forward. His manner was pleasant and apologetic.

'I'm afraid I startled you,' he said. 'I had to come back for something.'

'Back for something,' cried Mr Dinsmead. His face was purple, his veins swelling. 'Back for what, I should like to know?'

'Some tea,' said Mortimer.

With a swift gesture he took something from his pocket, and, taking up one of the teacups from the table, emptied some of its contents into a little test-tube he held in his left hand.

'What—what are you doing?' gasped Mr Dinsmead. His face had gone chalky-white, the purple dying out as if by magic. Mrs Dinsmead gave a thin, high, frightened cry.

'You read the papers, I think, Mr Dinsmead? I am sure you do. Sometimes one reads accounts of a whole family being poisoned, some of them recover, some do not. In this case, *one would not*. The first explanation would be the tinned brawn you were eating, but supposing the doctor to be a suspicious man, not easily taken in by the tinned food theory? There is a packet of arsenic in your larder. On the shelf below it is a packet of tea. There is a convenient hole in the top shelf, what more natural to suppose then that the arsenic found its way into the tea by accident? Your son Johnnie might be blamed for carelessness, nothing more.'

'I—I don't know what you mean,' gasped Dinsmead.

'I think you do,' Mortimer took up a second teacup and filled a second test-tube. He fixed a red label to one and a blue label to the other.

'The red-labelled one,' he said, 'contains tea from your daughter Charlotte's cup, the other from your daughter Magdalen's. I am prepared to swear that in the first I shall find four or five times the amount of arsenic than in the latter.'

'You are mad,' said Dinsmead.

'Oh! dear me, no. I am nothing of the kind. You told me today, Mr Dinsmead, that Magdalen *is* your daughter. Charlotte was the child you adopted, the child who was so like her mother that when I held a miniature of that mother in my hand today I mistook it for one of Charlotte herself. Your own daughter was to inherit the fortune, and since it might be impossible to keep your supposed daughter Charlotte out of sight, and someone who knew the mother might have realized the truth of the resemblance, you decided on, well—a pinch of white arsenic at the bottom of a teacup.'

Mrs Dinsmead gave a sudden high cackle, rocking herself to and fro in violent hysterics.

'Tea,' she squeaked, 'that's what he said, tea, not lemonade.'

'Hold your tongue, can't you?' roared her husband wrathfully.

Mortimer saw Charlotte looking at him, wide-eyed, wondering, across the table. Then he felt a hand on his arm, and Magdalen dragged him out of earshot.

'Those,' she pointed at the phials—'Daddy. You won't—'

Mortimer laid his hand on her shoulder. 'My child,' he

said, 'you don't believe in the past. I do. I believe in the atmosphere of this house. If he had not come to it, perhaps—I say *perhaps*—your father might not have conceived the plan he did. I keep these two test-tubes to safeguard Charlotte now and in the future. Apart from that, I shall do nothing, in gratitude, if you will, to that hand that wrote S.O.S.'

# THE ADVENTURE OF THE
# EGYPTIAN TOMB

I have always considered that one of the most thrilling and dramatic of the many adventures I have shared with Poirot was that of our investigation into the strange series of deaths which followed upon the discovery and opening of the Tomb of King Men-her-Ra.

Hard upon the discovery of the Tomb of Tutankh-Amen by Lord Carnarvon, Sir John Willard and Mr Bleibner of New York, pursuing their excavations not far from Cairo, in the vicinity of the Pyramids of Gizeh, came unexpectedly on a series of funeral chambers. The greatest interest was aroused by their discovery. The Tomb appeared to be that of King Men-her-Ra, one of those shadowy kings of the Eighth Dynasty, when the Old Kingdom was falling to decay. Little was known about this period, and the discoveries were fully reported in the newspapers.

An event soon occurred which took a profound hold on the public mind. Sir John Willard died quite suddenly of heart failure.

The more sensational newspapers immediately took the opportunity of reviving all the old superstitious stories connected with the ill luck of certain Egyptian treasures. The unlucky Mummy at the British Museum, that hoary old chestnut, was dragged out with fresh zest, was quietly denied by the Museum, but nevertheless enjoyed all its usual vogue.

A fortnight later Mr Bleibner died of acute blood poisoning, and a few days afterwards a nephew of his shot himself in New York. The 'Curse of Men-her-Ra' was the talk of the day, and the magic power of dead-and-gone Egypt was exalted to a fetish point.

It was then that Poirot received a brief note from Lady Willard, widow of the dead archaeologist, asking him to go and see her at her house in Kensington Square. I accompanied him.

Lady Willard was a tall, thin woman, dressed in deep mourning. Her haggard face bore eloquent testimony to her recent grief.

'It is kind of you to have come so promptly, Monsieur Poirot.'

'I am at your service, Lady Willard. You wished to consult me?'

'You are, I am aware, a detective, but it is not only as a detective that I wish to consult you. You are a man of original views, I know, you have imagination, experience of the world, tell me, Monsieur Poirot, what are your views on the supernatural?'

Poirot hesitated for a moment before he replied. He seemed to be considering. Finally he said:

'Let us not misunderstand each other, Lady Willard. It is not a general question that you are asking me there. It has a personal application, has it not? You are referring obliquely to the death of your late husband?'

'That is so,' she admitted.

'You want me to investigate the circumstances of his death?'

'I want you to ascertain for me exactly how much is newspaper chatter, and how much may be said to be founded on fact? Three deaths, Monsieur Poirot—each one explicable taken by itself, but taken together surely an almost unbelievable coincidence, and all within a month of the opening of the tomb! It may be mere superstition, it may be some potent curse from the past that operates in ways undreamed of by modern science. The fact remains—three deaths! And

I am afraid, Monsieur Poirot, horribly afraid. It may not yet be the end.'

'For whom do you fear?'

'For my son. When the news of my husband's death came I was ill. My son, who has just come down from Oxford, went out there. He brought the—the body home, but now he has gone out again, in spite of my prayers and entreaties. He is so fascinated by the work that he intends to take his father's place and carry on the system of excavations. You may think me a foolish, credulous woman, but, Monsieur Poirot, I am afraid. Supposing that the spirit of the dead King is not yet appeased? Perhaps to you I seem to be talking nonsense—'

'No, indeed, Lady Willard,' said Poirot quickly. 'I, too, believe in the force of superstition, one of the greatest forces the world has ever known.'

I looked at him in surprise. I should never have credited Poirot with being superstitious. But the little man was obviously in earnest.

'What you really demand is that I shall protect your son? I will do my utmost to keep him from harm.'

'Yes, in the ordinary way, but against an occult influence?'

'In volumes of the Middle Ages, Lady Willard, you will find many ways of counteracting black magic. Perhaps they knew more than we moderns with all our boasted science. Now let us come to facts, that I may have guidance. Your husband had always been a devoted Egyptologist, hadn't he?'

'Yes, from his youth upwards. He was one of the greatest living authorities upon the subject.'

'But Mr Bleibner, I understand, was more or less of an amateur?'

'Oh, quite. He was a very wealthy man who dabbled freely in any subject that happened to take his fancy. My husband managed to interest him in Egyptology, and it was his money that was so useful in financing the expedition.'

'And the nephew? What do you know of his tastes? Was he with the party at all?'

'I do not think so. In fact I never knew of his existence

till I read of his death in the paper. I do not think he and Mr Bleibner can have been at all intimate. He never spoke of having any relations.'

'Who are the other members of the party?'

'Well, there's Dr Tosswill, a minor official connected with the British Museum; Mr Schneider of the Metropolitan Museum in New York; a young American secretary; Dr Ames, who accompanies the expedition in his professional capacity; and Hassan, my husband's devoted native servant.'

'Do you remember the name of the American secretary?'

'Harper, I think, but I cannot be sure. He had not been with Mr Bleibner very long, I know. He was a very pleasant young fellow.'

'Thank you, Lady Willard.'

'If there is anything else—'

'For the moment, nothing. Leave it now in my hands, and be assured that I will do all that is humanly possible to protect your son.'

They were not exactly reassuring words, and I observed Lady Willard wince as he uttered them. Yet, at the same time, the fact that he had not pooh-poohed her fears seemed in itself to be a relief to her.

For my part I had never before suspected that Poirot had so deep a vein of superstition in his nature. I tackled him on the subject as we went homewards. His manner was grave and earnest.

'But yes, Hastings. I believe in these things. You must not underrate the force of superstition.'

'What are we going to do about it?'

'*Toujours pratique*, the good Hastings! *Eh bien*, to begin with we are going to cable to New York for fuller details of young Mr Bleibner's death.'

He duly sent off his cable. The reply was full and precise. Young Rupert Bleibner had been in low water for several years. He had been a beach-comber and a remittance man in several South Sea islands, but had returned to New York two years ago, where he had rapidly sunk lower and lower.

The most significant thing, to my mind, was that he had recently managed to borrow enough money to take him to Egypt. 'I've a good friend there I can borrow from,' he had declared. Here, however, his plans had gone awry. He had returned to New York cursing his skinflint of an uncle who cared more for the bones of dead and gone kings than his own flesh and blood. It was during his sojourn in Egypt that the death of Sir John Willard had occurred. Rupert had plunged once more into his life of dissipation in New York, and then, without warning, he had committed suicide, leaving behind him a letter which contained some curious phrases. It seemed written in a sudden fit of remorse. He referred to himself as a leper and an outcast, and the letter ended by declaring that such as he were better dead.

A shadowy theory leapt into my brain. I had never really believed in the vengeance of a long dead Egyptian king. I saw here a more modern crime. Supposing this young man had decided to do away with his uncle—preferably by poison. By mistake, Sir John Willard receives the fatal dose. The young man returns to New York, haunted by his crime. The news of his uncle's death reaches him. He realizes how unnecessary his crime has been, and stricken with remorse takes his own life.

I outlined my solution to Poirot. He was interested.

'It is ingenious what you have thought of there—decidedly it is ingenious. It may even be true. But you leave out of count the fatal influence of the Tomb.'

I shrugged my shoulders.

'You still think that has something to do with it?'

'So much so, *mon ami*, that we start for Egypt tomorrow.'

'What?' I cried, astonished.

'I have said it.' An expression of conscious heroism spread over Poirot's face. Then he groaned. 'But oh,' he lamented, 'the sea! The hateful sea!'

It was a week later. Beneath our feet was the golden sand of the desert. The hot sun poured down overhead. Poirot, the picture of misery, wilted by my side. The little man was not a good traveller. Our four days' voyage from Marseilles had been one long agony to him. He had landed at Alexandria the wraith of his former self, even his usual neatness had deserted him. We had arrived in Cairo and had driven out at once to the Mena House Hotel, right in the shadow of the Pyramids.

The charm of Egypt had laid hold of me. Not so Poirot. Dressed precisely the same as in London, he carried a small clothes-brush in his pocket and waged an unceasing war on the dust which accumulated on his dark apparel.

'And my boots,' he wailed. 'Regard them, Hastings. My boots, of the neat patent leather, usually so smart and shining. See, the sand is inside them, which is painful, and outside them, which outrages the eyesight. Also the heat, it causes my moustaches to become limp—but limp!'

'Look at the Sphinx,' I urged. 'Even I can feel the mystery and the charm it exhales.'

Poirot looked at it discontentedly.

'It has not the air happy,' he declared. 'How could it, half-buried in sand in that untidy fashion. Ah, this cursed sand!'

'Come, now, there's a lot of sand in Belgium,' I reminded him, mindful of a holiday spent at Knocke-sur-mer in the midst of 'Les dunes impeccables' as the guide-book had phrased it.

'Not in Brussels,' declared Poirot. He gazed at the Pyramids thoughtfully. 'It is true that they, at least, are of a shape solid and geometrical, but their surface is of an unevenness most unpleasing. And the palm-trees I like them not. Not even do they plant them in rows!'

I cut short his lamentations, by suggesting that we should start for the camp. We were to ride there on camels, and the beasts were patiently kneeling, waiting for us to mount, in charge of several picturesque boys headed by a voluble dragoman.

I pass over the spectacle of Poirot on a camel. He started

by groans and lamentations and ended by shrieks, gesticu-
lations and invocations to the Virgin Mary and every Saint
in the calendar. In the end, he descended ignominiously and
finished the journey on a diminutive donkey. I must admit
that a trotting camel is no joke for the amateur. I was stiff
for several days.

At last we neared the scene of the excavations. A sunburnt
man with a grey beard, in white clothes and wearing a
helmet, came to meet us.

'Monsieur Poirot and Captain Hastings? We received your
cable. I'm sorry that there was no one to meet you in Cairo.
An unforeseen event occurred which completely disorgan-
ized our plans.'

Poirot paled. His hand, which had stolen to his clothes-
brush, stayed its course.

'Not another death?' he breathed.

'Yes.'

'Sir Guy Willard?' I cried.

'No, Captain Hastings. My American colleague, Mr
Schneider.'

'And the cause?' demanded Poirot.

'Tetanus.'

I blanched. All around me I seemed to feel an atmosphere
of evil, subtle and menacing. A horrible thought flashed
across me. Supposing I were next?

'*Mon Dieu*,' said Poirot, in a very low voice, 'I do not
understand this. It is horrible. Tell me, monsieur, there is no
doubt that it was tetanus?'

'I believe not. But Dr Ames will tell you more than I can
do.'

'Ah, of course, you are not the doctor.'

'My name is Tosswill.'

This, then, was the British expert described by Lady Willard
as being a minor official at the British Museum. There was
something at once grave and steadfast about him that took
my fancy.

'If you will come with me,' continued Dr Tosswill. 'I will

take you to Sir Guy Willard. He was most anxious to be informed as soon as you should arrive.'

We were taken across the camp to a large tent. Dr Tosswill lifted up the flap and we entered. Three men were sitting inside.

'Monsieur Poirot and Captain Hastings have arrived, Sir Guy,' said Tosswill.

The youngest of the three men jumped up and came forward to greet us. There was a certain impulsiveness in his manner which reminded me of his mother. He was not nearly so sunburnt as the others, and that fact, coupled with a certain haggardness round the eyes, made him look older than his twenty-two years. He was clearly endeavouring to bear up under a severe mental strain.

He introduced his two companions, Dr Ames, a capable-looking man of thirty-odd, with a touch of greying hair at the temples, and Mr Harper, the secretary, a pleasant lean young man wearing the national insignia of horn-rimmed spectacles.

After a few minutes' desultory conversation the latter went out, and Dr Tosswill followed him. We were left alone with Sir Guy and Dr Ames.

'Please ask any questions you want to ask, Monsieur Poirot,' said Willard. 'We are utterly dumbfounded at this strange series of disasters, but it isn't—it can't be, anything but coincidence.'

There was a nervousness about his manner which rather belied the words. I saw that Poirot was studying him keenly.

'Your heart is really in this work, Sir Guy?'

'Rather. No matter what happens, or what comes of it, the work is going on. Make up your mind to that.'

Poirot wheeled round on the other.

'What have you to say to that, *monsieur le docteur*?'

'Well,' drawled the doctor, 'I'm not for quitting myself.'

Poirot made one of those expressive grimaces of his.

'Then, *évidemment*, we must find out just how we stand. When did Mr Schneider's death take place?'

'Three days ago.'

'You are sure it was tetanus?'

'Dead sure.'

'It couldn't have been a case of strychnine poisoning, for instance?'

'No, Monsieur Poirot, I see what you're getting at. But it was a clear case of tetanus.'

'Did you not inject anti-serum?'

'Certainly we did,' said the doctor drily. 'Every conceivable thing that could be done was tried.'

'Had you the anti-serum with you?'

'No. We procured it from Cairo.'

'Have there been any other cases of tetanus in the camp?'

'No, not one.'

'Are you certain that the death of Mr Bleibner was not due to tetanus?'

'Absolutely plumb certain. He had a scratch upon his thumb which became poisoned, and septicaemia set in. It sounds pretty much the same to a layman, I dare say, but the two things are entirely different.'

'Then we have four deaths—all totally dissimilar, one heart failure, one blood poisoning, one suicide and one tetanus.'

'Exactly, Monsieur Poirot.'

'Are you certain that there is nothing which might link the four together?'

'I don't quite understand you?'

'I will put it plainly. Was any act committed by those four men which might seem to denote disrespect to the spirit of Men-her-Ra?'

The doctor gazed at Poirot in astonishment.

'You're talking through your hat, Monsieur Poirot. Surely you've not been guyed into believing all that fool talk?'

'Absolute nonsense,' muttered Willard angrily.

Poirot remained placidly immovable, blinking a little out of his green cat's eyes.

'So you do not believe it, *monsieur le docteur*?'

'No, sir, I do not,' declared the doctor emphatically. 'I am a scientific man, and I believe only what science teaches.'

'Was there no science then in Ancient Egypt?' asked Poirot softly. He did not wait for a reply, and indeed Dr Ames seemed rather at a loss for the moment. 'No, no, do not answer me, but tell me this. What do the native workmen think?'

'I guess,' said Dr Ames, 'that, where white folk lose their heads, natives aren't going to be far behind. I'll admit that they're getting what you might call scared—but they've no cause to be.'

'I wonder,' said Poirot non-committally.

Sir Guy leant forward.

'Surely,' he cried incredulously, 'you cannot believe in— oh, but the thing's absurd! You can know nothing of Ancient Egypt if you think that.'

For answer Poirot produced a little book from his pocket— an ancient tattered volume. As he held it out I saw its title, *The Magic of the Egyptians and Chaldeans*. Then, wheeling round, he strode out of the tent. The doctor stared at me.

'What is his little idea?'

The phrase, so familiar on Poirot's lips, made me smile as it came from another.

'I don't know exactly,' I confessed. 'He's got some plan of exorcizing the evil spirits, I believe.'

I went in search of Poirot, and found him talking to the lean-faced young man who had been the late Mr Bleibner's secretary.

'No,' Mr Harper was saying, 'I've only been six months with the expedition. Yes, I knew Mr Bleibner's affairs pretty well.'

'Can you recount to me anything concerning his nephew?'

'He turned up here one day, not a bad-looking fellow. I'd never met him before, but some of the others had—Ames, I think, and Schneider. The old man wasn't at all pleased to see him. They were at it in no time, hammer and tongs. "Not a cent," the old man shouted. "Not one cent now or when I'm dead. I intend to leave my money to the further-ance of my life's work. I've been talking it over with Mr

Schneider today." And a bit more of the same. Young Bleibner lit out for Cairo right away.'

'Was he in perfectly good health at the time?'

'The old man?'

'No, the young one.'

'I believe he did mention there was something wrong with him. But it couldn't have been anything serious, or I should have remembered.'

'One thing more, has Mr Bleibner left a will?'

'So far as we know, he has not.'

'Are you remaining with the expedition, Mr Harper?'

'No, sir, I am not. I'm for New York as soon as I can square up things here. You may laugh if you like, but I'm not going to be this blasted Men-her-Ra's next victim. He'll get me if I stop here.'

The young man wiped the perspiration from his brow.

Poirot turned away. Over his shoulder he said with a peculiar smile:

'Remember, he got one of his victims in New York.'

'Oh, hell!' said Mr Harper forcibly.

'That young man is nervous,' said Poirot thoughtfully. 'He is on the edge, but absolutely on the edge.'

I glanced at Poirot curiously, but his enigmatical smile told me nothing. In company with Sir Guy Willard and Dr Tosswill we were taken round the excavations. The principal finds had been removed to Cairo, but some of the tomb furniture was extremely interesting. The enthusiasm of the young baronet was obvious, but I fancied that I detected a shade of nervousness in his manner as though he could not quite escape from the feeling of menace in the air. As we entered the tent which had been assigned to us, for a wash before joining the evening meal, a tall dark figure in white robes stood aside to let us pass with a graceful gesture and a murmured greeting in Arabic. Poirot stopped.

'You are Hassan, the late Sir John Willard's servant?'

'I served my Lord Sir John, now I serve his son.' He took a step nearer to us and lowered his voice. 'You are a wise one, they say, learned in dealing with evil spirits. Let the young master depart from here. There is evil in the air around us.'

And with an abrupt gesture, not waiting for a reply, he strode away.

'Evil in the air,' muttered Poirot. 'Yes, I feel it.'

Our meal was hardly a cheerful one. The floor was left to Dr Tosswill, who discoursed at length upon Egyptian antiquities. Just as we were preparing to retire to rest, Sir Guy caught Poirot by the arm and pointed. A shadowy figure was moving amidst the tents. It was no human one: I recognized distinctly the dog-headed figure I had seen carved on the walls of the tomb.

My blood froze at the sight.

'*Mon Dieu*!' murmured Poirot, crossing himself vigorously. 'Anubis, the jackal-headed, the god of departing souls.'

'Someone is hoaxing us,' cried Dr Tosswill, rising indignantly to his feet.

'It went into your tent, Harper,' muttered Sir Guy, his face dreadfully pale.

'No,' said Poirot, shaking his head, 'into that of the Dr Ames.'

The doctor stared at him incredulously; then, repeating Dr Tosswill's words, he cried:

'Someone is hoaxing us. Come, we'll soon catch the fellow.'

He dashed energetically in pursuit of the shadowy apparition. I followed him, but, search as we would, we could find no trace of any living soul having passed that way. We returned, somewhat disturbed in mind, to find Poirot taking energetic measures, in his own way, to ensure his personal safety. He was busily surrounding our tent with various diagrams and inscriptions which he was drawing in the sand. I recognized the five-pointed star or Pentagon many times repeated. As was his wont, Poirot was at the same time delivering an impromptu lecture on witchcraft and magic in general, White magic as opposed to Black, with various references to the Ka and the Book of the Dead thrown in.

It appeared to excite the liveliest contempt in Dr Tosswill, who drew me aside, literally snorting with rage.

'Balderdash, sir,' he exclaimed angrily. 'Pure balderdash. The man's an imposter. He doesn't know the difference between the superstitions of the Middle Ages and the beliefs of Ancient Egypt. Never have I heard such a hotch-potch of ignorance and credulity.'

I calmed the excited expert, and joined Poirot in the tent. My little friend was beaming cheerfully.

'We can now sleep in peace,' he declared happily. 'And I can do with some sleep. My head, it aches abominably. Ah, for a good *tisane*!'

As though in answer to prayer, the flap of the tent was lifted and Hassan appeared, bearing a steaming cup which he offered to Poirot. It proved to be camomile tea, a beverage of which he is inordinately fond. Having thanked Hassan and refused his offer of another cup for myself, we were left alone once more. I stood at the door of the tent some time after undressing, looking out over the desert.

'A wonderful place,' I said aloud, 'and a wonderful work. I can feel the fascination. This desert life, this probing into the heart of a vanished civilization. Surely, Poirot, you, too, must feel the charm?'

I got no answer, and I turned, a little annoyed. My annoyance was quickly changed to concern. Poirot was lying back across the rude couch, his face horribly convulsed. Beside him was the empty cup. I rushed to his side, then dashed out and across the camp to Dr Ames's tent.

'Dr Ames!' I cried. 'Come at once.'

'What's the matter?' said the doctor, appearing in pyjamas.

'My friend. He's ill. Dying. The camomile tea. Don't let Hassan leave the camp.'

Like a flash the doctor ran to our tent. Poirot was lying as I left him.

'Extraordinary,' cried Ames. 'Looks like a seizure—or—

what did you say about something he drank?' He picked up the empty cup.

'Only I did not drink it!' said a placid voice.

We turned in amazement. Poirot was sitting up on the bed. He was smiling.

'No,' he said gently. 'I did not drink it. While my good friend Hastings was apostrophizing the night, I took the opportunity of pouring it, not down my throat, but into a little bottle. That little bottle will go to the analytical chemist. No'—as the doctor made a sudden movement—'as a sensible man, you will understand that violence will be of no avail. During Hastings' absence to fetch you, I have had time to put the bottle in safe keeping. Ah, quick, Hastings, hold him!'

I misunderstood Poirot's anxiety. Eager to save my friend, I flung myself in front of him. But the doctor's swift movement had another meaning. His hand went to his mouth, a smell of bitter almonds filled the air, and he swayed forward and fell.

'Another victim,' said Poirot gravely, 'but the last. Perhaps it is the best way. He has three deaths on his head.'

'Dr Ames?' I cried, stupefied. 'But I thought you believed in some occult influence?'

'You misunderstood me, Hastings. What I meant was that I believe in the terrific force of superstition. Once get it firmly established that a series of deaths are supernatural, and you might almost stab a man in broad daylight, and it would still be put down to the curse, so strongly is the instinct of the supernatural implanted in the human race. I suspected from the first that a man was taking advantage of that instinct. The idea came to him, I imagine, with the death of Sir John Willard. A fury of superstition arose at once. As far as I could see, nobody could derive any particular profit from Sir John's death. Mr Bleibner was a different case. He was a man of great wealth. The information I received from New York contained several suggestive points. To begin with, young Bleibner was reported to have said he had a good friend in

Egypt from whom he could borrow. It was tacitly understood that he meant his uncle, but it seemed to me that in that case he would have said so outright. The words suggest some boon companion of his own. Another thing, he scraped up enough money to take him to Egypt, his uncle refused outright to advance him a penny, yet he was able to pay the return passage to New York. Someone must have lent him the money.'

'All that was very thin,' I objected.

'But there was more. Hastings, there occur often enough words spoken metaphorically which are taken literally. The opposite can happen too. In this case, words which were meant literally were taken metaphorically. Young Bleibner wrote plainly enough: "I am a leper", but nobody realized that he shot himself because he believed that he contracted the dread disease of leprosy.'

'What?' I ejaculated.

'It was the clever invention of a diabolical mind. Young Bleibner was suffering from some minor skin trouble; he had lived in the South Sea Islands, where the disease is common enough. Ames was a former friend of his, and a well-known medical man, he would never dream of doubting his word. When I arrived here, my suspicions were divided between Harper and Dr Ames, but I soon realized that only the doctor could have perpetrated and concealed the crimes, and I learnt from Harper that he was previously acquainted with young Bleibner. Doubtless the latter at some time or another had made a will or had insured his life in favour of the doctor. The latter saw his chance of acquiring wealth. It was easy for him to inoculate Mr Bleibner with the deadly germs. Then the nephew, overcome with despair at the dread news his friend had conveyed to him, shot himself. Mr Bleibner, whatever his intentions, had made no will. His fortune would pass to his nephew and from him to the doctor.'

'And Mr Schneider?'

'We cannot be sure. He knew young Bleibner too,

remember, and may have suspected something, or, again, the doctor may have thought that a further death motiveless and purposeless would strengthen the coils of superstition. Furthermore, I will tell you an interesting psychological fact, Hastings. A murderer has always a strong desire to repeat his successful crime, the performance of it grows upon him. Hence my fears for young Willard. The figure of Anubis you saw tonight was Hassan dressed up by my orders. I wanted to see if I could frighten the doctor. But it would take more than the supernatural to frighten him. I could see that he was not entirely taken in by my pretences of belief in the occult. The little comedy I played for him did not deceive him. I suspected that he would endeavour to make me the next victim. Ah, but in spite of *la mer maudite*, the heat abominable, and the annoyances of the sand, the little grey cells still functioned!'

Poirot proved to be perfectly right in his premises. Young Bleibner, some years ago, in a fit of drunken merriment, had made a jocular will, leaving 'my cigarette-case you admire so much and everything else of which I die possessed which will be principally debts to my good friend Robert Ames who once saved my life from drowning'.

The case was hushed up as far as possible, and, to this day, people talk of the remarkable series of deaths in connection with the Tomb of Men-her-Ra as a triumphal proof of the vengeance of a bygone king upon the desecrators of his tomb—a belief which, as Poirot pointed out to me, is contrary to all Egyptian belief and thought.

# THE FOURTH MAN

Canon Parfitt panted a little. Running for trains was not much of a business for a man of his age. For one thing his figure was not what it was and with the loss of his slender silhouette went an increasing tendency to be short of breath. This tendency the Canon himself always referred to, with dignity, as '*My heart*, you know!'

He sank into the corner of the first-class carriage with a sigh of relief. The warmth of the heated carriage was most agreeable to him. Outside the snow was falling. Lucky to get a corner seat on a long night journey. Miserable business if you didn't. There ought to be a sleeper on this train.

The other three corners were already occupied, and noting this fact Canon Parfitt became aware that the man in the far corner was smiling at him in gentle recognition. He was a clean-shaven man with a quizzical face and hair just turning grey on the temples. His profession was so clearly the law that no one could have mistaken him for anything else for a moment. Sir George Durand was, indeed, a very famous lawyer.

'Well, Parfitt,' he remarked genially, 'you had a run for it, didn't you?'

'Very bad for my heart, I'm afraid,' said the Canon. 'Quite a coincidence meeting you, Sir George. Are you going far north?'

'Newcastle,' said Sir George laconically. 'By the way,' he added, 'do you know Dr Campbell Clark?'

The man sitting on the same side of the carriage as the Canon inclined his head pleasantly.

'We met on the platform,' continued the lawyer. 'Another coincidence.'

Canon Parfitt looked at Dr Campbell Clark with a good deal of interest. It was a name of which he had often heard. Dr Clark was in the forefront as a physician and mental specialist, and his last book, *The Problem of the Unconscious Mind*, had been the most discussed book of the year.

Canon Parfitt saw a square jaw, very steady blue eyes and reddish hair untouched by grey, but thinning rapidly. And he received also the impression of a very forceful personality.

By a perfectly natural association of ideas the Canon looked across to the seat opposite him, half-expecting to receive a glance of recognition there also, but the fourth occupant of the carriage proved to be a total stranger—a foreigner, the Canon fancied. He was a slight dark man, rather insignificant in appearance. Huddled in a big overcoat, he appeared to be fast asleep.

'Canon Parfitt of Bradchester?' inquired Dr Campbell Clark in a pleasant voice.

The Canon looked flattered. Those 'scientific sermons' of his had really made a great hit—especially since the Press had taken them up. Well, that was what the Church needed—good modern up-to-date stuff.

'I have read your book with great interest, Dr Campbell Clark,' he said. 'Though it's a bit technical here and there for me to follow.'

Durand broke in.

'Are you for talking or sleeping, Canon?' he asked. 'I'll confess at once that I suffer from insomnia and that therefore I'm in favour of the former.'

'Oh! certainly. By all means,' said the Canon. 'I seldom sleep on these night journeys, and the book I have with me is a very dull one.'

'We are at any rate a representative gathering,' remarked

the doctor with a smile. 'The Church, the Law, the Medical Profession.'

'Not much we couldn't give an opinion on between us, eh?' laughed Durand. 'The Church for the spiritual view, myself for the purely worldly and legal view, and you, Doctor, with the widest field of all, ranging from the purely pathological to the—super-psychological! Between us three we should cover any ground pretty completely, I fancy.'

'Not so completely as you imagine, I think,' said Dr Clark. 'There's another point of view, you know, that you left out, and that's rather an important one.'

'Meaning?' queried the lawyer.

'The point of view of the Man in the Street.'

'Is that so important? Isn't the Man in the Street usually wrong?'

'Oh! almost always. But he has the thing that all expert opinion must lack—the personal point of view. In the end, you know, you can't get away from personal relationships. I've found that in my profession. For every patient who comes to me genuinely ill, at least five come who have nothing whatever the matter with them except an inability to live happily with the inmates of the same house. They call it everything—from housemaid's knee to writer's cramp, but it's all the same thing, the raw surface produced by mind rubbing against mind.'

'You have a lot of patients with "nerves", I suppose,' the Canon remarked disparagingly. His own nerves were excellent.

'Ah! and what do you mean by that?' The other swung round on him, quick as a flash. 'Nerves! People use that word and laugh after it, just as you did. "Nothing the matter with so and so," they say. "Just nerves." But, good God, man, you've got the crux of everything there! You can get at a mere bodily ailment and heal it. But at this day we know very little more about the obscure causes of the hundred and one forms of nervous disease than we did in—well, the reign of Queen Elizabeth!'

'Dear me,' said Canon Parfitt, a little bewildered by this onslaught. 'Is that so?'

'Mind you, it's a sign of grace,' Dr Campbell Clark went on. 'In the old days we considered man a simple animal, body and soul—with stress laid on the former.'

'Body, soul and spirit,' corrected the clergyman mildly.

'Spirit?' The doctor smiled oddly. 'What do you parsons mean exactly by spirit? You've never been very clear about it, you know. All down the ages you've funked an exact definition.'

The Canon cleared his throat in preparation for speech, but to his chagrin he was given no opportunity. The doctor went on.

'Are we even sure the word is spirit—might it not be *spirits*?'

'Spirits?' Sir George Durand questioned, his eyebrows raised quizzically.

'Yes.' Campbell Clark's gaze transferred itself to him. He leaned forward and tapped the other man lightly on the breast. 'Are you so sure,' he said gravely, 'that there is only one occupant of this structure—for that is all it is, you know—this desirable residence to be let furnished—for seven, twenty-one, forty-one, seventy-one—whatever it may be!— years? And in the end the tenant moves his things out—little by little—and then goes out of the house altogether—and down comes the house, a mass of ruin and decay. You're the master of the house—we'll admit that, but aren't you ever conscious of the presence of others—soft-footed serv- ants, hardly noticed, except for the work they do—work that you're not conscious of having done? Or friends—moods that take hold of you and make you, for the time being, a "different man" as the saying goes? You're the king of the castle, right enough, but be very sure the "dirty rascal" is there too.'

'My dear Clark,' drawled the lawyer. 'You make me posi- tively uncomfortable. Is my mind really a battleground of conflicting personalities? Is that Science's latest?'

It was the doctor's turn to shrug his shoulders.

'Your body is,' he said drily. 'If the body, why not the mind?'

'Very interesting,' said Canon Parfitt. 'Ah! Wonderful science—wonderful science.'

And inwardly he thought to himself: 'I can get a most arresting sermon out of that idea.'

But Dr Campbell Clark had leant back in his seat, his momentary excitement spent.

'As a matter of fact,' he remarked in a dry professional manner, 'it is a case of dual personality that takes me to Newcastle tonight. Very interesting case. Neurotic subject, of course. But quite genuine.'

'Dual personality,' said Sir George Durand thoughtfully. 'It's not so very rare, I believe. There's loss of memory as well, isn't there? I know the matter cropped up in a case in the Probate Court the other day.'

Dr Clark nodded.

'The classic case, of course,' he said, 'was that of Felicie Bault. You may remember hearing of it?'

'Of course,' said Canon Parfitt. 'I remember reading about it in the papers—but quite a long time ago—seven years at least.'

Dr Campbell Clark nodded.

'That girl became one of the most famous figures in France. Scientists from all over the world came to see her. She had no less than four distinct personalities. They were known as Felicie 1, Felicie 2, Felicie 3, etc.'

'Wasn't there some suggestion of deliberate trickery?' asked Sir George alertly.

'The personalities of Felicie 3 and Felicie 4 were a little open to doubt,' admitted the doctor. 'But the main facts remain. Felicie Bault was a Brittany peasant girl. She was the third of a family of five; the daughter of a drunken father and a mentally defective mother. In one of his drinking bouts the father strangled the mother and was, if I remember rightly, transported for life. Felicie was then five years of age. Some charitable people interested themselves in the children and Felicie was brought up and educated by an English maiden lady who had a kind of home for destitute children. She could make very little of Felicie, however. She describes the girl as abnormally slow and stupid, only taught to read and write with the greatest difficulty and clumsy with her hands. This lady, Miss Slater, tried to fit the girl for domestic service, and did indeed find her several places when she was of an age to take them. But she never stayed long anywhere owing to her stupidity and also her intense laziness.'

The doctor paused for a minute, and the Canon, re-crossing his legs, and arranging his travelling rug more closely round him, was suddenly aware that the man opposite him had moved very slightly. His eyes, which had formerly been shut, were now open, and something in them, something mocking and indefinable, startled the worthy Canon. It was as though the man were listening and gloating secretly over what he heard.

'There is a photograph taken of Felicie Bault at the age of seventeen,' continued the doctor. 'It shows her as a loutish peasant girl, heavy of build. There is nothing in that picture to indicate that she was soon to be one of the most famous persons in France.

'Five years later, when she was 22, Felicie Bault had a severe nervous illness, and on recovery the strange phenomena began to manifest themselves. The following are facts attested to by many eminent scientists. The personality called Felicie 1 was undistinguishable from the Felicie Bault of the last twenty-two years. Felicie 1 wrote French badly and haltingly, she spoke no foreign languages and was unable to play the piano. Felicie 2, on the contrary, spoke Italian fluently and German moderately. Her handwriting was quite dissimilar to that of Felicie 1, and she wrote fluent and expressive French. She could discuss politics and art and she was passionately fond of playing the piano. Felicie 3 had many points in common with Felicie 2. She was intelligent and apparently well educated, but in moral character she was a total contrast. She appeared, in fact, an utterly depraved creature—but depraved in a Parisian and not a provincial way. She knew all the Paris *argot*, and the expressions of the chic *demi monde*. Her language was filthy and she would rail against religion and so-called "good people" in the most blasphemous terms. Finally there was Felicie 4—a dreamy, almost half-witted creature, distinctly pious and professedly clairvoyant, but this fourth personality was very unsatisfactory and elusive and has been sometimes thought to be a deliberate trickery on the part of Felicie 3—a kind of joke played by her on a credulous public. I may say that (with the possible exception of Felicie 4) each personality was distinct and separate and had no knowledge of the others. Felicie 2 was undoubtedly the most predominant and would last sometimes for a fortnight at a time, then Felicie 1 would appear abruptly for a day or two. After that, perhaps Felicie 3 or 4, but the two latter seldom remained in command for more than a few hours. Each change was accompanied by severe headache and heavy sleep, and in each case there was complete loss of memory of the other states, the personality in question taking up life where she had left it, unconscious of the passage of time.'

'Remarkable,' murmured the Canon. 'Very remarkable. As yet we know next to nothing of the marvels of the universe.'

'We know that there are some very astute impostors in it,' remarked the lawyer drily.

'The case of Felicie Bault was investigated by lawyers as well as by doctors and scientists,' said Dr Campbell Clark quickly. 'Maître Quimbellier, you remember, made the most thorough investigation and confirmed the views of the scientists. And after all, why should it surprise us so much? We come across the double-yolked egg, do we not? And the twin banana? Why not the double soul—or in this case the quadruple soul—in the single body?'

'The double soul?' protested the Canon.

Dr Campbell Clark turned his piercing blue eyes on him.

'What else can we call it? That is to say—if the personality is the soul?'

'It is a good thing such a state of affairs is only in the nature of a "freak",' remarked Sir George. 'If the case were common, it would give rise to pretty complications.'

'The condition is, of course, quite abnormal,' agreed the doctor. 'It was a great pity that a longer study could not have been made, but all that was put an end to by Felicie's unexpected death.'

'There was something queer about that, if I remember rightly,' said the lawyer slowly.

Dr Campbell Clark nodded.

'A most unaccountable business. The girl was found one morning dead in bed. She had clearly been strangled. But to everyone's stupefaction it was presently proved beyond doubt that she had actually strangled herself. The marks on her neck were those of her own fingers. A method of suicide which, though not physically impossible, must have necessitated terrific muscular strength and almost superhuman will power. What had driven the girl to such straits has never been found out. Of course her mental balance must always have been precarious. Still, there it is. The curtain has been rung down for ever on the mystery of Felicie Bault.'

It was then that the man in the far corner laughed.

The other three men jumped as though shot. They had totally forgotten the existence of the fourth amongst them. As they stared towards the place where he sat, still huddled in his overcoat, he laughed again.

'You must excuse me, gentlemen,' he said, in perfect English that had, nevertheless, a foreign flavour.

He sat up, displaying a pale face with a small jet-black moustache.

'Yes, you must excuse me,' he said, with a mock bow. 'But really! in science, is the last word ever said?'

'You know something of the case we have been discussing?' asked the doctor courteously.

'Of the case? No. But I knew her.'

'Felicie Bault?'

'Yes. And Annette Ravel also. You have not heard of Annette Ravel, I see? And yet the story of the one is the story of the other. Believe me, you know nothing of Felicie Bault if you do not also know the history of Annette Ravel.'

He drew out his watch and looked at it.

'Just half an hour before the next stop. I have time to tell you the story—that is, if you care to hear it?'

'Please tell it to us,' said the doctor quietly.

'Delighted,' said the Canon. 'Delighted.'

Sir George Durand merely composed himself in an attitude of keen attention.

'My name, gentlemen,' began their strange travelling companion, 'is Raoul Letardeau. You have spoken just now of an English lady, Miss Slater, who interested herself in works of charity. I was born in that Brittany fishing village and when my parents were both killed in a railway accident it was Miss Slater who came to the rescue and saved me from the equivalent of your English workhouse. There were some twenty children under her care, girls and boys. Amongst these children were Felicie Bault and Annette Ravel. If I cannot make you understand the personality of Annette, gentlemen, you will understand nothing. She was the child of what you call a *"fille de joie"* who had died of consumption abandoned by her lover. The mother had been a dancer, and Annette, too, had the desire to dance. When I saw her first she was eleven years old, a little shrimp of a thing with eyes that alternately mocked and promised—a little creature all fire and life. And at once— yes, at once—she made me her slave. It was "Raoul, do this for me." "Raoul, do that for me." And me, I obeyed. Already I worshipped her, and she knew it.

'We would go down to the shore together, we three—for Felicie would come with us. And there Annette would pull off her shoes and stockings and dance on the sand. And then when she sank down breathless, she would tell us of what she meant to do and to be.

'"See you, I shall be famous. Yes, exceedingly famous. I will have hundreds and thousands of silk stockings—the finest silk. And I shall live in an exquisite apartment. All my lovers shall be young and handsome as well as being rich. And when I dance all Paris shall come to see me. They will yell and call and shout and go mad over my dancing. And in the winters I shall not dance. I shall go south to the sunlight. There are villas there with orange trees. I shall have one of them. I shall lie in the sun on silk cushions, eating oranges. As for you, Raoul, I will never forget you, however rich and famous I shall be. I will protect you and advance your career. Felicie here shall be my maid—no, her hands are too clumsy. Look at them, how large and coarse they are."

'Felicie would grow angry at that. And then Annette would go on teasing her.

'"She is so ladylike, Felicie—so elegant, so refined. She is a princess in disguise—ha, ha."

'"My father and mother were married, which is more than yours were," Felicie would growl out spitefully.

'"Yes, and your father killed your mother. A pretty thing, to be a murderer's daughter."

'"Your father left your mother to rot," Felicie would rejoin.

'"Ah! yes." Annette became thoughtful. "*Pauvre Maman*. One must keep strong and well. It is everything to keep strong and well."

'"I am as strong as a horse," Felicie boasted.

'And indeed she was. She had twice the strength of any other girl in the Home. And she was never ill.

'But she was stupid, you comprehend, stupid like a brute beast. I often wondered why she followed Annette round as she did. It was, with her, a kind of fascination. Sometimes, I think, she actually hated Annette, and indeed Annette was not kind to her. She jeered at her slowness and stupidity, and baited her in front of the others. I have seen Felicie grow quite white with rage. Sometimes I have thought that she would fasten her fingers round Annette's neck and choke the life out of her. She was not nimble-witted enough to reply to Annette's taunts, but she did learn in time to make one retort which never failed. That was a reference to her own health and strength. She had learned (what I had always known) that Annette envied her her strong physique, and she struck instinctively at the weak spot in her enemy's armour.

'One day Annette came to me in great glee.

'"Raoul," she said. "We shall have fun today with that stupid Felicie. We shall die of laughing."

'"What are you going to do?"

'"Come behind the little shed, and I will tell you."

'It seemed that Annette had got hold of some book. Part of it she did not understand, and indeed the whole thing was much over her head. It was an early work on hypnotism.

'"A bright object, they say. The brass knob of my bed, it twirls round. I made Felicie look at it last night. 'Look at it steadily,' I said. 'Do not take your eyes off it.' And then I twirled it. Raoul, I was frightened. Her eyes looked so queer— so queer. 'Felicie, you will do what I say always,' I said. 'I will do what you say always, Annette,' she answered. And then—and then—I said: 'Tomorrow you will bring a tallow candle out into the playground at twelve o'clock and start to eat it. And if anyone asks you, you will say that is it the best *galette* you ever tasted.' Oh! Raoul, think of it!"

'"But she'll never do such a thing," I objected.

'"The book says so. Not that I can quite believe it—but, oh! Raoul, if the book is all true, how we shall amuse ourselves!"

'I, too, thought the idea very funny. We passed word round to the comrades and at twelve o'clock we were all in the playground. Punctual to the minute, out came Felicie with a stump of candle in her hand. Will you believe me, Messieurs, she began solemnly to nibble at it? We were all in hysterics! Every now and then one or other of the children would go up to her and say solemnly: "It is good, what you eat there, eh, Felicie?" And she would answer: "But, yes, it is the best *galette* I ever tasted." And then we would shriek with laughter. We laughed at last so loud that the noise seemed to wake up Felicie to a realization of what she was doing. She blinked her eyes in a puzzled way, looked at the candle, then at us. She passed her hand over her forehead.

'"But what is it that I do here?" she muttered.

'"You are eating a candle," we screamed.

'"*I* made you do it. *I* made you do it," cried Annette, dancing about.

'Felicie stared for a moment. Then she went slowly up to Annette.

'"So it is you—it is you who have made me ridiculous? I seem to remember. Ah! I will kill you for this."

'She spoke in a very quiet tone, but Annette rushed suddenly away and hid behind me.

'"Save me, Raoul! I am afraid of Felicie. It was only a joke, Felicie. Only a joke."

'"I do not like these jokes," said Felicie. "You understand? I hate you. I hate you all."

'She suddenly burst out crying and rushed away.

'Annette was, I think, scared by the result of her exper-iment, and did not try to repeat it. But from that day on, her ascendancy over Felicie seemed to grow stronger.

'Felicie, I now believe, always hated her, but nevertheless she could not keep away from her. She used to follow Annette around like a dog.

'Soon after that, Messieurs, employment was found for me, and I only came to the Home for occasional holidays. Annette's desire to become a dancer was not taken seriously, but she developed a very pretty singing voice as she grew older and Miss Slater consented to her being trained as a singer.

'She was not lazy, Annette. She worked feverishly, without rest. Miss Slater was obliged to prevent her doing too much. She spoke to me once about her.

'"You have always been fond of Annette," she said.

"Persuade her not to work too hard. She has a little cough lately that I do not like."

'My work took me far afield soon afterwards. I received one or two letters from Annette at first, but then came silence. For five years after that I was abroad.

'Quite by chance, when I returned to Paris, my attention was caught by a poster advertising Annette Ravelli with a picture of the lady. I recognized her at once. That night I went to the theatre in question. Annette sang in French and Italian. On the stage she was wonderful. Afterwards I went to her dressing-room. She received me at once.

'"Why, Raoul," she cried, stretching out her whitened hands to me. "This is splendid. Where have you been all these years?"

'I would have told her, but she did not really want to listen.'

'"You see, I have very nearly arrived!"

'She waved a triumphant hand round the room filled with bouquets.

'"The good Miss Slater must be proud of your success."

'"That old one? No, indeed. She designed me, you know, for the Conservatoire. Decorous concert singing. But me, I am an artist. It is here, on the variety stage, that I can express myself."

'Just then a handsome middle-aged man came in. He was very distinguished. By his manner I soon saw that he was Annette's protector. He looked sideways at me, and Annette explained.

'"A friend of my infancy. He passes through Paris, sees my picture on a poster *et voilà!*"

'The man was then very affable and courteous. In my presence he produced a ruby and diamond bracelet and clasped it on Annette's wrist. As I rose to go, she threw me a glance of triumph and a whisper.

'"I arrive, do I not? You see? All the world is before me."

'But as I left the room, I heard her cough, a sharp dry cough. I knew what it meant, that cough. It was the legacy of her consumptive mother.

'I saw her next two years later. She had gone for refuge to Miss Slater. Her career had broken down. She was in a state of advanced consumption for which the doctors said nothing could be done.

'Ah! I shall never forget her as I saw her then! She was lying in a kind of shelter in the garden. She was kept out-doors night and day. Her cheeks were hollow and flushed, her eyes bright and feverish and she coughed repeatedly.

'She greeted me with a kind of desperation that startled me.

'"It is good to see you, Raoul. You know what they say— that I may not get well? They say it behind my back, you understand. To me they are soothing and consolatory. But it is not true, Raoul, it is not true! I shall not permit myself to die. Die? With beautiful life stretching in front of me? It is the will to live that matters. All the great doctors say that nowadays. I am not one of the feeble ones who let go. Already I feel myself infinitely better—infinitely better, do you hear?"

'She raised herself on her elbow to drive her words home, then fell back, attacked by a fit of coughing that racked her thin body.

'"The cough—it is nothing," she gasped. "And haemorrhages do not frighten me. I shall surprise the doctors. It is the will that counts. Remember, Raoul, I am going to live."

'It was pitiful, you understand, pitiful.

'Just then, Felicie Bault came out with a tray. A glass of hot milk. She gave it to Annette and watched her drink it with an expression that I could not fathom. There was a kind of smug satisfaction in it.

'Annette too caught the look. She flung the glass down angrily, so that it smashed to bits.

'"You see her? That is how she always looks at me. She is glad I am going to die! Yes, she gloats over it. She who is well and strong. Look at her, never a day's illness, that one! And all for nothing. What good is that great carcass of hers to her? What can she make of it?"

'Felicie stooped and picked up the broken fragments of glass.

'"I do not mind what she says," she observed in a singsong voice. "What does it matter? I am a respectable girl, I am. As for her. She will be knowing the fires of Purgatory before very long. I am a Christian, I say nothing."

'"You hate me, cried Annette. "You have always hated me. Ah! but I can charm you, all the same. I can make you do what I want. See now, if I ask you to, you would go down on your knees before me now on the grass."

'"You are absurd," said Felicie uneasily.

'"But, yes, you will do it. You will. To please me. Down on your knees. I ask it of you, I, Annette. Down on your knees, Felicie."

'Whether it was the wonderful pleading in the voice, or some deeper motive, Felicie obeyed. She sank slowly to her knees, her arms spread wide, her face vacant and stupid.

'Annette flung her head back and laughed—peal upon peal of laughter.

'"Look at her, with her stupid face! How ridiculous she looks. You can get up now, Felicie, thank you! It is of no use to scowl at me. I am your mistress. You have to do what I say."

'She lay back on her pillows exhausted. Felicie picked up the tray and moved slowly away. Once she looked back over her shoulder, and the smouldering resentment in her eyes startled me.

'I was not there when Annette died. But it was terrible, it seems. She clung to life. She fought against death like a madwoman. Again and again she gasped out: "I will not die—do you hear me? I will not die. I will live—live—"

'Miss Slater told me all this when I came to see her six months later.

'"My poor Raoul," she said kindly. "You loved her, did you not?"

'"Always—always. But of what use could I be to her? Let

us not talk of it. She is dead—she so brilliant, so full of burning life . . ."

'Miss Slater was a sympathetic woman. She went on to talk of other things. She was very worried about Felicie, so she told me. The girl had had a queer sort of nervous breakdown, and ever since she had been very strange in manner.

'"You know," said Miss Slater, after a momentary hesitation, "that she is learning the piano?"

'I did not know it, and was very much surprised to hear it. Felicie—learning the piano! I would have declared the girl would not know one note from another.

'"She has talent, they say," continued Miss Slater. "I can't understand it. I have always put her down as—well, Raoul, you know yourself, she was always a stupid girl."

'I nodded.

'"She is so strange in her manner sometimes—I really don't know what to make of it."

'A few minutes later I entered the Salle de Lecture. Felicie was playing the piano. She was playing the air that I had heard Annette sing in Paris. You understand, Messieurs, it gave me quite a turn. And then, hearing me, she broke off suddenly and looked round at me, her eyes full of mockery and intelligence. For a moment I thought—Well, I will not tell you what I thought.

'"*Tiens*!" she said. "So it is you—*Monsieur* Raoul."

'I cannot describe the way she said it. To Annette I had never ceased to be Raoul. But Felicie, since we had met as grown-ups, always addressed me as *Monsieur* Raoul. But the way she said it now was different—as though the *Monsieur*, slightly stressed, was somehow very amusing.

'"Why, Felicie," I stammered. "You look quite different today."

'"Do I?" she said reflectively. "It is odd, that. But do not be so solemn, Raoul—decidedly I shall call you Raoul—did we not play together as children?—Life was made for laughter. Let us talk of the poor Annette—she who is dead and buried. Is she in Purgatory, I wonder, or where?"

'And she hummed a snatch of song—untunefully enough, but the words caught my attention.

'"Felicie," I cried. "You speak Italian?"

'"Why not, Raoul? I am not as stupid as I pretend to be, perhaps." She laughed at my mystification.

'"I don't understand—" I began.

'"But I will tell you. I am a very fine actress, though no one suspects it. I can play many parts—and play them very well."

'She laughed again and ran quickly out of the room before I could stop her.

'I saw her again before I left. She was asleep in an armchair. She was snoring heavily. I stood and watched her, fascinated, yet repelled. Suddenly she woke with a start. Her eyes, dull and lifeless, met mine.

'"Monsieur Raoul," she muttered mechanically.

'"Yes, Felicie, I am going now. Will you play to me again before I go?"

'"I? Play? You are laughing at me, Monsieur Raoul."

'"Don't you remember playing to me this morning?"

'She shook her head.

'"I play? How can a poor girl like me play?"

'She paused for a minute as though in thought, then beckoned me nearer.

'"Monsieur Raoul, there are strange things going on in this house! They play tricks upon you. They alter the clocks. Yes, yes, I know what I am saying. And it is all her doing."

'"Whose doing?" I asked, startled.

'"That Annette's. That wicked one's. When she was alive she always tormented me. Now that she is dead, she comes back from the dead to torment me."

'I stared at Felicie. I could see now that she was in an extremity of terror, her eyes staring from her head.

'"She is bad, that one. She is bad, I tell you. She would take the bread from your mouth, the clothes from your back, *the soul from your body* . . ."

'She clutched me suddenly.

'"I am afraid, I tell you—afraid. I hear her voice—not in my ear—no, not in my ear. Here, in my head—" She tapped her forehead. "She will drive me away—drive me away altogether, and then what shall I do, what will become of me?"

'Her voice rose almost to a shriek. She had in her eyes the look of the terrified brute beast at bay . . .

'Suddenly she smiled, a pleasant smile, full of cunning, with something in it that made me shiver.

'"If it should come to it, Monsieur Raoul, I am very strong with my hands—very strong with my hands."

'I had never noticed her hands particularly before. I looked at them now and shuddered in spite of myself. Squat brutal fingers, and as Felicie had said, terribly strong . . . I cannot explain to you the nausea that swept over me. With hands such as these her father must have strangled her mother . . .

'That was the last time I ever saw Felicie Bault. Immediately afterwards I went abroad—to South America. I returned from there two years after her death. Something I had read in the newspapers of her life and sudden death. I have heard fuller details tonight—from you—gentlemen! Felicie 3 and Felicie 4—I wonder? She was a good actress, you know!'

The train suddenly slackened speed. The man in the corner sat erect and buttoned his overcoat more closely.

'What is your theory?' asked the lawyer, leaning forward.

'I can hardly believe—' began Canon Parfitt, and stopped.

The doctor said nothing. He was gazing steadily at Raoul Letardeau.

'*The clothes from your back, the soul from your body,*' quoted the Frenchman lightly. He stood up. 'I say to you, Messieurs, that the history of Felicie Bault is the history of Annette Ravel. You did not know her, gentlemen. I did. *She was very fond of life . . .*'

His hand on the door, ready to spring out, he turned suddenly and bending down tapped Canon Parfitt on the chest.

'M. le docteur over there, he said just now, that all *this*'—

his hand smote the Canon's stomach, and the Canon winced—'was only a residence. Tell me, if you find a burglar in your house what do you do? Shoot him, do you not?'

'No,' cried the Canon. 'No, indeed—I mean—not in this country.'

But he spoke the last words to empty air. The carriage door banged.

The clergyman, the lawyer and the doctor were alone. The fourth corner was vacant.

# THE IDOL HOUSE OF ASTARTE

'And now, Dr Pender, what are you going to tell us?'

The old clergyman smiled gently.

'My life has been passed in quiet places,' he said. 'Very few eventful happenings have come my way. Yet once, when I was a young man, I had one very strange and tragic experience.'

'Ah!' said Joyce Lemprière encouragingly.

'I have never forgotten it,' continued the clergyman. 'It made a profound impression on me at the time, and to this day by a slight effort of memory I can feel again the awe and horror of that terrible moment when I saw a man stricken to death by apparently no mortal agency.'

'You make me feel quite creepy, Pender,' complained Sir Henry.

'It made me feel creepy, as you call it,' replied the other. 'Since then I have never laughed at the people who use the word atmosphere. There is such a thing. There are certain places imbued and saturated with good or evil influences which can make their power felt.'

'That house, The Larches, is a very unhappy one,' remarked Miss Marple. 'Old Mr Smithers lost all his money and had to leave it, then the Carslakes took it and Johnny Carslake fell downstairs and broke his leg and Mrs Carslake had to go away to the south of France for her health, and now the Burdens have got it and I hear that poor Mr Burden has got to have an operation almost immediately.'

'There is, I think, rather too much superstition about such matters,' said Mr Petherick. 'A lot of damage is done to property by foolish reports heedlessly circulated.'

'I have known one or two "ghosts" that have had a very robust personality,' remarked Sir Henry with a chuckle.

'I think,' said Raymond, 'we should allow Dr Pender to go on with his story.'

Joyce got up and switched off the two lamps, leaving the room lit only by the flickering firelight.

'Atmosphere,' she said. 'Now we can get along.'

Dr Pender smiled at her, and leaning back in his chair and taking off his pince-nez, he began his story in a gentle reminiscent voice.

'I don't know whether any of you know Dartmoor at all. The place I am telling you about is situated on the borders of Dartmoor. It was a very charming property, though it had been on the market without finding a purchaser for several years. The situation was perhaps a little bleak in winter, but the views were magnificent and there were certain curious and original features about the property itself. It was bought by a man called Haydon—Sir Richard Haydon. I had known him in his college days, and though I had lost sight of him for some years, the old ties of friendship still held, and I accepted with pleasure his invitation to go down to Silent Grove, as his new purchase was called.

'The house party was not a very large one. There was Richard Haydon himself, and his cousin, Elliot Haydon. There was a Lady Mannering with a pale, rather inconspicuous daughter called Violet. There was a Captain Rogers and his wife, hard riding, weather-beaten people, who lived only for horses and hunting. There was also a young Dr Symonds and there was Miss Diana Ashley. I knew something about the last named. Her picture was very often in the Society papers and she was one of the notorious beauties of the Season. Her appearance was indeed very striking. She was dark and tall, with a beautiful skin of an even tint of pale cream, and her half closed dark eyes set slantways in her head gave her a curiously piquant oriental appearance. She had, too, a wonderful speaking voice, deep-toned and bell-like.

'I saw at once that my friend Richard Haydon was very much attracted by her, and I guessed that the whole party was merely arranged as a setting for her. Of her own feelings I was not so sure. She was capricious in her favours. One day talking to Richard and excluding everyone else from her notice, and another day she would favour his cousin, Elliot, and appear hardly to notice that such a person as Richard existed, and then again she would bestow the most bewitching smiles upon the quiet and retiring Dr Symonds.

'On the morning after my arrival our host showed us all over the place. The house itself was unremarkable, a good solid house built of Devonshire granite. Built to withstand time and exposure. It was unromantic but very comfortable. From the windows of it one looked out over the panorama of the Moor, vast rolling hills crowned with weather-beaten Tors.

'On the slopes of the Tor nearest to us were various hut circles, relics of the bygone days of the late Stone Age. On another hill was a barrow which had recently been excavated, and in which certain bronze implements had been found. Haydon was by way of being interested in antiquarian matters and he talked to us with a great deal of energy and enthusiasm. This particular spot, he explained, was particularly rich in relics of the past.

'Neolithic hut dwellers, Druids, Romans, and even traces of the early Phoenicians were to be found.

'"But this place is the most interesting of all," he said "You know its name—Silent Grove. Well, it is easy enough to see what it takes its name from."

'He pointed with his hand. That particular part of the country was bare enough—rocks, heather and bracken, but about a hundred yards from the house there was a densely planted grove of trees.

'"That is a relic of very early days," said Haydon, "The

trees have died and been replanted, but on the whole it has been kept very much as it used to be—perhaps in the time of the Phoenician settlers. Come and look at it."

'We all followed him. As we entered the grove of trees a curious oppression came over me. I think it was the silence. No birds seemed to nest in these trees. There was a feeling about it of desolation and horror. I saw Haydon looking at me with a curious smile.

'"Any feeling about this place, Pender?" he asked me. "Antagonism now? Or uneasiness?"

'"I don't like it," I said quietly.

'"You are within your rights. This was a stronghold of one of the ancient enemies of your faith. This is the Grove of Astarte."

'"Astarte?"

'"Astarte, or Ishtar, or Ashtoreth, or whatever you choose to call her. I prefer the Phoenician name of Astarte. There is, I believe, one known Grove of Astarte in this country— in the North on the Wall. I have no evidence, but I like to believe that we have a true and authentic Grove of Astarte here. Here, within this dense circle of trees, sacred rites were performed."

'"Sacred rites," murmured Diana Ashley. Her eyes had a dreamy faraway look. "What were they, I wonder?"

'"Not very reputable by all accounts," said Captain Rogers with a loud unmeaning laugh. "Rather hot stuff, I imagine."

'Haydon paid no attention to him.

'"In the centre of the Grove there should be a Temple," he said. "I can't run to Temples, but I have indulged in a little fancy of my own."

'We had at that moment stepped out into a little clearing in the centre of the trees. In the middle of it was something not unlike a summerhouse made of stone. Diana Ashley looked inquiringly at Haydon.

'"I call it The Idol House," he said. "It is the Idol House of Astarte."

'He led the way up to it. Inside, on a rude ebony pillar,

there reposed a curious little image representing a woman with crescent horns, seated on a lion.

'"Astarte of the Phoenicians," said Haydon, "the Goddess of the Moon."

'"The Goddess of the Moon," cried Diana. "Oh, do let us have a wild orgy tonight. Fancy dress. And we will come out here in the moonlight and celebrate the rites of Astarte."

'I made a sudden movement and Elliot Haydon, Richard's cousin, turned quickly to me.

'"You don't like all this, do you, Padre?" he said.

'"No," I said gravely. "I don't."

'He looked at me curiously. "But it is only tomfoolery. Dick can't know that this really is a sacred grove. It is just a fancy of his; he likes to play with the idea. And anyway, if it were—"

'"If it were?"

'"Well—" he laughed uncomfortably. "You don't believe in that sort of thing, do you? You, a parson."

'"I am not sure that as a parson I ought not to believe in it."

'"But that sort of thing is all finished and done with."

'"I am not so sure," I said musingly. "I only know this: I am not as a rule a sensitive man to atmosphere, but ever since I entered this grove of trees I have felt a curious impression and sense of evil and menace all round me."

'He glanced uneasily over his shoulder.

'"Yes," he said, "it is—it is queer, somehow. I know what you mean but I suppose it is only our imagination makes us feel like that. What do you say, Symonds?"

'The doctor was silent a minute or two before he replied. Then he said quietly:

'"I don't like it. I can't tell you why. But somehow or other, I don't like it."

'At that moment Violet Mannering came across to me.

'"I hate this place," she cried. "I hate it. Do let's get out of it."

'We moved away and the others followed us. Only Diana

Ashley lingered. I turned my head over my shoulder and saw her standing in front of the Idol House gazing earnestly at the image within it.

'The day was an unusually hot and beautiful one and Diana Ashley's suggestion of a Fancy Dress party that evening was received with general favour. The usual laughing and whispering and frenzied secret sewing took place and when we all made our appearance for dinner there were the usual outcries of merriment. Rogers and his wife were Neolithic hut dwellers—explaining the sudden lack of hearth rugs. Richard Haydon called himself a Phoenician sailor, and his cousin was a Brigand Chief, Dr Symonds was a chef, Lady Mannering was a hospital nurse, and her daughter was a Circassian slave. I myself was arrayed somewhat too warmly as a monk. Diana Ashley came down last and was somewhat of a disappointment to all of us, being wrapped in a shapeless black domino.

'"The Unknown," she declared airily. "That is what I am. Now for goodness' sake let's go in to dinner."

'After dinner we went outside. It was a lovely night, warm and soft, and the moon was rising.

'We wandered about and chatted and the time passed quickly enough. It must have been an hour later when we realized that Diana Ashley was not with us.

'"Surely she has not gone to bed," said Richard Haydon.

'Violet Mannering shook her head.

'"Oh, no," she said. "I saw her going off in that direction about a quarter of an hour ago." She pointed as she spoke towards the grove of trees that showed black and shadowy in the moonlight.

'"I wonder what she is up to," said Richard Haydon, "some devilment, I swear. Let's go and see."

'We all trooped off together, somewhat curious as to what Miss Ashley had been up to. Yet I, for one, felt a curious reluctance to enter that dark foreboding belt of trees. Something stronger than myself seemed to be holding me back and urging me not to enter. I felt more definitely convinced than ever of the essential evilness of the spot. I think that some of the others experienced the same sensations that I did, though they would have been loath to admit it. The trees were so closely planted that the moonlight could not penetrate. There were a dozen soft sounds all round us, whisperings and sighings. The feeling was eerie in the extreme, and by common consent we all kept close together.

'Suddenly we came out into the open clearing in the middle of the grove and stood rooted to the spot in amazement, for there, on the threshold of the Idol House, stood a shimmering figure wrapped tightly round in diaphanous gauze and with two crescent horns rising from the dark masses of her hair.

'"My God!" said Richard Haydon, and the sweat sprang out on his brow.

'But Violet Mannering was sharper.

'"Why, it's Diana," she exclaimed. "What has she done to herself? Oh, she looks quite different somehow!"

'The figure in the doorway raised her hands. She took a step forward and chanted in a high sweet voice.

'"I am the Priestess of Astarte," she crooned. "Beware how you approach me, for I hold death in my hand."

'"Don't do it, dear," protested Lady Mannering. "You give us the creeps, you really do."

'Haydon sprang forward towards her.

'"My God, Diana!" he cried. "You are wonderful."

'My eyes were accustomed to the moonlight now and I could see more plainly. She did, indeed, as Violet had said, look quite different. Her face was more definitely oriental, and her eyes more of slits with something cruel in their gleam, and the strange smile on her lips was one that I had never seen there before.

'"Beware," she cried warningly. "Do not approach the Goddess. If anyone lays a hand on me it is death."

'"You are wonderful, Diana," cried Haydon, "but do stop it. Somehow or other I—I don't like it."

'He was moving towards her across the grass and she flung out a hand towards him.

'"Stop," she cried. "One step nearer and I will smite you with the magic of Astarte."

'Richard Haydon laughed and quickened his pace, when all at once a curious thing happened. He hesitated for a moment, then seemed to stumble and fall headlong.

'He did not get up again, but lay where he had fallen prone on the ground.

'Suddenly Diana began to laugh hysterically. It was a strange horrible sound breaking the silence of the glade.

'With an oath Elliot sprang forward.

'"I can't stand this," he cried, "get up, Dick, get up, man."

'But still Richard Haydon lay where he had fallen. Elliot Haydon reached his side, knelt by him and turned him gently over. He bent over him, peering in his face.

'Then he rose sharply to his feet and stood swaying a little.

'"Doctor," he said. "Doctor, for God's sake come. I—I think he is dead."

'Symonds ran forward and Elliot rejoined us walking very slowly. He was looking down at his hands in a way I didn't understand.

'At that moment there was a wild scream from Diana.

'"I have killed him," she cried. "Oh, my God! I didn't mean to, but I have killed him."

'And she fainted dead away, falling in a crumpled heap on the grass.

'There was a cry from Mrs Rogers.

'"Oh, do let us get away from this dreadful place," she wailed, "anything might happen to us here. Oh, it's awful!"

'Elliot got hold of me by the shoulder.

'"It can't be, man," he murmured. "I tell you it can't *be*. A man cannot be killed like that. It is—it's against Nature."

'I tried to soothe him.

'"There is some explanation," I said. "Your cousin must

have had some unsuspected weakness of the heart. The shock and excitement—"

'He interrupted me.

'"You don't understand," he said. He held up his hands for me to see and I noticed a red stain on them.

'"Dick didn't die of shock, he was stabbed—stabbed to the heart, and *there is no weapon*."

'I stared at him incredulously. At that moment Symonds rose from his examination of the body and came towards us. He was pale and shaking all over.

'"Are we all mad?" he said. "What is this place—that things like this can happen in it?"

'"Then it is true," I said.

'He nodded.

'"The wound is such as would be made by a long thin dagger, but—there is no dagger there."

'We all looked at each other.

'"But it must be there," cried Elliot Haydon. "It must have dropped out. It must be on the ground somewhere. Let us look."

'We peered about vainly on the ground. Violet Mannering said suddenly:

'"Diana had something in her hand. A kind of dagger. I saw it. I saw it glitter when she threatened him."

'Elliot Haydon shook his head.

'"He never even got within three yards of her," he objected.

'Lady Mannering was bending over the prostrate girl on the ground.

'"There is nothing in her hand now," she announced, "and I can't see anything on the ground. Are you sure you saw it, Violet? I didn't."

'Dr Symonds came over to the girl.

'"We must get her to the house," he said. "Rogers, will you help?"

'Between us we carried the unconscious girl back to the house. Then we returned and fetched the body of Sir Richard.'

Dr Pender broke off apologetically and looked round.

'One would know better nowadays,' he said, 'owing to the prevalence of detective fiction. Every street boy knows that a body must be left where it is found. But in these days we had not the same knowledge, and accordingly we carried the body of Richard Haydon back to his bedroom in the square granite house and the butler was despatched on a bicycle in search of the police—a ride of some twelve miles.

'It was then that Elliot Haydon drew me aside.

'"Look here," he said. "I am going back to the grove. That weapon has got to be found."

'"If there was a weapon," I said doubtfully.

'He seized my arm and shook it fiercely. "You have got that superstitious stuff into your head. You think his death was supernatural; well, I am going back to the grove to find out."

'I was curiously averse to his doing so. I did my utmost to dissuade him, but without result. The mere idea of that thick circle of trees was abhorrent to me and I felt a strong premonition of further disaster. But Elliot was entirely pig-headed. He was, I think, scared himself, but would not admit it. He went off fully armed with determination to get to the bottom of the mystery.

'It was a very dreadful night, none of us could sleep, or attempt to do so. The police, when they arrived, were frankly incredulous of the whole thing. They evinced a strong desire to cross-examine Miss Ashley, but there they had to reckon with Dr Symonds, who opposed the idea vehemently. Miss Ashley had come out of her faint or trance and he had given her a long sleeping draught. She was on no account to be disturbed until the following day.

'It was not until about seven o'clock in the morning that anyone thought about Elliot Haydon, and then Symonds suddenly asked where he was. I explained what Elliot had done and Symonds's grave face grew a shade graver. "I wish he hadn't. It is—it is foolhardy," he said.

'"You don't think any harm can have happened to him?"

'"I hope not. I think, Padre, that you and I had better go and see."

'I knew he was right, but it took all the courage in my command to nerve myself for the task. We set out together and entered once more that ill-fated grove of trees. We called him twice and got no reply. In a minute or two we came into the clearing, which looked pale and ghostly in the early morning light. Symonds clutched my arm and I uttered a muttered exclamation. Last night when we had seen it in the moonlight there had been the body of a man lying face downwards on the grass. Now in the early morning light the same sight met our eyes. Elliot Haydon was lying on the exact spot where his cousin had been.

'"My God!" said Symonds. "*It has got him too!*"

'We ran together over the grass. Elliot Haydon was unconscious but breathing feebly and this time there was no doubt of what had caused the tragedy. A long thin bronze weapon remained in the wound.

'"Got him through the shoulder, not through the heart. That is lucky," commented the doctor. "On my soul, I don't know what to think. At any rate he is not dead and he will be able to tell us what happened."

'But that was just what Elliot Haydon was not able to do. His description was vague in the extreme. He had hunted about vainly for the dagger and at last giving up the search had taken up a stand near the Idol House. It was then that he became increasingly certain that someone was watching him from the belt of trees. He fought against this impression but was not able to shake it off. He described a cold strange wind that began to blow. It seemed to come not from the trees but from the interior of the Idol House. He turned round, peering inside it. He saw the small figure of the Goddess and he felt he was under an optical delusion. The figure seemed to grow larger and larger. Then he suddenly received something that felt like a blow between his temples which sent him reeling back, and as he fell he was conscious of a sharp burning pain in his left shoulder.

'The dagger was identified this time as being the identical one which had been dug up in the barrow on the hill, and which had been bought by Richard Haydon. Where he had kept it, in the house or in the Idol House in the grove, none seemed to know.

'The police were of the opinion, and always will be, that he was deliberately stabbed by Miss Ashley, but in view of our combined evidence that she was never within three yards of him, they could not hope to support the charge against her. So the thing has been and remains a mystery.'

There was a silence.

'There doesn't seem anything to say,' said Joyce Lemprière at length. 'It is all so horrible—and uncanny. Have you no explanation for yourself, Dr Pender?'

The old man nodded. 'Yes,' he said. 'I have an explanation—a kind of explanation, that is. Rather a curious one—but to my mind it still leaves certain factors unaccounted for.'

'I have been to séances,' said Joyce, 'and you may say what you like, very queer things can happen. I suppose one can explain it by some kind of hypnotism. The girl really turned herself into a Priestess of Astarte, and I suppose somehow or other she must have stabbed him. Perhaps she threw the dagger that Miss Mannering saw in her hand.'

'Or it might have been a javelin,' suggested Raymond West. 'After all, moonlight is not very strong. She might have had a kind of spear in her hand and stabbed him at a distance, and then I suppose mass hypnotism comes into account. I mean, you were all prepared to see him stricken down by supernatural means and so you saw it like that.'

'I have seen many wonderful things done with weapons and knives at music halls,' said Sir Henry. 'I suppose it is possible that a man could have been concealed in the belt of trees, and that he might from there have thrown a knife or a dagger with sufficient accuracy—agreeing, of course, that he was a professional. I admit that that seems rather far-fetched, but it seems the only really feasible theory. You remember that the other man was distinctly under the impression that there was someone in the grove of trees watching him. As to Miss Mannering saying that Miss Ashley had a dagger in her hand and the others saying she hadn't, that doesn't surprise me. If you had had my experience you would know that five persons' account of the same thing will differ so widely as to be almost incredible.'

Mr Petherick coughed.

'But in all these theories we seem to be overlooking one essential fact,' he remarked. 'What became of the weapon? Miss Ashley could hardly get rid of a javelin standing as she was in the middle of an open space; and if a hidden murderer had thrown a dagger, then the dagger would still have been in the wound when the man was turned over. We must, I think, discard all far-fetched theories and confine ourselves to sober fact.'

'And where does sober fact lead us?'

'Well, one thing seems quite clear. No one was near the man when he was stricken down, so the only person who *could* have stabbed him was he himself. Suicide, in fact.'

'But why on earth should he wish to commit suicide?' asked Raymond West incredulously.

The lawyer coughed again. 'Ah, that is a question of theory once more,' he said. 'At the moment I am not concerned with theories. It seems to me, excluding the supernatural in which I do not for one moment believe, that that was the only way things could have happened. He stabbed himself, and as he fell his arms flew out, wrenching the dagger from the wound and flinging it far into the zone of the trees. That is, I think, although somewhat unlikely, a possible happening.'

'I don't like to say, I am sure,' said Miss Marple. 'It all perplexes me very much indeed. But curious things do happen. At Lady Sharpley's garden party last year the man who was arranging the clock golf tripped over one of the numbers—quite unconscious he was—and didn't come round for about five minutes.'

'Yes, dear Aunt,' said Raymond gently, 'but he wasn't stabbed, was he?'

'Of course not, dear,' said Miss Marple. 'That is what I am telling you. Of course there is only one way that poor Sir Richard could have been stabbed, but I do wish I knew what caused him to stumble in the first place. Of course, it might have been a tree root. He would be looking at the girl, of course, and when it is moonlight one does trip over things.'

'You say that there is only one way that Sir Richard could have been stabbed, Miss Marple,' said the clergyman, looking at her curiously.

'It is very sad and I don't like to think of it. He was a right-handed man, was he not? I mean to stab himself in the left shoulder he must have been. I was always so sorry for poor Jack Baynes in the War. He shot himself in the foot, you remember, after very severe fighting at Arras. He told me about it when I went to see him in hospital, and very ashamed of it he was. I don't expect this poor man, Elliot Haydon, profited much by his wicked crime.'

'Elliot Haydon,' cried Raymond. 'You think he did it?'

'I don't see how anyone else could have done it,' said Miss Marple, opening her eyes in gentle surprise. 'I mean if, as Mr Petherick so wisely says, one looks at the facts and disregards all that atmosphere of heathen goddesses which I don't think is very nice. He went up to him first and turned him over, and of course to do that he would have to have had his back to them all, and being dressed as a brigand chief he would be sure to have a weapon of some kind in his belt. I remember dancing with a man dressed as a brigand chief when I was a young girl. He had five kinds of knives and daggers, and I can't tell you how awkward and uncomfortable it was for his partner.'

All eyes were turned towards Dr Pender.

'I knew the truth,' said he, 'five years after that tragedy occurred. It came in the shape of a letter written to me by Elliot Haydon. He said in it that he fancied that I had always suspected him. He said it was a sudden temptation. He too loved Diana Ashley, but he was only a poor struggling barrister. With Richard out of the way and inheriting his title and estates, he saw a wonderful prospect opening up before him. The dagger had jerked out of his belt as he knelt down by his cousin, and almost before he had time to think he drove it in and returned it to his belt again. He stabbed himself later in order to divert suspicion. He wrote to me on the eve of starting on an expedition to the South Pole in case, as he said, he should never come back. I do not think that he meant to come back, and I know that, as Miss Marple has said, his crime profited him nothing. "For five years," he wrote, "I have lived in Hell. I hope, at least, that I may expiate my crime by dying honourably."'

There was a pause.

'And he did die honourably,' said Sir Henry. 'You have changed the names in your story, Dr Pender, but I think I recognize the man you mean.'

'As I said,' went on the old clergyman, 'I do not think that explanation quite covers the facts. I still think there was an evil influence in that grove, an influence that directed Elliot Haydon's action. Even to this day I can never think without a shudder of The Idol House of Astarte.'

# THE GIPSY

Macfarlane had often noticed that his friend, Dickie Carpenter, had a strange aversion to gipsies. He had never known the reason for it. But when Dickie's engagement to Esther Lawes was broken off, there was a momentary tearing down of reserves between the two men.

Macfarlane had been engaged to the younger sister, Rachel, for about a year. He had known both the Lawes girls since they were children. Slow and cautious in all things, he had been unwilling to admit to himself the growing attraction that Rachel's childlike face and honest brown eyes had for him. Not a beauty like Esther, no! But unutterably truer and sweeter. With Dickie's engagement to the elder sister, the bond between the two men seemed to be drawn closer.

And now, after a few brief weeks, that engagement was off again, and Dickie, simple Dickie, hard hit. So far in his young life all had gone so smoothly. His career in the Navy had been well chosen. His craving for the sea was inborn. There was something of the Viking about him, primitive and direct, a nature on which subtleties of thought were wasted. He belonged to that inarticulate order of young Englishmen who dislike any form of emotion, and who find it peculiarly hard to explain their mental processes in words . . .

Macfarlane, that dour Scot, with a Celtic imagination hidden away somewhere, listened and smoked while his friend floundered along in a sea of words. He had known an unburdening was coming. But he had expected the subject matter to be different. To begin with, anyway, there was no mention of Esther Lawes. Only, it seemed, the story of a childish terror.

'It all started with a dream I had when I was a kid. Not a nightmare exactly. She—the gipsy, you know—would just come into any old dream—even a good dream (or a kid's idea of what's good—a party and crackers and things). I'd be enjoying myself no end, and then I'd feel, I'd *know*, that if I looked up, *she*'d be there, standing as she always stood, watching me . . . With sad eyes, you know, as though she understood something that I didn't . . . Can't explain why it rattled me so—but it did! Every time! I used to wake up howling with terror, and my old nurse used to say: "There! Master Dickie's had one of his gipsy dreams again!"'

'Ever been frightened by real gipsies?'

'Never saw one till later. That was queer, too. I was chasing a pup of mine. He'd run away. I got through the garden door, and along one of the forest paths. We lived in the New Forest then, you know. I came to a sort of clearing at the end, with a wooden bridge over a stream. And just beside it a gipsy was standing—with a red handkerchief over her head—just the same as in my dream. And at once I was frightened! She looked at me, you know . . . Just the same look—as though she knew something I didn't, and was sorry about it . . . And then she said quite quietly, nodding her head at me: "*I shouldn't go that way, if I were you.*" I can't tell you why, but it frightened me to death. I dashed past her on to the bridge. I suppose it was rotten. Anyway, it gave way, and I was chucked into the stream. It was running pretty fast, and I was nearly drowned. Beastly to be nearly drowned. I've never forgotten it. And I felt it had all to do with the gipsy . . .'

'Actually, though, she warned you against it?'

'I suppose you could put it like that,' Dickie paused, then went on: 'I've told you about this dream of mine, not because it has anything to do with what happened after (at least, I suppose it hasn't), but because it's the jumping off point, as it were. You'll understand now what I mean by the "gipsy feeling." So I'll go on to that first night at the Lawes'. I'd just come back from the west coast then. It was awfully rum to be in England again. The Lawes were old friends of my people's. I hadn't seen the girls since I was about seven, but young Arthur was a great pal of mine, and after he died, Esther used to write to me, and send me out papers. Awfully jolly letters, she wrote! Cheered me up no end. I always wished I was a better hand at writing back. I was awfully keen to see her. It seemed odd to know a girl quite well from her letters, and not otherwise. Well, I went down to the Lawes' place first thing. Esther was away when I arrived, but was expected back that evening. I sat next to Rachel at dinner, and as I looked up and down the long table a queer feeling came over me. I felt someone was watching me, and it made me uncomfortable. Then I saw her—'

'Saw who—'

'Mrs Haworth—what I'm telling you about.'

It was on the tip of Macfarlane's tongue to say: 'I thought you were telling me about Esther Lawes.' But he remained silent, and Dickie went on.

'There was something about her quite different from all the rest. She was sitting next to old Lawes—listening to him very gravely with her head bent down. She had some of that red tulle stuff round her neck. It had got torn, I think, anyway it stood up behind her head like little tongues of flame . . . I said to Rachel: "Who's that woman over there. Dark—with a red scarf?"

'"Do you mean Alistair Haworth? She's got a red scarf. But she's fair. *Very* fair."

'So she was, you know. Her hair was a lovely pale shining yellow. Yet I could have sworn positively she was dark. Queer what tricks one's eyes play on one . . . After dinner, Rachel introduced us, and we walked up and down in the garden. We talked about reincarnation . . .'

'Rather out of your line, Dickie!'

'I suppose it is. I remember saying that it seemed to be a jolly sensible way of accounting for how one seems to know some people right off—as if you'd met them before. She said: "You mean lovers . . ." There was something queer about the way she said it—something soft and eager. It reminded me of something—but I couldn't remember what. We went on jawing a bit, and then old Lawes called us from the terrace—said Esther had come, and wanted to see me. Mrs Haworth put her hand on my arm and said: "You're going in?" "Yes," I said. "I suppose we'd better," and then—then—'

'Well?'

'It sounds such rot. Mrs Haworth said: "*I shouldn't go in if I were you . . .*"' He paused. 'It frightened me, you know. It frightened me badly. That's why I told you about the dream . . . Because, you see, she said it just the same way—quietly, as though she knew something I didn't. It wasn't just a pretty woman who wanted to keep me out in the garden with her. Her voice was just kind—and very sorry. Almost as though she knew what was to come . . . I suppose it was rude, but I turned and left her—almost ran to the house. It seemed like safety. I knew then that I'd been afraid of her from the first. It was a relief to see old Lawes. Esther was there beside him . . .' He hesitated a minute and then muttered rather obscurely: 'There was no question—the moment I saw her. I knew I'd got it in the neck.'

Macfarlane's mind flew swiftly to Esther Lawes. He had once heard her summed up as 'Six foot one of Jewish perfection.' A shrewd portrait, he thought, as he remembered her unusual height and the long slenderness of her, the marble whiteness of her face with its delicate down-drooping nose, and the black splendour of hair and eyes. Yes, he did not wonder that the boyish simplicity of Dickie had capitulated. Esther could never have made his own pulses beat one jot faster, but he admitted her magnificence.

'And then,' continued Dickie, 'we got engaged.'

'At once?'

'Well, after about a week. It took her about a fortnight after that to find out that she didn't care after all . . .' He gave a short bitter laugh.

'It was the last evening before I went back to the old ship. I was coming back from the village through the woods—and then I saw *her*—Mrs Haworth, I mean. She had on a red tam-o'-shanter, and—just for a minute, you know—it made me jump! I've told you about my dream, so you'll understand . . . Then we walked along a bit. Not that there was a word Esther couldn't have heard, you know . . .'

'No?' Macfarlane looked at his friend curiously. Strange how people told you things of which they themselves were unconscious!

'And then, when I was turning to go back to the house, she stopped me. She said: "You'll be home soon enough. *I shouldn't go back too soon if I were you* . . ." And then *I knew*—that there was something beastly waiting for me . . . and . . . as soon as I got back Esther met me, and told me—that she'd found out she didn't really care . . .'

Macfarlane grunted sympathetically. 'And Mrs Haworth?' he asked.

'I never saw her again—until tonight.'

'Tonight?'

'Yes. At the doctor johnny's nursing home. They had a look at my leg, the one that got messed up in that torpedo business. It's worried me a bit lately. The old chap advised an operation—it'll be quite a simple thing. Then as I left the place, I ran into a girl in a red jumper over her nurse's things, and she said: "*I wouldn't have that operation, if I were you* . . ." Then I saw it was Mrs Haworth. She passed on so quickly I couldn't stop her. I met another nurse, and asked about her. But she said there wasn't anyone of that name in the home . . . Queer . . .'

'Sure it was her?'

'Oh! yes, you see—she's very beautiful . . .' He paused, and then added: 'I shall have the old op, of course—but—but in case my number *should* be up—'

'Rot!'

'Of course it's rot. But all the same I'm glad I told you about this gipsy business . . . You know, there's more of it if only I could remember . . .'

Macfarlane walked up the steep moorland road. He turned in at the gate of the house near the crest of the hill. Setting his jaw squarely, he pulled the bell.

'Is Mrs Haworth in?'

'Yes, sir. I'll tell her.' The maid left him in a low long room, with windows that gave on the wildness of the moorland. He frowned a little. Was he making a colossal ass of himself?

Then he started. A low voice was singing overhead:

> *'The gipsy woman*
> *Lives on the moor—'*

The voice broke off. Macfarlane's heart beat a shade faster. The door opened.

The bewildering, almost Scandinavian fairness of her came as a shock. In spite of Dickie's description, he had imagined her gipsy dark . . . And he suddenly remembered Dickie's words, and the peculiar tone of them. *'You see, she's very beautiful . . .'* Perfect unquestionable beauty is rare, and perfect unquestionable beauty was what Alistair Haworth possessed.

He caught himself up, and advanced towards her. 'I'm afraid you don't know me from Adam. I got your address from the Lawes. But—I'm a friend of Dickie Carpenter's.'

She looked at him closely for a minute or two. Then she said: 'I was going out. Up on the moor. Will you come too?'

She pushed open the window, and stepped out on the hillside. He followed her. A heavy, rather foolish-looking man was sitting in a basket-chair smoking.

'My husband! We're going out on the moor, Maurice.

And then Mr Macfarlane will come back to lunch with us. You will, won't you?'

'Thanks very much.' He followed her easy stride up the hill, and thought to himself: 'Why? Why, on God's earth, marry *that*?'

Alistair made her way to some rocks. 'We'll sit here. And you shall tell me—what you came to tell me.'

'You knew?'

'I always know when bad things are coming. It is bad, isn't it? About Dickie?'

'He underwent a slight operation—quite successfully. But his heart must have been weak. He died under the anaesthetic.'

What he expected to see on her face, he scarcely knew—hardly that look of utter eternal weariness . . . He heard her murmur: 'Again—to wait—so long—so long . . .' She looked up: 'Yes, what were you going to say?'

'Only this. Someone warned him against this operation. A nurse. He thought it was you. Was it?'

She shook her head. 'No, it wasn't me. But I've got a cousin who is a nurse. She's rather like me in a dim light. I dare say that was it.' She looked up at him again. 'It doesn't matter, does it?' And then suddenly her eyes widened. She drew in her breath. 'Oh!' she said. 'Oh! How funny! You don't understand . . .'

Macfarlane was puzzled. She was still staring at him.

'I thought you did . . . You *should* do. You look as though you'd got it, too . . .'

'Got what?'

'The gift—curse—call it what you like. I believe you have. Look hard at that hollow in the rocks. Don't think of anything, just look . . . Ah!' she marked his slight start. 'Well—you saw something?'

'It must have been imagination. Just for a second I saw it full of blood!'

She nodded. 'I knew you had it. That's the place where the old sun-worshippers sacrificed victims. I knew that before

anyone told me. And there are times when I know just how
they felt about it—almost as though I'd been there myself
. . . And there's something about the moor that makes me
feel as though I were coming back home . . . Of course it's
natural that I should have the gift. I'm a Ferguesson. There's
second sight in the family. And my mother was a medium
until my father married her. Cristine was her name. She was
rather celebrated.'

'Do you mean by "the gift" the power of being able to
see things before they happen?'

'Yes, forwards or backwards—it's all the same. For instance,
I saw you wondering why I married Maurice—oh! yes, you
did!—It's simply because I've always known that there's
something dreadful hanging over him . . . I wanted to save
him from it . . . Women are like that. With my gift, I ought
to be able to prevent it happening . . . if one ever can . . .
I couldn't help Dickie. And Dickie wouldn't understand . . .
He was afraid. He was very young.'

'Twenty-two.'

'And I'm thirty. But I didn't mean that. There are so many
ways of being divided, length and height and breadth . . .
but to be divided by time is the worst way of all . . .' She
fell into a long brooding silence.

The low peal of a gong from the house below roused
them.

At lunch, Macfarlane watched Maurice Haworth. He was
undoubtedly madly in love with his wife. There was the
unquestioning happy fondness of a dog in his eyes. Macfarlane
marked also the tenderness of her response, with its hint of
maternity. After lunch he took his leave.

'I'm staying down at the inn for a day or so. May I come
and see you again? Tomorrow, perhaps?'

'Of course. But—'

'But what—'

She brushed her hand quickly across her eyes. 'I don't
know. I—I fancied that we shouldn't meet again—that's all
. . . Goodbye.'

He went down the road slowly. In spite of himself, a cold hand seemed tightening round his heart. Nothing in her words, of course, but—

A motor swept round the corner. He flattened himself against the hedge . . . only just in time. A curious greyish pallor crept across his face . . .

'Good Lord, my nerves are in a rotten state,' muttered Macfarlane, as he awoke the following morning. He reviewed the events of the afternoon before dispassionately. The motor, the short-cut to the inn and the sudden mist that had made him lose his way with the knowledge that a dangerous bog was no distance off. Then the chimney pot that had fallen off the inn, and the smell of burning in the night which he had traced to a cinder on his hearthrug. Nothing in it at all! Nothing at all—but for her words, and that deep unacknowledged certainty in his heart that she *knew* . . .

He flung off his bedclothes with sudden energy. He must go up and see her first thing. That would break the spell. That is, *if he got there safely* . . . Lord, what a fool he was!

He could eat little breakfast. Ten o'clock saw him starting up the road. At ten-thirty his hand was on the bell. Then, and not till then, he permitted himself to draw a long breath of relief.

'Is Mrs Haworth in?'

It was the same elderly woman who had opened the door before. But her face was different—ravaged with grief.

'Oh! sir, oh! sir, you haven't heard then?'

'Heard what?'

'Miss Alistair, the pretty lamb. It was her tonic. She took it every night. The poor captain is beside himself, he's nearly mad. He took the wrong bottle off the shelf in the dark . . . They sent for the doctor, but he was too late—'

And swiftly there recurred to Macfarlane the words: '*I've always known there was something dreadful hanging over him. I ought to be able to prevent it happening—if one ever can—*' Ah!

but one couldn't cheat Fate . . . Strange fatality of vision that had destroyed where it sought to save . . .

The old servant went on: 'My pretty lamb! So sweet and gentle she was, and so sorry for anything in trouble. Couldn't bear anyone to be hurt.' She hesitated, then added: 'Would you like to go up and see her, sir? I think, from what she said, that you must have known her long ago. A *very* long time ago, she said . . .'

Macfarlane followed the old woman up the stairs, into the room over the drawing-room where he had heard the voice singing the day before. There was stained glass at the top of the windows. It threw a red light on the head of the bed . . . *A gipsy with a red handkerchief over her head* . . . Nonsense, his nerves were playing tricks again. He took a long last look at Alistair Haworth.

'There's a lady to see you, sir.'

'Eh?' Macfarlane looked at the landlady abstractedly. 'Oh! I beg your pardon, Mrs Rowse, I've been seeing ghosts.'

'Not really, sir? There's queer things to be seen on the moor after nightfall, I know. There's the white lady, and the Devil's blacksmith, and the sailor and the gipsy—'

'What's that? A sailor and a gipsy?'

'So they say, sir. It was quite a tale in my young days. Crossed in love they were, a while back . . . But they've not walked for many a long day now.'

'No? I wonder if perhaps—they will again now . . .'

'Lor! sir, what things you do say! About that young lady—'

'What young lady?'

'The one that's waiting to see you. She's in the parlour. Miss Lawes, she said her name was.'

'Oh!'

Rachel! He felt a curious feeling of contraction, a shifting of perspective. He had been peeping through at another world. He had forgotten Rachel, for Rachel belonged to this life only . . . Again that curious shifting of perspective, that slipping back to a world of three dimensions only.

He opened the parlour door. Rachel—with her honest brown eyes. And suddenly, like a man awakening from a dream, a warm rush of glad reality swept over him. He was alive—alive! He thought: 'There's only one life one can be *sure* about! This one!'

'Rachel!' he said, and, lifting her chin, he kissed her lips.

# PHILOMEL COTTAGE

'Goodbye, darling.'

'Goodbye, sweetheart.'

Alix Martin stood leaning over the small rustic gate, watching the retreating figure of her husband as he walked down the road in the direction of the village.

Presently he turned a bend and was lost to sight, but Alix still stayed in the same position, absent-mindedly smoothing a lock of the rich brown hair which had blown across her face, her eyes far away and dreamy.

Alix Martin was not beautiful, nor even, strictly speaking, pretty. But her face, the face of a woman no longer in her first youth, was irradiated and softened until her former colleagues of the old office days would hardly have recognized her. Miss Alex King had been a trim business-like young woman, efficient, slightly brusque in manner, obviously capable and matter-of-fact.

Alix had graduated in a hard school. For fifteen years, from the age of eighteen until she was thirty-three, she had kept herself (and for seven years of the time an invalid mother) by her work as a shorthand typist. It was the struggle for existence which had hardened the soft lines of her girlish face.

True, there had been romance—of a kind—Dick Windyford, a fellow-clerk. Very much of a woman at heart, Alix had always known without seeming to know that he cared. Outwardly they had been friends, nothing more. Out of his slender salary Dick had been hard put to it to provide for the schooling of a younger brother. For the moment he could not think of marriage.

And then suddenly deliverance from daily toil had come to the girl in the most unexpected manner. A distant cousin had died, leaving her money to Alix—a few thousand pounds, enough to bring in a couple of hundred a year. To Alix it was freedom, life, independence. Now she and Dick need wait no longer.

But Dick reacted unexpectedly. He had never directly spoken of his love to Alix; now he seemed less inclined to do so than ever. He avoided her, became morose and gloomy. Alix was quick to realize the truth. She had become a woman of means. Delicacy and pride stood in the way of Dick's asking her to be his wife.

She liked him none the worse for it, and was indeed deliberating as to whether she herself might not take the first step, when for the second time the unexpected descended upon her.

She met Gerald Martin at a friend's house. He fell violently in love with her and within a week they were engaged. Alix, who had always considered herself 'not the falling-in-love kind', was swept clean off her feet.

Unwittingly she had found the way to arouse her former lover. Dick Windyford had come to her stammering with rage and anger.

'The man's a perfect stranger to you! You know nothing about him!'

'I know that I love him.'

'How can you know—in a week?'

'It doesn't take everyone eleven years to find out that they're in love with a girl,' cried Alix angrily.

His face went white.

'I've cared for you ever since I met you. I thought that you cared also.'

Alix was truthful.

'I thought so too,' she admitted. 'But that was because I didn't know what love was.'

Then Dick had burst out again. Prayers, entreaties, even threats—threats against the man who had supplanted him. It was amazing to Alix to see the volcano that existed beneath the reserved exterior of the man she had thought she knew so well.

Her thoughts went back to that interview now, on this sunny morning, as she leant on the gate of the cottage. She had been married a month, and she was idyllically happy. Yet, in the momentary absence of the husband who was everything to her, a tinge of anxiety invaded her perfect happiness. And the cause of that anxiety was Dick Windyford.

Three times since her marriage she had dreamed the same dream. The environment differed, but the main facts were always the same. *She saw her husband lying dead and Dick Windyford standing over him, and she knew clearly and distinctly that his was the hand which had dealt the fatal blow.*

But horrible though that was, there was something more horrible still—horrible, that was, on awakening, for in the dream it seemed perfectly natural and inevitable. *She, Alix Martin, was glad that her husband was dead*; she stretched out grateful hands to the murderer, sometimes she thanked him. The dream always ended the same way, with herself clasped in Dick Windyford's arms.

She had said nothing of this dream to her husband, but secretly it had perturbed her more than she liked to admit. Was it a warning—a warning against Dick Windyford?

Alix was roused from her thoughts by the sharp ringing of the telephone bell from within the house. She entered the cottage and picked up the receiver. Suddenly she swayed, and put out a hand against the wall.

'Who did you say was speaking?'

'Why, Alix, what's the matter with your voice? I wouldn't have known it. It's Dick.'

'Oh!' said Alix. 'Oh! Where—where are you?'

'At the Traveller's Arms—that's the right name, isn't it?

Or don't you even know of the existence of your village pub? I'm on my holiday—doing a bit of fishing here. Any objection to my looking you two good people up this evening after dinner?'

'No,' said Alix sharply. 'You mustn't come.'

There was a pause, and then Dick's voice, with a subtle alteration in it, spoke again.

'I beg your pardon,' he said formally. 'Of course I won't bother you—'

Alix broke in hastily. He must think her behaviour too extraordinary. It *was* extraordinary. Her nerves must be all to pieces.

'I only meant that we were—engaged tonight,' she explained, trying to make her voice sound as natural as possible. 'Won't you—won't you come to dinner tomorrow night?'

But Dick evidently noticed the lack of cordiality in her tone.

'Thanks very much,' he said, in the same formal voice, 'but I may be moving on any time. Depends if a pal of mine turns up or not. Goodbye, Alix.' He paused, and then added hastily, in a different tone: 'Best of luck to you, my dear.'

Alix hung up the receiver with a feeling of relief.

'He mustn't come here,' she repeated to herself. 'He mustn't come here. Oh, what a fool I am! To imagine myself into a state like this. All the same, I'm glad he's not coming.'

She caught up a rustic rush hat from a table, and passed out into the garden again, pausing to look up at the name carved over the porch: Philomel Cottage.

'Isn't it a very fanciful name?' she had said to Gerald once before they were married. He had laughed.

'You little Cockney,' he had said, affectionately. 'I don't believe you have ever heard a nightingale. I'm glad you haven't. Nightingales should sing only for lovers. We'll hear them together on a summer's evening outside our own home.'

And at the remembrance of how they had indeed heard

them, Alix, standing in the doorway of her home, blushed happily.

It was Gerald who had found Philomel Cottage. He had come to Alix bursting with excitement. He had found the very spot for them—unique—a gem—the chance of a life-time. And when Alix had seen it she too was captivated. It was true that the situation was rather lonely—they were two miles from the nearest village—but the cottage itself was so exquisite with its old-world appearance, and its solid comfort of bathrooms, hot-water system, electric light, and telephone, that she fell a victim to its charm immediately. And then a hitch occurred. The owner, a rich man who had made it his whim, declined to let it. He would only sell.

Gerald Martin, though possessed of a good income, was unable to touch his capital. He could raise at most a thousand pounds. The owner was asking three. But Alix, who had set her heart on the place, came to the rescue. Her own capital was easily realized, being in bearer bonds. She would contribute half of it to the purchase of the home. So Philomel Cottage became their very own, and never for a minute had Alix regretted the choice. It was true that servants did not appreciate the rural solitude—indeed, at the moment they had none at all—but Alix, who had been starved of domestic life, thoroughly enjoyed cooking dainty little meals and looking after the house.

The garden, which was magnificently stocked with flowers, was attended by an old man from the village who came twice a week.

As she rounded the corner of the house, Alix was surprised to see the old gardener in question busy over the flower-beds. She was surprised because his days for work were Mondays and Fridays, and today was Wednesday.

'Why, George, what are you doing here?' she asked, as she came towards him.

The old man straightened up with a chuckle, touching the brim of an aged cap.

'I thought as how you'd be surprised, ma'am. But 'tis this way. There be a fête over to Squire's on Friday, and I sez to myself, I sez, neither Mr Martin nor yet his good lady won't take it amiss if I comes for once on a Wednesday instead of a Friday.'

'That's quite all right,' said Alix. 'I hope you'll enjoy yourself at the fête.'

'I reckon to,' said George simply. 'It's a fine thing to be able to eat your fill and know all the time as it's not you as is paying for it. Squire allus has a proper sit-down tea for 'is tenants. Then I thought too, ma'am, as I might as well see you before you goes away so as to learn your wishes for the borders. You have no idea when you'll be back, ma'am, I suppose?'

'But I'm not going away.'

George stared.

'Bain't you going to Lunnon tomorrow?'

'No. What put such an idea into your head?'

George jerked his head over his shoulder.

'Met Maister down to village yesterday. He told me you was both going away to Lunnon tomorrow, and it was uncertain when you'd be back again.'

'Nonsense,' said Alix, laughing. 'You must have misunderstood him.'

All the same, she wondered exactly what it could have been that Gerald had said to lead the old man into such a curious mistake. Going to London? She never wanted to go to London again.

'I hate London,' she said suddenly and harshly.

'Ah!' said George placidly. 'I must have been mistook somehow, and yet he said it plain enough, it seemed to me. I'm glad you're stopping on here. I don't hold with all this gallivanting about, and I don't think nothing of Lunnon. *I've* never needed to go there. Too many moty cars—that's the trouble nowadays. Once people have got a moty car, blessed if they can stay still anywheres. Mr Ames, wot used to have this house—nice peaceful sort of gentleman he was until he

bought one of them things. Hadn't had it a month before
he put up this cottage for sale. A tidy lot he'd spent on it
too, with taps in all the bedrooms, and the electric light and
all. "You'll never see your money back," I sez to him. "But,"
he sez to me, "I'll get every penny of two thousand pounds
for this house." And, sure enough, he did.'

'He got three thousand,' said Alix, smiling.

'Two thousand,' repeated George. 'The sum he was asking
was talked of at the time.'

'It really was three thousand,' said Alix.

'Ladies never understand figures,' said George,
unconvinced. 'You'll not tell me that Mr Ames had the face
to stand up to you and say three thousand brazen-like in a
loud voice?'

'He didn't say it to me,' said Alix; 'he said it to my
husband.'

George stooped again to his flower-bed.

'The price was two thousand,' he said obstinately.

Alix did not trouble to argue with him. Moving to one of
the farther beds, she began to pick an armful of flowers.

As she moved with her fragrant posy towards the house,
Alix noticed a small dark-green object peeping from between
some leaves in one of the beds. She stooped and picked it
up, recognizing it for her husband's pocket diary.

She opened it, scanning the entries with some amusement.
Almost from the beginning of their married life she had
realized that the impulsive and emotional Gerald had the
uncharacteristic virtues of neatness and method. He was
extremely fussy about meals being punctual, and always
planned his day ahead with the accuracy of a timetable.

Looking through the diary, she was amused to notice the
entry on the date of May 14th: 'Marry Alix St Peter's 2.30.'

'The big silly,' murmured Alix to herself, turning the pages.
Suddenly she stopped.

'"Wednesday, June 18th"—why, that's today.'

In the space for that day was written in Gerald's neat,

precise hand: '9 p.m.' Nothing else. What had Gerald planned to do at 9 p.m.? Alix wondered. She smiled to herself as she realized that had this been a story, like those she had so often read, the diary would doubtless have furnished her with some sensational revelation. It would have had in it for certain the name of another woman. She fluttered the back pages idly. There were dates, appointments, cryptic references to business deals, but only one woman's name— her own.

Yet as she slipped the book into her pocket and went on with her flowers to the house, she was aware of a vague uneasiness. Those words of Dick Windyford's recurred to her almost as though he had been at her elbow repeating them: 'The man's a perfect stranger to you. You know nothing about him.'

It was true. What did she know about him? After all, Gerald was forty. In forty years there must have been women in his life . . .

Alix shook herself impatiently. She must not give way to these thoughts. She had a far more instant preoccupation to deal with. Should she, or should she not, tell her husband that Dick Windyford had rung her up?

There was the possibility to be considered that Gerald might have already run across him in the village. But in that case he would be sure to mention it to her immediately upon his return, and matters would be taken out of her hands. Otherwise—what? Alix was aware of a distinct desire to say nothing about it.

If she told him, he was sure to suggest asking Dick Windyford to Philomel Cottage. Then she would have to explain that Dick had proposed himself, and that she had made an excuse to prevent his coming. And when he asked her why she had done so, what could she say? Tell him her dream? But he would only laugh—or worse, see that she attached an importance to it which he did not.

In the end, rather shamefacedly, Alix decided to say nothing. It was the first secret she had ever kept from her husband, and the consciousness of it made her feel ill at ease.

When she heard Gerald returning from the village shortly before lunch, she hurried into the kitchen and pretended to be busy with the cooking so as to hide her confusion.

It was evident at once that Gerald had seen nothing of Dick Windyford. Alix felt at once relieved and embarrassed. She was definitely committed now to a policy of concealment.

It was not until after their simple evening meal, when they were sitting in the oak-beamed living-room with the windows thrown open to let in the sweet night air scented with the perfume of the mauve and white stocks outside, that Alix remembered the pocket diary.

'Here's something you've been watering the flowers with,' she said, and threw it into his lap.

'Dropped it in the border, did I?'

'Yes; I know all your secrets now.'

'Not guilty,' said Gerald, shaking his head.

'What about your assignation at nine o'clock tonight?'

'Oh! that—' he seemed taken aback for a moment; then he smiled as though something afforded him particular amusement. 'It's an assignation with a particularly nice girl, Alix. She's got brown hair and blue eyes, and she's very like you.'

'I don't understand,' said Alix, with mock severity. 'You're evading the point.'

'No, I'm not. As a matter of fact, that's a reminder that I'm going to develop some negatives tonight, and I want you to help me.'

Gerald Martin was an enthusiastic photographer. He had a somewhat old-fashioned camera, but with an excellent lens, and he developed his own plates in a small cellar which he had had fitted up as a dark-room.

'And it must be done at nine o'clock precisely,' said Alix teasingly.

Gerald looked a little vexed.

'My dear girl,' he said, with a shade of testiness in his manner, 'one should always plan a thing for a definite time. Then one gets through one's work properly.'

Alix sat for a minute or two in silence, watching her husband as he lay in his chair smoking, his dark head flung back and the clear-cut lines of his clean-shaven face showing up against the sombre background. And suddenly, from some unknown source, a wave of panic surged over her, so that she cried out before she could stop herself, 'Oh, Gerald, I wish I knew more about you!'

Her husband turned an astonished face upon her.

'But, my dear Alix, you do know all about me. I've told you of my boyhood in Northumberland, of my life in South Africa, and these last ten years in Canada which have brought me success.'

'Oh! business!' said Alix scornfully.

Gerald laughed suddenly.

'I know what you mean—love affairs. You women are all the same. Nothing interests you but the personal element.'

Alix felt her throat go dry, as she muttered indistinctly: 'Well, but there must have been—love affairs. I mean—if I only knew—'

There was silence again for a minute or two. Gerald Martin was frowning, a look of indecision on his face. When he spoke it was gravely, without a trace of his former bantering manner.

'Do you think it wise, Alix—this—Bluebeard's chamber business? There have been women in my life; yes, I don't deny it. You wouldn't believe me if I denied it. But I can swear to you truthfully that not one of them meant anything to me.'

There was a ring of sincerity in his voice which comforted the listening wife.

'Satisfied, Alix?' he asked, with a smile. Then he looked at her with a shade of curiosity.

'What has turned your mind on to these unpleasant subjects tonight of all nights?'

Alix got up, and began to walk about restlessly.

'Oh, I don't know,' she said. 'I've been nervy all day.'

'That's odd,' said Gerald, in a low voice, as though speaking to himself. 'That's very odd.'

'Why is it odd?'

'Oh, my dear girl, don't flash out at me so. I only said it was odd, because, as a rule, you're so sweet and serene.'

Alix forced a smile.

'Everything's conspired to annoy me today,' she confessed. 'Even old George had got some ridiculous idea into his head that we were going away to London. He said you had told him so.'

'Where did you see him?' asked Gerald sharply.

'He came to work today instead of Friday.'

'Damned old fool,' said Gerald angrily.

Alix stared in surprise. Her husband's face was convulsed with rage. She had never seen him so angry. Seeing her astonishment Gerald made an effort to regain control of himself.

'Well, he is a damned old fool,' he protested.

'What can you have said to make him think that?'

'I? I never said anything. At least—oh, yes, I remember; I made some weak joke about being "off to London in the morning", and I suppose he took it seriously. Or else he didn't hear properly. You undeceived him, of course?'

He waited anxiously for her reply.

'Of course, but he's the sort of old man who if once he gets an idea in his head—well, it isn't so easy to get it out again.'

Then she told him of George's insistence on the sum asked for the cottage.

Gerald was silent for a minute or two, then he said slowly:

'Ames was willing to take two thousand in cash and the remaining thousand on mortgage. That's the origin of that mistake, I fancy.'

'Very likely,' agreed Alix.

Then she looked up at the clock, and pointed to it with a mischievous finger.

'We ought to be getting down to it, Gerald. Five minutes behind schedule.'

A very peculiar smile came over Gerald Martin's face.

'I've changed my mind,' he said quietly; 'I shan't do any photography tonight.'

A woman's mind is a curious thing. When she went to bed that Wednesday night Alix's mind was contented and at rest. Her momentarily assailed happiness reasserted itself, triumphant as of yore.

But by the evening of the following day she realized that some subtle forces were at work undermining it. Dick Windyford had not rung up again, nevertheless she felt what she supposed to be his influence at work. Again and again those words of his recurred to her: '*The man's a perfect stranger. You know nothing about him.*' And with them came the memory of her husband's face, photographed clearly on her brain, as he said, 'Do you think it wise, Alix, this—Bluebeard's chamber business?' Why had he said that?

There had been warning in them—a hint of menace. It was as though he had said in effect: 'You had better not pry into my life, Alix. You may get a nasty shock if you do.'

By Friday morning Alix had convinced herself that there *had* been a woman in Gerald's life—a Bluebeard's chamber that he had sedulously sought to conceal from her. Her jealousy, slow to awaken, was now rampant.

Was it a woman he had been going to meet that night at 9 p.m.? Was his story of photographs to develop a lie invented upon the spur of the moment?

Three days ago she would have sworn that she knew her husband through and through. Now it seemed to her that he was a stranger of whom she knew nothing. She remembered his unreasonable anger against old George, so at variance with his usual good-tempered manner. A small thing, perhaps, but it showed her that she did not really know the man who was her husband.

There were several little things required on Friday from the village. In the afternoon Alix suggested that she should go for them whilst Gerald remained in the garden; but somewhat to her surprise he opposed this plan vehemently, and insisted on going himself whilst she remained at home. Alix was forced to give way to him, but his insistence surprised and alarmed her. Why was he so anxious to prevent her going to the village?

Suddenly an explanation suggested itself to her which made the whole thing clear. Was it not possible that, whilst saying nothing to her, Gerald had indeed come across Dick Windyford? Her own jealousy, entirely dormant at the time of their marriage, had only developed afterwards. Might it not be the same with Gerald? Might he not be anxious to prevent her seeing Dick Windyford again? This explanation was so consistent with the facts, and so comforting to Alix's perturbed mind, that she embraced it eagerly.

Yet when tea-time had come and passed she was restless and ill at ease. She was struggling with a temptation that had assailed her ever since Gerald's departure. Finally, pacifying her conscience with the assurance that the room did need a thorough tidying, she went upstairs to her husband's dressing-room. She took a duster with her to keep up the pretence of housewifery.

'If I were only sure,' she repeated to herself. 'If I could only be *sure*.'

In vain she told herself that anything compromising would have been destroyed ages ago. Against that she argued that men do sometimes keep the most damning piece of evidence through an exaggerated sentimentality.

In the end Alix succumbed. Her cheeks burning with the shame of her action, she hunted breathlessly through packets of letters and documents, turned out the drawers, even went through the pockets of her husband's clothes. Only two drawers eluded her; the lower drawer of the chest of drawers and the small right-hand drawer of the writing-desk were both locked. But Alix was by now lost to all shame. In one of these drawers she was convinced that she would find evidence of this imaginary woman of the past who obsessed her.

She remembered that Gerald had left his keys lying care-lessly on the sideboard downstairs. She fetched them and tried them one by one. The third key fitted the writing-table drawer. Alix pulled it open eagerly. There was a cheque-book and a wallet well stuffed with notes, and at the back of the drawer a packet of letters tied up with a piece of tape.

Her breath coming unevenly, Alix untied the tape. Then a deep burning blush overspread her face, and she dropped the letters back into the drawer, closing and relocking it. For the letters were her own, written to Gerald Martin before she married him.

She turned now to the chest of drawers, more with a wish to feel that she had left nothing undone than from any expectation of finding what she sought.

To her annoyance none of the keys on Gerald's bunch fitted the drawer in question. Not to be defeated, Alix went into the other rooms and brought back a selection of keys with her. To her satisfaction the key of the spare room wardrobe also fitted the chest of drawers. She unlocked the drawer and pulled it open. But there was nothing in it but a roll of newspaper clippings already dirty and discoloured with age.

Alix breathed a sigh of relief. Nevertheless, she glanced at the clippings, curious to know what subject had interested Gerald so much that he had taken the trouble to keep the dusty roll. They were nearly all American papers, dated some seven years ago, and dealing with the trial of the notorious swindler and bigamist, Charles Lemaitre. Lemaitre had been suspected of doing away with his women victims. A skeleton had been found beneath the floor of one of the houses he had rented, and most of the women he had 'married' had never been heard of again.

He had defended himself from the charges with consum-mate skill, aided by some of the best legal talent in the United States. The Scottish verdict of 'Not Proven' might perhaps have stated the case best. In its absence, he was found Not Guilty on the capital charge, though sentenced to a long term of imprisonment on the other charges preferred against him.

Alix remembered the excitement caused by the case at the time, and also the sensation aroused by the escape of Lemaitre some three years later. He had never been recaptured. The personality of the man and his extraordinary power over women had been discussed at great length in the English papers at the time, together with an account of his excitability in court, his passionate protestations, and his occasional sudden physical collapses, due to the fact that he had a weak heart, though the ignorant accredited it to his dramatic powers.

There was a picture of him in one of the clippings Alix held, and she studied it with some interest—a long-bearded, scholarly-looking gentleman.

Who was it the face reminded her of? Suddenly, with a shock, she realized that it was Gerald himself. The eyes and brow bore a strong resemblance to his. Perhaps he had kept the cutting for that reason. Her eyes went on to the paragraph beside the picture. Certain dates, it seemed, had been entered in the accused's pocket-book, and it was contended that these were dates when he had done away with his victims. Then a woman gave evidence and identified the prisoner positively by the fact that he had a mole on his left wrist, just below the palm of the hand.

Alix dropped the papers and swayed as she stood. *On his left wrist, just below the palm, her husband had a small scar . . .*

The room whirled round her. Afterwards it struck her as strange that she should have leaped at once to such absolute certainty. Gerald Martin was Charles Lemaitre! She knew it, and accepted it in a flash. Disjointed fragments whirled through her brain, like pieces of a jigsaw puzzle fitting into place.

The money paid for the house—her money—her money only; the bearer bonds she had entrusted to his keeping. Even her dream appeared in its true significance. Deep down in her, her subconscious self had always feared Gerald Martin and wished to escape from him. And it was to Dick Windyford this self of hers had looked for help. That, too, was why she was able to accept the truth too easily, without doubt or hesitation. She was to have been another of Lemaitre's victims. Very soon, perhaps . . .

A half-cry escaped her as she remembered something. *Wednesday, 9 p.m.* The cellar, with the flagstones that were so easily raised! Once before he had buried one of his victims in a cellar. It had been all planned for Wednesday night. But to write it down beforehand in that methodical manner—insanity! No, it was logical. Gerald always made a memorandum of his engagements; murder was to him a business proposition like any other.

But what had saved her? What could possibly have saved her? Had he relented at the last minute? No. In a flash the answer came to her—*old George.*

She understood now her husband's uncontrollable anger. Doubtless he had paved the way by telling everyone he met that they were going to London the next day. Then George had come to work unexpectedly, had mentioned London to her, and she had contradicted the story. Too risky to do away with her that night, with old George repeating that conversation. But what an escape! If she had not happened to mention that trivial matter—Alix shuddered.

And then she stayed motionless as though frozen to stone. She had heard the creak of the gate into the road. *Her husband had returned.*

For a moment Alix stayed as though petrified, then she crept on tiptoe to the window, looking out from behind the shelter of the curtain.

Yes, it was her husband. He was smiling to himself and humming a little tune. In his hand he held an object which almost made the terrified girl's heart stop beating. It was a brand-new spade.

Alix leaped to a knowledge born of instinct. *It was to be tonight . . .*

But there was still a chance. Gerald, humming his little tune, went round to the back of the house.

Without hesitating a moment, she ran down the stairs and out of the cottage. But just as she emerged from the door, her husband came round the other side of the house.

'Hallo,' he said, 'where are you running off to in such a hurry?'

Alix strove desperately to appear calm and as usual. Her chance was gone for the moment, but if she was careful not to arouse his suspicions, it would come again later. Even now, perhaps . . .

'I was going to walk to the end of the lane and back,' she said in a voice that sounded weak and uncertain in her own ears.

'Right,' said Gerald. 'I'll come with you.'

'No—please, Gerald. I'm—nervy, headachy—I'd rather go alone.'

He looked at her attentively. She fancied a momentary suspicion gleamed in his eye.

'What's the matter with you, Alix? You're pale—trembling.'

'Nothing.' She forced herself to be brusque—smiling. 'I've got a headache, that's all. A walk will do me good.'

'Well, it's no good your saying you don't want me,' declared Gerald, with his easy laugh. 'I'm coming, whether you want me or not.'

She dared not protest further. If he suspected that she *knew* . . .

With an effort she managed to regain something of her normal manner. Yet she had an uneasy feeling that he looked at her sideways every now and then, as though not quite satisfied. She felt that his suspicions were not completely allayed.

When they returned to the house he insisted on her lying down, and brought some eau-de-cologne to bathe her temples. He was, as ever, the devoted husband. Alix felt herself as helpless as though bound hand and foot in a trap.

Not for a minute would he leave her alone. He went with her into the kitchen and helped her to bring in the simple cold dishes she had already prepared. Supper was a meal that choked her, yet she forced herself to eat, and even to appear gay and natural. She knew now that she was fighting for her life. She was alone with this man, miles from help, absolutely at his mercy. Her only chance was so to lull his suspicions that he would leave her alone for a few moments—long enough for her to get to the telephone in the hall and summon assistance. That was her only hope now.

A momentary hope flashed over her as she remembered how he had abandoned his plan before. Suppose she told him that Dick Windyford was coming up to see them that evening?

The words trembled on her lips—then she rejected them hastily. This man would not be baulked a second time. There was a determination, an elation, underneath his calm bearing that sickened her. She would only precipitate the crime. He would murder her there and then, and calmly ring up Dick Windyford with a tale of having been suddenly called away. Oh! if only Dick Windyford were coming to the house this evening! If Dick . . .

A sudden idea flashed into her mind. She looked sharply sideways at her husband as though she feared that he might read her mind. With the forming of a plan, her courage was reinforced. She became so completely natural in manner that she marvelled at herself.

She made the coffee and took it out to the porch where they often sat on fine evenings.

'By the way,' said Gerald suddenly, 'we'll do those photographs later.'

Alix felt a shiver run through her, but she replied nonchalantly, 'Can't you manage alone? I'm rather tired tonight.'

'It won't take long.' He smiled to himself. 'And I can promise you you won't be tired afterwards.'

The words seemed to amuse him. Alix shuddered. Now or never was the time to carry out her plan.

She rose to her feet.

'I'm just going to telephone to the butcher,' she announced nonchalantly. 'Don't you bother to move.'

'To the butcher? At this time of night?'

'His shop's shut, of course, silly. But he's in his house all right. And tomorrow's Saturday, and I want him to bring me some veal cutlets early, before someone else grabs them off him. The old dear will do anything for me.'

She passed quickly into the house, closing the door behind her. She heard Gerald say, 'Don't shut the door,' and was quick with her light reply, 'It keeps the moths out. I hate moths. Are you afraid I'm going to make love to the butcher, silly?'

Once inside, she snatched down the telephone receiver and gave the number of the Traveller's Arms. She was put through at once.

'Mr Windyford? Is he still there? Can I speak to him?'

Then her heart gave a sickening thump. The door was pushed open and her husband came into the hall.

'Do go away, Gerald,' she said pettishly. 'I hate anyone listening when I'm telephoning.'

He merely laughed and threw himself into a chair.

'Sure it really is the butcher you're telephoning to?' he quizzed.

Alix was in despair. Her plan had failed. In a minute Dick Windyford would come to the phone. Should she risk all and cry out an appeal for help?

And then, as she nervously depressed and released the little key in the receiver she was holding, which permits the voice to be heard or not heard at the other end, another plan flashed into her head.

'It will be difficult,' she thought to herself. 'It means keeping my head, and thinking of the right words, and not faltering for a moment, but I believe I could do it. I *must* do it.'

And at that minute she heard Dick Windyford's voice at the other end of the phone.

Alix drew a deep breath. Then she depressed the key firmly and spoke.

'*Mrs Martin speaking—from Philomel Cottage. Please come* (she released the key) tomorrow morning with six nice veal cutlets (she depressed the key again). *It's very important* (she released the key). Thank you so much, Mr Hexworthy: you won't mind my ringing you up so late. I hope, but those veal cutlets are really a matter of (she depressed the key again) *life or death* (she released it). Very well—tomorrow morning (she depressed it) *as soon as possible.*'

She replaced the receiver on the hook and turned to face her husband, breathing hard.

'So that's how you talk to your butcher, is it?' said Gerald.

'It's the feminine touch,' said Alix lightly.

She was simmering with excitement. He had suspected nothing. Dick, even if he didn't understand, would come.

She passed into the sitting-room and switched on the electric light. Gerald followed her.

'You seem very full of spirits now?' he said, watching her curiously.

'Yes,' said Alix. 'My headache's gone.'

She sat down in her usual seat and smiled at her husband as he sank into his own chair opposite her. She was saved. It was only five and twenty past eight. Long before nine o'clock Dick would have arrived.

'I didn't think much of that coffee you gave me,' complained Gerald. 'It tasted very bitter.'

'It's a new kind I was trying. We won't have it again if you don't like it, dear.'

Alix took up a piece of needlework and began to stitch. Gerald read a few pages of his book. Then he glanced up at the clock and tossed the book away.

'Half-past eight. Time to go down to the cellar and start work.'

The sewing slipped from Alix's fingers.

'Oh, not yet. Let us wait until nine o'clock.'

'No, my girl—half-past eight. That's the time I fixed. You'll be able to get to bed all the earlier.'

'But I'd rather wait until nine.'

'You know when I fix a time I always stick to it. Come along, Alix. I'm not going to wait a minute longer.'

Alix looked up at him, and in spite of herself she felt a wave of terror slide over her. The mask had been lifted. Gerald's hands were twitching, his eyes were shining with excitement, he was continually passing his tongue over his dry lips. He no longer cared to conceal his excitement.

Alix thought, 'It's true—*he can't wait*—he's like a madman.'

He strode over to her, and jerked her on to her feet with a hand on her shoulder.

'Come on, my girl—or I'll carry you there.'

His tone was gay, but there was an undisguised ferocity behind it that appalled her. With a supreme effort she jerked herself free and clung cowering against the wall. She was powerless. She couldn't get away—she couldn't do anything—and he was coming towards her.

'Now, Alix—'

'No—no.'

She screamed, her hands held out impotently to ward him off.

'Gerald—stop—I've got something to tell you, something to confess—'

He did stop.

'To confess?' he said curiously.

'Yes, to confess.' She had used the words at random, but she went on desperately, seeking to hold his arrested attention.

A look of contempt swept over his face.

'A former lover, I suppose,' he sneered.

'No,' said Alix. 'Something else. You'd call it, I expect—yes, you'd call it a crime.'

And at once she saw that she had struck the right note. Again his attention was arrested, held. Seeing that, her nerve came back to her. She felt mistress of the situation once more.

'You had better sit down again,' she said quietly.

She herself crossed the room to her old chair and sat down. She even stooped and picked up her needlework. But behind her calmness she was thinking and inventing feverishly: for the story she invented must hold his interest until help arrived.

'I told you,' she said slowly, 'that I had been a shorthand typist for fifteen years. That was not entirely true. There were two intervals. The first occurred when I was twenty-two. I came across a man, an elderly man with a little property. He fell in love with me and asked me to marry him. I accepted. We were married.' She paused. 'I induced him to insure his life in my favour.'

She saw a sudden keen interest spring up in her husband's face, and went on with renewed assurance:

'During the war I worked for a time in a hospital dispensary. There I had the handling of all kinds of rare drugs and poisons.'

She paused reflectively. He was keenly interested now, not a doubt of it. The murderer is bound to have an interest in murder. She had gambled on that, and succeeded. She stole a glance at the clock. It was five and twenty to nine.

'There is one poison—it is a little white powder. A pinch of it means death. You know something about poisons perhaps?'

She put the question in some trepidation. If he did, she would have to be careful.

'No,' said Gerald: 'I know very little about them.'

She drew a breath of relief.

'You have heard of hyoscine, of course? This is a drug that acts much the same way, but is absolutely untraceable. Any doctor would give a certificate of heart failure. I stole a small quantity of this drug and kept it by me.'

She paused, marshalling her forces.

'Go on,' said Gerald.

'No. I'm afraid. I can't tell you. Another time.'

'Now,' he said impatiently. 'I want to hear.'

'We had been married a month. I was very good to my elderly husband, very kind and devoted. He spoke in praise of me to all the neighbours. Everyone knew what a devoted wife I was. I always made his coffee myself every evening. One evening, when we were alone together, I put a pinch of the deadly alkaloid in his cup—'

Alix paused, and carefully re-threaded her needle. She, who had never acted in her life, rivalled the greatest actress in the world at this moment. She was actually living the part of the cold-blooded poisoner.

'It was very peaceful. I sat watching him. Once he gasped a little and asked for air. I opened the window. Then he said he could not move from his chair. *Presently he died.*'

She stopped, smiling. It was a quarter to nine. Surely they would come soon.

'How much,' said Gerald, 'was the insurance money?'

'About two thousand pounds. I speculated with it, and lost it. I went back to my office work. But I never meant to remain there long. Then I met another man. I had stuck to my maiden name at the office. He didn't know I had been married before. He was a younger man, rather good-looking, and quite well-off. We were married quietly in Sussex. He didn't want to insure his life, but of course he made a will in my favour. He liked me to make his coffee myself just as my first husband had done.'

Alix smiled reflectively, and added simply, 'I make very good coffee.'

Then she went on:

'I had several friends in the village where we were living. They were very sorry for me, with my husband dying suddenly of heart failure one evening after dinner. I didn't quite like the doctor. I don't think he suspected me, but he was certainly very surprised at my husband's sudden death. I don't quite know why I drifted back to the office again. Habit, I suppose. My second husband left about four thousand pounds. I didn't speculate with it this time; I invested it. Then, you see—'

But she was interrupted. Gerald Martin, his face suffused with blood, half-choking, was pointing a shaking forefinger at her.

'The coffee—my God! the coffee!'

She stared at him.

'I understand now why it was bitter. You devil! You've been up to your tricks again.'

His hands gripped the arms of his chair. He was ready to spring upon her.

'You've poisoned me.'

Alix had retreated from him to the fireplace. Now, terrified, she opened her lips to deny—and then paused. In another minute he would spring upon her. She summoned all her strength. Her eyes held his steamy, compellingly.

'Yes,' she said. 'I poisoned you. Already the poison is working. At this minute you can't move from your chair—you can't move—'

If she could keep him there—even a few minutes . . .

Ah! what was that? Footsteps on the road. The creak of the gate. Then footsteps on the path outside. The outer door opening.

'*You can't move,*' she said again.

Then she slipped past him and fled headlong from the room to fall fainting into Dick Windyford's arms.

'My God! Alix,' he cried.

Then he turned to the man with him, a tall stalwart figure in policeman's uniform.

'Go and see what's been happening in that room.'

He laid Alix carefully down on a couch and bent over her.

'My little girl,' he murmured. 'My poor little girl. What have they been doing to you?'

Her eyelids fluttered and her lips just murmured his name.

Dick was aroused by the policeman's touching him on the arm.

'There's nothing in that room, sir, but a man sitting in a

chair. Looks as though he'd had some kind of bad fright, and—'

'Yes?'

'Well, sir, he's—dead.'

They were startled by hearing Alix's voice. She spoke as though in some kind of dream, her eyes still closed.

'*And presently,*' she said, almost as though she were quoting from something, '*he died*—'

# THE LAMP

It was undoubtedly an old house. The whole square was old, with that disapproving dignified old age often met with in a cathedral town. But No. 19 gave the impression of an elder among elders; it had a veritable patriarchal solemnity; it towered greyest of the grey, haughtiest of the haughty, chillest of the chill. Austere, forbidding, and stamped with that particular desolation attaching to all houses that have been long untenanted, it reigned above the other dwellings.

In any other town it would have been freely labelled 'haunted', but Weyminster was averse from ghosts and considered them hardly respectable except at the appanage of a 'county family'. So No. 19 was never alluded to as a haunted house; but nevertheless it remained, year after year, 'To be Let or Sold.'

Mrs Lancaster looked at the house with approval as she drove up with the talkative house agent, who was in an unusually hilarious mood at the idea of getting No. 19 off his books. He inserted the key in the door without ceasing his appreciative comments.

'How long has the house been empty?' inquired Mrs Lancaster, cutting short his flow of language rather brusquely.

Mr Raddish (of Raddish and Foplow) became slightly confused.

'Er—er—some time,' he remarked blandly.

'So I should think,' said Mrs Lancaster drily.

The dimly lighted hall was chill with a sinister chill. A more imaginative woman might have shivered, but this woman happened to be eminently practical. She was tall with much dark brown hair just tinged with grey and rather cold blue eyes.

She went over the house from attic to cellar, asking a pertinent question from time to time. The inspection over, she came back into one of the front rooms looking out on the square and faced the agent with a resolute mien.

'What is the matter with the house?'

Mr Raddish was taken by surprise.

'Of course, an unfurnished house is always a little gloomy,' he parried feebly.

'Nonsense,' said Mrs Lancaster. 'The rent is ridiculously low for such a house—purely nominal. There must be some reason for it. I suppose the house is haunted?'

Mr Raddish gave a nervous little start but said nothing.

Mrs Lancaster eyed him keenly. After a few moments she spoke again.

'Of course that is all nonsense, I don't believe in ghosts or anything of that sort, and personally it is no deterrent to my taking the house; but servants, unfortunately, are very credulous and easily frightened. It would be kind of you to tell me exactly what—what thing *is* supposed to haunt this place.'

'I—er—really don't know,' stammered the house agent.

'I am sure you must,' said the lady quietly. 'I cannot take the house without knowing. What was it? A murder?'

'Oh! no,' cried Mr Raddish, shocked by the idea of anything so alien to the respectability of the square. 'It's—it's only a child.'

'A child?'

'Yes.'

'I don't know the story exactly,' he continued reluctantly. 'Of course, there are all kinds of different versions, but I believe that about thirty years ago a man going by the name of Williams took No. 19. Nothing was known of him; he

kept no servants; he had no friends; he seldom went out
in the day time. He had one child, a little boy. After he had
been there about two months, he went up to London, and
had barely set foot in the metropolis before he was recognized as being a man "wanted" by the police on some
charge—exactly what, I do not know. But it must have been
a grave one, because, sooner than give himself up, he shot
himself. Meanwhile, the child lived on here, alone in the
house. He had food for a little time, and he waited day after
day for his father's return. Unfortunately, it had been
impressed upon him that he was never under any circumstances to go out of the house or speak to anyone. He was
a weak, ailing, little creature, and did not dream of diso-
beying this command. In the night, the neighbours, not
knowing that his father had gone away, often heard him
sobbing in the awful loneliness and desolation of the empty
house.'

Mr Raddish paused.

'And—er—the child starved to death,' he concluded, in
the same tones as he might have announced that it had just
begun to rain.

'And it is the child's ghost that is supposed to haunt the
place?' asked Mrs Lancaster.

'It is nothing of consequence really,' Mr Raddish hastened
to assure her. 'There's nothing *seen*, not *seen*, only people
say, ridiculous, of course, but they do say they hear—the
child—crying, you know.'

Mrs Lancaster moved towards the front door.

'I like the house very much,' she said. 'I shall get nothing
as good for the price. I will think it over and let you know.'

'It really looks very cheerful, doesn't it, Papa?'

Mrs Lancaster surveyed her new domain with approval.
Gay rugs, well-polished furniture, and many knick-knacks,
had quite transformed the gloomy aspect of No. 19.

She spoke to a thin, bent old man with stooping shoulders
and a delicate mystical face. Mr Winburn did not resemble

his daughter; indeed no greater contrast could be imagined than that presented by her resolute practicalness and his dreamy abstraction.

'Yes,' he answered with a smile, 'no one would dream the house was haunted.'

'Papa, don't talk nonsense! On our first day too.'

Mr Winburn smiled.

'Very well, my dear, we will agree that there are no such things as ghosts.'

'And please,' continued Mrs Lancaster, 'don't say a word before Geoff. He's so imaginative.'

Geoff was Mrs Lancaster's little boy. The family consisted of Mr Winburn, his widowed daughter, and Geoffrey.

Rain had begun to beat against the window—pitter-patter, pitter-patter.

'Listen,' said Mr Winburn. 'Is it not like little footsteps?'

'It is more like rain,' said Mrs Lancaster, with a smile.

'But *that, that* is a footstep,' cried her father, bending forward to listen.

Mrs Lancaster laughed outright.

'That's Geoff coming downstairs.'

Mr Winburn was obliged to laugh too. They were having tea in the hall, and he had been sitting with his back to the staircase. He now turned his chair round to face it.

Little Geoffrey was coming down, rather slowly and sedately, with a child's awe of a strange place. The stairs were of polished oak, uncarpeted. He came across and stood by his mother. Mr Winburn gave a slight start. As the child was crossing the floor, he distinctly heard another pair of footsteps on the stairs, as of someone following Geoffrey. Dragging footsteps, curiously painful they were. Then he shrugged his shoulders incredulously. 'The rain, no doubt,' he thought.

'I'm looking at the spongecakes,' remarked Geoff with the admirably detached air of one who points out an interesting fact.

His mother hastened to comply with the hint.

'Well, Sonny, how do you like your new home?' she asked.

'Lots,' replied Geoffrey with his mouth generously filled. 'Pounds and pounds and pounds.' After this last assertion, which was evidently expressive of the deepest contentment, he relapsed into silence, only anxious to remove the sponge-cake from the sight of man in the least time possible.

Having bolted the last mouthful, he burst forth into speech.

'Oh! Mummy, there's attics here, Jane says; and can I go at once and *eggz*plore them? And there might be a secret door, Jane says there isn't, but I think there must be, and, anyhow, I know there'll be *pipes, water pipes* (with a face full of ecstasy) and can I play with them. and, oh! can I go and see the Boi-i-ler?' He spun out the last word with such evident rapture that his grandfather felt ashamed to reflect that this peerless delight of childhood only conjured up to his imagination the picture of hot water that wasn't hot, and heavy and numerous plumber's bills.

'We'll see about the attics tomorrow, darling,' said Mrs Lancaster. 'Suppose you fetch your bricks and build a nice house, or an engine.'

'Don't want to build an 'ouse.'

'*House*.'

'House, or h'engine h'either.'

'Build a boiler,' suggested his grandfather.

Geoffrey brightened.

'With pipes?'

'Yes, lots of pipes.'

Geoffrey ran away happily to fetch his bricks.

The rain was still falling. Mr Winburn listened. Yes, it must have been the rain he had heard; but it did sound like footsteps.

He had a queer dream that night.

He dreamt that he was walking through a town, a great city it seemed to him. But it was a children's city; there were no grown-up people there, nothing but children, crowds of them. In his dream they all rushed to the stranger

crying: 'Have you brought him?' It seemed that he understood what they meant and shook his head sadly. When
they saw this, the children turned away and began to cry,
sobbing bitterly.

The city and the children faded away and he awoke to
find himself in bed, but the sobbing was still in his ears.
Though wide awake, he heard it distinctly; and he remembered that Geoffrey slept on the floor below, while this sound
of a child's sorrow descended from above. He sat up and
struck a match. Instantly the sobbing ceased.

Mr Winburn did not tell his daughter of the dream or its
sequel. That it was no trick of his imagination, he was
convinced; indeed soon afterwards he heard it again in the
day time. The wind was howling in the chimney but *this*
was a separate sound—distinct, unmistakable; pitiful little
heart-broken sobs.

He found out too, that he was not the only one to hear
them. He overheard the housemaid saying to the parlour
maid that she 'didn't think as that there nurse was kind to
Master Geoffrey, she'd 'eard 'im crying 'is little 'eart out only
that very morning.' Geoffrey had come down to breakfast
and lunch beaming with health and happiness; and Mr
Winburn knew that it was not Geoff who had been crying,
but that other child whose dragging footsteps had startled
him more than once.

Mrs Lancaster alone never heard anything. Her ears were
not perhaps attuned to catch sounds from another world.

Yet one day she also received a shock.

'Mummy,' said Geoff plaintively. 'I wish you'd let me play
with that little boy.'

Mrs Lancaster looked up from her writing-table with a
smile.

'What little boy, dear?'

'I don't know his name. He was in an attic, sitting on the
floor crying, but he ran away when he saw me. I suppose
he was *shy* (with slight contempt), not like a *big* boy, and

then, when I was in the nursery building, I saw him standing in the door watching me build, and he looked so awful lonely and as though he wanted to play wiv me. I said: "Come and build a h'engine," but he didn't say nothing, just looked as—as though he saw a lot of chocolates, and his Mummy had told him not to touch them.' Geoff sighed, sad personal reminiscences evidently recurring to him. 'But when I asked Jane who he was and told her I wanted to play wiv him, she said there wasn't no little boy in the 'ouse and not to tell naughty stories. I don't love Jane at all.'

Mrs Lancaster got up.

'Jane was right. There was no little boy.'

'But I saw him. Oh! Mummy, do let me play wiv him, he did look so awful lonely and unhappy. I *do* want to do something to "make him better".'

Mrs Lancaster was about to speak again, but her father shook his head.

'Geoff,' he said very gently, 'that poor little boy *is* lonely, and perhaps you may do something to comfort him; but you must find out how by yourself—like a puzzle—do you see?'

'Is it because I am getting *big* I must do it all my lone?'

'Yes, because you are getting big.'

As the boy left the room, Mrs Lancaster turned to her father impatiently.

'Papa, this is absurd. To encourage the boy to believe the servants' idle tales!'

'No servant has told the child anything,' said the old man gently. 'He's seen—what I *hear*, what I could see perhaps if I were his age.'

'But it's such nonsense! Why don't I see it or hear it?'

Mr Winburn smiled, a curiously tired smile, but did not reply.

'Why?' repeated his daughter. 'And why did you tell him he could help the—the—thing. It's—it's all so impossible.'

The old man looked at her with his thoughtful glance.

'Why not?' he said. 'Do you remember these words:

> *'What Lamp has Destiny to guide*
> *Her little Children stumbling in the Dark?*
> *"A Blind Understanding," Heaven replied.*

'Geoffrey has that—a blind understanding. All children possess it. It is only as we grow older that we lose it, that we cast it away from us. Sometimes, when we are quite old, a faint gleam comes back to us, but the Lamp burns brightest in childhood. That is why I think Geoffrey may help.'

'I don't understand,' murmured Mrs Lancaster feebly.

'No more do I. That—that child is in trouble and wants—to be set free. But how? I do not know, but—it's awful to think of it—sobbing its heart out—a *child*.'

A month after this conversation Geoffrey fell very ill. The east wind had been severe, and he was not a strong child. The doctor shook his head and said that it was a grave case. To Mr Winburn he divulged more and confessed that the case was quite hopeless. 'The child would never have lived to grow up, under any circumstances,' he added. 'There has been serious lung trouble for a long time.'

It was when nursing Geoff that Mrs Lancaster became aware of that—other child. At first the sobs were an indistinguishable part of the wind, but gradually they became more distinct, more unmistakable. Finally she heard them in moments of dead calm: a child's sobs—dull, hopeless, heartbroken.

Geoff grew steadily worse and in his delirium he spoke of the 'little boy' again and again. 'I do want to help him get away, I do!' he cried.

Succeeding the delirium there came a state of lethargy. Geoffrey lay very still, hardly breathing, sunk in oblivion. There was nothing to do but wait and watch. Then there came a still night, clear and calm, without one breath of wind.

Suddenly the child stirred. His eyes opened. He looked past his mother toward the open door. He tried to speak and she bent down to catch the half breathed words.

'All right, I'm comin',' he whispered; then he sank back.

The mother felt suddenly terrified, she crossed the room to her father. Somewhere near them the other child was laughing. Joyful, contented, triumphant and silvery laughter echoed through the room.

'I'm frightened; I'm frightened,' she moaned.

He put his arm round her protectingly. A sudden gust of wind made them both start, but it passed swiftly and left the air quiet as before.

The laughter had ceased and there crept to them a faint sound, so faint as hardly to be heard, but growing louder till they could distinguish it. Footsteps—light footsteps, swiftly departing.

Pitter-patter, pitter-patter, they ran—those well-known halting little feet. Yet—surely—now *other* footsteps suddenly mingled with them, moving with a quicker and a lighter tread.

With one accord they hastened to the door.

Down, down, down, past the door, close to them, pitter-patter, pitter-patter, went the unseen feet of the little children *together*.

Mrs Lancaster looked up wildly.

'There are *two* of them—*two!*'

Grey with sudden fear, she turned towards the cot in the corner, but her father restrained her gently, and pointed away.

'There,' he said simply.

Pitter-patter, pitter-patter—fainter and fainter.

And then—silence.

# THE DREAM

Hercule Poirot gave the house a steady appraising glance. His eyes wandered a moment to its surroundings, the shops, the big factory building on the right, the blocks of cheap mansion flats opposite.

Then once more his eyes returned to Northway House, relic of an earlier age—an age of space and leisure, when green fields had surrounded its well-bred arrogance. Now it was an anachronism, submerged and forgotten in the hectic sea of modern London, and not one man in fifty could have told you where it stood.

Furthermore, very few people could have told you to whom it belonged, though its owner's name would have been recognized as one of the world's richest men. But money can quench publicity as well as flaunt it. Benedict Farley, that eccentric millionaire, chose not to advertise his choice of residence. He himself was rarely seen, seldom making a public appearance. From time to time, he appeared at board meetings, his lean figure, beaked nose, and rasping voice easily dominating the assembled directors. Apart from that, he was just a well-known figure of legend. There were his strange meannesses, his incredible generosities, as well as more personal details—his famous patchwork dressing-gown, now reputed to be twenty-eight years old, his invariable diet of cabbage soup and caviare, his hatred of cats. All these things the public knew.

Hercule Poirot knew them also. It was all he did know

of the man he was about to visit. The letter which was in his coat pocket told him little more.

After surveying this melancholy landmark of a past age for a minute or two in silence, he walked up the steps to the front door and pressed the bell, glancing as he did so at the neat wrist-watch which had at last replaced an old favourite—the large turnip-faced watch of earlier days. Yes, it was exactly nine-thirty. As ever, Hercule Poirot was exact to the minute.

The door opened after just the right interval. A perfect specimen of the genus butler stood outlined against the lighted hall.

'Mr Benedict Farley?' asked Hercule Poirot.

The impersonal glance surveyed him from head to foot, inoffensively but effectively.

*En gros et en détail*, thought Hercule Poirot to himself with appreciation.

'You have an appointment, sir?' asked the suave voice.

'Yes.'

'Your name, sir?'

'Monsieur Hercule Poirot.'

The butler bowed and drew back. Hercule Poirot entered the house. The butler closed the door behind him.

But there was yet one more formality before the deft hands took hat and stick from the visitor.

'You will excuse me, sir. I was to ask for a letter.' With deliberation Poirot took from his pocket the folded letter and handed it to the butler. The latter gave it a mere glance, then returned it with a bow. Hercule Poirot returned it to his pocket. Its contents were simple.

*Northway House, W.8*
*M. Hercule Poirot*
    *Dear Sir,*
*Mr Benedict Farley would like to have the benefit of your advice. If convenient to yourself he would be glad if you would*

*call upon him at the above address at 9.30 tomorrow (Thursday) evening.*

> *Yours truly,*
> *Hugo Cornworthy*
> *(Secretary)*
> *P.S. Please bring this letter with you.*

Deftly the butler relieved Poirot of hat, stick and overcoat. He said:

'Will you please come up to Mr Cornworthy's room?'

He led the way up the broad staircase. Poirot followed him, looking with appreciation at such *objets d'art* as were of an opulent and florid nature! His taste in art was always somewhat bourgeois.

On the first floor the butler knocked on a door.

Hercule Poirot's eyebrows rose very slightly. It was the first jarring note. For the best butlers do not knock at doors—and yet indubitably this was a first-class butler!

It was, so to speak, the first intimation of contact with the eccentricity of a millionaire.

A voice from within called out something. The butler threw open the door. He announced (and again Poirot sensed the deliberate departure from orthodoxy):

'The gentleman you are expecting, sir.'

Poirot passed into the room. It was a fair-sized room, very plainly furnished in a workmanlike fashion. Filing cabinets, books of reference, a couple of easy-chairs, and a large and imposing desk covered with neatly docketed papers. The corners of the room were dim, for the only light came from a big green-shaded reading lamp which stood on a small table by the arm of one of the easy-chairs. It was placed so as to cast its full light on anyone approaching from the door. Hercule Poirot blinked a little, realizing that the lamp bulb was at least 150 watts. In the arm-chair sat a thin figure in a patchwork dressing-gown—Benedict Farley. His head was stuck forward in a characteristic attitude, his beaked nose projecting like that of a bird. A crest of white hair like that of a cockatoo rose above his forehead. His eyes glittered behind thick lenses as he peered suspiciously at his visitor.

'Hey,' he said at last—and his voice was shrill and harsh, with a rasping note in it. 'So you're Hercule Poirot, hey?'

'At your service,' said Poirot politely and bowed, one hand on the back of the chair.

'Sit down—sit down,' said the old man testily.

Hercule Poirot sat down—in the full glare of the lamp. From behind it the old man seemed to be studying him attentively.

'How do I know you're Hercule Poirot—hey?' he demanded fretfully. 'Tell me that—hey?'

Once more Poirot drew the letter from his pocket and handed it to Farley.

'Yes,' admitted the millionaire grudgingly. 'That's it. That's what I got Cornworthy to write.' He folded it up and tossed it back. 'So you're the fellow, are you?'

With a little wave of his hand Poirot said:

'I assure you there is no deception!'

Benedict Farley chuckled suddenly.

'That's what the conjurer says before he takes the goldfish out of the hat! Saying that is part of the trick, you know!'

Poirot did not reply. Farley said suddenly:

'Think I'm a suspicious old man, hey? So I am. Don't trust anybody! That's my motto. Can't trust anybody when you're rich. No, no, it doesn't do.'

'You wished,' Poirot hinted gently, 'to consult me?'

The old man nodded.

'That's right. Always buy the best. That's my motto. Go to the expert and don't count the cost. You'll notice, M. Poirot, I haven't asked you your fee. I'm not going to! Send me in the bill later—I shan't cut up rough over it. Damned fools at the dairy thought they could charge me two and nine for eggs when two and seven's the market price—lot of swindlers! I won't be swindled. But the man at the top's different. He's worth the money. I'm at the top myself—I know.'

Hercule Poirot made no reply. He listened attentively, his head poised a little on one side.

Behind his impassive exterior he was conscious of a feeling of disappointment. He could not exactly put his finger on it. So far Benedict Farley had run true to type—that is, he had conformed to the popular idea of himself; and yet—Poirot was disappointed.

'The man,' he said disgustedly to himself, 'is a mounte-bank—nothing but a mountebank!'

He had known other millionaires, eccentric men too, but in nearly every case he had been conscious of a certain force, an inner energy that had commanded his respect. If they had worn a patchwork dressing-gown, it would have been because they liked wearing such a dressing-gown. But the dressing-gown of Benedict Farley, or so it seemed to Poirot, was essentially a stage property. And the man himself was essentially stagy. Every word he spoke was uttered, so Poirot felt assured, sheerly for effect.

He repeated again unemotionally, 'You wished to consult me, Mr Farley?'

Abruptly the millionaire's manner changed.

He leaned forward. His voice dropped to a croak.

'Yes. Yes . . . I want to hear what you've got to say—what you think . . . Go to the top! That's my way! The best doctor—the best detective—it's between the two of them.'

'As yet, Monsieur, I do not understand.'

'Naturally,' snapped Farley. 'I haven't begun to tell you.'

He leaned forward once more and shot out an abrupt question.

'What do you know, M. Poirot, about dreams?'

The little man's eyebrows rose. Whatever he had expected, it was not this.

'For that, M. Farley, I should recommend Napoleon's *Book of Dreams*—or the latest practising psychologist from Harley Street.'

Benedict Farley said soberly, 'I've tried both . . .'

There was a pause, then the millionaire spoke, at first almost in a whisper, then with a voice growing higher and higher.

'It's the same dream—night after night. And I'm afraid, I tell you—I'm afraid . . . It's always the same. I'm sitting in my room next door to this. Sitting at my desk, writing. There's a clock there and I glance at it and see the time— exactly twenty-eight minutes past three. Always the same time, you understand.

'*And when I see the time, M. Poirot, I know I've got to do it.* I don't want to do it—I loathe doing it—but I've got to . . .'

His voice had risen shrilly.

Unperturbed, Poirot said, 'And what is it that you have to do?'

'At twenty-eight minutes past three,' Benedict Farley said hoarsely, 'I open the second drawer down on the right of my desk, take out the revolver that I keep there, load it and walk over to the window. And then—and then—'

'Yes?'

Benedict Farley said in a whisper:

'*Then I shoot myself . . .*'

There was silence.

Then Poirot said, 'That is your dream?'

'Yes.'

'The same every night?'

'Yes.'

'What happens after you shoot yourself?'

'I wake up.'

Poirot nodded his head slowly and thoughtfully. 'As a matter of interest, do you keep a revolver in that particular drawer?'

'Yes.'

'Why?'

'I have always done so. It is as well to be prepared.'

'Prepared for what?'

Farley said irritably, 'A man in my position has to be on his guard. All rich men have enemies.'

Poirot did not pursue the subject. He remained silent for a moment or two, then he said:

'Why exactly did you send for me?'

'I will tell you. First of all I consulted a doctor—three doctors to be exact.'

'Yes?'

'The first told me it was all a question of diet. He was an elderly man. The second was a young man of the modern school. He assured me that it all hinged on a certain event that took place in infancy at that particular time of day— three twenty-eight. I am so determined, he says, not to remember the event, that I symbolize it by destroying myself. That is his explanation.'

'And the third doctor?' asked Poirot.

Benedict Farley's voice rose in shrill anger.

'He's a young man too. He has a preposterous theory! He asserts that I, myself, am tired of life, that my life is so unbearable to me that I deliberately want to end it! But since to acknowledge that fact would be to acknowledge that essentially I am a failure, I refuse in my waking moments to face the truth. But when I am asleep, all inhibitions are removed, and I proceed to do that *which I really wish to do*. I put an end to myself.'

'His view is that you really wish, unknown to yourself, to commit suicide?' said Poirot.

Benedict Farley cried shrilly:

'And that's impossible—impossible! I'm perfectly happy! I've got everything I want—everything money can buy! It's fantastic—unbelievable even to suggest a thing like that!'

Poirot looked at him with interest. Perhaps something in the shaking hands, the trembling shrillness of the voice, warned him that the denial was *too* vehement, that its very insistence was in itself suspect. He contented himself with saying:

'And where do I come in, Monsieur?'

Benedict Farley calmed down suddenly. He tapped with an emphatic finger on the table beside him.

'There's another possibility. And if it's right, you're the man to know about it! You're famous, you've had hundreds of cases—fantastic, improbable cases! You'd know if anyone does.'

'Know what?'

Farley's voice dropped to a whisper.

'Supposing someone wants to kill me . . . Could they do it this way? Could they make me dream that dream night after night?'

'Hypnotism, you mean?'

'Yes.'

Hercule Poirot considered the question.

'It would be possible, I suppose,' he said at last. 'It is more a question for a doctor.'

'You don't know of such a case in your experience?'

'Not precisely on those lines, no.'

'You see what I'm driving at? I'm made to dream the same dream, night after night, night after night—and then—one day the suggestion is too much for me—*and I act upon it*. I do what I've dreamed of so often—kill myself!'

Slowly Hercule Poirot shook his head.

'You don't think that is possible?' asked Farley.

'*Possible?*' Poirot shook his head. 'That is not a word I care to meddle with.'

'But you think it improbable?'

'Most improbable.'

Benedict Farley murmured. 'The doctor said so too . . .' Then his voice rising shrilly again, he cried out, 'But why do I have this dream? Why? Why?'

Hercule Poirot shook his head. Benedict Farley said abruptly, 'You're sure you've never come across anything like this in your experience?'

'Never.'

'That's what I wanted to know.'

Delicately, Poirot cleared his throat.

'You permit,' he said, 'a question?'

'What is it? What is it? Say what you like.'

'Who is it you suspect of wanting to kill you?' Farley snapped out, 'Nobody. Nobody at all.'

'But the idea presented itself to your mind?' Poirot persisted.

'I wanted to know—if it was a possibility.'

'Speaking from my own experience, I should say No. Have you ever been hypnotized, by the way?'

'Of course not. D'you think I'd lend myself to such tomfoolery?'

'Then I think one can say that your theory is definitely improbable.'

'But the dream, you fool, the dream.'

'The dream is certainly remarkable,' said Poirot thoughtfully. He paused and then went on. 'I should like to see the scene of this drama—the table, the clock, and the revolver.'

'Of course, I'll take you next door.'

Wrapping the folds of his dressing-gown round him, the old man half-rose from his chair. Then suddenly, as though a thought had struck him, he resumed his seat.

'No,' he said. 'There's nothing to see there. I've told you all there is to tell.'

'But I should like to see for myself—'

'There's no need,' Farley snapped. 'You've given me your opinion. That's the end.'

Poirot shrugged his shoulders. 'As you please.' He rose to his feet. 'I am sorry, Mr Farley, that I have not been able to be of assistance to you.'

Benedict Farley was staring straight ahead of him. 'Don't want a lot of hanky-pankying around,' he growled out. 'I've told you the facts—you can't make anything of them. That closes the matter. You can send me a bill for the consultation fee.'

'I shall not fail to do so,' said the detective drily. He walked towards the door.

'Stop a minute.' The millionaire called him back. 'That letter—I want it.'

'The letter from your secretary?'

'Yes.'

Poirot's eyebrows rose. He put his hand into his pocket, drew out a folded sheet, and handed it to the old man. The latter scrutinized it, then put it down on the table beside him with a nod.

Once more Hercule Poirot walked to the door. He was puzzled. His busy mind was going over and over the story he had been told. Yet in the midst of his mental preoccupation, a nagging sense of something wrong obtruded itself. And that something had to do with himself—not with Benedict Farley.

With his hand on the door knob, his mind cleared. He, Hercule Poirot, had been guilty of an error! He turned back into the room once more.

'A thousand pardons! In the interest of your problem I have committed a folly! That letter I handed to you—by mischance I put my hand into my right-hand pocket instead of the left—'

'What's all this? What's all this?'

'The letter that I handed you just now—an apology from my laundress concerning the treatment of my collars.' Poirot was smiling, apologetic. He dipped into his left-hand pocket. 'This is *your* letter.'

Benedict Farley snatched at it—grunted: 'Why the devil can't you mind what you're doing?'

Poirot retrieved his laundress's communication, apologized gracefully once more, and left the room.

He paused for a moment outside on the landing. It was a spacious one. Directly facing him was a big old oak settle with a refectory table in front of it. On the table were magazines. There were also two arm-chairs and a table with flowers. It reminded him a little of a dentist's waiting-room.

The butler was in the hall below waiting to let him out.

'Can I get you a taxi, sir?'

'No, I thank you. The night is fine. I will walk.'

Hercule Poirot paused a moment on the pavement waiting for a lull in the traffic before crossing the busy street.

A frown creased his forehead. 'No,' he said to himself. 'I do not understand at all. Nothing makes sense. Regrettable to have to admit it, but I, Hercule Poirot, am completely baffled.'

That was what might be termed the first act of the drama. The second act followed a week later. It opened with a telephone call from one John Stillingfleet, M.D.

He said with a remarkable lack of medical decorum:

'That you, Poirot, old horse? Stillingfleet here.'

'Yes, my friend. What is it?'

'I'm speaking from Northway House—Benedict Farley's.'

'Ah, yes?' Poirot's voice quickened with interest. 'What of—Mr Farley?'

'Farley's dead. Shot himself this afternoon.'

There was a pause, then Poirot said:

'Yes . . .'

'I notice you're not overcome with surprise. Know something about it, old horse?'

'Why should you think that?'

'Well, it isn't brilliant deduction or telepathy or anything like that. We found a note from Farley to you making an appointment about a week ago.'

'I see.'

'We've got a tame police inspector here—got to be careful, you know, when one of these millionaire blokes bumps himself off. Wondered whether you could throw any light on the case. If so, perhaps you'd come round?'

'I will come immediately.'

'Good for you, old boy. Some dirty work at the cross-roads—eh?'

Poirot merely repeated that he would set forth immediately.

'Don't want to spill the beans over the telephone? Quite right. So long.'

A quarter of an hour later Poirot was sitting in the library, a low long room at the back of Northway House on the ground floor. There were five other persons in the room: Inspector Barnett, Dr Stillingfleet, Mrs Farley, the widow of the millionaire, Joanna Farley, his only daughter, and Hugo Cornworthy, his private secretary.

Of these, Inspector Barnett was a discreet soldierly-looking man. Dr Stillingfleet, whose professional manner was entirely different from his telephonic style, was a tall, long-faced young man of thirty. Mrs Farley was obviously very much younger than her husband. She was a handsome dark-haired woman. Her mouth was hard and her black eyes gave absolutely no clue to her emotions. She appeared perfectly self-possessed. Joanna Farley had fair hair and a freckled face. The prominence of her nose and chin was clearly inherited from her father. Her eyes were intelligent and shrewd. Hugo Cornworthy was a good-looking young fellow, very correctly dressed. He seemed intelligent and efficient.

After greetings and introductions, Poirot narrated simply and clearly the circumstances of his visit and the story told him by Benedict Farley. He could not complain of any lack of interest.

'Most extraordinary story I've ever heard!' said the inspector. 'A dream, eh? Did you know anything about this, Mrs Farley?'

She bowed her head.

'My husband mentioned it to me. It upset him very much. I—I told him it was indigestion—his diet, you know, was very peculiar—and suggested his calling in Dr Stillingfleet.'

The young man shook his head. 'He didn't consult me. From M. Poirot's story, I gather he went to Harley Street.'

'I would like your advice on that point, Doctor,' said Poirot. 'Mr Farley told me that he consulted three specialists. What do you think of the theories they advanced?'

Stillingfleet frowned.

'It's difficult to say. You've got to take into account that what he passed on to you wasn't exactly what had been said to him. It was a layman's interpretation.'

'You mean he had got the phraseology wrong?'

'Not exactly. I mean they would put a thing to him in professional terms, he'd get the meaning a little distorted, and then recast it in his own language.'

'So that what he told me was not really what the doctors said.'

'That's what it amounts to. He's just got it all a little wrong, if you know what I mean.'

Poirot nodded thoughtfully. 'Is it known whom he consulted?' he asked.

Mrs Farley shook her head, and Joanna Farley remarked: 'None of us had any idea he had consulted anyone.'

'Did he speak to *you* about his dream?' asked Poirot.

The girl shook her head.

'And you, Mr Cornworthy?'

'No, he said nothing at all. I took down a letter to you at his dictation, but I had no idea why he wished to consult you. I thought it might possibly have something to do with some business irregularity.'

Poirot asked: 'And now as to the actual facts of Mr Farley's death?'

Inspector Barnett looked interrogatively at Mrs Farley and at Dr Stillingfleet, and then took upon himself the role of spokesman.

'Mr Farley was in the habit of working in his own room on the first floor every afternoon. I understand that there was a big amalgamation of business in prospect—'

He looked at Hugo Cornworthy who said, 'Consolidated Coachlines.'

'In connection with that,' continued Inspector Barnett, 'Mr Farley had agreed to give an interview to two members of the Press. He very seldom did anything of the kind—only about once in five years, I understand. Accordingly two reporters, one from the Associated Newsgroups, and one from Amalgamated Press-sheets, arrived at a quarter past three by appointment. They waited on the first floor outside Mr Farley's door—which was the customary place for people to wait who had an appointment with Mr Farley. At twenty past three a messenger arrived from the office of Consolidated Coachlines with some urgent papers. He was shown into Mr Farley's room where he handed over the documents. Mr Farley accompanied him to the door, and from there spoke to the two members of the Press. He said:

'"I'm sorry, gentlemen, to have to keep you waiting, but I have some urgent business to attend to. I will be as quick as I can."

'The two gentlemen, Mr Adams and Mr Stoddart, assured Mr Farley that they would await his convenience. He went back into his room, shut the door—and was never seen alive again!'

'Continue,' said Poirot.

'At a little after four o'clock,' went on the inspector, 'Mr Cornworthy here came out of his room which is next door to Mr Farley's and was surprised to see the two reporters still waiting. He wanted Mr Farley's signature to some letters and thought he had also better remind him that these two gentlemen were waiting. He accordingly went into Mr Farley's room. To his surprise he could not at first see Mr Farley and thought the room was empty. Then he caught sight of a boot sticking out behind the desk (which is placed in front of the window). He went quickly across and discovered Mr Farley lying there dead, with a revolver beside him.

'Mr Cornworthy hurried out of the room and directed the butler to ring up Dr Stillingfleet. By the latter's advice, Mr Cornworthy also informed the police.'

'Was the shot heard?' asked Poirot.

'No. The traffic is very noisy here, the landing window was open. What with lorries and motor horns it would be most unlikely if it had been noticed.'

Poirot nodded thoughtfully. 'What time is it supposed he died?' he asked.

Stillingfleet said:

'I examined the body as soon as I got here—that is, at thirty-two minutes past four. Mr Farley had been dead at least an hour.'

Poirot's face was very grave.

'So then, it seems possible that his death could have occurred at the time he mentioned to me—that is, at twenty-eight minutes past three.'

'Exactly,' said Stillingfleet.

'Any fingermarks on the revolver?'

'Yes, his own.'

'And the revolver itself?'

The inspector took up the tale.

'Was one which he kept in the second right-hand drawer of his desk, just as he told you. Mrs Farley has identified it positively. Moreover, you understand, there is only one entrance to the room, the door giving on to the landing. The two reporters were sitting exactly opposite that door and they swear that no one entered the room from the time Mr Farley spoke to them, until Mr Cornworthy entered it at a little after four o'clock.'

'So that there is every reason to suppose that Mr Farley committed suicide.'

Inspector Barnett smiled a little.

'There would have been no doubt at all but for one point.'

'And that?'

'The letter written to you.'

Poirot smiled too.

'I see! Where Hercule Poirot is concerned—immediately the suspicion of murder arises!'

'Precisely,' said the inspector drily. 'However, after your clearing up of the situation—'

Poirot interrupted him. 'One little minute.' He turned to Mrs Farley. 'Had your husband ever been hypnotized?'

'Never.'

'Had he studied the question of hypnotism? Was he interested in the subject?'

She shook her head. 'I don't think so.'

Suddenly her self-control seemed to break down. 'That horrible dream! It's uncanny! That he should have dreamed that—night after night—and then—it's as though he were—*hounded* to death!'

Poirot remembered Benedict Farley saying—'*I proceed to do that which I really wish to do. I put an end to myself.*'

He said, 'Had it ever occurred to you that your husband might be tempted to do away with himself?'

'No—at least—sometimes he was very queer . . .'

Joanna Farley's voice broke in clear and scornful. 'Father would never have killed himself. He was far too careful of himself.'

Dr Stillingfleet said, 'It isn't the people who threaten to commit suicide who usually do it, you know, Miss Farley. That's why suicides sometimes seem unaccountable.'

Poirot rose to his feet. 'Is it permitted,' he asked, 'that I see the room where the tragedy occurred?'

'Certainly. Dr Stillingfleet—'

The doctor accompanied Poirot upstairs.

Benedict Farley's room was a much larger one than the secretary's next door. It was luxuriously furnished with deep leather-covered arm-chairs, a thick pile carpet, and a superb outsize writing-desk.

Poirot passed behind the latter to where a dark stain on the carpet showed just before the window. He remembered the millionaire saying, '*At twenty-eight minutes past three I open the second drawer on the right of my desk, take out the revolver that I keep there, load it, and walk over to the window. And then—and then I shoot myself.*'

He nodded slowly. Then he said:

'The window was open like this?'

'Yes. But nobody could have got in that way.'

Poirot put his head out. There was no sill or parapet and no pipes near. Not even a cat could have gained access that way. Opposite rose the blank wall of the factory, a dead wall with no windows in it.

Stillingfleet said, 'Funny room for a rich man to choose as his own sanctum, with that outlook. It's like looking out on to a prison wall.'

'Yes,' said Poirot. He drew his head in and stared at the expanse of solid brick. 'I think,' he said, 'that that wall is important.'

Stillingfleet looked at him curiously. 'You mean—psychologically?'

Poirot had moved to the desk. Idly, or so it seemed, he picked up a pair of what are usually called lazy-tongs. He pressed the handles; the tongs shot out to their full length. Delicately, Poirot picked up a burnt match stump with them from beside a chair some feet away and conveyed it carefully to the waste-paper basket.

'When you've finished playing with those things . . .' said Stillingfleet irritably.

Hercule Poirot murmured, 'An ingenious invention,' and replaced the tongs neatly on the writing-table. Then he asked:

'Where were Mrs Farley and Miss Farley at the time of the—death?'

'Mrs Farley was resting in her room on the floor above this. Miss Farley was painting in her studio at the top of the house.'

Hercule Poirot drummed idly with his fingers on the table for a minute or two. Then he said:

'I should like to see Miss Farley. Do you think you could ask her to come here for a minute or two?'

'If you like.'

Stillingfleet glanced at him curiously, then left the room. In another minute or two the door opened and Joanna Farley came in.

'You do not mind, Mademoiselle, if I ask you a few questions?'

She returned his glance coolly. 'Please ask anything you choose.'

'Did you know that your father kept a revolver in his desk?'

'No.'

'Where were you and your mother—that is to say your stepmother—that is right?'

'Yes, Louise is my father's second wife. She is only eight years older than I am. You were about to say—?'

'Where were you and she on Thursday of last week? That is to say, on Thursday night.'

She reflected for a minute or two. 'Thursday? Let me see. Oh, yes, we had gone to the theatre. To see *Little Dog Laughed*.'

'Your father did not suggest accompanying you?'

'He never went out to theatres.'

'What did he usually do in the evenings?'

'He sat in here and read.'

'He was not a very sociable man?'

The girl looked at him directly. 'My father,' she said, 'had a singularly unpleasant personality. No one who lived in close association with him could possibly be fond of him.'

'That, Mademoiselle, is a very candid statement.'

'I am saving you time, M. Poirot. I realize quite well what you are getting at. My stepmother married my father for his money. I live here because I have no money to live else-where. There is a man I wish to marry—a poor man; my father saw to it that he lost his job. He wanted me, you see, to marry well—an easy matter since I was to be his heiress!'

'Your father's fortune passes to you?'

'Yes. That is, he left Louise, my stepmother, a quarter of a million free of tax, and there are other legacies, but the residue goes to me.' She smiled suddenly. 'So you see, M. Poirot, I had every reason to desire my father's death!'

'I see, Mademoiselle, that you have inherited your father's intelligence.'

She said thoughtfully, 'Father was clever . . . One felt that with him—that he had force—driving power—but it had all turned sour—bitter—there was no humanity left . . .'

Hercule Poirot said softly, '*Grand Dieu*, but what an imbe-cile I am . . .'

Joanna Farley turned towards the door. 'Is there anything more?'

'Two little questions. These tongs here,' he picked up the lazy-tongs, 'were they always on the table?'

'Yes. Father used them for picking up things. He didn't like stooping.'

'One other question. Was your father's eyesight good?'

She stared at him.

'Oh, no—he couldn't see at all—I mean he couldn't see without his glasses. His sight had always been bad from a boy.'

'But with his glasses?'

'Oh, he could see all right then, of course.'

'He could read newspapers and fine print?'

'Oh, yes.'

'That is all, Mademoiselle.'

She went out of the room.

Poirot murmured, 'I was stupid. It was there, all the time, under my nose. And because it was so near I could not see it.'

He leaned out of the window once more. Down below, in the narrow way between the house and the factory, he saw a small dark object.

Hercule Poirot nodded, satisfied, and went downstairs again.

The others were still in the library. Poirot addressed himself to the secretary:

'I want you, Mr Cornworthy, to recount to me in detail the exact circumstances of Mr Farley's summons to me. When, for instance, did Mr Farley dictate that letter?'

'On Wednesday afternoon—at five-thirty, as far as I can remember.'

'Were there any special directions about posting it?'

'He told me to post it myself.'

'And you did so?'

'Yes.'

'Did he give any special instructions to the butler about admitting me?'

'Yes. He told me to tell Holmes (Holmes is the butler) that a gentleman would be calling at nine-thirty. He was to ask the gentleman's name. He was also to ask to see the letter.'

'Rather peculiar precaution to take, don't you think?'

Cornworthy shrugged his shoulders.

'Mr Farley,' he said carefully, 'was rather a peculiar man.'

'Any other instructions?'

'Yes. He told me to take the evening off.'

'Did you do so?'

'Yes, immediately after dinner I went to the cinema.'

'When did you return?'

'I let myself in about a quarter past eleven.'

'Did you see Mr Farley again that evening?'

'No.'

'And he did not mention the matter the next morning?'

'No.'

Poirot paused a moment, then resumed, 'When I arrived I was not shown into Mr Farley's own room.'

'No. He told me that I was to tell Holmes to show you into my room.'

'Why was that? Do you know?'

Cornworthy shook his head. 'I never questioned any of Mr Farley's orders,' he said drily. 'He would have resented it if I had.'

'Did he usually receive visitors in his own room?'

'Usually, but not always. Sometimes he saw them in my room.'

'Was there any reason for that?'

Hugo Cornworthy considered.

'No—I hardly think so—I've never really thought about it.'

Turning to Mrs Farley, Poirot asked:

'You permit that I ring for your butler?'

'Certainly, M. Poirot.'

Very correct, very urbane, Holmes answered the bell.

'You rang, madam?'

Mrs Farley indicated Poirot with a gesture. Holmes turned politely. 'Yes, sir?'

'What were your instructions, Holmes, on the Thursday night when I came here?'

Holmes cleared his throat, then said:

'After dinner Mr Cornworthy told me that Mr Farley expected a Mr Hercule Poirot at nine-thirty. I was to ascertain the gentleman's name, and I was to verify the information by glancing at a letter. Then I was to show him up to Mr Cornworthy's room.'

'Were you also told to knock on the door?'

An expression of distaste crossed the butler's countenance.

'That was one of Mr Farley's orders. I was always to knock when introducing visitors—business visitors, that is,' he added.

'Ah, that puzzled me! Were you given any other instructions concerning me?'

'No, sir. When Mr Cornworthy had told me what I have just repeated to you he went out.'

'What time was that?'

'Ten minutes to nine, sir.'

'Did you see Mr Farley after that?'

'Yes, sir, I took him up a glass of hot water as usual at nine o'clock.'

'Was he then in his own room or in Mr Cornworthy's?'

'He was in his own room, sir.'

'You noticed nothing unusual about that room?'

'Unusual? No, sir.'

'Where were Mrs Farley and Miss Farley?'

'They had gone to the theatre, sir.'

'Thank you, Holmes, that will do.'

Holmes bowed and left the room. Poirot turned to the millionaire's widow.

'One more question, Mrs Farley. Had your husband good sight?'

'No. Not without his glasses.'

'He was very short-sighted?'

'Oh, yes, he was quite helpless without his spectacles.'

'He had several pairs of glasses?'

'Yes.'

'Ah,' said Poirot. He leaned back. 'I think that that concludes the case . . .'

There was silence in the room. They were all looking at the little man who sat there complacently stroking his moustache. On the inspector's face was perplexity, Dr Stillingfleet was frowning, Cornworthy merely stared uncomprehendingly, Mrs Farley gazed in blank astonishment, Joanna Farley looked eager.

Mrs Farley broke the silence.

'I don't understand, M. Poirot.' Her voice was fretful. 'The dream—'

'Yes,' said Poirot. 'That dream was very important.'

Mrs Farley shivered. She said:

'I've never believed in anything supernatural before—but now—to dream it night after night beforehand—'

'It's extraordinary,' said Stillingfleet. 'Extraordinary! If we hadn't got your word for it, Poirot, and if you hadn't had it straight from the horse's mouth—' he coughed in embarrassment, and readopting his professional manner, 'I beg your pardon, Mrs Farley. If Mr Farley himself had not told that story—'

'Exactly,' said Poirot. His eyes, which had been half-closed, opened suddenly. They were very green. *'If Benedict Farley hadn't told me—'*

He paused a minute, looking round at a circle of blank faces.

'There are certain things, you comprehend, that happened that evening which I was quite at a loss to explain. First, why make such a point of my bringing that letter with me?'

'Identification,' suggested Cornworthy.

'No, no, my dear young man. Really that idea is too ridiculous. There must be some much more valid reason. For not only did Mr Farley require to see that letter produced, but he definitely demanded that I should leave it behind me. And moreover even then he did not destroy it! It was found among his papers this afternoon. *Why did he keep it?*'

Joanna Farley's voice broke in. 'He wanted, in case anything happened to him, that the facts of his strange dream should be made known.'

Poirot nodded approvingly.

'You are astute, Mademoiselle. That must be—that can only be—the point of the keeping of the letter. When Mr Farley was dead, the story of that strange dream was to be told! That dream was very important. That dream, Mademoiselle, was *vital*!

'I will come now,' he went on, 'to the second point. After hearing his story I ask Mr Farley to show me the desk and the revolver. He seems about to get up to do so, then suddenly refuses. Why did he refuse?'

This time no one advanced an answer.

'I will put that question differently. *What was there in that next room that Mr Farley did not want me to see?*'

There was still silence.

'Yes,' said Poirot, 'it is difficult, that. And yet there was some reason—some *urgent* reason why Mr Farley received me in his secretary's room and refused point blank to take me into his own room. *There was something in that room he could not afford to have me see.*

'And now I come to the third inexplicable thing that happened on that evening. Mr Farley, just as I was leaving, requested me to hand him the letter I had received. By inadvertence I handed him a communication from my laundress. He glanced at it and laid it down beside him. Just before I left the room I discovered my error—and rectified it! After that I left the house and—I admit it—I was completely at sea! The whole affair and especially that last incident seemed to me quite inexplicable.'

He looked round from one to the other.

'You do not see?'

Stillingfleet said, 'I don't really see how your laundress comes into it, Poirot.'

'My laundress,' said Poirot, 'was very important. That miserable woman who ruins my collars, was, for the first time in her life, useful to somebody. Surely you see—it is so obvious. Mr Farley glanced at that communication—*one glance* would have told him that it was the wrong letter—

and yet he knew nothing. Why? *Because he could not see it properly!'*

Inspector Barnett said sharply, 'Didn't he have his glasses on?'

Hercule Poirot smiled. 'Yes,' he said. 'He had his glasses on. That is what makes it so very interesting.'

He leaned forward.

'Mr Farley's dream was very important. He dreamed, you see, that he committed suicide. And a little later on, he did commit suicide. That is to say he was alone in a room and was found there with a revolver by him, and no one entered or left the room at the time that he was shot. What does that mean? It means, does it not, that it *must* be suicide!'

'Yes,' said Stillingfleet.

Hercule Poirot shook his head.

'On the contrary,' he said. 'It was murder. An unusual and a very cleverly planned murder.'

Again he leaned forward, tapping the table, his eyes green and shining.

'Why did Mr Farley not allow me to go into his own room that evening? What was there in there that I must not be allowed to see? I think, my friends, that there was—Benedict Farley himself!'

He smiled at the blank faces.

'Yes, yes, it is not nonsense what I say. Why could the Mr Farley to whom I had been talking not realize the difference between two totally dissimilar letters? Because, *mes amis*, he was a man of *normal sight* wearing a pair of very powerful glasses. Those glasses would render a man of normal eyesight practically blind. Isn't that so, Doctor?'

Stillingfleet murmured, 'That's so—of course.'

'Why did I feel that in talking to Mr Farley I was talking to a *mountebank*, to an actor playing a part! Consider the setting. The dim room, the green-shaded light turned blindingly away from the figure in the chair. What did I see—the famous patchwork dressing-gown, the beaked nose (faked with that useful substance, nose putty) the white crest of

hair, the powerful lenses concealing the eyes. What evidence
is there that Mr Farley ever had a dream? Only the story I
was told and the evidence of *Mrs Farley*. What evidence is
there that Benedict Farley kept a revolver in his desk? Again
only the story told me and the word of Mrs Farley. Two
people carried this fraud through—Mrs Farley and Hugo
Cornworthy. Cornworthy wrote the letter to me, gave
instructions to the butler, went out ostensibly to the cinema,
but let himself in again immediately with a key, went to his
room, made himself up, and played the part of Benedict
Farley.

'And so we come to this afternoon. The opportunity for
which Mr Cornworthy has been waiting arrives. There are
two witnesses on the landing to swear that no one goes in
or out of Benedict Farley's room. Cornworthy waits until a
particularly heavy batch of traffic is about to pass. Then he
leans out of his window, and with the lazy-tongs which he
has purloined from the desk next door he holds an object
against the window of that room. Benedict Farley comes to
the window. Cornworthy snatches back the tongs and as
Farley leans out, and the lorries are passing outside,
Cornworthy shoots him with the revolver that he has ready.
There is a blank wall opposite, remember. There can be no
witness of the crime. Cornworthy waits for over half an
hour, then gathers up some papers, conceals the lazy-tongs
and the revolver between them and goes out on to the
landing and into the next room. He replaces the tongs on
the desk, lays down the revolver after pressing the dead
man's fingers on it, and hurries out with the news of Mr
Farley's "suicide".

'He arranges that the letter to me shall be found and that
I shall arrive with my story—the story I heard *from Mr Farley's
own lips*—of his extraordinary "dream"—the strange compul-
sion he felt to kill himself! A few credulous people will
discuss the hypnotism theory—but the main result will be
to confirm without a doubt that the actual hand that held
the revolver was Benedict Farley's own.'

Hercule Poirot's eyes went to the widow's face—he noted with satisfaction the dismay—the ashy pallor—the blind fear . . .

'And in due course,' he finished gently, 'the happy ending would have been achieved. A quarter of a million and two hearts that beat as one . . .'

John Stillingfleet, M.D., and Hercule Poirot walked along the side of Northway House. On their right was the towering wall of the factory. Above them, on their left, were the windows of Benedict Farley's and Hugo Cornworthy's rooms. Hercule Poirot stopped and picked up a small object—a black stuffed cat.

'*Voilà*,' he said. 'That is what Cornworthy held in the lazy-tongs against Farley's window. You remember, he hated cats? Naturally he rushed to the window.'

'Why on earth didn't Cornworthy come out and pick it up after he'd dropped it?'

'How could he? To do so would have been definitely suspicious. After all, if this object were found what would anyone think—that some child had wandered round here and dropped it.'

'Yes,' said Stillingfleet with a sigh. 'That's probably what the ordinary person *would* have thought. But not good old Hercule! D'you know, old horse, up to the very last minute I thought you were leading up to some subtle theory of high-falutin' psychological "suggested" murder? I bet those two thought so too! Nasty bit of goods, the Farley. Goodness, how she cracked! Cornworthy might have got away with it if she hadn't had hysterics and tried to spoil your beauty by going for you with her nails. I only got her off you just in time.'

He paused a minute and then said:

'I rather like the girl. Grit, you know, and brains. I suppose I'd be thought to be a fortune hunter if I had a shot at her . . .?'

'You are too late, my friend. There is already someone *sur le tapis*. Her father's death has opened the way to happiness.'

'Take it all round, *she* had a pretty good motive for bumping off the unpleasant parent.'

'Motive and opportunity are not enough,' said Poirot. 'There must also be the criminal temperament!'

'I wonder if you'll ever commit a crime, Poirot?' said Stillingfleet. 'I bet you could get away with it all right. As a matter of fact, it would be *too* easy for you—I mean the thing would be off as definitely too unsporting.'

'That,' said Poirot, 'is a typical English idea.'

# WIRELESS

'Above all, avoid worry and excitement,' said Dr Meynell, in the comfortable fashion affected by doctors.

Mrs Harter, as is often the case with people hearing these soothing but meaningless words, seemed more doubtful than relieved.

'There is a certain cardiac weakness,' continued the doctor fluently, 'but nothing to be alarmed about. I can assure you of that.

'All the same,' he added, 'it might be as well to have a lift installed. Eh? What about it?'

Mrs Harter looked worried.

Dr Meynell, on the contrary, looked pleased with himself. The reason he liked attending rich patients rather than poor ones was that he could exercise his active imagination in prescribing for their ailments.

'Yes, a lift,' said Dr Meynell, trying to think of something else even more dashing—and failing. 'Then we shall avoid all undue exertion. Daily exercise on the level on a fine day, but avoid walking up hills. And above all,' he added happily, 'plenty of distraction for the mind. Don't dwell on your health.'

To the old lady's nephew, Charles Ridgeway, the doctor was slightly more explicit.

'Do not misunderstand me,' he said. 'Your aunt may live for years, probably will. At the same time shock or over-exertion might carry her off like that!' He snapped his fingers.

'She must lead a very quiet life. No exertion. No fatigue. But, of course, she must not be allowed to brood. She must be kept cheerful and the mind well distracted.'

'Distracted,' said Charles Ridgeway thoughtfully.

Charles was a thoughtful young man. He was also a young man who believed in furthering his own inclinations whenever possible.

That evening he suggested the installation of a wireless set.

Mrs Harter, already seriously upset at the thought of the lift, was disturbed and unwilling. Charles was fluent and persuasive.

'I do not know that I care for these new-fangled things.' said Mrs Harter piteously. 'The waves, you know—the electric waves. They might affect me.'

Charles in a superior and kindly fashion pointed out the futility of this idea.

Mrs Harter, whose knowledge of the subject was of the vaguest, but who was tenacious of her own opinion, remained unconvinced.

'All that electricity,' she murmured timorously. 'You may say what you like, Charles, but some people *are* affected by electricity. I always have a terrible headache before a thunderstorm. I know that.'

She nodded her head triumphantly.

Charles was a patient young man. He was also persistent.

'My dear Aunt Mary,' he said, 'let me make the thing clear to you.'

He was something of an authority on the subject. He delivered now quite a lecture on the theme; warming to his task, he spoke of bright-emitter valves, of dull-emitter valves, of high frequency and low frequency, of amplification and of condensers.

Mrs Harter, submerged in a sea of words that she did not understand, surrendered.

'Of course, Charles,' she murmured, 'if you really think—'

'My dear Aunt Mary,' said Charles enthusiastically. 'It is

the very thing for you, to keep you from moping and all that.'

The lift prescribed by Dr Meynell was installed shortly afterwards and was very nearly the death of Mrs Harter since, like many other old ladies, she had a rooted objection to strange men in the house. She suspected them one and all of having designs on her old silver.

After the lift the wireless set arrived. Mrs Harter was left to contemplate the, to her, repellent object—a large ungainly-looking box, studded with knobs.

It took all Charles' enthusiasm to reconcile her to it.

Charles was in his element, he turned knobs, discoursing eloquently the while.

Mrs Harter sat in her high-backed chair, patient and polite, with a rooted conviction in her own mind that these new-fangled notions were neither more nor less than un-mitigated nuisances.

'Listen, Aunt Mary, we are on to Berlin, isn't that splendid? Can you hear the fellow?'

'I can't hear anything except a good deal of buzzing and clicking,' said Mrs Harter.

Charles continued to twirl knobs. 'Brussels,' he announced with enthusiasm.

'Is it really?' said Mrs Harter with no more than a trace of interest.

Charles again turned knobs and an unearthly howl echoed forth into the room.

'Now we seem to be on to the Dogs' Home,' said Mrs Harter, who was an old lady with a certain amount of spirit.

'Ha, ha!' said Charles, 'you will have your joke, won't you, Aunt Mary? Very good that!'

Mrs Harter could not help smiling at him. She was very fond of Charles. For some years a niece, Miriam Harter, had lived with her. She had intended to make the girl her heiress, but Miriam had not been a success. She was impatient and obviously bored by her aunt's society. She was always out, 'gadding about' as Mrs Harter called it. In the end, she had entangled herself with a young man of whom her aunt thoroughly disapproved. Miriam had been returned to her mother with a curt note much as if she had been goods on approval. She had married the young man in question and Mrs Harter usually sent her a handkerchief case or a table-centre at Christmas.

Having found nieces disappointing, Mrs Harter turned her attention to nephews. Charles, from the first, had been an unqualified success. He was always pleasantly deferential to his aunt, and listened with an appearance of intense interest to the reminiscences of her youth. In this he was a great contrast to Miriam, who had been frankly bored and showed it. Charles was never bored, he was always good-tempered, always gay. He told his aunt many times a day that she was a perfectly marvellous old lady.

Highly satisfied with her new acquisition, Mrs Harter had written to her lawyer with instructions as to the making of a new will. This was sent to her, duly approved by her and signed.

And now even in the matter of the wireless, Charles was soon proved to have won fresh laurels.

Mrs Harter, at first antagonistic, became tolerant and finally fascinated. She enjoyed it very much better when Charles was out. The trouble with Charles was that he could not leave the thing alone. Mrs Harter would be seated in her chair comfortably listening to a symphony concert or a lecture on Lucrezia Borgia or Pond Life, quite happy and at peace with the world. Not so Charles. The harmony would be shattered by discordant shrieks while he enthusiastically attempted to get foreign stations. But on those evenings when Charles was dining out with friends Mrs Harter enjoyed the wireless very much indeed. She would turn on two switches, sit in her high-backed chair and enjoy the programme of the evening.

It was about three months after the wireless had been installed that the first eerie happening occurred. Charles was absent at a bridge party.

The programme for that evening was a ballad concert. A well-known soprano was singing 'Annie Laurie', and in the middle of 'Annie Laurie' a strange thing happened. There was a sudden break, the music ceased for a moment, the buzzing, clicking noise continued and then that too died away. There was dead silence, and then very faintly a low buzzing sound was heard.

Mrs Harter got the impression, why she did not know, that the machine was tuned into somewhere very far away, and then clearly and distinctly a voice spoke, a man's voice with a faint Irish accent.

*'Mary—can you hear me, Mary? It is Patrick speaking . . . I am coming for you soon. You will be ready, won't you, Mary?'*

Then, almost immediately, the strains of 'Annie Laurie' once more filled the room.

Mrs Harter sat rigid in her chair, her hands clenched on each arm of it. Had she been dreaming? Patrick! Patrick's voice! Patrick's voice in this very room, speaking to her. No, it must be a dream, a hallucination perhaps. She must just have dropped off to sleep for a minute or two. A curious thing to have dreamed—that her dead husband's voice should speak to her over the ether. It frightened her just a little. What were the words he had said?

*'I am coming for you soon, Mary. You will be ready, won't you?'*

Was it, could it be a premonition? Cardiac weakness. Her heart. After all, she was getting on in years.

'It's a warning—that's what it is,' said Mrs Harter, rising slowly and painfully from her chair, and added characteristically:

'All that money wasted on putting in a lift!'

She said nothing of her experience to anyone, but for the next day or two she was thoughtful and a little preoccupied.

And then came the second occasion. Again she was alone in the room. The wireless, which had been playing an orchestral selection, died away with the same suddenness as before. Again there was silence, the sense of distance, and finally

Patrick's voice, not as it had been in life—but a voice rarefied, far away, with a strange unearthly quality.

*'Patrick speaking to you, Mary. I will be coming for you very soon now . . .'*

Then click, buzz, and the orchestral selection was in full swing again.

Mrs Harter glanced at the clock. No, she had not been asleep this time. Awake and in full possession of her faculties, she had heard Patrick's voice speaking. It was no hallucination, she was sure of that. In a confused way she tried to think over all that Charles had explained to her of the theory of ether waves.

Could it be Patrick had *really* spoken to her? That his actual voice had been wafted through space? There were missing wave lengths or something of that kind. She remembered Charles speaking of 'gaps in the scale'. Perhaps the missing waves explained all the so-called psychological phenomena? No, there was nothing inherently impossible in the idea. Patrick had spoken to her. He had availed himself of modern science to prepare her for what must soon be coming.

Mrs Harter rang the bell for her maid, Elizabeth.

Elizabeth was a tall gaunt woman of sixty. Beneath an unbending exterior she concealed a wealth of affection and tenderness for her mistress.

'Elizabeth,' said Mrs Harter when her faithful retainer had appeared, 'you remember what I told you? The top left-hand drawer of my bureau. It is locked, the long key with the white label. Everything is there ready.'

'Ready, ma'am?'

'For my burial,' snorted Mrs Harter. 'You know perfectly well what I mean, Elizabeth. You helped me to put the things there yourself.'

Elizabeth's face began to work strangely.

'Oh, ma'am,' she wailed, 'don't dwell on such things. I thought you was a sight better.'

'We have all got to go sometime or another,' said Mrs Harter practically. 'I am over my three score years and ten,

Elizabeth. There, there, don't make a fool of yourself. If you must cry, go and cry somewhere else.'

Elizabeth retired, still sniffing.

Mrs Harter looked after her with a good deal of affection.

'Silly old fool, but faithful,' she said, 'very faithful. Let me see, was it a hundred pounds or only fifty I left her? It ought to be a hundred. She has been with me a long time.'

The point worried the old lady and the next day she sat down and wrote to her lawyer asking if he would send her will so that she might look over it. It was that same day that Charles startled her by something he said at lunch.

'By the way, Aunt Mary,' he said, 'who is that funny old josser up in the spare room? The picture over the mantel-piece, I mean. The old johnny with the beaver and side whiskers?'

Mrs Harter looked at him austerely.

'That is your Uncle Patrick as a young man,' she said.

'Oh, I say, Aunt Mary, I am awfully sorry. I didn't mean to be rude.'

Mrs Harter accepted the apology with a dignified bend of the head.

Charles went on rather uncertainly:

'I just wondered. You see—'

He stopped undecidedly and Mrs Harter said sharply:

'Well? What were you going to say?'

'Nothing,' said Charles hastily. 'Nothing that makes sense, I mean.'

For the moment the old lady said nothing more, but later that day, when they were alone together, she returned to the subject.

'I wish you would tell me, Charles, what it was made you ask me about that picture of your uncle.'

Charles looked embarrassed.

'I told you, Aunt Mary. It was nothing but a silly fancy of mine—quite absurd.'

'Charles,' said Mrs Harter in her most autocratic voice, 'I insist upon knowing.'

'Well, my dear aunt, if you will have it, I fancied I saw him—the man in the picture, I mean—looking out of the end window when I was coming up the drive last night. Some effect of the light, I suppose. I wondered who on earth he could be, the face was so—early Victorian, if you know what I mean. And then Elizabeth said there was no one, no visitor or stranger in the house, and later in the evening I happened to drift into the spare room, and there was the picture over the mantelpiece. My man to the life! It is quite easily explained, really, I expect. Subconscious and all that. Must have noticed the picture before without realizing that I had noticed it, and then just fancied the face at the window.'

'The end window?' said Mrs Harter sharply.

'Yes, why?'

'Nothing,' said Mrs Harter.

But she was startled all the same. That room had been her husband's dressing-room.

That same evening, Charles again being absent, Mrs Harter sat listening to the wireless with feverish impatience. If for the third time she heard the mysterious voice, it would prove to her finally and without a shadow of doubt that she was really in communication with some other world.

Although her heart beat faster, she was not surprised when the same break occurred, and after the usual interval of deathly silence the faint far-away Irish voice spoke once more.

'Mary—you are prepared now . . . On Friday I shall come for you . . . Friday at half past nine . . . Do not be afraid—there will be no pain . . . Be ready . . .'

Then almost cutting short the last word, the music of the orchestra broke out again, clamorous and discordant.

Mrs Harter sat very still for a minute or two. Her face had gone white and she looked blue and pinched round the lips.

Presently she got up and sat down at her writing desk. In a somewhat shaky hand she wrote the following lines:

*Tonight, at 9.15, I have distinctly heard the voice of my
dead husband. He told me that he would come for me on
Friday night at 9.30. If I should die on that day and at
that hour I should like the facts made known so as to prove
beyond question the possibility of communicating with the
spirit world.*
   MARY HARTER.

Mrs Harter read over what she had written, enclosed it
in an envelope and addressed the envelope. Then she rang
the bell which was promptly answered by Elizabeth. Mrs
Harter got up from her desk and gave the note she had just
written to the old woman.

'Elizabeth,' she said, 'if I should die on Friday night I
should like that note given to Dr Meynell. No'—as Elizabeth
appeared to be about to protest—'do not argue with me.
You have often told me you believe in premonitions. I have
a premonition now. There is one thing more. I have left you
in my will £50. I should like you to have £100. If I am not
able to go to the bank myself before I die Mr Charles will
see to it.'

As before, Mrs Harter cut short Elizabeth's tearful protests.
In pursuance of her determination, the old lady spoke to
her nephew on the subject the following morning.

'Remember, Charles, that if anything should happen to
me, Elizabeth is to have an extra £50.'

'You are very gloomy these days, Aunt Mary,' said Charles
cheerfully. 'What is going to happen to you? According to
Dr Meynell, we shall be celebrating your hundredth birthday
in twenty years or so!'

Mrs Harter smiled affectionately at him but did not answer.
After a minute or two she said:

'What are you doing on Friday evening, Charles?'

Charles looked a trifle surprised.

'As a matter of fact, the Ewings asked me to go in and
play bridge, but if you would rather I stayed at home—'

'No,' said Mrs Harter with determination. 'Certainly not.

I mean it, Charles. On that night of all nights I should much rather be alone.'

Charles looked at her curiously, but Mrs Harter vouchsafed no further information. She was an old lady of courage and determination. She felt that she must go through with her strange experience single-handed.

Friday evening found the house very silent. Mrs Harter sat as usual in her straight-backed chair drawn up to the fireplace. All her preparations were made. That morning she had been to the bank, had drawn out £50 in notes and had handed them over to Elizabeth despite the latter's tearful protests. She had sorted and arranged all her personal belongings and had labelled one or two pieces of jewellery with the names of friends or relations. She had also written out a list of instructions for Charles. The Worcester tea service was to go to Cousin Emma. The Sèvres jars to young William, and so on.

Now she looked at the long envelope she held in her hand and drew from it a folded document. This was her will sent to her by Mr Hopkinson in accordance with her instructions. She had already read it carefully, but now she looked over it once more to refresh her memory. It was a short, concise document. A bequest of £50 to Elizabeth Marshall in consideration of faithful service, two bequests of £500 to a sister and a first cousin, and the remainder to her beloved nephew Charles Ridgeway.

Mrs Harter nodded her head several times. Charles would be a very rich man when she was dead. Well, he had been a dear good boy to her. Always kind, always affectionate, and with a merry tongue which never failed to please her.

She looked at the clock. Three minutes to the half hour. Well she was ready. And she was calm—quite calm. Although she repeated these last words to herself several times, her heart beat strangely and unevenly. She hardly realized it herself, but she was strung up to a fine point of overwrought nerves.

Half past nine. The wireless was switched on. What would she hear? A familiar voice announcing the weather forecast or that far-away voice belonging to a man who had died twenty-five years before?

But she heard neither. Instead there came a familiar sound, a sound she knew well but which tonight made her feel as though an icy hand were laid on her heart. A fumbling at the door . . .

It came again. And then a cold blast seemed to sweep through the room. Mrs Harter had now no doubt what her sensations were. She was afraid . . . She was more than afraid—she was terrified . . .

And suddenly there came to her the thought: *Twenty-five years is a long time. Patrick is a stranger to me now.*

Terror! That was what was invading her.

A soft step outside the door—a soft halting footstep. Then the door swung silently open . . .

Mrs Harter staggered to her feet, swaying slightly from side to side, her eyes fixed on the doorway, something slipped from her fingers into the grate.

She gave a strangled cry which died in her throat. In the dim light of the doorway stood a familiar figure with chestnut beard and whiskers and an old-fashioned Victorian coat.

*Patrick had come for her!*

Her heart gave one terrified leap and stood still. She slipped to the ground in a huddled heap.

There Elizabeth found her, an hour later.

Dr Meynell was called at once and Charles Ridgeway was hastily recalled from his bridge party. But nothing could be done. Mrs Harter had gone beyond human aid.

It was not until two days later that Elizabeth remembered the note given to her by her mistress. Dr Meynell read it with great interest and showed it to Charles Ridgeway.

'A very curious coincidence,' he said. 'It seems clear that your aunt had been having hallucinations about her dead husband's voice. She must have strung herself up to such a point that the excitement was fatal and when the time actually came she died of the shock.'

'Auto-suggestion?' said Charles.

'Something of the sort. I will let you know the result of the autopsy as soon as possible, though I have no doubt of it myself.' In the circumstances an autopsy was desirable, though purely as a matter of form.

Charles nodded comprehendingly.

On the preceding night, when the household was in bed, he had removed a certain wire which ran from the back of the wireless cabinet to his bedroom on the floor above. Also, since the evening had been a chilly one, he had asked Elizabeth to light a fire in his room, and in that fire he had burned a chestnut beard and whiskers. Some Victorian clothing belonging to his late uncle he replaced in the camphor-scented chest in the attic.

As far as he could see, he was perfectly safe. His plan, the shadowy outline of which had first formed in his brain when Doctor Meynell had told him that his aunt might with due care live for many years, had succeeded admirably. A sudden shock, Dr Meynell had said. Charles, that affectionate young man, beloved of old ladies, smiled to himself.

When the doctor departed, Charles went about his duties mechanically. Certain funeral arrangements had to be finally settled. Relatives coming from a distance had to have trains looked out for them. In one or two cases they would have to stay the night. Charles went about it all efficiently and methodically, to the accompaniment of an undercurrent of his own thoughts.

*A very good stroke of business!* That was the burden of them. Nobody, least of all his dead aunt, had known in what perilous straits Charles stood. His activities, carefully concealed from the world, had landed him where the shadow of a prison loomed ahead.

Exposure and ruin had stared him in the face unless he could in a few short months raise a considerable sum of money. Well—that was all right now. Charles smiled to himself. Thanks to—yes, call it a practical joke—nothing criminal about *that*—he was saved. He was now a very rich man. He had no anxieties on the subject, for Mrs Harter had never made any secret of her intentions.

Chiming in very appositely with these thoughts, Elizabeth put her head round the door and informed him that Mr Hopkinson was here and would like to see him.

About time, too, Charles thought. Repressing a tendency to whistle, he composed his face to one of suitable gravity and repaired to the library. There he greeted the precise old gentleman who had been for over a quarter of a century the late Mrs Harter's legal adviser.

The lawyer seated himself at Charles' invitation and with a dry cough entered upon business matters.

'I did not quite understand your letter to me, Mr Ridgeway. You seemed to be under the impression that the late Mrs Harter's will was in our keeping?'

Charles stared at him.

'But surely—I've heard my aunt say as much.'

'Oh! quite so, quite so. It *was* in our keeping.'

'*Was?*'

'That is what I said. Mrs Harter wrote to us, asking that it might be forwarded to her on Tuesday last.'

An uneasy feeling crept over Charles. He felt a far-off premonition of unpleasantness.

'Doubtless it will come to light amongst her papers,' continued the lawyer smoothly.

Charles said nothing. He was afraid to trust his tongue. He had already been through Mrs Harter's papers pretty thoroughly, well enough to be quite certain that no will was amongst them. In a minute or two, when he had regained control of himself, he said so. His voice sounded unreal to himself, and he had a sensation as of cold water trickling down his back.

'Has anyone been through her personal effects?' asked the lawyer.

Charles replied that her own maid, Elizabeth, had done

so. At Mr Hopkinson's suggestion, Elizabeth was sent for. She came promptly, grim and upright, and answered the questions put to her.

She had been through all her mistress's clothes and personal belongings. She was quite sure that there had been no legal document such as a will amongst them. She knew what the will looked like—her mistress had had it in her hand only the morning of her death.

'You are sure of that?' asked the lawyer sharply.

'Yes, sir. She told me so, and she made me take fifty pounds in notes. The will was in a long blue envelope.'

'Quite right,' said Mr Hopkinson.

'Now I come to think of it,' continued Elizabeth, 'that same blue envelope was lying on this table the morning after—but empty. I laid it on the desk.'

'I remember seeing it there,' said Charles.

He got up and went over to the desk. In a minute or two he turned round with an envelope in his hand which he handed to Mr Hopkinson. The latter examined it and nodded his head.

'That is the envelope in which I despatched the will on Tuesday last.'

Both men looked hard at Elizabeth.

'Is there anything more, sir?' she inquired respectfully.

'Not at present, thank you.'

Elizabeth went towards the door.

'One minute,' said the lawyer. 'Was there a fire in the grate that evening?'

'Yes, sir, there was always a fire.'

'Thank you, that will do.'

Elizabeth went out. Charles leaned forward, resting a shaking hand on the table.

'What do you think? What are you driving at?'

Mr Hopkinson shook his head.

'We must still hope the will may turn up. If it does not—'

'Well, if it does not?'

'I am afraid there is only one conclusion possible. Your

aunt sent for that will in order to destroy it. Not wishing Elizabeth to lose by that, she gave her the amount of her legacy in cash.'

'But why?' cried Charles wildly. 'Why?'

Mr Hopkinson coughed. A dry cough.

'You have had no—er—disagreement with your aunt, Mr Ridgeway?' he murmured.

Charles gasped.

'No, indeed,' he cried warmly. 'We were on the kindest, most affectionate terms, right up to the end.'

'Ah!' said Mr Hopkinson, not looking at him.

It came to Charles with a shock that the lawyer did not believe him. Who knew what this dry old stick might not have heard? Rumours of Charles' doings might have come round to him. What more natural than that he should suppose that these same rumours had come to Mrs Harter, and the aunt and nephew should have had an altercation on the subject?

But it wasn't so! Charles knew one of the bitterest moments of his career. His lies had been believed. Now that he spoke the truth, belief was withheld. The irony of it!

Of course his aunt had never burnt the will! Of course—

His thoughts came to a sudden check. What was that picture rising before his eyes? An old lady with one hand clasped to her heart . . . something slipping . . . a paper . . . falling on the red-hot embers . . .

Charles' face grew livid. He heard a hoarse voice—his own—asking:

'If that will's never found—?'

'There is a former will of Mrs Harter's still extant. Dated September 1920. By it Mrs Harter leaves everything to her niece, Miriam Harter, now Miriam Robinson.'

What was the old fool saying? Miriam? Miriam with her nondescript husband, and her four whining brats. All his cleverness—for Miriam!

The telephone rang sharply at his elbow. He took up the receiver. It was the doctor's voice, hearty and kindly.

'That you Ridgeway? Thought you'd like to know. The autopsy's just concluded. Cause of death as I surmised. But as a matter of fact the cardiac trouble was much more serious than I suspected when she was alive. With the utmost care, she couldn't have lived longer than two months at the outside. Thought you'd like to know. Might console you more or less.'

'Excuse me,' said Charles, 'would you mind saying that again?'

'She couldn't have lived longer than two months,' said the doctor in a slightly louder tone. 'All things work out for the best, you know, my dear fellow—'

But Charles had slammed back the receiver on its hook. He was conscious of the lawyer's voice speaking from a long way off.

'Dear me, Mr Ridgeway, are you ill?'

Damn them all! The smug-faced lawyer. That poisonous old ass Meynell. No hope in front of him—only the shadow of the prison wall . . .

He felt that Somebody had been playing with him—playing with him like a cat with a mouse. Somebody must be laughing . . .

# THE WIFE OF THE KENITE

Herr Schaefer removed his hat and wiped his perspiring brow. He was hot. He was hungry and thirsty—especially the latter. But, above all, he was anxious. Before him stretched the yellow expanse of the veldt. Behind him, the line of the horizon was broken by the 'dumps' of the outlying portion of the Reef. And from far away, in the direction of Johannesburg, came a sound like distant thunder. But it was not thunder, as Herr Schaefer knew only too well. It was monotonous and regular, and represented the triumph of law and order over the forces of Revolution.

Incidentally, it was having a most wearing effect on the nerves of Herr Schaefer. The position in which he found himself was an unpleasant one. The swift efficient proclamation of martial law, followed by the dramatic arrival of Smuts with the tyres of his car shot flat, had had the effect of completely disorganising the carefully laid plans of Schaefer and his friends, and Schaefer himself had narrowly escaped being laid by the heels. For the moment he was at large, but the present was uncomfortable, and the future too problematical to be pleasant.

In good, sound German, Herr Schaefer cursed the country, the climate, the Rand and all workers thereon, and most especially his late employers, the Reds. As a paid agitator, he had done his work with true German efficiency, but his military upbringing, and his years of service with the German Army in Belgium, led him to admire the forcefulness of

Smuts, and to despise unfeignedly the untrained rabble, devoid of discipline, which had crumbled to pieces at the first real test.

'They are scum,' said Herr Schaefer, gloomily, moistening his cracked lips. 'Swine! No drilling. No order. No discipline. Ragged commandos riding loose about the veldt! Ah! If they had but one Prussian drill sergeant!'

Involuntarily his back straightened. For a year he had been endeavouring to cultivate a slouch which, together with a ragged beard, might make his apparent dealing in such innocent vegetable produce as cabbages, cauliflowers, and potatoes less open to doubt. A momentary shiver went down his spine as he reflected that certain papers might even now be in the hands of the military—papers whereon the word 'cabbage' stood opposite 'dynamite', and potatoes were labelled 'detonators'.

The sun was nearing the horizon. Soon the cool of the evening would set in. If he could only reach a friendly farm (there were one or two hereabouts, he knew), he would find shelter for the night, and explicit directions that might set him on the road to freedom on the morrow.

Suddenly his eyes narrowed appreciatively upon a point to his extreme left.

'Mealies!' said Herr Schaefer. 'Where there are mealies there is a farm not far off.'

His reasoning proved correct. A rough track led through the cultivated belt of land. He came first to a cluster of kraals, avoided them dextrously (since he had no wish to be seen if the farm should not prove to be one of those he sought), and skirting a slight rise, came suddenly upon the farm itself. It was the usual low building, with a corrugated roof, and a stoep running round two sides of it.

The sun was setting now, a red, angry blur on the horizon, and a woman was standing in the open doorway, looking out into the falling dusk. Herr Schaefer pulled his hat well over his eyes and came up the steps.

'Is this by any chance the farm of Mr Henshel?' he asked.

The woman nodded without speaking, staring at him with wide blue eyes. Schaefer drew a deep breath of relief, and looked back at her with a measure of appreciation. He admired the Dutch, wide-bosomed type such as this. A grand creature, with her full breast and her wide hips; not young, nearer forty than thirty, fair hair just touched with grey parted simply in the middle of her wide forehead, something grand and forceful about her, like a patriarch's wife of old.

'A fine mother of sons,' thought Herr Schaefer appreciatively. 'Also, let us hope, a good cook!'

His requirements of women were primitive and simple.

'Mr Henshel expects me, I think,' said the German, and added in a slightly lower tone: 'I am interested in potatoes.'

She gave the expected reply.

'We, too, are cultivators of vegetables.' She spoke the words correctly, but with a strong accent. Her English was evidently not her strong point and Schaefer put her down as belonging to one of those Dutch Nationalist families who forbid their children to use the interloper's tongue. With a big, work-stained hand, she pointed behind him.

'You come from Jo'burg—yes?'

He nodded.

'Things are finished there. I escaped by the skin of my teeth. Then I lost myself on the veldt. It is pure chance that I found my way here.'

The Dutch woman shook her head. A strange ecstatic smile irradiated her broad features.

'There is no chance—only God. Enter, then.'

Approving her sentiments, for Herr Schaefer liked a woman to be religious, he crossed the threshold. She drew back to let him pass, the smile still lingering on her face, and just for a moment the thought that there was something here he did not quite understand flashed across Herr Schaefer's mind. He dismissed the idea as of little importance.

The house was built, like most, in the form of an H. The inner hall, from which rooms opened out all round, was pleasantly cool. The table was spread in preparation for a meal. The woman showed him to a bedroom, and on his return to the hall, when he had removed the boots from his aching feet, he found Henshel awaiting him. An Englishman, this, with a mean, vacuous face, a little rat of a fellow drunk with catchwords and phrases. It was amongst such as he that most of Schaefer's work had lain, and he knew the type well. Abuse of capitalists, of the 'rich who batten on the poor', the iniquities of the Chamber of Mines, the heroic endurance of the miners—these were the topics on which Henshel expatiated, Schaefer nodding wearily with his mind fixed solely on food and drink.

At last the woman appeared, bearing a steaming tureen of soup. They sat down together and fell to. It was good soup. Henshel continued to talk; his wife was silent. Schaefer contented himself with monosyllables and appropriate grunts. When Mrs Henshel left the room to bring in the next course, he said appreciatively: 'Your wife is a good cook. You are lucky. Not all Dutch women cook well.'

Henshel stared at him.

'My wife is not Dutch.'

Schaefer looked his astonishment, but the shortness of Henshel's tone, and some unacknowledged uneasiness in himself forbade him asking further. It was odd, though. He had been so sure that she was Dutch.

After the meal, he sat on the stoep in the cool dusk smoking. Somewhere in the house behind him a door banged. It was followed by the noise of a horse's hoofs. Vaguely uneasy, he sat forward listening as they grew fainter in the distance, then started violently to find Mrs Henshel standing at his elbow with a steaming cup of coffee. She set it down on a little table beside him.

'My husband has ridden over to Cloete's—to make the arrangements for getting you away in the morning,' she explained.

'Oh! I see.'

Curious, how his uneasiness persisted.

'When will he be back?'

'Some time after midnight.'

His uneasiness was not allayed. Yet what was it that he feared? Surely not that Henshel would give him up to the police? No, the man was sincere enough—a red-hot Revolutionist. The fact of the matter was that he, Conrad Schaefer, had got nerves! A German soldier (Schaefer unconsciously always thought of himself as a soldier) had no business with nerves. He took up the cup beside him and drank it down, making a grimace as he did so. What filthy stuff this Boer coffee always was! Roasted acorns! He was sure of it—roasted acorns!

He put the cup down again, and as he did so, a deep sigh came from the woman standing by his side. He had almost forgotten her presence.

'Will you not sit down?' he asked, making no motion, however, to rise from his own seat.

She shook her head.

'I have to clear away, and wash the dishes, and make my house straight.'

Schaefer nodded an approving head.

'The children are already in bed, I suppose,' he said genially.

There was a pause before she answered.

'I have no children.'

Schaefer was surprised. From the first moment he saw her he had definitely associated her with motherhood.

She took up the cup and walked to the entrance door with it. Then she spoke over her shoulder.

'I had one child. It died . . .'

'Ach! I am sorry,' said Schaefer, kindly.

The woman did not answer. She stood there motionless. And suddenly Schaefer's uneasiness returned a hundred-fold. Only this time, he connected it definitely—not with the house, not with Henshel, but with this slow-moving, grandly fashioned woman—this wife of Henshel's who was neither English nor Dutch. His curiosity roused afresh, he asked her the question point blank. What nationality was she?

'Flemish.'

She said the word abruptly, then passed into the house, leaving Herr Schaefer disturbed and upset.

Flemish! That was it, was it? Flemish! His mind flew swiftly to and fro, from the mud flats of Belgium to the sun-baked plateaus of South Africa. Flemish! He didn't like it. Both the French and the Belgians were so extraordinarily unreasonable! They couldn't forget.

His mind felt curiously confused. He yawned two or three times, wide, gaping yawns. He must get to bed and sleep—sleep—. Pah! How bitter that coffee had been—he could taste it still.

A light sprang up in the house. He got up and made his way to the door. His legs felt curiously unsteady. Inside, the big woman was sitting reading by the light of a small oil lamp. Herr Schaefer felt strangely reassured at the sight of the heavy volume on her knee. The Bible! He approved of women reading the Bible. He was a religious man himself, with a thorough belief in the German God, the God of the Old Testament, a God of blood and battles, of thunder and lightning, of material rewards and dire material vengeance, swift to anger and terrible in wrath.

He stumbled to a chair (what *was* the matter with his legs?); and in a thick, strange voice, suppressing another terrific yawn, he asked her what chapter she was reading.

Her blue eyes, under their level brows met his, something inscrutable in their depths. So might have looked a prophetess of Israel.

'The fourth chapter of Judges.'

He nodded, yawning again. He *must* go to bed . . . but the effort to rise was too much for him . . . his eyelids closed . . .

'The fourth chapter of Judges.' What was the fourth chapter of Judges? His uneasiness returned, swelled into terror. Something was wrong . . . Judges . . . Sleep overcame him. He went down into the depths—and horror went with him . . .

He awoke, dragging himself back to consciousness . . . Time had passed—much time, he felt certain of it. Where was he?

He blinked up at the light—there were pains in his arms and legs . . . he felt sick . . . the taste of the coffee was still in his mouth . . . But what was this? He was lying on the floor, bound hand and foot with strips of towel, and standing over him was the sinister figure of the woman who was not Dutch. His wits came back to him in a flash of sheer desperate fear. He was in danger . . . great danger . . .

She marked the growth of consciousness in his eyes, and answered it as though he had actually spoken.

'Yes, I will tell you now. You remember passing through a place called Voogplaat, in Belgium?'

He recalled the name. Some twopenny-ha'penny village he had passed through with his regiment.

She nodded, and went on.

'You came to my door with some other soldiers. My man was away with the Belgian Army. My first man—not Henshel, I have only been married to him two years. The boy, my little one—he was only four years of age—ran out. He began to cry—what child would not? He feared the soldiers. You ordered him to stop. He could not. You seized a chopper—ah God!—and struck off his hand! You laughed, and said: "That hand will never wield a weapon against Germany."'

'It is not true,' cried Schaefer, shrilly, 'And even if it was—it was war!'

She paid no heed, but went on.

'I struck you in the face. What mother would not have done otherwise? You caught up the child . . . and dashed him against the wall . . .'

She stopped, her voice broken, her breast heaving . . .

Schaefer murmured feebly, abandoning the idea of denial.

'It was war . . . it was war . . .'

The sweat stood on his brow. He was alone with this woman, miles from help . . .

'I recognised you at once this afternoon in spite of your beard. You did not recognise me. You said it was chance led you here—but I knew it was God . . .'

Her bosom heaved, her eyes flashed with a fanatical light.

Her God was Schaefer's God—a God of vengeance. She was uplifted by the strange, stern frenzy of a Priestess of old.

'He has delivered you into my hands.'

Wild words poured from Schaefer, arguments, prayers, appeals for mercy, threats. And all left her untouched.

'God sent me another sign. When I opened the Bible tonight, I saw what He would have me do. *Blessed above women shall Jael, the wife of Heber the Kenite, be . . .'*

She stooped and took from the floor a hammer and some long, shining nails . . . A scream burst from Schaefer's throat. He remembered now the fourth chapter of Judges, that dramatic story of black inhospitality! Sisera fleeing from his enemies . . . a woman standing at the door of a tent . . . Jael, the wife of Heber the Kenite . . .

And sonorously, in her deep voice with the broad Flemish accent, her eyes shining as the Israelite woman's may have shone in bygone days, she spoke the words of triumph:

*'This is the day in which the Lord hath delivered mine enemy into my hand . . .'*

# THE MYSTERY OF THE BLUE JAR

Jack Hartington surveyed his topped drive ruefully. Standing by the ball, he looked back to the tee, measuring the distance. His face was eloquent of the disgusted contempt which he felt. With a sigh he drew out his iron, executed two vicious swings with it, annihilating in turn a dandelion and a tuft of grass, and then addressed himself firmly to the ball.

It is hard when you are twenty-four years of age, and your one ambition in life is to reduce your handicap at golf, to be forced to give time and attention to the problem of earning your living. Five and a half days out of the seven saw Jack imprisoned in a kind of mahogany tomb in the city. Saturday afternoon and Sunday were religiously devoted to the real business of life, and in an excess of zeal he had taken rooms at the small hotel near Stourton Heath links, and rose daily at the hour of six a.m. to get in an hour's practice before catching the 8.46 to town.

The only disadvantage to the plan was that he seemed constitutionally unable to hit anything at that hour in the morning. A foozled iron succeeded a muffed drive. His mashie shots ran merrily along the ground, and four putts seemed to be the minimum on any green.

Jack sighed, grasped his iron firmly and repeated to himself the magic words, 'Left arm right through, and don't look up.'

He swung back—and then stopped, petrified, as a shrill cry rent the silence of the summer's morning.

'Murder,' it called. 'Help! Murder!'

It was a woman's voice, and it died away at the end into a sort of gurgling sigh.

Jack flung down his club and ran in the direction of the sound. It had come from somewhere quite near at hand. This particular part of the course was quite wild country, and there were few houses about. In fact, there was only one near at hand, a small picturesque cottage, which Jack had often noticed for its air of old world daintiness. It was towards this cottage that he ran. It was hidden from him by a heather-covered slope, but he rounded this and in less than a minute was standing with his hand on the small latched gate.

There was a girl standing in the garden, and for a moment Jack jumped to the natural conclusion that it was she who had uttered the cry for help. But he quickly changed his mind.

She had a little basket in her hand, half full of weeds, and had evidently just straightened herself up from weeding a wide border of pansies. Her eyes, Jack noticed, were just like pansies themselves, velvety and soft and dark, and more violet than blue. She was like a pansy altogether, in her straight purple linen gown.

The girl was looking at Jack with an expression midway between annoyance and surprise.

'I beg your pardon,' said the young man. 'But did you cry out just now?'

'I? No, indeed.'

Her surprise was so genuine that Jack felt confused. Her voice was very soft and pretty with a slight foreign inflection.

'But you must have heard it,' he exclaimed. 'It came from somewhere just near here.'

She stared at him.

'I heard nothing at all.'

Jack in his turn stared at her. It was perfectly incredible that she should not have heard that agonized appeal for help. And yet her calmness was so evident that he could not believe she was lying to him.

'It came from somewhere close at hand,' he insisted.

She was looking at him suspiciously now.

'What did it say?' she asked.

'Murder—help! Murder!'

'Murder—help! murder,' repeated the girl. 'Somebody has played a trick on you, Monsieur. Who could be murdered here?'

Jack looked about him with a confused idea of discovering a dead body upon a garden path. Yet he was still perfectly sure that the cry he had heard was real and not a product of his imagination. He looked up at the cottage windows. Everything seemed perfectly still and peaceful.

'Do you want to search our house?' asked the girl drily.

She was so clearly sceptical that Jack's confusion grew deeper than ever. He turned away.

'I'm sorry,' he said. 'It must have come from higher up in the woods.'

He raised his cap and retreated. Glancing back over his shoulder, he saw that the girl had calmly resumed her weeding.

For some time he hunted through the woods, but could find no sign of anything unusual having occurred. Yet he was as positive as ever that he had really heard the cry. In the end, he gave up the search and hurried home to bolt his breakfast and catch the 8.46 by the usual narrow margin of a second or so. His conscience pricked him a little as he sat in the train. Ought he not to have immediately reported what he had heard to the police? That he had not done so was solely owing to the pansy girl's incredulity. She had clearly suspected him of romancing—possibly the police might do the same. *Was* he absolutely certain that he had heard the cry?

By now he was not nearly so positive as he had been—the natural result of trying to recapture a lost sensation. Was it some bird's cry in the distance that he had twisted into the semblance of a woman's voice?

But he rejected the suggestion angrily. It was a woman's voice, and he had heard it. He remembered looking at his watch just before the cry had come. As nearly as possible it must have been five and twenty minutes past seven when he had heard the call. That might be a fact useful to the police if—if anything should be discovered.

Going home that evening, he scanned the evening papers anxiously to see if there were any mention of a crime having been committed. But there was nothing, and he hardly knew whether to be relieved or disappointed.

The following morning was wet—so wet that even the most ardent golfer might have his enthusiasm damped. Jack rose at the last possible moment, gulped his breakfast, ran for the train and again eagerly scanned the papers. Still no mention of any gruesome discovery having been made. The evening papers told the same tale.

'Queer,' said Jack to himself, 'but there it is. Probably some blinking little boys having a game together up in the woods.'

He was out early the following morning. As he passed the cottage, he noted out of the tail of his eye that the girl was out in the garden again weeding. Evidently a habit of hers. He did a particularly good approach shot, and hoped that she had noticed it. As he teed up on the next tee, he glanced at his watch.

'Just five and twenty past seven,' he murmured. 'I wonder—'

The words were frozen on his lips. From behind him came the same cry which had so startled him before. A woman's voice, in dire distress.

'Murder—help! Murder!'

Jack raced back. The pansy girl was standing by the gate. She looked startled, and Jack ran up to her triumphantly, crying out:

'You heard it this time, anyway.'

Her eyes were wide with some emotion he could not fathom but he noticed that she shrank back from him as he approached, and even glanced back at the house, as though she meditated running to it for shelter.

She shook her head, staring at him.

'I heard nothing at all,' she said wonderingly.

It was as though she had struck him a blow between the eyes. Her sincerity was so evident that he could not disbelieve her. Yet he couldn't have imagined it—he couldn't—he couldn't—

He heard her voice speaking gently—almost with sympathy.

'You have had the shell-shock, yes?'

In a flash he understood her look of fear, her glance back at the house. She thought that he suffered from delusions . . .

And then, like a douche of cold water, came the horrible thought, was she right? *Did* he suffer from delusions? Obsessed by the horror of the thought, he turned and stumbled away without vouchsafing a word. The girl watched him go, sighed, shook her head, and bent down to her weeding again.

Jack endeavoured to reason matters out with himself. 'If I hear the damned thing again at twenty-five minutes past seven,' he said to himself, 'it's clear that I've got hold of a hallucination of some sort. But I won't hear it.'

He was nervous all that day, and went to bed early determined to put the matter to the proof the following morning.

As was perhaps natural in such a case, he remained awake half the night, and finally overslept himself. It was twenty past seven by the time he was clear of the hotel and running towards the links. He realized that he would not be able to get to the fatal spot by twenty-five past, but surely, if the voice was a hallucination pure and simple, he would hear it anywhere. He ran on, his eyes fixed on the hands of his watch.

Twenty-five past. From far off came the echo of a woman's voice, calling. The words could not be distinguished, but he was convinced that it was the same cry he had heard before, and that it came from the same spot, somewhere in the neighbourhood of the cottage.

Strangely enough, that fact reassured him. It might, after all, be a hoax. Unlikely as it seemed, the girl herself might be playing a trick on him. He set his shoulders resolutely, and took out a club from his golf bag. He would play the few holes up to the cottage.

The girl was in the garden as usual. She looked up this morning, and when he raised his cap to her, said good morning rather shyly . . . She looked, he thought, lovelier than ever.

'Nice day, isn't it?' Jack called out cheerily, cursing the unavoidable banality of the observation.

'Yes, indeed, it is lovely.'

'Good for the garden, I expect?'

The girl smiled a little, disclosing a fascinating dimple.

'Alas, no! For my flowers the rain is needed. See, they are all dried up.'

Jack accepted the invitation of her gesture, and came up to the low hedge dividing the garden from the course, looking over it into the garden.

'They seem all right,' he remarked awkwardly, conscious as he spoke of the girl's slightly pitying glance running over him.

'The sun is good, is it not?' she said. 'For the flowers one can always water them. But the sun gives strength and repairs the health. Monsieur is much better today, I can see.'

Her encouraging tone annoyed Jack intensely.

'Curse it all,' he said to himself. 'I believe she's trying to cure me by suggestion.'

'I'm perfectly well,' he said irritably.

'That is good then,' returned the girl quickly and soothingly.

Jack had the irritating feeling that she didn't believe him.

He played a few more holes and hurried back to breakfast. As he ate it, he was conscious, not for the first time, of the close scrutiny of a man who sat at the table next to him. He was a man of middle age, with a powerful forceful face. He had a small dark beard and very piercing grey eyes, and an ease and assurance of manner which placed him among the higher ranks of the professional classes. His name, Jack knew, was Lavington, and he had heard vague rumours as to his being a well-known medical specialist, but as Jack was not a frequenter of Harley Street, the name had conveyed little or nothing to him.

But this morning he was very conscious of the quiet observation under which he was being kept, and it frightened him a little. Was his secret written plainly in his face for all to see? Did this man, by reason of his professional calling, know that there was something amiss in the hidden grey matter?

Jack shivered at the thought. Was it true? Was he really going mad? Was the whole thing a hallucination, or was it a gigantic hoax?

And suddenly a very simple way of testing the solution occurred to him. He had hitherto been alone on his round. Supposing someone else was with him? Then one out of three things might happen. The voice might be silent. They might both hear it. Or—he only might hear it.

That evening he proceeded to carry his plan into effect. Lavington was the man he wanted with him. They fell into conversation easily enough—the older man might have been waiting for such an opening. It was clear that for some reason or other Jack interested him. The latter was able to come quite easily and naturally to the suggestion that they might play a few holes together before breakfast. The arrangement was made for the following morning.

They started out a little before seven. It was a perfect day, still and cloudless, but not too warm. The doctor was playing well, Jack wretchedly. His whole mind was intent on the forthcoming crisis. He kept glancing surreptitiously at his watch. They reached the seventh tee, between which and the hole the cottage was situated, about twenty past seven.

The girl, as usual, was in the garden as they passed. She did not look up.

Two balls lay on the green, Jack's near the hole, the doctor's some little distance away.

'I've got this for it,' said Lavington. 'I must go for it, I suppose.'

He bent down, judging the line he should take. Jack stood rigid, his eyes glued to his watch. It was exactly twenty-five minutes past seven.

The ball ran swiftly along the grass, stopped on the edge of the hole, hesitated and dropped in.

'Good putt,' said Jack. His voice sounded hoarse and unlike himself . . . He shoved his wrist watch farther up his arm with a sigh of overwhelming relief. Nothing had happened. The spell was broken.

'If you don't mind waiting a minute,' he said, 'I think I'll have a pipe.'

They paused a while on the eighth tee. Jack filled and lit the pipe with fingers that trembled a little in spite of himself. An enormous weight seemed to have lifted from his mind.

'Lord, what a good day it is,' he remarked, staring at the prospect ahead of him with great contentment. 'Go on, Lavington, your swipe.'

And then it came. Just at the very instant the doctor was hitting. A woman's voice, high and agonized.

'Murder—Help! Murder!'

The pipe fell from Jack's nerveless hand, as he spun round in the direction of the sound, and then, remembering, gazed breathlessly at his companion.

Lavington was looking down the course, shading his eyes.

'A bit short—just cleared the bunker, though, I think.'

He had heard nothing.

The world seemed to spin round with Jack. He took a step or two, lurching heavily. When he recovered himself, he was lying on the short turf, and Lavington was bending over him.

'There, take it easy now, take it easy.'

'What did I do?'

'You fainted, young man—or gave a very good try at it.'

'My God!' said Jack, and groaned.

'What's the trouble? Something on your mind?'

'I'll tell you in one minute, but I'd like to ask you something first.'

The doctor lit his own pipe and settled himself on the bank.

'Ask anything you like,' he said comfortably.

'You've been watching me for the last day or two. Why?'

Lavington's eyes twinkled a little.

'That's rather an awkward question. A cat can look at a king, you know.'

'Don't put me off. I'm in earnest. Why was it? I've a vital reason for asking.'

Lavington's face grew serious.

'I'll answer you quite honestly. I recognized in you all the signs of a man labouring under a sense of acute strain, and it intrigued me what that strain could be.'

'I can tell you that easily enough,' said Jack bitterly. 'I'm going mad.'

He stopped dramatically, but his statement not seeming to arouse the interest and consternation he expected, he repeated it.

'I tell you I'm going mad.'

'Very curious,' murmured Lavington. 'Very curious indeed.'

Jack felt indignant.

'I suppose that's all it does seem to you. Doctors are so damned callous.'

'Come, come, my young friend, you're talking at random. To begin with, although I have taken my degree, I do not practise medicine. Strictly speaking, I am not a doctor—not a doctor of the body, that is.'

Jack looked at him keenly.

'Of the mind?'

'Yes, in a sense, but more truly I call myself a doctor of the soul.'

'Oh!'

'I perceive the disparagement in your tone, and yet we must use some word to denote the active principle which can be separated and exist independently of its fleshy home, the body. You've got to come to terms with the soul, you know, young man, it isn't just a religious term invented by clergymen. But we'll call it the mind, or the subconscious self, or any term that suits you better. You took offence at my tone just now, but I can assure you that it really did strike me as very curious that such a well-balanced and perfectly normal young man as yourself should suffer from the delusion that he was going out of his mind.'

'I'm out of my mind all right. Absolutely barmy.'

'You will forgive me for saying so, but I don't believe it.'

'I suffer from delusions.'

'After dinner?'

'No, in the morning.'

'Can't be done,' said the doctor, relighting his pipe which had gone out.

'I tell you I hear things that no one else hears.'

'One man in a thousand can see the moons of Jupiter. Because the other nine hundred and ninety nine can't see them there's no reason to doubt that the moons of Jupiter exist, and certainly no reason for calling the thousandth man a lunatic.'

'The moons of Jupiter are a proved scientific fact.'

'It's quite possible that the delusions of today may be the proved scientific facts of tomorrow.'

In spite of himself, Lavington's matter-of-fact manner was having its effect upon Jack. He felt immeasurably soothed and cheered. The doctor looked at him attentively for a minute or two and then nodded.

'That's better,' he said. 'The trouble with you young fellows is that you're so cocksure nothing can exist outside your own philosophy that you get the wind up when something occurs to jolt you out of that opinion. Let's hear your grounds for believing that you're going mad, and we'll decide whether or not to lock you up afterwards.'

As faithfully as he could, Jack narrated the whole series of occurrences.

'But what I can't understand,' he ended, 'is why this morning it should come at half past seven—five minutes late.'

Lavington thought for a minute or two. Then—

'What's the time now by your watch?' he asked.

'Quarter to eight,' replied Jack, consulting it.

'That's simple enough, then. Mine says twenty to eight. Your watch is five minutes fast. That's a very interesting and important point—to me. In fact, it's invaluable.'

'In what way?'

Jack was beginning to get interested.

'Well, the obvious explanation is that on the first morning you *did* hear some such cry—may have been a joke, may not. On the following mornings, you suggestioned yourself to hear it at exactly the same time.'

'I'm sure I didn't.'

'Not consciously, of course, but the subconscious plays us some funny tricks, you know. But anyway, that explanation won't wash. If it was a case of suggestion, you would have heard the cry at twenty-five minutes past seven by your watch, and you could never have heard it when the time, as you thought, was past.'

'Well, then?'

'Well—it's obvious, isn't it? This cry for help occupies a perfectly definite place and time in space. The place is the vicinity of that cottage and the time is twenty-five minutes past seven.'

'Yes, but why should *I* be the one to hear it? I don't believe in ghosts and all that spook stuff—spirits rapping and all the rest of it. Why should I hear the damned thing?'

'Ah! that we can't tell at present. It's a curious thing that many of the best mediums are made out of confirmed sceptics. It isn't the people who are interested in occult phenomena who get the manifestations. Some people see and hear things that other people don't—we don't know why, and nine times out of ten they don't want to see or hear them, and are convinced that they are suffering from delusions—just as you were. It's like electricity. Some substances are good conductors, others are non-conductors, and for a long time we didn't know why, and had to be content just to accept the fact. Nowadays we do know why. Some day, no doubt, we shall know why you hear this thing and I and the girl don't. Everything's governed by natural law, you know— there's no such thing really as the supernatural. Finding out the laws that govern so called psychic phenomena is going to be a tough job—but every little helps.'

'But what am I going to *do?*' asked Jack.

Lavington chuckled.

'Practical, I see. Well, my young friend, you are going to have a good breakfast and get off to the city without worrying your head further about things you don't understand. I, on the other hand, am going to poke about, and see what I can find out about that cottage back there. That's where the mystery centres, I dare swear.'

Jack rose to his feet.

'Right, sir. I'm on, but, I say—'

'Yes?'

Jack flushed awkwardly.

'I'm sure the girl's all right,' he muttered.

Lavington looked amused.

'You didn't tell me she was a pretty girl! Well, cheer up, I think the mystery started before her time.'

Jack arrived home that evening in a perfect fever of curiosity. He was by now pinning his faith blindly to Lavington. The doctor had accepted the matter so naturally, had been so matter-of-fact and unperturbed by it, that Jack was impressed.

He found his new friend waiting for him in the hall when he came down for dinner, and the doctor suggested that they should dine together at the same table.

'Any news, sir?' asked Jack anxiously.

'I've collected the life history of Heather Cottage all right. It was tenanted first by an old gardener and his wife. The old man died, and the old woman went to her daughter.

Then a builder got hold of it, and modernized it with great success, selling it to a city gentleman who used it for week-ends. About a year ago, he sold it to some people called Turner—Mr and Mrs Turner. They seem to have been rather a curious couple from all I can make out. He was an Englishman, his wife was popularly supposed to be partly Russian, and was a very handsome exotic-looking woman. They lived very quietly, seeing no one, and hardly ever going outside the cottage garden. The local rumour goes that they were afraid of something—but I don't think we ought to rely on that.

'And then suddenly one day they departed, cleared out one morning early, and never came back. The agents here got a letter from Mr Turner, written from London, instructing him to sell up the place as quickly as possible. The furniture was sold off, and the house itself was sold to a Mr Mauleverer. He only actually lived in it a fortnight—then he advertised it to be let furnished. The people who have it now are a consumptive French professor and his daughter. They have been there just ten days.'

Jack digested this in silence.

'I don't see that that gets us any forrarder,' he said at last. 'Do you?'

'I rather want to know more about the Turners,' said Lavington quietly. 'They left very early in the morning, you remember. As far as I can make out, nobody actually saw them go. Mr Turner has been seen since—but I can't find anybody who has seen Mrs Turner.'

Jack paled.

'It can't be—you don't mean—'

'Don't excite yourself, young man. The influence of anyone at the point of death—and especially of violent death—upon their surroundings is very strong. Those surroundings might conceivably absorb that influence, transmitting it in turn to a suitably tuned receiver—in this case yourself.'

'But why me?' murmured Jack rebelliously. 'Why not someone who could do some good?'

'You are regarding the force as intelligent and purposeful, instead of blind and mechanical. I do not believe myself in earthbound spirits, haunting a spot for one particular purpose. But the thing I have seen, again and again, until I can hardly believe it to be pure coincidence, is a kind of blind groping towards justice—a subterranean moving of blind forces, always working obscurely towards that end . . .'

He shook himself—as though casting off some obsession that pre-occupied him, and turned to Jack with a ready smile.

'Let us banish the subject—for tonight at all events,' he suggested.

Jack agreed readily enough, but did not find it so easy to banish the subject from his own mind.

During the weekend, he made vigorous inquiries of his own, but succeeded in eliciting little more than the doctor had done. He had definitely given up playing golf before breakfast.

The next link in the chain came from an unexpected quarter. On getting back one day, Jack was informed that a young lady was waiting to see him. To his intense surprise it proved to be the girl of the garden—the pansy girl, as he always called her in his own mind. She was very nervous and confused.

'You will forgive me, Monsieur, for coming to seek you like this? But there is something I want to tell you—I—'

She looked round uncertainly.

'Come in here,' said Jack promptly, leading the way into the now deserted 'Ladies' Drawing-room' of the hotel, a dreary apartment, with a good deal of red plush about it. 'Now, sit down, Miss, Miss—'

'Marchaud, Monsieur, Felise Marchaud.'

'Sit down, Mademoiselle Marchaud, and tell me all about it.'

Felise sat down obediently. She was dressed in dark green today, and the beauty and charm of the proud little face was more evident than ever. Jack's heart beat faster as he sat down beside her.

'It is like this,' explained Felise. 'We have been here but a short time, and from the beginning we hear the house—our so sweet little house—is haunted. No servant will stay in it. That does not matter so much—me, I can do the *ménage* and cook easily enough.'

'Angel,' thought the infatuated young man. 'She's wonderful.'

But he maintained an outward semblance of businesslike attention.

'This talk of ghosts, I think it is all folly—that is until four days ago. Monsieur, four nights running, I have had the same dream. A lady stands there—she is beautiful, tall and very fair. In her hands she holds a blue china jar. She is distressed—very distressed, and continually she holds out the jar to me, as though imploring me to do something with it—but alas! she cannot speak, and I—I do not know what she asks. That was the dream for the first two nights—but the night before last, there was more of it. She and the blue jar faded away, and suddenly I heard her voice crying out—I know it is her voice, you comprehend—and, oh! Monsieur, the words she says are those you spoke to me that morning. "Murder—Help! Murder!" I awoke in terror. I say to myself— it is a nightmare, the words you heard are an accident. But last night the dream came again. Monsieur, what is it? You too have heard. What shall we do?'

Felise's face was terrified. Her small hands clasped themselves together, and she gazed appealingly at Jack. The latter affected an unconcern he did not feel.

'That's all right, Mademoiselle Marchaud. You mustn't worry. I tell you what I'd like you to do, if you don't mind, repeat the whole story to a friend of mine who is staying here, a Dr Lavington.'

Felise signified her willingness to adopt this course, and Jack went off in search of Lavington. He returned with him a few minutes later.

Lavington gave the girl a keen scrutiny as he acknowledged Jack's hurried introductions. With a few reassuring words, he soon put the girl at her ease, and he, in his turn, listened attentively to her story.

'Very curious,' he said, when she had finished. 'You have told your father of this?'

Felise shook her head.

'I have not liked to worry him. He is very ill still'—her eyes filled with tears—'I keep from him anything that might excite or agitate him.'

'I understand,' said Lavington kindly. 'And I am glad you came to us, Mademoiselle Marchaud. Hartington here, as you know, had an experience something similar to yours. I think I may say that we are well on the track now. There is nothing else that you can think of?'

Felise gave a quick movement.

'Of course! How stupid I am. It is the point of the whole story. Look, Monsieur, at what I found at the back of one of the cupboards where it had slipped behind the shelf.'

She held out to them a dirty piece of drawing-paper on which was executed roughly in water colours a sketch of a woman. It was a mere daub, but the likeness was probably good enough. It represented a tall fair woman, with something subtly un-English about her face. She was standing by a table on which was standing a blue china jar.

'I only found it this morning,' explained Felise. 'Monsieur le docteur, that is the face of the woman I saw in my dream, and that is the identical blue jar.'

'Extraordinary,' commented Lavington. 'The key to the mystery is evidently the blue jar. It looks like a Chinese jar to me, probably an old one. It seems to have a curious raised pattern over it.'

'It is Chinese,' declared Jack. 'I have seen an exactly similar one in my uncle's collection—he is a great collector of Chinese porcelain, you know, and I remember noticing a jar just like this a short time ago.'

'The Chinese jar,' mused Lavington. He remained a minute or two lost in thought, then raised his head suddenly, a curious light shining in his eyes. 'Hartington, how long has your uncle had that jar?'

'How long? I really don't know.'

'Think. Did he buy it lately?'

'I don't know—yes, I believe he did, now I come to think of it. I'm not very interested in porcelain myself, but I remember his showing me his "recent acquisitions", and this was one of them.'

'Less than two months ago? The Turners left Heather Cottage just two months ago.'

'Yes, I believe it was.'

'Your uncle attends country sales sometimes?'

'He's always tooling round to sales.'

'Then there is no inherent improbability in our assuming that he bought this particular piece of porcelain at the sale of the Turners' things. A curious coincidence—or perhaps what I call the groping of blind justice. Hartington, you must find out from your uncle at once where he bought this jar.'

Jack's face fell.

'I'm afraid that's impossible. Uncle George is away on the Continent. I don't even know where to write to him.'

'How long will he be away?'

'Three weeks to a month at least.'

There was a silence. Felise sat looking anxiously from one man to the other.

'Is there nothing that we can do?' she asked timidly.

'Yes, there is one thing,' said Lavington, in a tone of suppressed excitement. 'It is unusual, perhaps, but I believe that it will succeed. Hartington, you must get hold of that jar. Bring it down here, and, if Mademoiselle permits, we will spend a night at Heather Cottage, taking the blue jar with us.'

Jack felt his skin creep uncomfortably.

'What do you think will happen?' he asked uneasily.

'I have not the slightest idea—but I honestly believe that the mystery will be solved and the ghost laid. Quite possibly there may be a false bottom to the jar and something is concealed inside it. If no phenomena occur, we must use our own ingenuity.'

Felise clasped her hands.

'It is a wonderful idea,' she exclaimed.

Her eyes were alight with enthusiasm. Jack did not feel nearly so enthusiastic—in fact, he was inwardly funking it badly, but nothing would have induced him to admit the fact before Felise. The doctor acted as though his suggestion were the most natural one in the world.

'When can you get the jar?' asked Felise, turning to Jack.

'Tomorrow,' said the latter, unwillingly.

He had to go through with it now, but the memory of the frenzied cry for help that had haunted him each morning was something to be ruthlessly thrust down and not thought about more than could be helped.

He went to his uncle's house the following evening, and took away the jar in question. He was more than ever convinced when he saw it again that it was the identical one pictured in the water colour sketch, but carefully as he looked it over he could see no sign that it contained a secret receptacle of any kind.

It was eleven o'clock when he and Lavington arrived at Heather Cottage. Felise was on the look-out for them, and opened the door softly before they had time to knock.

'Come in,' she whispered. 'My father is asleep upstairs, and we must not wake him. I have made coffee for you in here.'

She led the way into the small cosy sitting room. A spirit lamp stood in the grate, and bending over it, she brewed them both some fragrant coffee.

Then Jack unfastened the Chinese jar from its many wrappings. Felise gasped as her eyes fell on it.

'But yes, but yes,' she cried eagerly. 'That is it—I would know it anywhere.'

Meanwhile Lavington was making his own preparations. He removed all the ornaments from a small table and set it in the middle of the room. Round it he placed three chairs.

Then, taking the blue jar from Jack, he placed it in the centre of the table.

'Now,' he said, 'we are ready. Turn off the lights, and let us sit round the table in the darkness.'

The others obeyed him. Lavington's voice spoke again out of the darkness.

'Think of nothing—or of everything. Do not force the mind. It is possible that one of us has mediumistic powers. If so, that person will go into a trance. Remember, there is nothing to fear. Cast out fear from your hearts, and drift—drift—'

His voice died away and there was silence. Minute by minute, the silence seemed to grow more pregnant with possibilities. It was all very well for Lavington to say 'Cast out fear'. It was not fear that Jack felt—it was panic. And he was almost certain that Felise felt the same way. Suddenly he heard her voice, low and terrified.

'Something terrible is going to happen. I feel it.'

'Cast out fear', said Lavington. 'Do not fight against the influence.'

The darkness seemed to get darker and the silence more acute. And nearer and nearer came that indefinable sense of menace.

Jack felt himself choking—stifling—the evil thing was very near . . .

And then the moment of conflict passed. He was drifting, drifting down stream—his lids closed—peace—darkness . . .

Jack stirred slightly. His head was heavy—heavy as lead. Where was he?

Sunshine . . . birds . . . He lay staring up at the sky.

Then it all came back to him. The sitting. The little room. Felise and the doctor. What had happened?

He sat up, his head throbbing unpleasantly, and looked round him. He was lying in a little copse not far from the cottage. No one else was near him. He took out his watch. To his amazement it registered half past twelve.

Jack struggled to his feet, and ran as fast as he could in the direction of the cottage. They must have been alarmed by his failure to come out of the trance, and carried him out into the open air.

Arrived at the cottage, he knocked loudly on the door. But there was no answer, and no signs of life about it. They must have gone off to get help. Or else—Jack felt an indefinable fear invade him. What had happened last night?

He made his way back to the hotel as quickly as possible. He was about to make some inquiries at the office, when he was diverted by a colossal punch in the ribs which nearly knocked him off his feet. Turning in some indignation, he beheld a white-haired old gentleman wheezing with mirth.

'Didn't expect me, my boy. Didn't expect me, hey?' said this individual.

'Why, Uncle George, I thought you were miles away—in Italy somewhere.'

'Ah! but I wasn't. Landed at Dover last night. Thought I'd motor up to town and stop here to see you on the way. And what did I find? Out all night, hey? Nice goings on—'

'Uncle George,' Jack checked him firmly. 'I've got the most extraordinary story to tell you. I dare say you won't believe it.'

'I dare say I shan't,' laughed the old man. 'But do your best, my boy.'

'But I must have something to eat,' continued Jack. 'I'm famished.'

He led the way to the dining-room, and over a substantial repast, he narrated the whole story.

'And God knows what's become of them,' he ended.

His uncle seemed on the verge of apoplexy.

'The jar,' he managed to ejaculate at last. 'THE BLUE JAR! What's become of that?'

Jack stared at him in non-comprehension, but submerged in the torrent of words that followed he began to understand.

It came with a rush: 'Ming—unique—gem of my collection—worth ten thousand pounds at least—offer from Hoggenheimer,

the American millionaire—only one of its kind in the world—
Confound it, sir, what have you done with my BLUE JAR?'

Jack rushed from the room. He must find Lavington. The
young lady at the office eyed him coldly.

'Dr Lavington left late last night—by motor. He left a note
for you.'

Jack tore it open. It was short and to the point.

*My dear young friend,*

*Is the day of the supernatural over? Not quite—especially
when tricked out in new scientific language. Kindest regards
from Felise, invalid father, and myself. We have twelve hours
start, which ought to be ample.*

> *Yours ever,*
> *Ambrose Lavington,*
> Doctor of the Soul.

# THE STRANGE CASE OF SIR ARTHUR CARMICHAEL

*(Taken from the notes of the late Dr Edward Carstairs, M.D.,
the eminent psychologist.)*

I am perfectly aware that there are two distinct ways of
looking at the strange and tragic events which I have set
down here. My own opinion has never wavered. I have
been persuaded to write the story out in full, and indeed I
believe it to be due to science that such strange and inexplicable facts should not be buried in oblivion.

It was a wire from my friend, Dr Settle, that first introduced me to the matter. Beyond mentioning the name
Carmichael, the wire was not explicit, but in obedience to
it I took the 12.20 train from Paddington to Wolden, in
Herefordshire.

The name of Carmichael was not unfamiliar to me. I had
been slightly acquainted with the late Sir William Carmichael
of Wolden, though I had seen nothing of him for the last
eleven years. He had, I knew, one son, the present baronet,
who must now be a young man of about twenty-three. I
remembered vaguely having heard some rumours about Sir
William's second marriage, but could recall nothing definite
unless it were a vague impression detrimental to the second
Lady Carmichael.

Settle met me at the station.

'Good of you to come,' he said as he wrung my hand.

'Not at all. I understand this is something in my line?'

'Very much so.'

'A mental case, then?' I hazarded. 'Possessing some unusual features?'

We had collected my luggage by this time and were seated in a dog-cart driving away from the station in the direction of Wolden, which lay about three miles away. Settle did not answer for a minute or two. Then he burst out suddenly.

'The whole thing's incomprehensible! Here is a young man, twenty-three years of age, thoroughly normal in every respect. A pleasant amiable boy, with no more than his fair share of conceit, not brilliant intellectually perhaps, but an excellent type of the ordinary upper-class young Englishman. Goes to bed in his usual health one evening, and is found the next morning wandering about the village in a semi-idiotic condition, incapable of recognizing his nearest and dearest.'

'Ah!' I said, stimulated. This case promised to be interesting. 'Complete loss of memory? And this occurred—?'

'Yesterday morning. The 9th of August.'

'And there has been nothing—no shock that you know of—to account for this state?'

'Nothing.'

I had a sudden suspicion.

'Are you keeping anything back?'

'N—no.'

His hesitation confirmed my suspicion.

'I must know everything.'

'It's nothing to do with Arthur. It's to do with—with the house.'

'With the house,' I repeated, astonished.

'You've had a great deal to do with that sort of thing, haven't you, Carstairs? You've "tested" so-called haunted houses. What's your opinion of the whole thing?'

'In nine cases out of ten, fraud,' I replied. 'But the tenth—well, I have come across phenomena that are absolutely unexplainable from the ordinary materialistic standpoint. I am a believer in the occult.'

Settle nodded. We were just turning in at the Park gates. He pointed with his whip at a low-lying white mansion on the side of a hill.

'That's the house,' he said. 'And—there's *something* in that house, something uncanny—horrible. We all feel it . . . And I'm not a superstitious man . . .'

'What form does it take?' I asked.

He looked straight in front of him. 'I'd rather you knew nothing. You see, if you—coming here unbiased—knowing nothing about it—see it too—well—'

'Yes,' I said, 'it's better so. But I should be glad if you will tell me a little more about the family.'

'Sir William,' said Settle, 'was twice married. Arthur is the child of his first wife. Nine years ago he married again, and the present Lady Carmichael is something of a mystery. She is only half English, and, I suspect, has Asiatic blood in her veins.'

He paused.

'Settle,' I said, 'you don't like Lady Carmichael.'

He admitted it frankly. 'No, I don't. There has always seemed to be something sinister about her. Well, to continue, by his second wife Sir William had another child, also a boy, who is now eight years old. Sir William died three years ago, and Arthur came into the title and place. His stepmother and half-brother continued to live with him at Wolden. The estate, I must tell you, is very much impoverished. Nearly the whole of Sir Arthur's income goes to keeping it up. A few hundreds a year was all Sir William could leave his wife, but fortunately Arthur has always got on splendidly with his stepmother, and has been only too delighted to have her live with him. Now—'

'Yes?'

'Two months ago Arthur became engaged to a charming girl, a Miss Phyllis Patterson.' He added, lowering his voice with a touch of emotion: 'They were to have been married next month. She is staying here now. You can imagine her distress—'

I bowed my head silently.

We were driving up close to the house now. On our right the green lawn sloped gently away. And suddenly I saw a most charming picture. A young girl was coming slowly across the lawn to the house. She wore no hat, and the sunlight enhanced the gleam of her glorious golden hair. She carried a great basket of roses, and a beautiful grey Persian cat twined itself lovingly round her feet as she walked.

I looked at Settle interrogatively.

'That is Miss Patterson,' he said.

'Poor girl,' I said, 'poor girl. What a picture she makes with the roses and her grey cat.'

I heard a faint sound and looked quickly round at my friend. The reins had slipped out of his fingers, and his face was quite white.

'What's the matter?' I exclaimed.

He recovered himself with an effort.

'Nothing,' he said, 'nothing.'

In a few moments more we had arrived, and I was following him into the green drawing-room, where tea was laid out.

A middle-aged but still beautiful woman rose as we entered and came forward with an outstretched hand.

'This is my friend, Dr Carstairs, Lady Carmichael.'

I cannot explain the instinctive wave of repulsion that swept over me as I took the proffered hand of this charming and stately woman who moved with the dark and languorous grace that recalled Settle's surmise of Oriental blood.

'It is very good of you to come, Dr Carstairs,' she said in a low musical voice, 'and to try and help us in our great trouble.'

I made some trivial reply and she handed me my tea.

In a few minutes the girl I had seen on the lawn outside entered the room. The cat was no longer with her, but she still carried the basket of roses in her hand. Settle introduced me and she came forward impulsively.

'Oh! Dr Carstairs, Dr Settle has told us so much about you. I have a feeling that you will be able to do something for poor Arthur.'

Miss Patterson was certainly a very lovely girl, though her cheeks were pale, and her frank eyes were outlined with dark circles.

'My dear young lady,' I said reassuringly, 'indeed you must not despair. These cases of lost memory, or secondary personality, are often of very short duration. At any minute the patient may return to his full powers.'

She shook her head. 'I can't believe in this being a second personality,' she said. '*This* isn't Arthur at all. It is *no* personality of his. It isn't *him*. I—'

'Phyllis, dear,' said Lady Carmichael's soft voice, 'here is your tea.'

And something in the expression of her eyes as they rested on the girl told me that Lady Carmichael had little love for her prospective daughter-in-law.

Miss Patterson declined the tea, and I said, to ease the conversation: 'Isn't the pussy cat going to have a saucer of milk?'

She looked at me rather strangely.

'The—pussy cat?'

'Yes, your companion of a few moments ago in the garden—'

I was interrupted by a crash. Lady Carmichael had upset the tea kettle, and the hot water was pouring all over the floor. I remedied the matter, and Phyllis Patterson looked questioningly at Settle. He rose.

'Would you like to see your patient now, Carstairs?'

I followed him at once. Miss Patterson came with us. We went upstairs and Settle took a key from his pocket.

'He sometimes has a fit of wandering,' he explained. 'So I usually lock the door when I'm away from the house.'

He turned the key in the lock and we went in.

A young man was sitting on the window seat where the last rays of the westerly sun struck broad and yellow. He sat curiously still, rather hunched together, with every muscle relaxed. I thought at first that he was quite unaware of our presence until I suddenly saw that, under immovable lids, he was watching us closely. His eyes dropped as they met mine, and he blinked. But he did not move.

'Come, Arthur,' said Settle cheerfully. 'Miss Patterson and a friend of mine have come to see you.'

But the young fellow in the window seat only blinked. Yet a moment or two later I saw him watching us again—furtively and secretly.

'Want your tea?' asked Settle, still loudly and cheerfully, as though talking to a child.

He set on the table a cup full of milk. I lifted my eyebrows in surprise, and Settle smiled.

'Funny thing,' he said, 'the only drink he'll touch is milk.'

In a moment or two, without undue haste, Sir Arthur uncoiled himself, limb by limb, from his huddled position, and walked slowly over to the table. I recognized suddenly that his movements were absolutely silent, his feet made no sound as they trod. Just as he reached the table he gave a tremendous stretch, poised on one leg forward, the other stretching out behind him. He prolonged this exercise to its utmost extent, and then yawned. Never have I seen such a yawn! It seemed to swallow up his entire face.

He now turned his attention to the milk, bending down to the table until his lips touched the fluid.

Settle answered my inquiring look.

'Won't make use of his hands at all. Seems to have returned to a primitive state. Odd, isn't it?'

I felt Phyllis Patterson shrink against me a little, and I laid my hand soothingly on her arm.

The milk was finished at last, and Arthur Carmichael stretched himself once more, and then with the same quiet noiseless footsteps he regained the window seat, where he sat, huddled up as before, blinking at us.

Miss Patterson drew us out into the corridor. She was trembling all over.

'Oh! Dr Carstairs,' she cried. 'It *isn't* him—that thing in there isn't Arthur! I should feel—I should know—'

I shook my head sadly.

'The brain can play strange tricks, Miss Patterson.'

I confess that I was puzzled by the case. It presented unusual features. Though I had never seen young Carmichael before there was something about his peculiar manner of walking, and the way he blinked, that reminded me of someone or something that I could not quite place.

Our dinner that night was a quiet affair, the burden of conversation being sustained by Lady Carmichael and myself. When the ladies had withdrawn Settle asked me my impression of my hostess.

'I must confess,' I said, 'that for no cause or reason I dislike her intensely. You are quite right, she has Eastern blood, and, I should say, possesses marked occult powers. She is a woman of extraordinary magnetic force.'

Settle seemed on the point of saying something, but checked himself and merely remarked after a minute or two: 'She is absolutely devoted to her little son.'

We sat in the green drawing-room again after dinner. We had just finished coffee and were conversing rather stiffly on the topics of the day when the cat began to miaow piteously for admission outside the door. No one took any notice, and, as I am fond of animals, after a moment or two I rose.

'May I let the poor thing in?' I asked Lady Carmichael.

Her face seemed very white, I thought, but she made a faint gesture of the head which I took as assent and, going to the door, I opened it. But the corridor outside was quite empty.

'Strange,' I said, 'I could have sworn I heard a cat.'

As I came back to my chair I noticed they were all watching me intently. It somehow made me feel a little uncomfortable.

We retired to bed early. Settle accompanied me to my room.

'Got everything you want?' he asked, looking around.

'Yes, thanks.'

He still lingered rather awkwardly as though there was something he wanted to say but could not quite get out.

'By the way,' I remarked, 'you said there was something uncanny about this house? As yet it seems most normal.'

'You call it a cheerful house?'

'Hardly that, under the circumstances. It is obviously under the shadow of a great sorrow. But as regards any abnormal influence, I should give it a clean bill of health.'

'Good night,' said Settle abruptly. 'And pleasant dreams.'

Dream I certainly did. Miss Patterson's grey cat seemed to have impressed itself upon my brain. All night long, it seemed to me, I dreamt of the wretched animal.

Awaking with a start, I suddenly realized what had brought the cat so forcibly into my thoughts. The creature was miaowing persistently outside my door. Impossible to sleep with that racket going on. I lit my candle and went to the door. But the passage outside my room was empty, though the miaowing still continued. A new idea struck me. The unfortunate animal was shut up somewhere, unable to get out. To the left was the end of the passage, where Lady Carmichael's room was situated. I turned therefore to the right and had taken but a few paces when the noise broke out again from behind me. I turned sharply and the sound came again, this time distinctly on the *right* of me.

Something, probably a draught in the corridor, made me shiver, and I went sharply back to my room. Everything was silent now, and I was soon asleep once more—to wake to another glorious summer's day.

As I was dressing I saw from my window the disturber of my night's rest. The grey cat was creeping slowly and stealthily across the lawn. I judged its object of attack to be a small flock of birds who were busy chirruping and preening themselves not far away.

And then a very curious thing happened. The cat came straight on and passed through the midst of the birds, its fur almost brushing against them—and the birds did not fly away. I could not understand it—the thing seemed incomprehensible.

So vividly did it impress me that I could not refrain from mentioning it at breakfast.

'Do you know?' I said to Lady Carmichael, 'that you have a very unusual cat?'

I heard the quick rattle of a cup on a saucer, and I saw Phyllis Patterson, her lips parted and her breath coming quickly, gazing earnestly at me.

There was a moment's silence, and then Lady Carmichael said in a distinctly disagreeable manner: 'I think you must have made a mistake. There is no cat here. I have never had a cat.'

It was evident that I had managed to put my foot in it badly, so I hastily changed the subject.

But the matter puzzled me. Why had Lady Carmichael declared there was no cat in the house? Was it perhaps Miss Patterson's, and its presence concealed from the mistress of the house? Lady Carmichael might have one of those strange antipathies to cats which are so often met with nowadays. It hardly seemed a plausible explanation, but I was forced to rest content with it for the moment.

Our patient was still in the same condition. This time I made a thorough examination and was able to study him more closely than the night before. At my suggestion it was arranged that he should spend as much time with the family as possible. I hoped not only to have a better opportunity of observing him when he was off his guard, but the ordinary everyday routine might awaken some gleam of intelligence. His demeanour, however, remained unchanged. He was quiet and docile, seemed vacant, but was in point of fact, intensely and rather slyly watchful. One thing certainly came as a surprise to me, the intense affection he displayed towards his stepmother. Miss Patterson he ignored completely, but he always managed to sit as near Lady Carmichael as possible, and once I saw him rub his head against her shoulder in a dumb expression of love.

I was worried about the case. I could not but feel that there was some clue to the whole matter which had so far escaped me.

'This is a very strange case,' I said to Settle.

'Yes,' said he, 'it's very—suggestive.'

He looked at me—rather furtively, I thought.

'Tell me,' he said. 'He doesn't—remind you of anything?'

The words struck me disagreeably, reminding me of my impression of the day before.

'Remind me of what?' I asked.

He shook his head.

'Perhaps it's my fancy,' he muttered. 'Just my fancy.'

And he would say no more on the matter.

Altogether there was mystery shrouding the affair. I was still obsessed with that baffling feeling of having missed the clue that should elucidate it to me. And concerning a lesser matter there was also mystery. I mean that trifling affair of the grey cat. For some reason or other the thing was getting on my nerves. I dreamed of cats—I continually fancied I heard him. Now and then in the distance I caught a glimpse of the beautiful animal. And the fact that there was some mystery connected with it fretted me unbearably. On a sudden impulse I applied one afternoon to the footman for information.

'Can you tell me anything,' I said, 'about the cat I see?'

'The cat, sir?' He appeared politely surprised.

'Wasn't there—isn't there—a cat?'

'Her ladyship *had* a cat, sir. A great pet. Had to be put away though. A great pity, as it was a beautiful animal.'

'A grey cat?' I asked slowly.

'Yes, sir. A Persian.'

'And you say it was destroyed?'

'Yes, sir.'

'You're quite sure it was destroyed?'

'Oh! quite sure, sir. Her ladyship wouldn't have him sent to the vet—but did it herself. A little less than a week ago now. He's buried out there under the copper beech, sir.' And he went out of the room, leaving me to my meditations.

Why had Lady Carmichael affirmed so positively that she had never had a cat?

I felt an intuition that this trifling affair of the cat was in some way significant. I found Settle and took him aside.

'Settle,' I said. 'I want to ask you a question. Have you, or have you not, both seen and heard a cat in this house?'

He did not seem surprised at the question. Rather did he seem to have been expecting it.

'I've heard it,' he said. 'I've not seen it.'

'But that first day,' I cried. 'On the lawn with Miss Patterson!'

He looked at me very steadily.

'I saw Miss Patterson walking across the lawn. Nothing else.'

I began to understand. 'Then,' I said, 'the cat—?'

He nodded.

'I wanted to see if you—unprejudiced—would hear what we all hear . . .?'

'You all hear it then?'

He nodded again.

'It's strange,' I murmured thoughtfully. 'I never heard of a cat haunting a place before.'

I told him what I had learnt from the footman, and he expressed surprise.

'That's news to me. I didn't know that.'

'But what does it mean?' I asked helplessly.

He shook his head. 'Heaven only knows! But I'll tell you, Carstairs—I'm afraid. The—thing's voice sounds—menacing.'

'Menacing?' I said sharply. 'To whom?'

He spread out his hands. 'I can't say.'

It was not till that evening after dinner that I realized the meaning of his words. We were sitting in the green drawing-room, as on the night of my arrival, when it came—the loud insistent miaowing of a cat outside the door. But this time it was unmistakably angry in its tone—a fierce cat yowl, long-drawn and menacing. And then as it ceased the brass hook outside the door was rattled violently as by a cat's paw.

Settle started up.

'I swear that's real,' he cried.

He rushed to the door and flung it open.

There was nothing there.

He came back mopping his brow. Phyllis was pale and trembling, Lady Carmichael deathly white. Only Arthur, squatting contentedly like a child, his head against his stepmother's knee, was calm and undisturbed.

Miss Patterson laid her hand on my arm as we went upstairs.

'Oh! Dr Carstairs,' she cried. 'What is it? What does it all mean?'

'We don't know yet, my dear young lady,' I said. 'But I mean to find out. But you mustn't be afraid. I am convinced there is no danger to you personally.'

She looked at me doubtfully. 'You think that?'

'I am sure of it,' I answered firmly. I remembered the loving way the grey cat had twined itself round her feet, and I had no misgivings. The menace was not for her.

I was some time dropping off to sleep, but at length I fell into an uneasy slumber from which I awoke with a sense of shock. I heard a scratching sputtering noise as of something being violently ripped or torn. I sprang out of bed and rushed out into the passage. At the same moment Settle burst out of his room opposite. The sound came from our left.

'You hear it, Carstairs?' he cried. 'You hear it?'

We came swiftly up to Lady Carmichael's door. Nothing had passed us, but the noise had ceased. Our candles glittered blankly on the shiny panels of Lady Carmichael's door. We stared at one another.

'You know what it was?' he half whispered.

I nodded. 'A cat's claws ripping and tearing something.' I shivered a little. Suddenly I gave an exclamation and lowered the candle I held.

'Look here, Settle.'

'Here' was a chair that rested against the wall—and the seat of it was ripped and torn in long strips . . .

We examined it closely. He looked at me and I nodded.

'Cat's claws,' he said, drawing in his breath sharply. 'Unmistakable.' His eyes went from the chair to the closed door. 'That's the person who is menaced. Lady Carmichael!'

I slept no more that night. Things had come to a pass where something must be done. As far as I knew there was only one person who had the key to the situation. I suspected Lady Carmichael of knowing more than she chose to tell.

She was deathly pale when she came down the next morning, and only toyed with the food on her plate. I was sure that only an iron determination kept her from breaking down. After breakfast I requested a few words with her. I went straight to the point.

'Lady Carmichael,' I said. 'I have reason to believe that you are in very grave danger.'

'Indeed?' She braved it out with wonderful unconcern.

'There is in this house,' I continued, 'A Thing—a Presence—that is obviously hostile to you.'

'What nonsense,' she murmured scornfully. 'As if I believed in any rubbish of that kind.'

'The chair outside your door,' I remarked drily, 'was ripped to ribbons last night.'

'Indeed?' With raised eyebrows she pretended surprise, but I saw that I had told her nothing she did not know. 'Some stupid practical joke, I suppose.'

'It was not that,' I replied with some feeling. 'And I want you to tell me—for your own sake—' I paused.

'Tell you what?' she queried.

'Anything that can throw light on the matter,' I said gravely.

She laughed.

'I know nothing,' she said. 'Absolutely nothing.'

And no warnings of danger could induce her to relax the statement. Yet I was convinced that she *did* know a great deal more than any of us, and held some clue to the affair of which we were absolutely ignorant. But I saw that it was quite impossible to make her speak.

I determined, however, to take every precaution that I could, convinced as I was that she was menaced by a very real and immediate danger. Before she went to her room the following night Settle and I made a thorough examination of it. We had agreed that we would take it in turns to watch in the passage.

I took the first watch, which passed without incident, and at three o'clock Settle relieved me. I was tired after my sleepless night the day before, and dropped off at once. And I had a very curious dream.

I dreamed that the grey cat was sitting at the foot of my bed and that its eyes were fixed on mine with a curious pleading. Then, with the ease of dreams, I knew that the creature wanted me to follow it. I did so, and it led me down the great staircase and right to the opposite wing of the house to a room which was obviously the library. It paused there at one side of the room and raised its front paws till they rested on one of the lower shelves of books, while it gazed at me once more with that same moving look of appeal.

Then—cat and library faded, and I awoke to find that morning had come.

Settle's watch had passed without incident, but he was keenly interested to hear of my dream. At my request he took me to the library, which coincided in every particular with my vision of it. I could even point out the exact spot where the animal had given me that last sad look.

We both stood there in silent perplexity. Suddenly an idea occurred to me, and I stooped to read the title of the book in that exact place. I noticed that there was a gap in the line.

'Some book has been taken out of here,' I said to Settle.

He stooped also to the shelf.

'Hallo,' he said. 'There's a nail at the back here that has torn off a fragment of the missing volume.'

He detached the little scrap of paper with care. It was not more than an inch square—but on it were printed two significant words: 'The cat . . .'

We looked at each other.

'This thing gives me the creeps,' said Settle. 'It's simply horribly uncanny.'

'I'd give anything to know,' I said, 'what book it is that is missing from here. Do you think there is any way of finding out?'

'Maybe a catalogue somewhere. Perhaps Lady Carmichael—'

I shook my head.

'Lady Carmichael will tell you nothing.'

'You think so?'

'I am sure of it. While we are guessing and feeling about in the dark Lady Carmichael *knows*. And for reasons of her own she will say nothing. She prefers to run a most horrible risk sooner than break silence.'

The day passed with an uneventfulness that reminded me of the calm before a storm. And I had a strange feeling that the problem was near solution. I was groping about in the dark, but soon I should see. The facts were all there, ready, waiting for the little flash of illumination that should weld them together and show out their significance.

And come it did! In the strangest way!

It was when we were all sitting together in the green drawing-room as usual after dinner. We had been very silent. So noiseless indeed was the room that a little mouse ran across the floor—and in an instant the thing happened.

With one long spring Arthur Carmichael leapt from his chair. His quivering body was swift as an arrow on the mouse's track. It had disappeared behind the wainscoting, and there he crouched—watchful—his body still trembling with eagerness.

It was horrible! I have never known such a paralysing moment. I was no longer puzzled as to that something that Arthur Carmichael reminded me of with his stealthy feet and watching eyes. And in a flash an explanation, wild, incredible, unbelievable, swept into my mind. I rejected it as impossible—unthinkable! But I could not dismiss it from my thoughts.

I hardly remember what happened next. The whole thing seemed blurred and unreal. I know that somehow we got upstairs and said our goodnights briefly, almost with a dread of meeting each other's eyes, lest we should see there some confirmation of our own fears.

Settle established himself outside Lady Carmichael's door to take the first watch, arranging to call me at 3 a.m. I had no special fears for Lady Carmichael; I was too taken up with my fantastic impossible theory. I told myself it was impossible—but my mind returned to it, fascinated.

And then suddenly the stillness of the night was disturbed. Settle's voice rose in a shout, calling me. I rushed out into the corridor.

He was hammering and pounding with all his might on Lady Carmichael's door.

'Devil take the woman!' he cried. 'She's locked it!'

'But—'

'*It's* in there, man! In with her! Can't you hear it?'

From behind the locked door a long-drawn cat yowl sounded fiercely. And then following it a horrible scream—and another . . . I recognized Lady Carmichael's voice.

'The door!' I yelled. 'We must break it in. In another minute we shall be too late.'

We set our shoulders against it, and heaved with all our might. It gave with a crash—and we almost fell into the room.

Lady Carmichael lay on the bed bathed in blood. I have seldom seen a more horrible sight. Her heart was still beating, but her injuries were terrible, for the skin of the throat was all ripped and torn . . . Shuddering, I whispered: 'The Claws . . .' A thrill of superstitious horror ran over me.

I dressed and bandaged the wounds carefully and suggested to Settle that the exact nature of the injuries had better be kept secret, especially from Miss Patterson. I wrote out a telegram for a hospital nurse, to be despatched as soon as the telegraph office was open.

The dawn was now stealing in at the window. I looked out on the lawn below.

'Get dressed and come out,' I said abruptly to Settle. 'Lady Carmichael will be all right now.'

He was soon ready, and we went out into the garden together.

'What are you going to do?'

'Dig up the cat's body,' I said briefly. 'I must be sure—'

I found a spade in a toolshed and we set to work beneath the large copper beech tree. At last our digging was rewarded. It was not a pleasant job. The animal had been dead a week. But I saw what I wanted to see.

'That's the cat,' I said. 'The identical cat I saw the first day I came here.'

Settle sniffed. An odour of bitter almonds was still perceptible.

'Prussic acid,' he said.

I nodded.

'What are you thinking?' he asked curiously.

'What you think too!'

My surmise was no new one to him—it had passed through his brain also, I could see.

'It's impossible,' he murmured. 'Impossible! It's against all science—all nature . . .' His voice tailed off in a shudder. 'That mouse last night,' he said. 'But—oh! it couldn't be!'

'Lady Carmichael,' I said, 'is a very strange woman. She has occult powers—hypnotic powers. Her forebears came from the East. Can we know what use she might have made of these powers over a weak lovable nature such as Arthur Carmichael's? And remember, Settle, if Arthur Carmichael remains a hopeless imbecile, devoted to her, the whole property is practically hers and her son's—whom you have told me she adores. And Arthur was going to be married!'

'But what are we going to do, Carstairs?'

'There's nothing to be done,' I said. 'We'll do our best though to stand between Lady Carmichael and vengeance.'

Lady Carmichael improved slowly. Her injuries healed themselves as well as could be expected—the scars of that terrible assault she would probably bear to the end of her life.

I had never felt more helpless. The power that defeated us was still at large, undefeated, and though quiescent for the minute we could hardly regard it as doing otherwise than biding its time. I was determined upon one thing. As soon as Lady Carmichael was well enough to be moved she must be taken away from Wolden. There was just a chance that the terrible manifestation might be unable to follow her. So the days went on.

I had fixed September 18th as the date of Lady Carmichael's removal. It was on the morning of the 14th when the unexpected crisis arose.

I was in the library discussing details of Lady Carmichael's case with Settle when an agitated housemaid rushed into the room.

'Oh! sir,' she cried. 'Be quick! Mr Arthur—he's fallen into the pond. He stepped on the punt and it pushed off with him, and he overbalanced and fell in! I saw it from the window.'

I waited for no more, but ran straight out of the room followed by Settle. Phyllis was just outside and had heard the maid's story. She ran with us.

'But you needn't be afraid,' she cried. 'Arthur is a magnificent swimmer.'

I felt forebodings, however, and redoubled my pace. The surface of the pond was unruffled. The empty punt floated lazily about—but of Arthur there was no sign.

Settle pulled off his coat and his boots. 'I'm going in,' he said. 'You take the boat-hook and fish about from the other punt. It's not very deep.'

Very long the time seemed as we searched vainly. Minute followed minute. And then, just as we were despairing, we found him, and bore the apparently lifeless body of Arthur Carmichael to shore.

As long as I live I shall never forget the hopeless agony of Phyllis's face.

'Not—not—' her lips refused to frame the dreadful word.

'No, no, my dear,' I cried. 'We'll bring him round, never fear.'

But inwardly I had little hope. He had been under water for half an hour. I sent off Settle to the house for hot blankets and other necessaries, and began myself to apply artificial respiration.

We worked vigorously with him for over an hour but there was no sign of life. I motioned to Settle to take my place again, and I approached Phyllis.

'I'm afraid,' I said gently, 'that it is no good. Arthur is beyond our help.'

She stayed quite still for a moment and then suddenly flung herself down on the lifeless body.

'Arthur!' she cried desperately. 'Arthur! Come back to me! Arthur—come back—come back!'

Her voice echoed away into silence. Suddenly I touched Settle's arm. 'Look!' I said.

A faint tinge of colour had crept into the drowned man's face. I felt his heart.

'Go on with the respiration,' I cried. 'He's coming round!'

The moments seemed to fly now. In a marvellously short time his eyes opened.

Then suddenly I realized a difference. *These were intelligent eyes, human eyes* . . .

They rested on Phyllis.

'Hallo! Phil,' he said weakly. 'Is it you? I thought you weren't coming until tomorrow.'

She could not yet trust herself to speak but she smiled at him. He looked round with increasing bewilderment.

'But, I say, where am I? And—how rotten I feel! What's the matter with me? Hallo, Dr Settle!'

'You've been nearly drowned—that's what's the matter,' returned Settle grimly.

Sir Arthur made a grimace.

'I've always heard it was beastly coming back afterwards! But how did it happen? Was I walking in my sleep?'

Settle shook his head.

'We must get him to the house,' I said, stepping forward.

He stared at me, and Phyllis introduced me. 'Dr Carstairs, who is staying here.'

We supported him between us and started for the house. He looked up suddenly as though struck by an idea.

'I say, doctor, this won't knock me up for the 12th, will it?'

'The 12th?' I said slowly, 'you mean the 12th of August?'

'Yes—next Friday.'

'Today is the 14th of September,' said Settle abruptly.

His bewilderment was evident.

'But—but I thought it was the 8th of August? I must have been ill then?'

Phyllis interposed rather quickly in her gentle voice.

'Yes,' she said, 'you've been very ill.'

He frowned. 'I can't understand it. I was perfectly all right when I went to bed last night—at least of course it wasn't really last night. I had dreams though, I remember, dreams . . .' His brow furrowed itself still more as he strove to remember. 'Something—what was it? Something dreadful—someone had done it to me—and I was angry— desperate . . . And then I dreamed I was a cat—yes, a cat! Funny, wasn't it? But it wasn't a funny dream. It was more—horrible! But I can't remember. It all goes when I think.'

I laid my hand on his shoulder. 'Don't try to think, Sir Arthur,' I said gravely. 'Be content—to forget.'

He looked at me in a puzzled way and nodded. I heard Phyllis draw a breath of relief. We had reached the house.

'By the way,' said Sir Arthur suddenly, 'where's the mater?'

'She has been—ill,' said Phyllis after a momentary pause.

'Oh! poor old mater!' His voice rang with genuine concern. 'Where is she? In her room?'

'Yes,' I said, 'but you had better not disturb—'

The words froze on my lips. The door of the drawing-room

opened and Lady Carmichael, wrapped in a dressing-gown, came out into the hall.

Her eyes were fixed on Arthur, and if ever I have seen a look of absolute guilt-stricken terror I saw it then. Her face was hardly human in its frenzied terror. Her hand went to her throat.

Arthur advanced towards her with boyish affection.

'Hello, mater! So you've been knocked up too? I say, I'm awfully sorry.'

She shrank back before him, her eyes dilating. Then suddenly, with a shriek of a doomed soul, she fell backwards through the open door.

I rushed and bent over her, then beckoned to Settle.

'Hush,' I said. 'Take him upstairs quietly and then come down again. Lady Carmichael is dead.'

He returned in a few minutes.

'What was it?' he asked. 'What caused it?'

'Shock,' I said grimly. 'The shock of seeing Arthur Carmichael, the *real* Arthur Carmichael, restored to life! Or you may call it, as I prefer to, the judgement of God!'

'You mean—' he hesitated.

I looked at him in the eyes so that he understood.

'A life for a life,' I said significantly.

'But—'

'Oh! I know that a strange and unforeseen accident permitted the spirit of Arthur Carmichael to return to his body. But, nevertheless, Arthur Carmichael was murdered.'

He looked at me half fearfully. 'With prussic acid?' he asked in a low tone.

'Yes,' I answered. 'With prussic acid.'

Settle and I have never spoken of our belief. It is not one likely to be credited. According to the orthodox point of view Arthur Carmichael merely suffered from loss of memory, Lady Carmichael lacerated her own throat in a temporary fit of mania, and the apparition of the Grey Cat was mere imagination.

But there are two facts that to my mind are unmistakable.

One is the ripped chair in the corridor. The other is even more significant. A catalogue of the library was found, and after exhaustive search it was proved that the missing volume was an ancient and curious work on the possibilities of the metamorphosis of human beings into animals!

One thing more. I am thankful to say that Arthur knows nothing. Phyllis has locked the secret of those weeks in her own heart, and she will never, I am sure, reveal them to the husband she loves so dearly, and who came back across the barrier of the grave at the call of her voice.

# THE BLUE GERANIUM

'When I was down here last year—' said Sir Henry Clithering, and stopped.

His hostess, Mrs Bantry, looked at him curiously.

The Ex-Commissioner of Scotland Yard was staying with old friends of his, Colonel and Mrs Bantry, who lived near St Mary Mead.

Mrs Bantry, pen in hand, had just asked his advice as to who should be invited to make a sixth guest at dinner that evening.

'Yes?' said Mrs Bantry encouragingly. 'When you were here last year?'

'Tell me,' said Sir Henry, 'do you know a Miss Marple?'

Mrs Bantry was surprised. It was the last thing she had expected.

'Know Miss Marple? Who doesn't! The typical old maid of fiction. Quite a dear, but hopelessly behind the times. Do you mean you would like me to ask *her* to dinner?'

'You are surprised?'

'A little, I must confess. I should hardly have thought you—but perhaps there's an explanation?'

'The explanation is simple enough. When I was down here last year we got into the habit of discussing unsolved mysteries—there were five or six of us—Raymond West, the novelist, started it. We each supplied a story to which we knew the answer, but nobody else did. It was supposed to be an exercise in the deductive faculties—to see who could get nearest the truth.'

'Well?'

'Like in the old story—we hardly realized that Miss Marple was playing; but we were very polite about it—didn't want to hurt the old dear's feelings. And now comes the cream of the jest. The old lady outdid us every time!'

'What?'

'I assure you—straight to the truth like a homing pigeon.'

'But how extraordinary! Why, dear old Miss Marple has hardly ever been out of St Mary Mead.'

'Ah! But according to her, that has given her unlimited opportunities of observing human nature—under the micro-scope as it were.'

'I suppose there's something in that,' conceded Mrs Bantry. 'One would at least know the petty side of people. But I don't think we have any really exciting criminals in our midst. I think we must try her with Arthur's ghost story after dinner. I'd be thankful if she'd find a solution to that.'

'I didn't know that Arthur believed in ghosts?'

'Oh! he doesn't. That's what worries him so. And it happened to a friend of his, George Pritchard—a most prosaic person. It's really rather tragic for poor George. Either this extraordinary story is true—or else—'

'Or else what?'

Mrs Bantry did not answer. After a minute or two she said irrelevantly:

'You know, I like George—everyone does. One can't believe that he—but people do do such extraordinary things.'

Sir Henry nodded. He knew, better than Mrs Bantry, the extraordinary things that people did.

So it came about that that evening Mrs Bantry looked round her dinner table (shivering a little as she did so, because the dining-room, like most English dining-rooms, was extremely cold) and fixed her gaze on the very upright old lady sitting on her husband's right. Miss Marple wore black lace mittens; an old lace fichu was draped round her shoulders and another piece of lace surmounted her white hair. She was talking animatedly to the elderly doctor, Dr Lloyd, about the Workhouse and the suspected shortcomings of the District Nurse.

Mrs Bantry marvelled anew. She even wondered whether Sir Henry had been making an elaborate joke—but there seemed no point in that. Incredible that what he had said could be really true.

Her glance went on and rested affectionately on her red-faced broad-shouldered husband as he sat talking horses to Jane Helier, the beautiful and popular actress. Jane, more beautiful (if that were possible) off the stage than on, opened enormous blue eyes and murmured at discreet intervals: 'Really?' 'Oh fancy!' 'How extraordinary!' She knew nothing whatever about horses and cared less.

'Arthur,' said Mrs Bantry, 'you're boring poor Jane to distraction. Leave horses alone and tell her your ghost story instead. You know . . . George Pritchard.'

'Eh, Dolly? Oh! but I don't know—'

'Sir Henry wants to hear it too. I was telling him something about it this morning. It would be interesting to hear what everyone has to say about it.'

'Oh do!' said Jane. 'I love ghost stories.'

'Well—' Colonel Bantry hesitated. 'I've never believed much in the supernatural. But this—

'I don't think any of you know George Pritchard. He's one of the best. His wife—well, she's dead now, poor woman. I'll just say this much: she didn't give George any too easy a time when she was alive. She was one of those semi-invalids—I believe she had really something wrong with her, but whatever it was she played it for all it was worth. She was capricious, exacting, unreasonable. She complained from morning to night. George was expected to wait on her hand and foot, and every thing he did was always wrong and he got cursed for it. Most men, I'm fully convinced, would have hit her over the head with a hatchet long ago. Eh, Dolly, isn't that so?'

'She was a dreadful woman,' said Mrs Bantry with conviction. 'If George Pritchard had brained her with a hatchet, and there had been any woman on the jury, he would have been triumphantly acquitted.'

'I don't quite know how this business started. George was rather vague about it. I gather Mrs Pritchard had always had a weakness for fortune tellers, palmists, clairvoyantes—anything of that sort. George didn't mind. If she found amusement in it well and good. But he refused to go into rhapsodies himself, and that was another grievance.

'A succession of hospital nurses was always passing through the house, Mrs Pritchard usually becoming dissatisfied with them after a few weeks. One young nurse had been very keen on this fortune telling stunt, and for a time Mrs Pritchard had been very fond of her. Then she suddenly fell out with her and insisted on her going. She had back another nurse who had been with her previously—an older woman, experienced and tactful in dealing with a neurotic patient. Nurse Copling, according to George, was a very good sort—a sensible woman to talk to. She put up with Mrs Pritchard's tantrums and nervestorms with complete indifference.

'Mrs Pritchard always lunched upstairs, and it was usual at lunch time for George and the nurse to come to some arrangement for the afternoon. Strictly speaking, the nurse went off from two to four, but "to oblige" as the phrase goes, she would sometimes take her time off after tea if George wanted to be free for the afternoon. On this occasion, she mentioned that she was going to see a sister at Golders Green and might be a little late returning. George's face fell, for he had arranged to play a round of golf. Nurse Copling, however, reassured him.

'"We'll neither of us be missed, Mr Pritchard." A twinkle came into her eye. "Mrs Pritchard's going to have more exciting company than ours."

'"Who's that?"

'"Wait a minute," Nurse Copling's eyes twinkled more than ever. "Let me get it right. *Zarida, Psychic Reader of the Future*."

'"Oh Lord!" groaned George. "That's a new one, isn't it?"

'"Quite new. I believe my predecessor, Nurse Carstairs, sent her along. Mrs Pritchard hasn't seen her yet. She made me write, fixing an appointment for this afternoon."

'"Well, at any rate, I shall get my golf," said George, and he went off with the kindliest feelings towards Zarida, the Reader of the Future.

'On his return to the house, he found Mrs Pritchard in a state of great agitation. She was, as usual, lying on her invalid couch, and she had a bottle of smelling salts in her hand which she sniffed at frequent intervals.

'"George," she exclaimed. "What did I tell you about this house? The moment I came into it, I *felt* there was something wrong! Didn't I tell you so at the time?"

'Repressing his desire to reply, "You always do," George said, "No, I can't say I remember it."

'"You never do remember anything that has to do with me. Men are all extraordinarily callous—but I really believe that you are even more insensitive than most."

'"Oh, come now, Mary dear, that's not fair."

'"Well, as I was telling you, this woman *knew* at once! She—she actually blenched—if you know what I mean—as she came in at the door, and she said: "There is evil here—evil and danger. I feel it."'

'Very unwisely George laughed.

'"Well, you have had your money's worth this afternoon."

'His wife closed her eyes and took a long sniff from her smelling bottle.

'"How you hate me! You would jeer and laugh if I were dying."

'George protested and after a minute or two she went on.

'"You may laugh, but I shall tell you the whole thing.

This house is definitely dangerous to me—the woman said so."

'George's formerly kind feeling towards Zarida underwent a change. He knew his wife was perfectly capable of insisting on moving to a new house if the caprice got hold of her.

'"What else did she say?" he asked.

'"She couldn't tell me very much. She was so upset. One thing she did say. I had some violets in a glass. She pointed at them and cried out:

'"Take those away. No blue flowers—never have blue flowers. *Blue flowers are fatal to you—remember that.*"'

'"And you know," added Mrs Pritchard, "I always have told you that blue as a colour is repellent to me. I feel a natural instinctive sort of warning against."

'George was much too wise to remark that he had never heard her say so before. Instead he asked what the mysterious Zarida was like. Mrs Pritchard entered with gusto upon a description.

'"Black hair in coiled knobs over her ears—her eyes were half closed—great black rims round them—she had a black veil over her mouth and chin—and she spoke in a kind of singing voice with a marked foreign accent—Spanish, I think—"

'"In fact all the usual stock-in-trade," said George cheerfully.

'His wife immediately closed her eyes.

'"I feel extremely ill," she said. "Ring for nurse. Unkindness upsets me, as you know only too well."

'It was two days later that Nurse Copling came to George with a grave face.

'"Will you come to Mrs Pritchard, please. She has had a letter which upsets her greatly."

'He found his wife with the letter in her hand. She held it out to him.

'"Read it," she said.

'George read it. It was on heavily scented paper, and the writing was big and black.

'*I have seen the future. Be warned before it is too late. Beware of the Full Moon. The Blue Primrose means Warning; the Blue Hollyhock means Danger; the Blue Geranium means Death . . .*

'Just about to burst out laughing, George caught Nurse Copling's eye. She made a quick warning gesture. He said rather awkwardly, "The woman's probably trying to frighten you, Mary. Anyway there aren't such things as blue primroses and blue geraniums."

'But Mrs Pritchard began to cry and say her days were numbered. Nurse Copling came out with George upon the landing.

'"Of all the silly tomfoolery," he burst out.

'"I suppose it is."

'Something in the nurse's tone struck him, and he stared at her in amazement.

'"Surely, nurse, you don't believe—"

'"No, no, Mr Pritchard. I don't believe in reading the future—that's nonsense. What puzzles me is the *meaning* of this. Fortune-tellers are usually out for what they can get. But this woman seems to be frightening Mrs Pritchard with no advantage to herself. I can't see the point. There's another thing—"

'"Yes?"

'"Mrs Pritchard says that something about Zarida was faintly familiar to her."

'"Well?"

'"Well, I don't like it, Mr Pritchard, that's all."

'"I didn't know you were so superstitious, nurse."

'"I'm not superstitious; but I know when a thing is fishy."

'It was about four days after this that the first incident happened. To explain it to you, I shall have to describe Mrs Pritchard's room—'

'You'd better let me do that,' interrupted Mrs Bantry. 'It was papered with one of those new wallpapers where you apply clumps of flowers to make a kind of herbaceous border. The effect is almost like being in a garden—though, of course, the flowers are all wrong. I mean they simply couldn't be in bloom all at the same time—'

'Don't let a passion for horticultural accuracy run away with you, Dolly,' said her husband. 'We all know you're an enthusiastic gardener.'

'Well, it *is* absurd,' protested Mrs Bantry. 'To have bluebells and daffodils and lupins and hollyhocks and Michaelmas daisies all grouped together.'

'Most unscientific,' said Sir Henry. 'But to proceed with the story.'

'Well, among these massed flowers were primroses, clumps of yellow and pink primroses and—oh go on, Arthur, this is your story—'

Colonel Bantry took up the tale.

'Mrs Pritchard rang her bell violently one morning. The household came running—thought she was in extremis; not at all. She was violently excited and pointing at the wallpaper; and there sure enough was *one blue primrose* in the midst of the others . . .'

'Oh!' said Miss Helier, 'how creepy!'

'The question was: Hadn't the blue primrose always been there? That was George's suggestion and the nurse's. But Mrs Pritchard wouldn't have it at any price. She had never noticed it till that very morning and the night before had been full moon. She was very upset about it.'

'I met George Pritchard that same day and he told me about it,' said Mrs Bantry. 'I went to see Mrs Pritchard and did my best to ridicule the whole thing; but without success. I came away really concerned, and I remember I met Jean Instow and told her about it. Jean is a queer girl. She said, "So she's really upset about it?" I told her that I thought the woman was perfectly capable of dying of fright—she was really abnormally superstitious.

'I remember Jean rather startled me with what she said next. She said, "Well, that might be all for the best, mightn't it?" And she said it so coolly, in so matter-of-fact a tone that I was really—well, shocked. Of course I know it's done nowadays—to be brutal and outspoken; but I never get used to it. Jean smiled at me rather oddly and said, "You don't like my saying that—but it's true. What use is Mrs Pritchard's life to her? None at all; and it's hell for George Pritchard. To have his wife frightened out of existence would be the best thing that could happen to him." I said, "George is most awfully good to her always." And she said, "Yes, he deserves a reward, poor dear. He's a very attractive person, George Pritchard. The last nurse thought so—the pretty one—what was her name? Carstairs. That was the cause of the row between her and Mrs P."

'Now I didn't like hearing Jean say that. Of course one had *wondered*—'

Mrs Bantry paused significantly.

'Yes, dear,' said Miss Marple placidly. 'One always does. Is Miss Instow a pretty girl? I suppose she plays golf?'

'Yes. She's good at all games. And she's nice-looking, attractive-looking, very fair with a healthy skin, and nice steady blue eyes. Of course we always have felt that she and George Pritchard—I mean if things had been different—they are so well suited to one another.'

'And they were friends?' asked Miss Marple.

'Oh yes. Great friends.'

'Do you think, Dolly,' said Colonel Bantry plaintively, 'that I might be allowed to go on with my story?'

'Arthur,' said Mrs Bantry resignedly, 'wants to get back to his ghosts.'

'I had the rest of the story from George himself,' went on the Colonel. 'There's no doubt that Mrs Pritchard got the wind up badly towards the end of the next month. She marked off on a calendar the day when the moon would be full, and on that night she had both the nurse and then George into her room and made them study the wallpaper carefully. There were pink hollyhocks and red ones, but there were no blue amongst them. Then when George left the room she locked the door—'

'And in the morning there was a large blue hollyhock,' said Miss Helier joyfully.

'Quite right,' said Colonel Bantry. 'Or at any rate, nearly

right. One flower of a hollyhock just above her head had turned blue. It staggered George; and of course the more it staggered him the more he refused to take the thing seriously. He insisted that the whole thing was some kind of practical joke. He ignored the evidence of the locked door and the fact that Mrs Pritchard discovered the change before anyone—even Nurse Copling—was admitted.

'It staggered George; and it made him unreasonable. His wife wanted to leave the house, and he wouldn't let her. He was inclined to believe in the supernatural for the first time, but he wasn't going to admit it. He usually gave in to his wife, but this time he wouldn't. Mary was not to make a fool of herself, he said. The whole thing was the most infernal nonsense.

'And so the next month sped away. Mrs Pritchard made less protest than one would have imagined. I think she was superstitious enough to believe that she couldn't escape her fate. She repeated again and again: "The blue primrose—warning. The blue hollyhock—danger. The blue geranium—*death*." And she would lie looking at the clump of pinky-red geraniums nearest her bed.

'The whole business was pretty nervy. Even the nurse caught the infection. She came to George two days before full moon and begged him to take Mrs Pritchard away. George was angry.

'"If all the flowers on that damned wall turned into blue devils it couldn't kill anyone!" he shouted.

'"It might. Shock has killed people before now."

'"Nonsense," said George.

'George has always been a shade pig-headed. You can't drive him. I believe he had a secret idea that his wife worked the change herself and that it was all some morbid hysterical plan of hers.

'Well, the fatal night came. Mrs Pritchard locked the door as usual. She was very calm—in almost an exalted state of mind. The nurse was worried by her state—wanted to give her a stimulant, an injection of strychnine, but Mrs Pritchard refused. In a way, I believe, she was enjoying herself. George said she was.'

'I think that's quite possible,' said Mrs Bantry. 'There must have been a strange sort of glamour about the whole thing.'

'There was no violent ringing of a bell the next morning. Mrs Pritchard usually woke about eight. When, at eight-thirty, there was no sign from her, nurse rapped loudly on the door. Getting no reply, she fetched George, and insisted on the door being broken open. They did so with the help of a chisel.

'One look at the still figure on the bed was enough for Nurse Copling. She sent George to telephone for the doctor, but it was too late. Mrs Pritchard, he said, must have been dead at least eight hours. Her smelling salts lay by her hand on the bed, *and on the wall beside her one of the pinky-red geraniums was a bright deep blue*.'

'Horrible,' said Miss Helier with a shiver.

Sir Henry was frowning.

'No additional details?'

Colonel Bantry shook his head, but Mrs Bantry spoke quickly.

'The gas.'

'What about the gas?' asked Sir Henry.

'When the doctor arrived there was a slight smell of gas, and sure enough he found the gas ring in the fireplace very slightly turned on; but so little it couldn't have mattered.'

'Did Mr Pritchard and the nurse not notice it when they first went in?'

'The nurse said she did notice a slight smell. George said he didn't notice gas, but something made him feel very queer and overcome; but he put that down to shock—and probably it was. At any rate there was no question of gas poisoning. The smell was scarcely noticeable.'

'And that's the end of the story?'

'No, it isn't. One way and another, there was a lot of talk. The servants, you see, had overheard things—had heard, for instance, Mrs Pritchard telling her husband that he hated her and would jeer if she were dying. And also more recent remarks. She had said one day, apropos of his refusing to leave the house: "Very well, when I am dead, I hope everyone will realize that you have killed me." And as ill luck would have it, he had been mixing some weed killer for the garden paths the day before. One of the younger servants had seen him and had afterwards seen him taking up a glass of hot milk for his wife.

'The talk spread and grew. The doctor had given a certificate—I don't know exactly in what terms—shock, syncope, heart failure, probably some medical terms meaning nothing much. However the poor lady had not been a month in her grave before an exhumation order was applied for and granted.'

'And the result of the autopsy was nil, I remember,' said Sir Henry gravely. 'A case, for once, of smoke without fire.'

'The whole thing is really very curious,' said Mrs Bantry. 'That fortune-teller, for instance—Zarida. At the address where she was supposed to be, no one had ever heard of any such person!'

'She appeared once—out of the blue,' said her husband, 'and then utterly vanished. Out of the *blue*—that's rather good!'

'And what is more,' continued Mrs Bantry, 'little Nurse Carstairs, who was supposed to have recommended her, had never even heard of her.'

They looked at each other.

'It's a mysterious story,' said Dr Lloyd. 'One can make guesses; but to guess—'

He shook his head.

'Has Mr Pritchard married Miss Instow?' asked Miss Marple in her gentle voice.

'Now why do you ask that?' inquired Sir Henry.

Miss Marple opened gentle blue eyes.

'It seems to me so important,' she said. 'Have they married?'

Colonel Bantry shook his head.

'We—well, we expected something of the kind—but it's eighteen months now. I don't believe they even see much of each other.'

'That is important,' said Miss Marple. 'Very important.'

'Then you think the same as I do,' said Mrs Bantry. 'You think—'

'Now, Dolly,' said her husband. 'It's unjustifiable—what you're going to say. You can't go about accusing people without a shadow of proof.'

'Don't be so—so manly, Arthur. Men are always afraid to say *anything*. Anyway, this is all between ourselves. It's just a wild fantastic idea of mine that possibly—only *possibly*— Jean Instow disguised herself as a fortune-teller. Mind you, she may have done it for a joke. I don't for a minute think that she meant any harm; but if she did do it, and if Mrs Pritchard was foolish enough to die of fright—well, that's what Miss Marple meant, wasn't it?'

'No, dear, not quite,' said Miss Marple. 'You see, if I were going to kill anyone—which, of course, I wouldn't dream of doing for a minute, because it would be very wicked, and besides I don't like killing—not even wasps, though I know it has to be, and I'm sure the gardener does it as humanely as possible. Let me see, what was I saying?'

'If you wished to kill anyone,' prompted Sir Henry.

'Oh yes. Well, if I did, I shouldn't be at all satisfied to trust to *fright*. I know one reads of people dying of it, but it seems a very uncertain sort of thing, and the most nervous people are far more brave than one really thinks they are. I should like something definite and certain, and make a thoroughly good plan about it.'

'Miss Marple,' said Sir Henry, 'you frighten me. I hope you will never wish to remove me. Your plans would be too good.'

Miss Marple looked at him reproachfully.

'I thought I had made it clear that I would never contemplate such wickedness,' she said. 'No, I was trying to put myself in the place of—er—a certain person.'

'Do you mean George Pritchard?' asked Colonel Bantry. 'I'll never believe it of George—though—mind you, even the nurse believes it. I went and saw her about a month afterwards, at the time of the exhumation. She didn't know how it was done—in fact, she wouldn't say anything at all—but it was clear enough that she believed George to be in some way responsible for his wife's death. She was convinced of it.'

'Well,' said Dr Lloyd, 'perhaps she wasn't so far wrong. And mind you, a nurse often *knows*. She can't say—she's got no proof—but she *knows*.'

Sir Henry leant forward.

'Come now, Miss Marple,' he said persuasively. 'You're lost in a daydream. Won't you tell us all about it?'

Miss Marple started and turned pink.

'I beg your pardon,' she said. 'I was just thinking about our District Nurse. A most difficult problem.'

'More difficult than the problem of the blue geranium?'

'It really depends on the primroses,' said Miss Marple. 'I mean, Mrs Bantry said they were yellow and pink. If it was a pink primrose that turned blue, of course, that fits in perfectly. But if it happened to be a yellow one—'

'It was a pink one,' said Mrs Bantry.

She stared. They all stared at Miss Marple.

'Then that seems to settle it,' said Miss Marple. She shook her head regretfully. 'And the wasp season and everything. And of course the gas.'

'It reminds you, I suppose, of countless village tragedies?' said Sir Henry.

'Not tragedies,' said Miss Marple. 'And certainly nothing criminal. But it does remind me a little of the trouble we are having with the District Nurse. After all, nurses are human beings, and what with having to be so correct in their behaviour and wearing those uncomfortable collars and being so thrown with the family—well, can you wonder that things sometimes happen?'

A glimmer of light broke upon Sir Henry.

'You mean Nurse Carstairs?'

'Oh no. Not Nurse Carstairs. Nurse *Copling*. You see, she had been there before, and very much thrown with Mr Pritchard, who you say is an attractive man. I dare say she thought, poor thing—well, we needn't go into that. I don't suppose she knew about Miss Instow, and of course afterwards, when she found out, it turned her against him and she tried to do all the harm she could. Of course the letter really gave her away, didn't it?'

'What letter?'

'Well, she wrote to the fortune-teller at Mrs Pritchard's request, and the fortune-teller came, apparently in answer to the letter. But later it was discovered that there never had been such a person at that address. So that shows that Nurse Copling was in it. She only pretended to write—so what could be more likely than that *she* was the fortune-teller herself?'

'I never saw the point about the letter,' said Sir Henry. 'That's a most important point, of course.'

'Rather a bold step to take,' said Miss Marple, 'because Mrs Pritchard might have recognized her in spite of the disguise—though of course if she had, the nurse could have pretended it was a joke.'

'What did you mean,' said Sir Henry, 'when you said that if you were a certain person you would not have trusted to fright?'

'One couldn't be *sure* that way,' said Miss Marple. 'No, I think that the warnings and the blue flowers were, if I may use a military term,' she laughed self-consciously—'*just camouflage.*'

'And the real thing?'

'I know,' said Miss Marple apologetically, 'that I've got wasps on the brain. Poor things, destroyed in their thousands—and usually on such a beautiful summer's day. But I remember thinking, when I saw the gardener shaking up the cyanide of potassium in a bottle with water, how like smelling-salts it looked. And if it were put in a smelling-salt bottle and substituted for the real one—well, the poor lady was in the habit of using her smelling-salts. Indeed you said they were found by her hand. Then, of course, while Mr Pritchard went to telephone to the doctor, the nurse would change it for the real bottle, and she'd just turn on the gas a little bit to mask any smell of almonds and in case anyone felt queer, and I always have heard that cyanide leaves no trace if you wait long enough. But, of course I may be wrong, and it may have been something entirely different in the bottle; but that doesn't really matter, does it?'

Miss Marple paused, a little out of breath.

Jane Helier leant forward and said, 'But the blue geranium, and the other flowers?'

'Nurses always have litmus paper, don't they?' said Miss Marple, 'for—well, for testing. Not a very pleasant subject. We won't dwell on it. I have done a little nursing myself.' She grew delicately pink. 'Blue turns red with acids, and red turns blue with alkalis. So easy to paste some red litmus over a red flower—near the bed, of course. And then, when the poor lady used her smelling-salts, the strong ammonia fumes would turn it blue. Really most ingenious. Of course, the geranium wasn't blue when they first broke into the room—nobody noticed it till afterwards. When nurse changed the bottles, she held the Sal Ammoniac against the wallpaper for a minute, I expect.'

'You might have been there, Miss Marple,' said Sir Henry.

'What worries me,' said Miss Marple, 'is poor Mr Pritchard and that nice girl, Miss Instow. Probably both suspecting each other and keeping apart—and life so very short.'

She shook her head.

'You needn't worry,' said Sir Henry. 'As a matter of fact I have something up my sleeve. A nurse has been arrested on a charge of murdering an elderly patient who had left her a legacy. It was done with cyanide of potassium substituted for smelling-salts. Nurse Copling trying the same trick again. Miss Instow and Mr Pritchard need have no doubts as to the truth.'

'Now isn't that nice?' cried Miss Marple. 'I don't mean about the new murder, of course. That's very sad, and shows how much wickedness there is in the world, and that if once you give way—which reminds me I *must* finish my little conversation with Dr Lloyd about the village nurse.'

# THE CALL OF WINGS

Silas Hamer heard it first on a wintry night in February. He and Dick Borrow had walked from a dinner given by Bernard Seldon, the nerve specialist. Borrow had been unusually silent, and Silas Hamer asked him with some curiosity what he was thinking about. Borrow's answer was unexpected.

'I was thinking, that of all these men tonight, only two amongst them could lay claim to happiness. And that these two, strangely enough, were you and I!'

The word 'strangely' was apposite, for no two men could be more dissimilar than Richard Borrow, the hard working East-end parson, and Silas Hamer, the sleek complacent man whose millions were a matter of household knowledge.

'It's odd, you know,' mused Borrow, 'I believe you're the only contented millionaire I've ever met.'

Hamer was silent a moment. When he spoke his tone had altered.

'I used to be a wretched shivering little newspaper boy. I wanted then—what I've got now!—the comfort and the luxury of money, not its power. I wanted money, not to wield as a force, but to spend lavishly—on myself! I'm frank about it, you see. Money can't buy everything, they say. Very true. But it can buy everything I want—therefore I'm satisfied. I'm a materialist, Borrow, out and out a materialist!'

The broad glare of the lighted thoroughfare confirmed this confession of faith. The sleek lines of Silas Hamer's body were amplified by the heavy fur-lined coat, and the white light emphasized the thick rolls of flesh beneath his chin. In contrast to him walked Dick Borrow, with the thin ascetic face and the star-gazing fanatical eyes.

'It's *you*,' said Hamer with emphasis, 'that I can't understand.'

Borrow smiled.

'I live in the midst of misery, want, starvation—all the ills of the flesh! And a predominant Vision upholds me. It's not easy to understand unless you believe in Visions, which I gather you don't.'

'I don't believe,' said Silas Hamer stolidly, 'in anything I can't see and hear and touch.'

'Quite so. That's the difference between us. Well, goodbye, the earth now swallows me up!'

They had reached the doorway of a lighted tube station, which was Borrow's route home.

Hamer proceeded alone. He was glad he had sent away the car tonight and elected to walk home. The air was keen and frosty, his senses were delightfully conscious of the enveloping warmth of the fur-lined coat.

He paused for an instant on the kerbstone before crossing the road. A great motor bus was heavily ploughing its way towards him. Hamer, with the feeling of infinite leisure, waited for it to pass. If he were to cross in front of it he would have to hurry—and hurry was distasteful to him.

By his side a battered derelict of the human race rolled drunkenly off the pavement. Hamer was aware of a shout, an ineffectual swerve of the motor bus, and then—he was looking stupidly, with a gradually awakening horror, at a limp inert heap of rags in the middle of the road.

A crowd gathered magically, with a couple of policemen and the bus driver as its nucleus. But Hamer's eyes were riveted in horrified fascination on that lifeless bundle that had once been a man—a man like himself! He shuddered as at some menace.

'Dahn't yer blime yerself, guv'nor,' remarked a rough-looking man at his side. 'Yer couldn't 'a done nothin'. 'E was done for anyways.'

Hamer stared at him. The idea that it was possible in any way to save the man had quite honestly never occurred to him. He scouted the notion now as an absurdity. Why if he had been so foolish, he might at this moment . . . His thoughts broke off abruptly, and he walked away from the crowd. He felt himself shaking with a nameless unquenchable dread. He was forced to admit to himself that he was *afraid*—horribly afraid—of Death . . . Death that came with dreadful swiftness and remorseless certainty to rich and poor alike . . .

He walked faster, but the new fear was still with him, enveloping him in its cold and chilling grasp.

He wondered at himself, for he knew that by nature he was no coward. Five years ago, he reflected, this fear would not have attacked him. For then Life had not been so sweet . . . Yes, that was it; love of Life was the key to the mystery. The zest of living was at its height for him; it knew but one menace, Death, the destroyer!

He turned out of the lighted thoroughfare. A narrow passageway, between high walls, offered a short-cut to the Square where his house, famous for its art treasures, was situated.

The noise of the street behind him lessened and faded, the soft thud of his own footsteps was the only sound to be heard.

And then out of the gloom in front of him came another sound. Sitting against the wall was a man playing the flute. One of the enormous tribe of street musicians, of course, but why had he chosen such a peculiar spot? Surely at this time of night the police—Hamer's reflections were interrupted suddenly as he realized with a shock that the man had no legs. A pair of crutches rested against the wall beside him. Hamer saw now that it was not a flute he was playing but a strange instrument whose notes were much higher and clearer than those of a flute.

The man played on. He took no notice of Hamer's approach. His head was flung far back on his shoulders, as though uplifted in the joy of his own music, and the notes poured out clearly and joyously, rising higher and higher . . .

It was a strange tune—strictly speaking, it was not a tune at all, but a single phrase, not unlike the slow turn given out by the violins of *Rienzi*, repeated again and again, passing from key to key, from harmony to harmony, but always rising and attaining each time to a greater and more boundless freedom.

It was unlike anything Hamer had ever heard. There was something strange about it, something inspiring—and uplifting . . . it . . . He caught frantically with both hands to a projection in the wall beside him. He was conscious of one thing only—*that he must keep down*—at all costs he must *keep down* . . .

He suddenly realized that the music had stopped. The legless man was reaching out for his crutches. And here was he, Silas Hamer, clutching like a lunatic at a stone buttress, for the simple reason that he had had the utterly preposterous notion—absurd on the face of it!—that he was rising from the ground—that the music was carrying him upwards . . .

He laughed. What a wholly mad idea! Of course his feet had never left the earth for a moment, but what a strange hallucination! The quick tap-tapping of wood on the pavement told him that the cripple was moving away. He looked after him until the man's figure was swallowed up in the gloom. An odd fellow!

He proceeded on his way more slowly; he could not efface from his mind the memory of that strange impossible sensation when the ground had failed beneath his feet . . .

And then on an impulse he turned and followed hurriedly in the direction the other had taken. The man could not have gone far—he would soon overtake him.

He shouted as soon as he caught sight of the maimed figure swinging itself slowly along.

'Hi! One minute.'

The man stopped and stood motionless until Hamer came abreast of him. A lamp burned just over his head and revealed every feature. Silas Hamer caught his breath in involuntary surprise. The man possessed the most singularly beautiful head he had ever seen. He might have been any age; assuredly he was not a boy, yet youth was the most predominant characteristic—youth and vigour in passionate intensity!

Hamer found an odd difficulty in beginning his conversation.

'Look here,' he said awkwardly, 'I want to know—what was that thing you were playing just now?'

The man smiled . . . With his smile the world seemed suddenly to leap into joyousness . . .

'It was an old tune—a very old tune . . . Years old—centuries old.'

He spoke with an odd purity and distinctness of enunciation, giving equal value to each syllable. He was clearly not an Englishman, yet Hamer was puzzled as to his nationality.

'You're not English? Where do you come from?'

Again the broad joyful smile.

'From over the sea, sir. I came—a long time ago—a very long time ago.'

'You must have had a bad accident. Was it lately?'

'Some time now, sir.'

'Rough luck to lose both legs.'

'It was well,' said the man very calmly. He turned his eyes with a strange solemnity on his interlocutor. 'They were evil.'

Hamer dropped a shilling in his hand and turned away. He was puzzled and vaguely disquieted. 'They were evil!' What a strange thing to say! Evidently an operation for some form of disease, but—how odd it had sounded.

Hamer went home thoughtful. He tried in vain to dismiss the incident from his mind. Lying in bed, with the first incipient sensation of drowsiness stealing over him, he heard a neighbouring clock strike one. One clear stroke and then silence—silence that was broken by a faint familiar sound

. . . Recognition came leaping. Hamer felt his heart beating quickly. It was the man in the passageway playing, somewhere not far distant . . .

The notes came gladly, the slow turn with its joyful call, the same haunting little phrase . . . 'It's uncanny,' murmured Hamer, 'it's uncanny. It's got wings to it . . .'

Clearer and clearer, higher and higher—each wave rising above the last, and catching *him* up with it. This time he did not struggle, he let himself go . . . Up—up . . . The waves of sound were carrying him higher and higher . . . Triumphant and free, they swept on.

Higher and higher . . . They had passed the limits of human sound now, but they still continued—rising, ever rising . . . Would they reach the final goal, the full perfection of height?

Rising . . .

*Something* was pulling—pulling him downwards. Something big and heavy and insistent. It pulled remorselessly—pulled him back, and down . . . down . . .

He lay in bed gazing at the window opposite. Then, breathing heavily and painfully, he stretched an arm out of bed. The movement seemed curiously cumbrous to him. The softness of the bed was oppressive, oppressive too were the heavy curtains over the window that blocked out the light and air. The ceiling seemed to press down upon him. He felt stifled and choked. He moved slightly under the bed clothes, and the weight of his body seemed to him the most oppressive of all . . .

'I want your advice, Seldon.'

Seldon pushed back his chair an inch or so from the table. He had been wondering what was the object of this tête-à-tête dinner. He had seen little of Hamer since the winter, and he was aware tonight of some indefinable change in his friend.

'It's just this,' said the millionaire. 'I'm worried about myself.'

Seldon smiled as he looked across the table.

'You're looking in the pink of condition.'

'It's not that.' Hamer paused a minute, then added quietly. 'I'm afraid I'm going mad.'

The nerve specialist glanced up with a sudden keen interest. He poured himself out a glass of port with a rather slow movement, and then said quietly, but with a sharp glance at the other man: 'What makes you think that?'

'Something that's happened to me. Something inexplicable, unbelievable. It can't be true, so I must be going mad.'

'Take your time,' said Seldon, 'and tell me about it.'

'I don't believe in the supernatural,' began Hamer. 'I never have. But this thing . . . Well, I'd better tell you the whole story from the beginning. It began last winter one evening after I had dined with you.'

Then briefly and concisely he narrated the events of his walk home and the strange sequel.

'That was the beginning of it all. I can't explain it to you properly—the feeling, I mean—but it was wonderful! Unlike anything I've ever felt or dreamed. Well, it's gone on ever since. Not every night, just now and then. The music, the feeling of being uplifted, the soaring flight . . . and then the terrible drag, the pull back to earth, and afterwards the pain, the actual physical pain of the awakening. It's like coming down from a high mountain—you know the pains in the ears one gets? Well, this is the same thing, but intensified— and with it goes the awful sense of *weight*—of being hemmed in, stifled . . .'

He broke off and there was a pause.

'Already the servants think I'm mad. I couldn't bear the roof and the walls—I've had a place arranged up at the top of the house, open to the sky, with no furniture or carpets, or any stifling things . . . But even then the houses all round are nearly as bad. It's open country I want, somewhere where one can breathe . . .' He looked across at Seldon. 'Well, what do you say? Can you explain it?'

'H'm,' said Seldon. 'Plenty of explanations. You've been

hypnotized, or you've hypnotized yourself. Your nerves have gone wrong. Or it may be merely a dream.'

Hamer shook his head. 'None of those explanations will do.'

'And there are others,' said Seldon slowly, 'but they're not generally admitted.'

'*You* are prepared to admit them?'

'On the whole, yes! There's a great deal we can't understand which can't possibly be explained normally. We've any amount to find out still, and I for one believe in keeping an open mind.'

'What do you advise me to do?' asked Hamer after a silence.

Seldon leaned forward briskly. 'One of several things. Go away from London, seek out your "open country". The dreams may cease.'

'I can't do that,' said Hamer quickly. 'It's come to this, that I can't do without them. I don't want to do without them.'

'Ah! I guessed as much. Another alternative, find this fellow, this cripple. You're endowing him now with all sorts of supernatural attributes. Talk to him. Break the spell.'

Hamer shook his head again.

'Why not?'

'I'm afraid,' said Hamer simply.

Seldon made a gesture of impatience. 'Don't believe in it all so blindly! This tune now, the medium that starts it all, what is it like?'

Hamer hummed it, and Seldon listened with a puzzled frown.

'Rather like a bit out of the Overture to *Rienzi*. There *is* something uplifting about it—it has wings. But I'm not carried off the earth! Now, these flights of yours, are they all exactly the same?'

'No, no.' Hamer leaned forward eagerly. 'They develop. Each time I see a little more. It's difficult to explain. You see, I'm always conscious of reaching a certain point—the music carries me there—not direct, but a succession of *waves*, each reaching higher than the last, until the highest point where one can go no further. I stay there until I'm dragged back. It isn't a place, it's more a *state*. Well, not just at first, but after a little while, I began to understand that there were other things all round me waiting until I was able to perceive them. Think of a kitten. It has eyes, but at first it can't see with them. It's blind and has to learn to see. Well, that was what it was to me. Mortal eyes and ears were no good to me, but there was something corresponding to them that hadn't yet been developed—something that wasn't *bodily* at all. And little by little that grew . . . there were sensations of light . . . then of sound . . . then of colour . . . All very vague and unformulated. It was more the knowledge of things than seeing or hearing them. First it was light, a light that grew stronger and clearer . . . then sand, great stretches of reddish sand . . . and here and there straight long lines of water like canals—'

Seldon drew in his breath sharply. '*Canals!* That's interesting. Go on.'

'But these things didn't matter—they didn't count any longer. The real things were the things I couldn't see yet—but I heard them . . . It was a sound like the rushing of wings . . . somehow, I can't explain why, it was glorious! There's nothing like it here. And then came another glory—*I saw them*—the Wings! Oh, Seldon, the Wings!'

'But what were they? Men—angels—birds?'

'I don't know. I couldn't see—not yet. But the colour of them! *Wing colour*—we haven't got it here—it's a wonderful colour.'

'Wing colour?' repeated Seldon. 'What's it like?'

Hamer flung up his hands impatiently. 'How can I tell you? Explain the colour blue to a blind person! It's a colour you've never seen—Wing colour!'

'Well?'

'Well? That's all. That's as far as I've got. But each time the coming back has been worse—more painful. I can't understand that. I'm convinced my body never leaves the bed. In this place I get to I'm convinced I've got no *physical* presence. Why should it hurt so confoundedly then?'

Seldon shook his head in silence.

'It's something awful—the coming back. The *pull* of it— then the pain, pain in every limb and every nerve, and my ears feel as though they were bursting. Then everything *presses* so, the weight of it all, the dreadful sense of imprisonment. I want light, air, space—above all *space* to breathe in! And I want freedom.'

'And what,' asked Seldon, 'of all the other things that used to mean so much to you?'

'That's the worst of it. I care for them still as much as, if not more than, ever. And these things, comfort, luxury, pleasure, seem to pull opposite ways to the Wings. It's a perpetual struggle between them—and I can't see how it's going to end.'

Seldon sat silent. The strange tale he had been listening to was fantastic enough in all truth. Was it all a delusion, a wild hallucination—or could it by any possibility be true? And if so, why *Hamer*, of all men . . .? Surely the materialist, the man who loved the flesh and denied the spirit, was the last man to see the sights of another world.

Across the table Hamer watched him anxiously.

'I suppose,' said Seldon slowly, 'that you can only wait. Wait and see what happens.'

'I can't! I tell you I can't! Your saying that shows you don't understand. It's tearing me in two, this awful struggle— this killing long-drawn-out fight between—between—' He hesitated.

'The flesh and the spirit?' suggested Seldon.

Hamer stared heavily in front of him. 'I suppose one might call it that. Anyway, it's unbearable . . . I can't get free . . .'

Again Bernard Seldon shook his head. He was caught up in the grip of the inexplicable. He made one more suggestion.

'If I were you,' he advised, 'I would get hold of that cripple.'

But as he went home he muttered to himself: '*Canals*—I wonder.'

Silas Hamer went out of the house the following morning with a new determination in his step. He had decided to take Seldon's advice and find the legless man. Yet inwardly he was convinced that his search would be in vain and that the man would have vanished as completely as though the earth had swallowed him up.

The dark buildings on either side of the passageway shut out the sunlight and left it dark and mysterious. Only in one place, half-way up it, there was a break in the wall, and through it there fell a shaft of golden light that illuminated with radiance a figure sitting on the ground. A figure—yes, it was the man!

The instrument of pipes leaned against the wall beside his crutches, and he was covering the paving stones with designs in coloured chalk. Two were completed, sylvan scenes of marvellous beauty and delicacy, swaying trees and a leaping brook that seemed alive.

And again Hamer doubted. Was this man a mere street musician, a pavement artist? Or was he something more . . .

Suddenly the millionaire's self-control broke down, and he cried fiercely and angrily: 'Who are you? For God's sake, who are you?'

The man's eyes met his, smiling.

'Why don't you answer? Speak, man, speak!'

Then he noticed that the man was drawing with incredible rapidity on a bare slab of stone. Hamer followed the movement with his eyes . . . A few bold strokes, and giant trees took form. Then, seated on a boulder . . . a man . . . playing an instrument of pipes. A man with a strangely beautiful face—*and goat's legs* . . .

The cripple's hand made a swift movement. The man still sat on the rock, but the goat's legs were gone. Again his eyes met Hamer's.

'They were evil,' he said.

Hamer stared, fascinated. For the face before him was the face of the picture, but strangely and incredibly beautified . . . Purified from all but an intense and exquisite joy of living.

Hamer turned and almost fled down the passageway into the bright sunlight, repeating to himself incessantly: 'It's impossible. Impossible . . . I'm mad—dreaming!' But the face haunted him—the face of Pan . . .

He went into the Park and sat on a chair. It was a deserted hour. A few nursemaids with their charges sat in the shade of the trees, and dotted here and there in the stretches of green, like islands in a sea, lay the recumbent forms of men . . .

The words 'a wretched tramp' were to Hamer an epitome of misery. But suddenly, today, he envied them . . .

They seemed to him of all created beings the only free ones. The earth beneath them, the sky above them, the world to wander in . . . they were not hemmed in or chained.

Like a flash it came to him that that which bound him so remorselessly was the thing he had worshipped and prized above all others—wealth! He had thought it the strongest thing on earth, and now, wrapped round by its golden strength, he saw the truth of his words. It was his money that held him in bondage . . .

But was it? Was that really it? Was there a deeper and more pointed truth that he had not seen? Was it the money or was it his own love of the money? He was bound in fetters of his own making; not wealth itself, but love of wealth was the chain.

He knew now clearly the two forces that were tearing at him, the warm composite strength of materialism that enclosed and surrounded him, and, opposed to it, the clear imperative call—he named it to himself the Call of the Wings.

And while the one fought and clung the other scorned war and would not stoop to struggle. It only called—called unceasingly . . . He heard it so clearly that it almost spoke in words.

'You cannot make terms with me,' it seemed to say. 'For

I am above all other things. If you follow my call you must give up all else and cut away the forces that hold you. For only the Free shall follow where I lead . . .'

'I can't,' cried Hamer. 'I can't . . .'

A few people turned to look at the big man who sat talking to himself.

So sacrifice was being asked of him, the sacrifice of that which was most dear to him, that which was part of himself.

*Part of himself*—he remembered the man without legs . . .

'What in the name of Fortune brings you here?' asked Borrow.

Indeed the East-end mission was an unfamiliar background to Hamer.

'I've listened to a good many sermons,' said the millionaire, 'all saying what could be done if you people had funds. I've come to tell you this: you can have funds.'

'Very good of you,' answered Borrow, with some surprise. 'A big subscription, eh?'

Hamer smiled drily. 'I should say so. Just every penny I've got.'

'*What?*'

Hamer rapped out details in a brisk businesslike manner. Borrow's head was whirling.

'You—you mean to say that you're making over your entire fortune to be devoted to the relief of the poor in the East End with myself appointed as trustee?'

'That's it.'

'But why—*why?*'

'I can't explain,' said Hamer slowly. 'Remember our talk about visions last February? Well, a vision has got hold of me.'

'It's splendid!' Borrow leaned forward, his eyes gleaming.

'There's nothing particularly splendid about it,' said Hamer grimly. 'I don't care a button about poverty in the East End. All they want is grit! *I* was poor enough—and I got out of it. But I've got to get rid of the money, and these tom-fool societies shan't get hold of it. You're a man I can trust. Feed bodies or souls with it—preferably the former. I've been hungry, but you can do as you like.'

'There's never been such a thing known,' stammered Borrow.

'The whole thing's done and finished with,' continued Hamer. 'The lawyers have fixed it up at last, and I've signed everything. I can tell you I've been busy this last fortnight. It's almost as difficult getting rid of a fortune as making one.'

'But you—you've kept *something?*'

'Not a penny,' said Hamer cheerfully. 'At least—that's not quite true. I've just twopence in my pocket.' He laughed.

He said goodbye to his bewildered friend, and walked out of the mission into the narrow evil-smelling streets. The words he had said so gaily just now came back to him with an aching sense of loss. 'Not a penny!' Of all his vast wealth he had kept nothing. He was afraid now—afraid of poverty and hunger and cold. Sacrifice had no sweetness for him.

Yet behind it all he was conscious that the weight and menace of things had lifted, he was no longer oppressed and bound down. The severing of the chain had seared and torn him, but the vision of freedom was there to strengthen him. His material needs might dim the Call, but they could not deaden it, for he knew it to be a thing of immortality that could not die.

There was a touch of autumn in the air, and the wind blew chill. He felt the cold and shivered, and then, too, he was hungry—he had forgotten to have any lunch. It brought the future very near to him. It was incredible that he should have given it all up; the ease, the comfort, the warmth! His body cried out impotently . . . And then once again there came to him a glad and uplifting sense of freedom.

Hamer hesitated. He was near the Tube station. He had twopence in his pocket. The idea came to him to journey by it to the Park where he had watched the recumbent idlers a fortnight ago. Beyond this whim he did not plan for the future. He believed honestly enough now that he was mad—

sane people did not act as he had done. Yet, if so, madness was a wonderful and amazing thing.

Yes, he would go now to the open country of the Park, and there was a special significance to him in reaching it by Tube. For the Tube represented to him all the horrors of buried, shut-in life . . . He would ascend from its imprisonment free to the wide green and the trees that concealed the menace of the pressing houses.

The lift bore him swiftly and relentlessly downward. The air was heavy and lifeless. He stood at the extreme end of the platform, away from the mass of people. On his left was the opening of the tunnel from which the train, snakelike, would presently emerge. He felt the whole place to be subtly evil. There was no one near him but a hunched-up lad sitting on a seat, sunk, it seemed, in a drunken stupor.

In the distance came the faint menacing roar of the train. The lad rose from his seat and shuffled unsteadily to Hamer's side, where he stood on the edge of the platform peering into the tunnel.

Then—it happened so quickly as to be almost incredible— he lost his balance and fell . . .

A hundred thoughts rushed simultaneously to Hamer's brain. He saw a huddled heap run over by a motor bus, and heard a hoarse voice saying: 'Dahn't yer blime yerself, guv'nor. Yer couldn't 'a done nothin'.' And with that came the knowledge that *this* life could only be saved, if it were saved, by himself. There was no one else near, and the train was close . . . It all passed through his mind with lightning rapidity. He experienced a curious calm lucidity of thought.

He had one short second in which to decide, and he knew in that moment that his fear of Death was unabated. He was horribly afraid. And then—was it not a forlorn hope? A useless throwing away of two lives?

To the terrified spectators at the other end of the platform there seemed no gap between the boy's fall and the man's jump after him—and then the train, rushing round the curve of the tunnel, powerless to pull up in time.

Swiftly Hamer caught up the lad in his arms. No natural gallant impulse swayed him, his shivering flesh was but obeying the command of the alien spirit that called for sacrifice. With a last effort he flung the lad forward on to the platform, falling himself . . .

Then suddenly his Fear died. The material world held him down no longer. He was free of his shackles. He fancied for a moment that he heard the joyous piping of Pan. Then— nearer and louder—swallowing up all else—came the glad rushing of innumerable Wings . . . enveloping and encircling him . . .

# THE FLOCK OF GERYON

'I really do apologize for intruding like this, M. Poirot.'

Miss Carnaby clasped her hands fervently round her handbag and leaned forward, peering anxiously into Poirot's face. As usual, she sounded breathless.

Hercule Poirot's eyebrows rose.

She said anxiously:

'You do remember me, don't you?'

Hercule Poirot's eyes twinkled. He said:

'I remember you as one of the most successful criminals I have ever encountered!'

'Oh dear me, M. Poirot, must you really say such things? You *were* so kind to me. Emily and I often talk about you, and if we see anything about you in the paper we cut it out at once and paste it in a book. As for Augustus, we have taught him a new trick. We say, "Die for Sherlock Holmes, die for Mr Fortune, die for Sir Henry Merrivale, and then *die for M. Hercule Poirot*" and he goes down and lies like a *log*—lies absolutely still without moving until we say the word!'

'I am gratified,' said Poirot. 'And how is *ce cher Auguste*?'

Miss Carnaby clasped her hands and became eloquent in praise of her Pekinese.

'Oh, M. Poirot, he's cleverer than ever. He knows *everything*. Do you know, the other day I was just admiring a baby in a pram and suddenly I felt a tug and there was Augustus trying his hardest to bite through his lead. Wasn't that clever?'

Poirot's eyes twinkled. He said:

'It looks to me as though Augustus shared these criminal tendencies we were speaking of just now!'

Miss Carnaby did not laugh. Instead, her nice plump face grew worried and sad. She said in a kind of gasp:

'Oh, M. Poirot, I'm so *worried*.'

Poirot said kindly:

'What is it?'

'Do you know, M. Poirot, I'm afraid—I really am afraid—that I must be a *hardened criminal*—if I may use such a term. Ideas come to me!'

'What kind of ideas?'

'The most extraordinary ideas! For instance, yesterday, a really most *practical* scheme for robbing a post office came into my head. I wasn't thinking about it—it just came! And another very ingenious way for evading custom duties . . . I feel convinced—quite convinced—that it would work.'

'It probably would,' said Poirot drily. 'That is the danger of your ideas.'

'It has worried me, M. Poirot, very much. Having been brought up with strict principles, as I have been, it is *most* disturbing that such lawless—such really *wicked*—ideas should come to me. The trouble is partly, I think, that I have a good deal of leisure time now. I have left Lady Hoggin and I am engaged by an old lady to read to her and write her letters every day. The letters are soon done and the moment I begin reading she goes to sleep, so I am left just sitting there—with an idle mind—and we all know the use the devil has for idleness.'

'Tcha, tcha,' said Poirot.

'Recently I have read a book—a very modern book, translated from the German. It throws a most interesting light on criminal tendencies. One must, so I understand, *sublimate* one's impulses! That, really, is why I came to you.'

'Yes?' said Poirot.

'You see, M. Poirot. I think that it is really not so much *wickedness* as a craving for excitement! My life has unfortunately been very humdrum. The—er—campaign of the Pekinese dogs, I sometimes feel, was the only time I really *lived*. Very reprehensible, of course, but, as my book says, one must not turn one's back on the truth. I came to you, M. Poirot, because I hoped it might be possible to—to subli-mate that craving for excitement by employing it, if I may put it that way, on the side of the angels.'

'Aha,' said Poirot. 'It is then as a colleague that you present yourself?'

Miss Carnaby blushed.

'It is very presumptuous of me, I know. But you were so *kind*—'

She stopped. Her eyes, faded blue eyes, had something in them of the pleading of a dog who hopes against hope that you will take him for a walk.

'It is an idea,' said Hercule Poirot slowly.

'I am, of course, not at all clever,' explained Miss Carnaby. 'But my powers of—of dissimulation are good. They have to be—otherwise one would be discharged from the post of companion immediately. And I have always found that to appear even stupider than one is, occasionally has good results.'

Hercule Poirot laughed. He said:

'You enchant me, Mademoiselle.'

'Oh dear, M. Poirot, what a very kind man you are. Then you do encourage me to *hope*? As it happens, I have just received a small legacy—a very small one, but it enables my sister and myself to keep and feed ourselves in a frugal manner so that I am not absolutely dependent on what I earn.'

'I must consider,' said Poirot, 'where your talents may best be employed. You have no idea yourself, I suppose?'

'You know, you must really be a thought reader, M. Poirot. I *have* been anxious lately about a friend of mine. I was going to consult you. Of course you may say it is all an old maid's fancy—just imagination. One is prone, perhaps, to exaggerate, and to see *design* where there may be only *coincidence*.'

'I do not think you would exaggerate, Miss Carnaby. Tell me what is on your mind.'

'Well, I have a friend, a very dear friend, though I have not seen very much of her of late years. Her name is Emmeline Clegg. She married a man in the North of England and he died a few years ago leaving her very comfortably off. She was unhappy and lonely after his death and I am afraid she is in some ways a rather foolish and perhaps credulous woman. Religion, M. Poirot, can be a great help and sustenance—but by that I mean orthodox religion.'

'You refer to the Greek Church?' asked Poirot.

Miss Carnaby looked shocked.

'Oh no, indeed. Church of England. And though I do not *approve* of Roman Catholics, they are at least *recognized*. And the Wesleyans and Congregationalists—they are all well-known respectable bodies. What I am talking about are these *odd* sects. They just spring up. They have a kind of emotional appeal but sometimes I have very grave doubts as to whether there is any true religious feeling behind them at all.'

'You think your friend is being victimized by a sect of this kind?'

'I do. Oh! I certainly do. The Flock of the Shepherd, they call themselves. Their headquarters is in Devonshire—a very lovely estate by the sea. The adherents go there for what they term a Retreat. That is a period of a fortnight—with religious services and rituals. And there are three big Festivals in the year, the Coming of the Pasture, the Full Pasture, and the Reaping of the Pasture.'

'Which last is stupid,' said Poirot. 'Because one does not reap pasture.'

'The whole thing is stupid,' said Miss Carnaby with warmth. 'The whole sect centres round the head of the movement, the Great Shepherd, he is called. A Dr Andersen. A very handsome-looking man, I believe, with a presence.'

'Which is attractive to the women, yes?'

'I am afraid so,' Miss Carnaby sighed. 'My father was a

very handsome man. Sometimes, it was most awkward in the parish. The rivalry in embroidering vestments—and the division of church work . . .'

She shook her head reminiscently.

'Are the members of the Great Flock mostly women?'

'At least three quarters of them, I gather. What men there are, are mostly *cranks*! It is upon the women that the success of the movement depends and—and on the *funds* they supply.'

'Ah,' said Poirot. 'Now we come to it. Frankly, you think the whole thing is a ramp?'

'Frankly, M. Poirot, I do. And another thing worries me. I happen to know that my poor friend is so bound up in this religion that she has recently made a will leaving all her property to the movement.'

Poirot said sharply:

'Was that—suggested to her?'

'In all fairness, no. It was entirely her own idea. The Great Shepherd had shown her a new way of life—so all that she had was to go on her death to the Great Cause. What really worries me is—'

'Yes—go on—'

'Several wealthy women have been among the devotees. In the last year *three* of them, no less, have died.'

'Leaving all their money to this sect?'

'Yes.'

'Their relations have made no protest? I should have thought it likely that there might have been litigation.'

'You see, M. Poirot, it is usually *lonely* women who belong to this gathering. People who have no very near relations or friends.'

Poirot nodded thoughtfully. Miss Carnaby hurried on:

'Of course I've no right to suggest anything at all. From what I have been able to find out, there was nothing *wrong* about any of these deaths. One, I believe, was *pneumonia* following *influenza* and another was attributed to gastric ulcer. There were absolutely no *suspicious circumstances*, if you know what I mean, and the deaths did not take place at Green Hills Sanctuary, but at their own homes. I've no doubt it is *quite* all right, but all the same I—well—I shouldn't like anything to happen to Emmie.'

She clasped her hands, her eyes appealed to Poirot.

Poirot himself was silent for some minutes. When he spoke there was a change in his voice. It was grave and deep.

He said:

'Will you give me, or will you find out for me, the names and addresses of these members of the sect who have recently died?'

'Yes indeed, M. Poirot.'

Poirot said slowly:

'Mademoiselle, I think you are a woman of great courage and determination. You have good histrionic powers. Would you be willing to undertake a piece of work that may be attended with considerable danger?'

'I should like nothing better,' said the adventurous Miss Carnaby.

Poirot said warningly:

'If there is a risk at all, it will be a grave one. You comprehend—either this is a mare's nest or it is *serious*. To find out which it is, it will be necessary for you yourself to become a member of the Great Flock. I would suggest that you exaggerate the amount of the legacy that you recently inherited. You are now a well-to-do woman with no very definite aim in life. You argue with your friend Emmeline about this religion she has adopted—assure her that it is all nonsense. She is eager to convert you. You allow yourself to be persuaded to go down to Green Hills Sanctuary. And there you fall a victim to the persuasive powers and magnetic influence of Dr Andersen. I think I can safely leave that part to you?'

Miss Carnaby smiled modestly. She murmured:

'I think I can manage *that* all right!'

\*

'Well, my friend, what have you got for me?'

Chief Inspector Japp looked thoughtfully at the little man who asked the question. He said ruefully:

'Not at all what I'd like to have, Poirot. I hate these long-haired, religious cranks like poison. Filling up women with a lot of mumbo-jumbo. But this fellow's being careful. There's nothing one can get hold of. All sounds a bit batty but harmless.'

'Have you learned anything about this Dr Andersen?'

'I've looked up his past history. He was a promising chemist and got chucked out of some German University. Seems his mother was Jewish. He was always keen on the study of Oriental Myths and Religions, spent all his spare time on that and has written various articles on the subject—some of the articles sound pretty crazy to me.'

'So it is possible that he is a genuine fanatic?'

'I'm bound to say it seems quite likely!'

'What about those names and addresses I gave you?'

'Nothing doing there. Miss Everitt died of ulcerative colitis. Doctor quite positive there was no hankypanky. Mrs Lloyd died of broncho-pneumonia. Lady Western died of tuberculosis. Had suffered from it many years ago—before she even met this bunch. Miss Lee died of typhoid—attributed to some salad she ate somewhere in the north of England. Three of them got ill and died in their own homes, and Mrs Lloyd died in a hotel in the south of France. As far as those deaths go, there's nothing to connect them with the Great Flock or with Andersen's place down in Devonshire. Must be pure coincidence. All absolutely O.K. and according to Cocker.'

Hercule Poirot sighed. He said:

'And yet, *mon cher*, I have a feeling that this is the tenth Labour of Hercules, and that this Dr Andersen is the Monster Geryon whom it is my mission to destroy.'

Japp looked at him anxiously.

'Look here, Poirot, you haven't been reading any queer literature yourself lately, have you?'

Poirot said with dignity:

'My remarks are, as always, apt, sound, and to the point.'

'You might start a new religion yourself,' said Japp, 'with the creed: "There is no one so clever as Hercule Poirot, Amen, D.C. Repeat *ad lib*."!'

'It is the peace here that I find so wonderful,' said Miss Carnaby, breathing heavily and ecstatically.

'I told you so, Amy,' said Emmeline Clegg.

The two friends were sitting on the slope of a hillside overlooking a deep and lovely blue sea. The grass was vivid green, the earth and the cliffs a deep, glowing red. The little estate now known as Green Hills Sanctuary was a promontory comprising about six acres. Only a narrow neck of land joined it to the mainland so that it was almost an island.

Mrs Clegg murmured sentimentally:

'The red land—the land of glow and promise—where threefold destiny is to be accomplished.'

Miss Carnaby sighed deeply and said:

'I thought the Master put it all so beautifully at the service last night.'

'Wait,' said her friend, 'for the festival tonight. The Full Growth of the Pasture!'

'I'm looking forward to it,' said Miss Carnaby.

'You will find it a wonderful spiritual experience,' her friend promised her.

Miss Carnaby had arrived at Green Hills Sanctuary a week previously. Her attitude on arrival had been: 'Now what's all this nonsense? Really, Emmie, a sensible woman like you—etc., etc.'

At a preliminary interview with Dr Andersen, she had conscientiously made her position quite clear.

'I don't want to feel that I am here under false pretences, Dr Andersen. My father was a clergyman of the Church of England and I have never wavered in my faith. I don't hold with heathen doctrines.'

The big, golden-haired man had smiled at her—a very sweet and understanding smile. He had looked indulgently at the plump, rather belligerent figure sitting so squarely in her chair.

'Dear Miss Carnaby,' he said. 'You are Mrs Clegg's friend, and as such welcome. And believe me, our doctrines are not heathen. Here all religions are welcomed, and all honoured equally.'

'Then they shouldn't be,' said the staunch daughter of the late Reverend Thomas Carnaby.

Leaning back in his chair, the Master murmured in his rich voice: 'In my Father's House are many mansions . . . Remember that, Miss Carnaby.'

As they left the presence, Miss Carnaby murmured to her friend: 'He really is a very handsome man.'

'Yes,' said Emmeline Clegg. 'And so wonderfully spiritual.'

Miss Carnaby agreed. It was true—she had felt it—an aura of unworldliness—of spirituality . . .

She took a grip upon herself. She was not here to fall a prey to the fascination, spiritual or otherwise, of the Great Shepherd. She conjured up a vision of Hercule Poirot. He seemed very far away, and curiously mundane . . .

'Amy,' said Miss Carnaby to herself. 'Take a grip upon yourself. Remember what you are here for . . .'

But as the days went on, she found herself surrendering only too easily to the spell of Green Hills. The peace, the simplicity, the delicious though simple food, the beauty of the services with their chants of Love and Worship, the simple moving words of the Master, appealing to all that was best and highest in humanity—here all the strife and ugliness of the world was shut out. Here was only Peace and Love . . .

And tonight was the great summer Festival, the Festival of the Full Pasture. And at it, she, Amy Carnaby, was to become initiated—to become one of the Flock.

The Festival took place in the white, glittering, concrete building, called by the Initiates the Sacred Fold. Here the devotees assembled just before the setting of the sun. They wore sheepskin cloaks and had sandals on their feet. Their arms were bare. In the centre of the Fold on a raised platform stood Dr Andersen. The big man, golden-haired and blue-eyed, with his fair beard and his handsome profile had never seemed more compelling. He was dressed in a green robe and carried a shepherd's crook of gold.

He raised this aloft and a deathly silence fell on the assembly.

'Where are my sheep?'

The answer came from the crowd.

*'We are here, O Shepherd.'*

'Lift up your hearts with joy and thanksgiving. This is the Feast of Joy.'

*'The Feast of Joy and we are joyful.'*

'There shall be no more sorrow for you, no more pain. All is joy!'

*'All is joy . . .'*

'How many heads has the Shepherd?'

*'Three heads, a head of gold, a head of silver, a head of sounding brass.'*

'How many bodies have the Sheep?'

*'Three bodies, a body of flesh, a body of corruption, and a body of light.'*

'How shall you be sealed in the Flock?'

*'By the Sacrament of Blood.'*

'Are you prepared for that Sacrament?'

*'We are.'*

'Bind your eyes and hold forth your right arm.'

The crowd obediently bound their eyes with the green scarves provided for the purpose. Miss Carnaby, like the rest, held her arm out in front of her.

The Great Shepherd moved along the lines of his Flock. There were little cries, moans of either pain or ecstasy.

Miss Carnaby, to herself, said fiercely:

'Most blasphemous, the whole thing! This kind of religious hysteria is to be deplored. I shall remain absolutely calm and observe the reactions of other people. I will *not* be carried away—I will *not . . .*'

The Great Shepherd had come to her. She felt her arm taken, held, there was a sharp, stinging pain like the prick of a needle. The Shepherd's voice murmured:

'*The Sacrament of Blood that brings joy . . .*'

He passed on.

Presently there came a command.

'Unveil and enjoy the pleasures of the spirit!'

The sun was just sinking. Miss Carnaby looked round her. At one with the others, she moved slowly out of the Fold. She felt suddenly uplifted, happy. She sank down on a soft, grassy bank. Why had she ever thought she was a lonely, unwanted, middle-aged woman? Life was wonderful—she herself was wonderful! She had the power of thought—of dreaming. There was nothing that she could not accomplish!

A great rush of exhilaration surged through her. She observed her fellow devotees round her—they seemed suddenly to have grown to an immense stature.

'*Like trees walking . . .*' said Miss Carnaby to herself reverently.

She lifted her hand. It was a purposeful gesture—with it she could command the earth. Cæsar, Napoleon, Hitler—poor, miserable, little fellows! They knew nothing of what she, Amy Carnaby, could do! Tomorrow she would arrange for world peace, for International Brotherhood. There should be no more Wars—no more Poverty—no more Disease. She, Amy Carnaby, would design a New World.

But there need be no hurry. Time was infinite . . . Minute succeeded minute, hour succeeded hour! Miss Carnaby's limbs felt heavy, but her mind was delightfully free. It could roam at will over the whole universe. She slept—but even as she slept she dreamt . . . Great spaces . . . vast buildings . . . a new and wonderful world . . .

Gradually the world shrank, Miss Carnaby yawned. She moved her stiff limbs. What had happened since yesterday? Last night she had dreamt . . .

There was a moon. By it, Miss Carnaby could just distinguish the figures on her watch. To her stupefaction the hands pointed to a quarter to ten. The sun, as she knew, had set at eight-ten. Only an hour and thirty-five minutes ago? Impossible. And yet—

'*Very* remarkable,' said Miss Carnaby to herself.

Hercule Poirot said:

'You must obey my instructions very carefully. You understand?'

'Oh yes, M. Poirot. You may rely on me.'

'You have spoken of your intention to benefit the cult?'

'Yes, M. Poirot. I spoke to the Master—excuse me, to Dr Andersen myself. I told him very emotionally what a wonderful revelation the whole thing had been—how I had come to scoff and remained to believe. I—really it seemed quite natural to say all these things. Dr Andersen, you know, has a lot of magnetic charm.'

'So I perceive,' said Hercule Poirot drily.

'His manner was most convincing. One really feels he doesn't care about money at all. "Give what you can," he said smiling in that wonderful way of his, "if you can give nothing, it does not matter. You are one of the Flock just the same." "Oh, Dr Andersen," I said, "I am not so badly off as *that*. I have just inherited a considerable amount of money from a distant relative and though I cannot actually touch any of the money until the legal formalities are all complied with, there is one thing I want to do at once." And then I explained that I was making a will and that I wanted to leave all I had to the Brotherhood. I explained that I had no near relatives.'

'And he graciously accepted the bequest?'

'He was very detached about it. Said it would be many long years before I passed over, that he could tell I was cut out for a long life of joy and spiritual fulfilment. He really speaks most *movingly*.'

'So it would seem.'

Poirot's tone was dry. He went on:

'You mentioned your health?'

'Yes, M. Poirot. I told him that I had had lung trouble, and that it had recurred more than once, but that a final treatment in a Sanatorium some years ago had, I hoped, quite cured me.'

'Excellent!'

'Though why it is necessary for me to say that I am consumptive when my lungs are as sound as a bell I really cannot see.'

'Be assured it *is* necessary. You mentioned your friend?'

'Yes. I told him (strictly in confidence) that dear Emmeline, besides the fortune she had inherited from her husband, would inherit an even larger sum shortly from an aunt who was deeply attached to her.'

'*Eh bien*, that ought to keep Mrs Clegg safe for the time being!'

'Oh, M. Poirot, do you really think there *is* anything wrong?'

'That is what I am going to endeavour to find out. Have you met a Mr Cole down at the Sanctuary?'

'There was a Mr Cole there last time I went down. A most peculiar man. He wears grass-green shorts and eats nothing but cabbage. He is a very ardent believer.'

'*Eh bien*, all progresses well—I make you my compliments on the work you have done—all is now set for the Autumn Festival.'

'Miss Carnaby—just a moment.'

Mr Cole clutched at Miss Carnaby, his eyes bright and feverish.

'I have had a Vision—a most remarkable Vision. I really must tell you about it.'

Miss Carnaby sighed. She was rather afraid of Mr Cole and his Visions. There were moments when she was decidedly of the opinion that Mr Cole was mad.

And she found these Visions of his sometimes very embarrassing. They recalled to her certain outspoken passages in that very modern German book on the Subconscious Mind which she had read before coming down to Devon.

Mr Cole, his eyes glistening, his lips twitching, began to talk excitedly.

'I had been meditating—reflecting on the Fullness of Life, on the Supreme Joy of Oneness—and then, you know, my eyes were opened and I *saw*—'

Miss Carnaby braced herself and hoped that what Mr Cole had seen would not be what he had seen the last time—which had been, apparently, a Ritual Marriage in ancient Sumeria between a god and goddess.

'I saw'—Mr Cole leant towards her, breathing hard, his eyes looking (yes, really they did) *quite* mad—'the Prophet Elijah descending from Heaven in his fiery chariot.'

Miss Carnaby breathed a sigh of relief. Elijah was much better, she didn't mind Elijah.

'Below,' went on Mr Cole, 'were the altars of Baal—hundreds and hundreds of them. A Voice cried to me: "Look, write and testify that which you shall see—"'

He stopped and Miss Carnaby murmured politely: 'Yes?'

'On the altars were the sacrifices, bound there, helpless, waiting for the knife. Virgins—hundreds of virgins—young beautiful, naked virgins—'

Mr Cole smacked his lips, Miss Carnaby blushed.

'Then came the ravens, the ravens of Odin, flying from the North. They met the ravens of Elijah—together they circled in the sky—they swooped, they plucked out the eyes of the victims—there was wailing and gnashing of teeth—and the Voice cried: "Behold a Sacrifice—for on this day shall Jehovah and Odin sign blood brotherhood!" Then the Priests fell upon their victims, they raised their knives—they mutilated their victims—'

Desperately Miss Carnaby broke away from her tormentor who was now slavering at the mouth in a kind of sadistic fervour:

'Excuse me one moment.'

She hastily accosted Lipscomb, the man who occupied the

Lodge which gave admission to Green Hills and who prov-
identially happened to be passing.

'I wonder,' she said, 'if you have found a brooch of mine.
I must have dropped it somewhere about the grounds.'

Lipscomb, who was a man immune from the general
sweetness and light of Green Hills, merely growled that he
hadn't seen any brooch. It wasn't *his* work to go about
looking for things. He tried to shake off Miss Carnaby but
she accompanied him, babbling about her brooch, till she
had put a safe distance between herself and the fervour of
Mr Cole.

At that moment, the Master himself came out of the Great
Fold and, emboldened by his benignant smile, Miss Carnaby
ventured to speak her mind to him.

Did he think that Mr Cole was quite—was quite—

The Master laid a hand on her shoulder.

'You must cast out Fear,' he said. 'Perfect Love casteth
out Fear . . .'

'But I think Mr Cole *is* mad. Those Visions he has—'

'As yet,' said the Master, 'he sees Imperfectly . . . through
the Glass of his own Carnal Nature. But the day will come
when he shall see Spiritually—Face to Face.'

Miss Carnaby was abashed. Of course, put like that—She
rallied to make a smaller protest.

'And really,' she said, 'need Lipscomb be so abominably
rude?'

Again the Master gave his Heavenly Smile.

'Lipscomb,' he said, 'is a faithful watch-dog. He is a
crude—a primitive soul—but faithful—utterly faithful.'

He strode on. Miss Carnaby saw him meet Mr Cole, pause,
put a hand on Mr Cole's shoulder. She hoped that the
Master's influence might alter the scope of future visions.

In any case, it was only a week now to the Autumn Festival.

On the afternoon preceding the Festival, Miss Carnaby met
Hercule Poirot in a small teashop in the sleepy little town
of Newton Woodbury. Miss Carnaby was flushed and even

more breathless than usual. She sat sipping tea and crumbling a rock bun between her fingers.

Poirot asked several questions to which she replied monosyllabically.

Then he said:

'How many will there be at the Festival?'

'I think a hundred and twenty. Emmeline is there, of course, and Mr Cole—really *he* has been *very* odd lately. He has visions. He described some of them to me—really most peculiar—I hope, I do hope, he is not *insane*. Then there will be quite a lot of new members—nearly twenty.'

'Good. You know what you have to do?'

There was a moment's pause before Miss Carnaby said in a rather odd voice:

'I know what you told me, M. Poirot . . .'

'*Très bien!*'

Then Amy Carnaby said clearly and distinctly:

'*But I am not going to do it.*'

Hercule Poirot stared at her. Miss Carnaby rose to her feet. Her voice came fast and hysterical.

'You sent me here to spy on Dr Andersen. You suspected him of all sorts of things. But he is a wonderful man—a great Teacher. I believe in him heart and soul! And I am not going to do your spying work any more, M. Poirot! I am one of the Sheep of the Shepherd. The Master has a new message for the World and from now on, I belong to him body and soul. And I'll pay for my own tea, please.'

With which slight anticlimax Miss Carnaby plonked down one and threepence and rushed out of the tea-shop.

'*Nom d'un nom d'un nom,*' said Hercule Poirot.

The waitress had to ask him twice before he realized that she was presenting the bill. He met the interested stare of a surly looking man at the next table, flushed, paid the check and got up and went out.

He was thinking furiously.

*

Once again the Sheep were assembled in the Great Fold. The Ritual Questions and Answers had been chanted.

'Are you prepared for the Sacrament?'

*'We are.'*

'Bind your eyes and hold out your right arm.'

The Great Shepherd, magnificent in his green robe, moved along the waiting lines. The cabbage-eating, vision-seeing Mr Cole, next to Miss Carnaby, gave a gulp of painful ecstasy as the needle pierced his flesh.

The Great Shepherd stood by Miss Carnaby. His hands touched her arm . . .

*'No, you don't. None of that . . .'*

Words incredible—unprecedented. A scuffle, a roar of anger. Green veils were torn from eyes—to see an unbelievable sight—the Great Shepherd struggling in the grasp of the sheep-skinned Mr Cole aided by another devotee.

In rapid professional tones, the erstwhile Mr Cole was saying:

'—and I have here a warrant for your arrest. I must warn you that anything you say may be used in evidence at your trial.'

There were other figures now at the door of the Sheep Fold—blue uniformed figures.

Someone cried: 'It's the *police*. They're taking the Master away. They're taking the Master . . .'

Everyone was shocked—horrified . . . to them the Great Shepherd was a martyr; suffering, as all great teachers suffer, from the ignorance and persecution of the outside world . . .

Meanwhile Detective Inspector Cole was carefully packing up the hypodermic syringe that had fallen from the Great Shepherd's hand.

'My brave colleague!'

Poirot shook Miss Carnaby warmly by the hand and introduced her to Chief Inspector Japp.

'First class work, Miss Carnaby,' said Chief Inspector Japp. 'We couldn't have done it without you and that's a fact.'

'Oh dear!' Miss Carnaby was flattered. 'It's so *kind* of you to say so. And I'm afraid, you know, that I've really *enjoyed* it all. The excitement, you know, and playing my part. I got quite carried away sometimes. I really felt I *was* one of those foolish women.'

'That's where your success lay,' said Japp. 'You were the genuine article. Nothing less would have taken that gentleman in! He's a pretty astute scoundrel.'

Miss Carnaby turned to Poirot.

'That was a terrible moment in the teashop. I didn't know *what* to do. I just had to act on the spur of the moment.'

'You were magnificent,' said Poirot warmly. 'For a moment I thought that either you or I had taken leave of our senses. I thought for one little minute that you *meant* it.'

'It was such a shock,' said Miss Carnaby. 'Just when we had been talking confidentially. I saw in the glass that Lipscomb, who keeps the Lodge of the Sanctuary, was sitting at the table behind me. I don't know now if it was an accident or if he had actually followed me. As I say, I had to do the best I could on the spur of the minute and trust that you would understand.'

Poirot smiled.

'I did understand. There was only one person sitting near enough to overhear anything we said and as soon as I left the teashop I arranged to have him followed when he came out. When he went straight back to the Sanctuary I understood that I could rely on you and that you would not let me down—but I was afraid because it increased the danger for you.'

'Was—was there really danger? What was there in the syringe?'

Japp said:

'Will you explain, or shall I?'

Poirot said gravely:

'Mademoiselle, this Dr Andersen had perfected a scheme of exploitation and murder—scientific murder. Most of his life has been spent in bacteriological research. Under a different name he has a chemical laboratory in Sheffield. There he makes cultures of various bacilli. It was his practice, at the Festivals, to inject into his followers a small but sufficient dose of Cannabis Indica—which is also known by the names of Hashish or Bhang. This gives delusions of grandeur and pleasurable enjoyment. It bound his devotees to him. These were the Spiritual Joys that he promised them.'

'Most remarkable,' said Miss Carnaby. 'Really a most remarkable sensation.'

Hercule Poirot nodded.

'That was his general stock in trade—a dominating personality, the power of creating mass hysteria and the reactions produced by this drug. But he had a second aim in view.

'Lonely women, in their gratitude and fervour, made wills leaving their money to the Cult. One by one, these women died. They died in their own homes and apparently of natural causes. Without being too technical I will try to explain. It is possible to make intensified cultures of certain bacteria. The bacillus Coli Communis, for instance, the cause of ulcerative colitis. Typhoid bacilli can be introduced into the system. So can the Pneumococcus. There is also what is termed Old Tuberculin which is harmless to a healthy person but which stimulates any old tubercular lesion into activity. You perceive the cleverness of the man? These deaths would occur in different parts of the country, with different doctors attending them and without any risk of arousing suspicion. He had also, I gather, cultivated a substance which had the power of delaying but intensifying the action of the chosen bacillus.'

'He's a devil, if there ever was one!' said Chief Inspector Japp.

Poirot went on:

'By my orders, you told him that you were a tuberculous subject. There was Old Tuberculin in the syringe when Cole arrested him. Since you were a healthy person it would not have harmed you, which is why I made you lay stress on your tubercular trouble. I was terrified that even now he *might* choose some other germ, but I respected your courage and I had to let you take the risk.'

'Oh, *that's* all right,' said Miss Carnaby brightly. 'I don't mind taking risks. I'm only frightened of bulls in fields and things like that. But have you enough evidence to *convict* this dreadful person?'

Japp grinned.

'Plenty of evidence,' he said. 'We've got his laboratory and his cultures and the whole layout!'

Poirot said:

'It is possible, I think, that he has committed a long line of murders. I may say that it was not because his mother was a Jewess that he was dismissed from that German University. That merely made a convenient tale to account for his arrival here and to gain sympathy for him. Actually, I fancy, he is of pure Aryan blood.'

Miss Carnaby sighed.

'*Qu'est ce qu'il y a?*' asked Poirot.

'I was thinking,' said Miss Carnaby, 'of a marvellous dream I had at the First Festival—hashish, I suppose. I arranged the whole world so beautifully! No wars, no poverty, no ill health, no ugliness . . .'

'It must have been a fine dream,' said Japp enviously.

Miss Carnaby jumped up. She said:

'I must get home. Emily has been so anxious. And dear Augustus has been missing me terribly, I hear.'

Hercule Poirot said with a smile:

'He was afraid, perhaps, that like him, you were going "to die for Hercule Poirot"!'

# THE RED SIGNAL

'No, but how too thrilling,' said pretty Mrs Eversleigh, opening her lovely, but slightly vacant eyes very wide. 'They always say women have a sixth sense; do you think it's true, Sir Alington?'

The famous alienist smiled sardonically. He had an unbounded contempt for the foolish pretty type, such as his fellow guest. Alington West was the supreme authority on mental disease, and he was fully alive to his own position and importance. A slightly pompous man of full figure.

'A great deal of nonsense is talked, I know that, Mrs Eversleigh. What does the term mean—a sixth sense?'

'You scientific men are always so severe. And it really is extraordinary the way one seems to positively know things sometimes—just know them, feel them, I mean—quite uncanny—it really is. Claire knows what I mean, don't you, Claire?'

She appealed to her hostess with a slight pout, and a tilted shoulder.

Claire Trent did not reply at once. It was a small dinner party, she and her husband, Violet Eversleigh, Sir Alington West, and his nephew, Dermot West, who was an old friend of Jack Trent's. Jack Trent himself, a somewhat heavy florid man, with a good-humoured smile, and a pleasant lazy laugh, took up the thread.

'Bunkum, Violet! Your best friend is killed in a railway accident. Straight away you remember that you dreamt of a black cat last Tuesday—marvellous, you felt all along that something was going to happen!'

'Oh, no, Jack, you're mixing up premonitions with intuition now. Come, now, Sir Alington, you must admit that premonitions are real?'

'To a certain extent, perhaps,' admitted the physician cautiously. 'But coincidence accounts for a good deal, and then there is the invariable tendency to make the most of a story afterwards—you've always got to take that into account.'

'I don't think there is any such thing as premonition,' said Claire Trent, rather abruptly. 'Or intuition, or a sixth sense, or any of the things we talk about so glibly. We go through life like a train rushing through the darkness to an unknown destination.'

'That's hardly a good simile, Mrs Trent,' said Dermot West, lifting his head for the first time and taking part in the discussion. There was a curious glitter in the clear grey eyes that shone out rather oddly from the deeply tanned face. 'You've forgotten the signals, you see.'

'The signals?'

'Yes, green if it's all right, and red—for danger!'

'Red—for danger—how thrilling!' breathed Violet Eversleigh.

Dermot turned from her rather impatiently.

'That's just a way of describing it, of course. Danger ahead! The red signal! Look out!'

Trent stared at him curiously.

'You speak as though it were an actual experience, Dermot, old boy.'

'So it is—has been, I mean.'

'Give us the yarn.'

'I can give you one instance. Out in Mesopotamia—just after the Armistice, I came into my tent one evening with the feeling strong upon me. Danger! Look out! Hadn't the ghost of a notion what it was all about. I made a round of the camp, fussed unnecessarily, took all precautions against an attack by hostile Arabs. Then I went back to my tent. As soon as I got inside, the feeling popped up again stronger than ever. Danger! In the end, I took a blanket outside, rolled myself up in it and slept there.'

'Well?'

'The next morning, when I went inside the tent, first thing I saw was a great knife arrangement—about half a yard long—struck down through my bunk, just where I would have lain. I soon found out about it—one of the Arab servants. His son had been shot as a spy. What have you got to say to that, Uncle Alington, as an example of what I call the red signal?'

The specialist smiled non-committally.

'A very interesting story, my dear Dermot.'

'But not one that you would accept unreservedly?'

'Yes, yes, I have no doubt that you had the premonition of danger, just as you state. But it is the origin of the premonition I dispute. According to you, it came from without, impressed by some outside source upon your mentality. But nowadays we find that nearly everything comes from within—from our subconscious self.'

'Good old subconscious,' cried Jack Trent. 'It's the jack-of-all-trades nowadays.'

Sir Alington continued without heeding the interruption.

'I suggest that by some glance or look this Arab had betrayed himself. Your conscious self did not notice or remember, but with your subconscious self it was otherwise. The subconscious never forgets. We believe, too, that it can reason and deduce quite independently of the higher or conscious will. Your subconscious self, then, believed that an attempt might be made to assassinate you, and succeeded in forcing its fear upon your conscious realization.'

'That sounds very convincing, I admit,' said Dermot, smiling.

'But not nearly so exciting,' pouted Mrs Eversleigh.

'It is also possible that you may have been subconsciously aware of the hate felt by the man towards you. What in old days used to be called telepathy certainly exists, though the conditions governing it are very little understood.'

'Have there been any other instances?' asked Claire of Dermot.

'Oh! yes, but nothing very pictorial—and I suppose they could all be explained under the heading of coincidence. I refused an invitation to a country house once, for no other reason than the hoisting of the "red signal". The place was burnt out during the week. By the way, Uncle Alington, where does the subconscious come in there?'

'I'm afraid it doesn't,' said Alington, smiling.

'But you've got an equally good explanation. Come, now. No need to be tactful with near relatives.'

'Well, then, nephew, I venture to suggest that you refused the invitation for the ordinary reason that you didn't much want to go, and that after the fire, you suggested to yourself that you had had a warning of danger, which explanation you now believe implicitly.'

'It's hopeless,' laughed Dermot. 'It's heads you win, tails I lose.'

'Never mind, Mr West,' cried Violet Eversleigh. 'I believe in your Red Signal implicitly. Is the time in Mesopotamia the last time you had it?'

'Yes—until—'

'I beg your pardon?'

'Nothing.'

Dermot sat silent. The words which had nearly left his lips were: 'Yes, *until tonight.*' They had come quite unbidden to his lips, voicing a thought which had as yet not been consciously realized, but he was aware at once that they were true. The Red Signal was looming up out of the darkness. Danger! Danger close at hand!

But why? What conceivable danger could there be here? Here in the house of his friends? At least—well, yes, there was that kind of danger. He looked at Claire Trent—her whiteness, her slenderness, the exquisite droop of her golden head. But that danger had been there for some time—it was never likely to get acute. For Jack Trent was his best friend, and more than his best friend, the man who had saved his life in Flanders and had been recommended for the VC for doing so. A good fellow, Jack, one of the best. Damned bad luck that he should have fallen in love with Jack's wife. He'd get over it some day, he supposed. A thing couldn't go on hurting like this for ever. One could starve it out—that was it, starve it out. It was not as though she would ever guess—and if she did guess, there was no danger of her caring. A statue, a beautiful statue, a thing of gold and ivory and pale pink coral . . . a toy for a king, not a real woman . . .

Claire . . . the very thought of her name, uttered silently, hurt him . . . He must get over it. He'd cared for women before . . . 'But not like this!' said something. 'Not like this.' Well, there it was. No danger there—heartache, yes, but not danger. Not the danger of the Red Signal. That was for something else.

He looked round the table and it struck him for the first time that it was rather an unusual little gathering. His uncle, for instance, seldom dined out in this small, informal way. It was not as though the Trents were old friends; until this evening Dermot had not been aware that he knew them at all.

To be sure, there was an excuse. A rather notorious medium was coming after dinner to give a *séance*. Sir Alington professed to be mildly interested in spiritualism. Yes, that was an excuse, certainly.

The word forced itself on his notice. An *excuse*. Was the *séance* just an excuse to make the specialist's presence at dinner natural? If so, what was the real object of his being here? A host of details came rushing into Dermot's mind, trifles unnoticed at the time, or, as his uncle would have said, unnoticed by the conscious mind.

The great physician had looked oddly, very oddly, at Claire more than once. He seemed to be watching her. She was uneasy under his scrutiny. She made little twitching motions with her hands. She was nervous, horribly nervous, and was it, could it be, *frightened*? Why was she frightened?

With a jerk, he came back to the conversation round the table. Mrs Eversleigh had got the great man talking upon his own subject.

'My dear lady,' he was saying, 'what *is* madness? I can assure you that the more we study the subject, the more difficult we find it to pronounce. We all practise a certain amount of self-deception, and when we carry it so far as to believe we are the Czar of Russia, we are shut up or restrained. But there is a long road before we reach that point. At what particular spot on it shall we erect a post and say, "On this side sanity, on the other madness?" It can't be done, you know. And I will tell you this, if the man suffering from a delusion happened to hold his tongue about it, in all probability we should never be able to distinguish him from a normal individual. The extraordinary sanity of the insane is a most interesting subject.'

Sir Alington sipped his wine with appreciation, and beamed upon the company.

'I've always heard they are very cunning,' remarked Mrs Eversleigh. 'Loonies, I mean.'

'Remarkably so. And suppression of one's particular delusion has a disastrous effect very often. All suppressions are dangerous, as psychoanalysis has taught us. The man who has a harmless eccentricity, and can indulge it as such, seldom goes over the border line. But the man'—he paused—'or woman who is to all appearance perfectly normal may be in reality a poignant source of danger to the community.'

His gaze travelled gently down the table to Claire, and then back again. He sipped his wine once more.

A horrible fear shook Dermot. Was *that* what he meant? Was *that* what he was driving at? Impossible, but—

'And all from suppressing oneself,' sighed Mrs Eversleigh. 'I quite see that one should be very careful always to—to express one's personality. The dangers of the other are frightful.'

'My dear Mrs Eversleigh,' expostulated the physician. 'You have quite misunderstood me. The cause of the mischief is in the physical matter of the brain—sometimes arising from some outward agency such as a blow; sometimes, alas, congenital.'

'Heredity is so sad,' sighed the lady vaguely. 'Consumption and all that.'

'Tuberculosis is not hereditary,' said Sir Alington drily.

'Isn't it? I always thought it was. But madness is! How dreadful. What else?'

'Gout,' said Sir Alington smiling. 'And colour blindness— the latter is rather interesting. It is transmitted direct to males, but is latent in females. So, while there are many colour-blind men, for a woman to be colour-blind, it must have been latent in her mother as well as present in her father—rather an unusual state of things to occur. That is what is called sex-limited heredity.'

'How interesting. But madness is not like that, is it?'

'Madness can be handed down to men or women equally,' said the physician gravely.

Claire rose suddenly, pushing back her chair so abruptly that it overturned and fell to the ground. She was very pale and the nervous motions of her fingers were very apparent.

'You—you will not be long, will you?' she begged. 'Mrs Thompson will be here in a few minutes now.'

'One glass of port, and I will be with you, for one,' declared Sir Alington. 'To see this wonderful Mrs Thompson's performance is what I have come for, is it not? Ha, ha! Not that I needed any inducement.' He bowed.

Claire gave a faint smile of acknowledgment and passed out of the room, her hand on Mrs Eversleigh's shoulder.

'Afraid I've been talking shop,' remarked the physician as he resumed his seat. 'Forgive me, my dear fellow.'

'Not at all,' said Trent perfunctorily.

He looked strained and worried. For the first time Dermot felt an outsider in the company of his friend. Between these two was a secret that even an old friend might not share.

And yet the whole thing was fantastic and incredible. What had he to go upon? Nothing but a couple of glances and a woman's nervousness.

They lingered over their wine but a very short time, and arrived up in the drawing-room just as Mrs Thompson was announced.

The medium was a plump middle-aged woman, atrociously dressed in magenta velvet, with a loud rather common voice.

'Hope I'm not late, Mrs Trent,' she said cheerily. 'You did say nine o'clock, didn't you?'

'You are quite punctual, Mrs Thompson,' said Claire in her sweet, slightly husky voice. 'This is our little circle.'

No further introductions were made, as was evidently the custom. The medium swept them all with a shrewd, penetrating eye.

'I hope we shall get some good results,' she remarked briskly. 'I can't tell you how I hate it when I go out and I can't give satisfaction, so to speak. It just makes me mad. But I think Shiromako (my Japanese control, you know) will be able to get through all right tonight. I'm feeling ever so fit, and I refused the welsh rabbit, fond of toasted cheese though I am.'

Dermot listened, half amused, half disgusted. How prosaic the whole thing was! And yet, was he not judging foolishly? Everything, after all, was natural—the powers claimed by mediums were natural powers, as yet imperfectly understood. A great surgeon might be wary of indigestion on the eve of a delicate operation. Why not Mrs Thompson?

Chairs were arranged in a circle, lights so that they could conveniently be raised or lowered. Dermot noticed that there was no question of *tests*, or of Sir Alington satisfying himself as to the conditions of the *séance*. No, this business of Mrs Thompson was only a blind. Sir Alington was here for quite another purpose. Claire's mother, Dermot remembered, had died abroad. There had been some mystery about her . . . Hereditary . . .

With a jerk he forced his mind back to the surroundings of the moment.

Everyone took their places, and the lights were turned out, all but a small red-shaded one on a far table.

For a while nothing was heard but the low even breathing of the medium. Gradually it grew more and more stertorous. Then, with a suddenness that made Dermot jump, a loud rap came from the far end of the room. It was repeated from the other side. Then a perfect crescendo of raps was heard. They died away, and a sudden high peal of mocking laughter rang through the room. Then silence, broken by a voice utterly unlike that of Mrs Thompson, a high-pitched quaintly inflected voice.

'I am here, gentlemen,' it said. 'Yess, I am here. You wish to ask me things?'

'Who are you? Shiromako?'

'Yess. I Shiromako. I pass over long time ago. I work. I very happy.'

Further details of Shiromako's life followed. It was all very flat and uninteresting, and Dermot had heard it often before. Everyone was happy, very happy. Messages were given from vaguely described relatives, the description being so loosely worded as to fit almost any contingency. An elderly lady, the mother of someone present, held the floor for some time, imparting copy book maxims with an air of refreshing novelty hardly borne out by her subject matter.

'Someone else want to get through now,' announced Shiromako. 'Got a very important message for one of the gentlemen.'

There was a pause, and then a new voice spoke, prefacing its remark with an evil demoniacal chuckle.

'Ha, ha! Ha, ha, ha! Better not go home. Better not go home. Take my advice.'

'Who are you speaking to?' asked Trent.

'One of you three. I shouldn't go home if I were him. Danger! Blood! Not very much blood—quite enough. No, don't go home.' The voice grew fainter. *Don't go home!*

It died away completely. Dermot felt his blood tingling. He was convinced that the warning was meant for him. Somehow or other, there was danger abroad tonight.

There was a sigh from the medium, and then a groan. She was coming round. The lights were turned on, and presently she sat upright, her eyes blinking a little.

'Go off well, my dear? I hope so.'

'Very good indeed, thank you, Mrs Thompson.'

'Shiromako, I suppose?'

'Yes, and others.'

Mrs Thompson yawned.

'I'm dead beat. Absolutely down and out. Does fairly take it out of you. Well, I'm glad it was a success. I was a bit afraid it mightn't be—afraid something disagreeable might happen. There's a queer feel about this room tonight.'

She glanced over each ample shoulder in turn, and then shrugged them uncomfortably.

'I don't like it,' she said. 'Any sudden deaths among any of you people lately?'

'What do you mean—among us?'

'Near relatives—dear friends? No? Well, if I wanted to be melodramatic, I'd say there was death in the air tonight. There, it's only my nonsense. Goodbye, Mrs Trent. I'm glad you've been satisfied.'

Mrs Thompson in her magenta velvet gown went out.

'I hope you've been interested, Sir Alington,' murmured Claire.

'A most interesting evening, my dear lady. Many thanks for the opportunity. Let me wish you good night. You are all going to a dance, are you not?'

'Won't you come with us?'

'No, no. I make it a rule to be in bed by half past eleven. Good night. Good night, Mrs Eversleigh. Ah! Dermot, I rather want to have a word with you. Can you come with me now? You can rejoin the others at the Grafton Galleries.'

'Certainly, uncle. I'll meet you there then, Trent.'

Very few words were exchanged between uncle and

nephew during the short drive to Harley Street. Sir Alington made a semi-apology for dragging Dermot away, and assured him that he would only detain him a few minutes.

'Shall I keep the car for you, my boy?' he asked, as they alighted.

'Oh, don't bother, uncle. I'll pick up a taxi.'

'Very good. I don't like to keep Charlson up later than I can help. Good night, Charlson. Now where the devil did I put my key?'

The car glided away as Sir Alington stood on the steps vainly searching his pockets.

'Must have left it in my other coat,' he said at length. 'Ring the bell, will you? Johnson is still up, I dare say.'

The imperturbable Johnson did indeed open the door within sixty seconds.

'Mislaid my key, Johnson,' explained Sir Alington. 'Bring a couple of whiskies and sodas into the library, will you?'

'Very good, Sir Alington.'

The physician strode on into the library and turned on the lights. He motioned to Dermot to close the door behind him after entering.

'I won't keep you long, Dermot, but there's just something I want to say to you. Is it my fancy, or have you a certain—tendresse, shall we say, for Mrs Jack Trent?'

The blood rushed to Dermot's face.

'Jack Trent is my best friend.'

'Pardon me, but that is hardly answering my question. I dare say that you consider my views on divorce and such matters highly puritanical, but I must remind you that you are my only near relative and that you are my heir.'

'There is no question of a divorce,' said Dermot angrily.

'There certainly is not, for a reason which I understand perhaps better than you do. That particular reason I cannot give you now, but I do wish to warn you. Claire Trent is not for you.'

The young man faced his uncle's gaze steadily.

'I do understand—and permit me to say, perhaps better

than you think. I know the reason for your presence at dinner tonight.'

'Eh?' The physician was clearly startled. 'How did you know that?'

'Call it a guess, sir. I am right, am I not, when I say that you were there in your—professional capacity.'

Sir Alington strode up and down.

'You are quite right, Dermot. I could not, of course, have told you so myself, though I am afraid it will soon be common property.'

Dermot's heart contracted.

'You mean that you have—made up your mind?'

'Yes, there is insanity in the family—on the mother's side. A sad case—a very sad case.'

'I can't believe it, sir.'

'I dare say not. To the layman there are few if any signs apparent.'

'And to the expert?'

'The evidence is conclusive. In such a case, the patient must be placed under restraint as soon as possible.'

'My God!' breathed Dermot. 'But you can't shut anyone up for nothing at all.'

'My dear Dermot! Cases are only placed under restraint when their being at large would result in danger to the community.

'Danger?'

'Very grave danger. In all probability a peculiar form of homicidal mania. It was so in the mother's case.'

Dermot turned away with a groan, burying his face in his hands. Claire—white and golden Claire!

'In the circumstances,' continued the physician comfortably, 'I felt it incumbent on me to warn you.'

'Claire,' murmured Dermot. 'My poor Claire.'

'Yes, indeed, we must all pity her.'

Suddenly Dermot raised his head.

'I don't believe it.'

'What?'

'I say I don't believe it. Doctors make mistakes. Everyone knows that. And they're always keen on their own speciality.'

'My dear Dermot,' cried Sir Alington angrily.

'I tell you I don't believe it—and anyway, even if it is so, I don't care. I love Claire. If she will come with me, I shall take her away—far away—out of the reach of meddling physicians. I shall guard her, care for her, shelter her with my love.'

'You will do nothing of the sort. Are you mad?'

Dermot laughed scornfully.

'*You* would say so, I dare say.'

'Understand me, Dermot.' Sir Alington's face was red with suppressed passion. 'If you do this thing—this shameful thing—it is the end. I shall withdraw the allowance I am now making you, and I shall make a new will leaving all I possess to various hospitals.'

'Do as you please with your damned money,' said Dermot in a low voice. 'I shall have the woman I love.'

'A woman who—'

'Say a word against her, and, by God! I'll kill you!' cried Dermot.

A slight clink of glasses made them both swing round. Unheard by them in the heat of their argument, Johnson had entered with a tray of glasses. His face was the imperturbable one of the good servant, but Dermot wondered how much he had overheard.

'That'll do, Johnson,' said Sir Alington curtly. 'You can go to bed.'

'Thank you, sir. Good night, sir.'

Johnson withdrew.

The two men looked at each other. The momentary interruption had calmed the storm.

'Uncle,' said Dermot. 'I shouldn't have spoken to you as I did. I can quite see that from your point of view you are perfectly right. But I have loved Claire Trent for a long time. The fact that Jack Trent is my best friend has hitherto stood in the way of my ever speaking of love to Claire herself. But

in these circumstances that fact no longer counts. The idea
that any monetary conditions can deter me is absurd. I think
we've both said all there is to be said. Good night.'

'Dermot—'

'It is really no good arguing further. Good night, Uncle
Alington. I'm sorry, but there it is.'

He went out quickly, shutting the door behind him. The
hall was in darkness. He passed through it, opened the front
door and emerged into the street, banging the door behind
him.

A taxi had just deposited a fare at a house farther along
the street and Dermot hailed it, and drove to the Grafton
Galleries.

In the door of the ballroom he stood for a minute bewildered, his head spinning. The raucous jazz music, the smiling
women—it was as though he had stepped into another world.

Had he dreamt it all? Impossible that that grim conversation with his uncle should have really taken place. There
was Claire floating past, like a lily in her white and silver
gown that fitted sheathlike to her slenderness. She smiled
at him, her face calm and serene. Surely it was all a dream.

The dance had stopped. Presently she was near him,
smiling up into his face. As in a dream he asked her to
dance. She was in his arms now, the raucous melodies had
begun again.

He felt her flag a little.

'Tired? Do you want to stop?'

'If you don't mind. Can we go somewhere where we can
talk? There is something I want to say to you.'

Not a dream. He came back to earth with a bump. Could
he ever have thought her face calm and serene? It was
haunted with anxiety, with dread. How much did she know?

He found a quiet corner, and they sat down side by side.

'Well,' he said, assuming a lightness he did not feel. 'You
said you had something you wanted to say to me?'

'Yes.' Her eyes were cast down. She was playing nervously
with the tassel of her gown. 'It's difficult—rather.'

'Tell me, Claire.'

'It's just this. I want you to—to go away for a time.'

He was astonished. Whatever he had expected, it was not this.

'You want me to go away? Why?'

'It's best to be honest, isn't it? I—I know that you are a—a gentleman and my friend. I want you to go away because I—I have let myself get fond of you.'

'Claire.'

Her words left him dumb—tongue-tied.

'Please do not think that I am conceited enough to fancy that you—that you would ever be likely to fall in love with me. It is only that—I am not very happy—and—oh! I would rather you went away.'

'Claire, don't you know that I have cared—cared damnably— ever since I met you?'

She lifted startled eyes to his face.

'You cared? You have cared a long time?'

'Since the beginning.'

'Oh!' she cried. 'Why didn't you tell me? Then? When I could have come to you! Why tell me now when it's too late. No, I'm mad—I don't know what I'm saying. I could never have come to you.'

'Claire, what did you mean when you said "now that it's too late?" Is it—is it because of my uncle? What he knows? What he thinks?'

She nodded dumbly, the tears running down her face.

'Listen, Claire, you're not to believe all that. You're not to think about it. Instead you will come away with me. We'll go to the South Seas, to islands like green jewels. You will be happy there, and I will look after you—keep you safe for always.'

His arms went round her. He drew her to him, felt her tremble at his touch. Then suddenly she wrenched herself free.

'Oh, no, please. Can't you see? I couldn't now. It would be ugly—ugly—ugly. All along I've wanted to be good—and now—it would be ugly as well.'

He hesitated, baffled by her words. She looked at him appealingly.

'Please,' she said. 'I want to be good . . .'

Without a word, Dermot got up and left her. For the moment he was touched and racked by her words beyond argument. He went for his hat and coat, running into Trent as he did so.

'Hallo, Dermot, you're off early.'

'Yes, I'm not in the mood for dancing tonight.'

'It's a rotten night,' said Trent gloomily. 'But you haven't got my worries.'

Dermot had a sudden panic that Trent might be going to confide in him. Not that—anything but that!

'Well, so long,' he said hurriedly. 'I'm off home.'

'Home, eh? What about the warning of the spirits?'

'I'll risk that. Good night, Jack.'

Dermot's flat was not far away. He walked there, feeling the need of the cool night air to calm his fevered brain.

He let himself in with his key and switched on the light in the bedroom.

And all at once, for the second time that night, the feeling that he had designated by the title of the Red Signal surged over him. So overpowering was it that for the moment it swept even Claire from his mind.

Danger! He was in danger. At this very moment, in this very room, he was in danger.

He tried in vain to ridicule himself free of the fear. Perhaps his efforts were secretly half-hearted. So far, the Red Signal had given him timely warning which had enabled him to avoid disaster. Smiling a little at his own superstition, he made a careful tour of the flat. It was possible that some malefactor had got in and was lying concealed there. But his search revealed nothing. His man Milson, was away, and the flat was absolutely empty.

He returned to his bedroom and undressed slowly, frowning to himself. The sense of danger was acute as ever. He went to a drawer to get out a handkerchief, and suddenly stood stock still. There was an unfamiliar lump in the middle of the drawer—something hard.

His quick nervous fingers tore aside the handkerchiefs and took out the object concealed beneath them. It was a revolver.

With the utmost astonishment Dermot examined it keenly. It was of a somewhat unfamiliar pattern, and one shot had been fired from it lately. Beyond that, he could make nothing of it. Someone had placed it in that drawer that very evening. It had not been there when he dressed for dinner—he was sure of that.

He was about to replace it in the drawer, when he was startled by a bell ringing. It rang again and again, sounding unusually loud in the quietness of the empty flat.

Who could it be coming to the front door at this hour? And only one answer came to the question—an answer instinctive and persistent.

'Danger—danger—danger . . .'

Led by some instinct for which he did not account, Dermot switched off his light, slipped on an overcoat that lay across a chair, and opened the hall door.

Two men stood outside. Beyond them Dermot caught sight of a blue uniform. A policeman!

'Mr West?' asked the foremost of the two men.

It seemed to Dermot that ages elapsed before he answered. In reality it was only a few seconds before he replied in a very fair imitation of his man's expressionless voice:

'Mr West hasn't come in yet. What do you want with him at this time of night?'

'Hasn't come in yet, eh? Very well, then, I think we'd better come in and wait for him.'

'No, you don't.'

'See here, my man, my name is Inspector Verall of Scotland Yard, and I've got a warrant for the arrest of your master. You can see it if you like.'

Dermot perused the proffered paper, or pretended to do so, asking in a dazed voice:

'What for? What's he done?'

'Murder. Sir Alington West of Harley Street.'

His brain in a whirl, Dermot fell back before his redoubtable visitors. He went into the sitting-room and switched on the light. The inspector followed him.

'Have a search round,' he directed the other man. Then he turned to Dermot.

'You stay here, my man. No slipping off to warn your master. What's your name, by the way?'

'Milson, sir.'

'What time do you expect your master in, Milson?'

'I don't know, sir, he was going to a dance, I believe. At the Grafton Galleries.'

'He left there just under an hour ago. Sure he's not been back here?'

'I don't think so, sir. I fancy I should have heard him come in.'

At this moment the second man came in from the adjoining room. In his hand he carried the revolver. He took it across to the inspector in some excitement. An expression of satisfaction flitted across the latter's face.

'That settles it,' he remarked. 'Must have slipped in and out without your hearing him. He's hooked it by now. I'd better be off. Cawley, you stay here, in case he should come back again, and you keep an eye on this fellow. He may know more about his master than he pretends.'

The inspector bustled off. Dermot endeavoured to get at the details of the affair from Cawley, who was quite ready to be talkative.

'Pretty clear case,' he vouchsafed. 'The murder was discovered almost immediately. Johnson, the manservant, had only just gone up to bed when he fancied he heard a shot, and came down again. Found Sir Alington dead, shot through the heart. He rang us up at once and we came along and heard his story.'

'Which made it a pretty clear case?' ventured Dermot.

'Absolutely. This young West came in with his uncle and

they were quarrelling when Johnson brought in the drinks. The old boy was threatening to make a new will, and your master was talking about shooting him. Not five minutes later the shot was heard. Oh! yes, clear enough. Silly young fool.'

Clear enough indeed. Dermot's heart sank as he realized the overwhelming nature of the evidence against him. Danger indeed—horrible danger! And no way out save that of flight. He set his wits to work. Presently he suggested making a cup of tea. Cawley assented readily enough. He had already searched the flat and knew there was no back entrance.

Dermot was permitted to depart to the kitchen. Once there he put the kettle on, and chinked cups and saucers industriously. Then he stole swiftly to the window and lifted the sash. The flat was on the second floor, and outside the window was a small wire lift used by tradesmen which ran up and down on its steel cable.

Like a flash Dermot was outside the window and swinging himself down the wire rope. It cut into his hands, making them bleed, but he went on desperately.

A few minutes later he was emerging cautiously from the back of the block. Turning the corner, he cannoned into a figure standing by the sidewalk. To his utter amazement he recognized Jack Trent. Trent was fully alive to the perils of the situation.

'My God! Dermot! Quick, don't hang about here.'

Taking him by the arm, he led him down a by-street, then down another. A lonely taxi was sighted and hailed and they jumped in, Trent giving the man his own address.

'Safest place for the moment. There we can decide what to do next to put those fools off the track. I came round here hoping to be able to warn you before the police got here, but I was too late.'

'I didn't even know that you had heard of it. Jack, you don't believe—'

'Of course not, old fellow, not for one minute. I know

you far too well. All the same, it's a nasty business for you. They came round asking questions—what time you got to the Grafton Galleries, when you left, etc. Dermot, who could have done the old boy in?'

'I can't imagine. Whoever did it put the revolver in my drawer, I suppose. Must have been watching us pretty closely.'

'That *séance* business was damned funny. *"Don't go home."* Meant for poor old West. He did go home, and got shot.'

'It applies to me to,' said Dermot. 'I went home and found a planted revolver and a police inspector.'

'Well, I hope it doesn't get me too,' said Trent. 'Here we are.'

He paid the taxi, opened the door with his latch-key, and guided Dermot up the dark stairs to his den, which was a small room on the first floor.

He threw open the door and Dermot walked in, whilst Trent switched on the light, and then came to join him.

'Pretty safe here for the time being,' he remarked. 'Now we can get our heads together and decide what is best to be done.'

'I've made a fool of myself,' said Dermot suddenly. 'I ought to have faced it out. I see more clearly now. The whole thing's a plot. What the devil are you laughing at?'

For Trent was leaning back in his chair, shaking with unrestrained mirth. There was something horrible in the sound—something horrible, too, about the man altogether. There was a curious light in his eyes.

'A damned clever plot,' he gasped out. 'Dermot, my boy, you're done for.'

He drew the telephone towards him.

'What are you going to do?' asked Dermot.

'Ring up Scotland Yard. Tell 'em their bird's here—safe under lock and key. Yes, I locked the door when I came in and the key's in my pocket. No good looking at that other door behind me. That leads into Claire's room, and she always locks it on her side. She's afraid of me, you know.

Been afraid of me a long time. She always knows when I'm thinking about that knife—a long sharp knife. No, you don't—'

Dermot had been about to make a rush at him, but the other had suddenly produced an ugly-looking revolver.

'That's the second of them,' chuckled Trent. 'I put the first of them in your drawer—after shooting old West with it—What are you looking at over my head? That door? It's no use, even if Claire was to open it—and she might to *you*—I'd shoot you before you got there. Not in the heart—not to kill, just wing you, so that you couldn't get away. I'm a jolly good shot, you know. I saved your life once. More fool I. No, no, I want you hanged—yes, hanged. It isn't you I want the knife for. It's Claire—pretty Claire, so white and soft. Old West knew. That's what he was here for tonight, to see if I was mad or not. He wanted to shut me up—so that I shouldn't get Claire with the knife. I was very cunning. I took his latchkey and yours too. I slipped away from the dance as soon as I got there. I saw you come out from his house, and I went in. I shot him and came away at once. Then I went to your place and left the revolver. I was at the Grafton Galleries again almost as soon as you were, and I put the latch-key back in your coat pocket when I was saying good night to you. I don't mind telling you all this. There's no one else to hear, and when you're being hanged I'd like you to know I did it . . . There's not a loophole of escape. It makes me laugh . . . God, how it makes me laugh! What are you thinking of? What the devil are you looking at?'

'I'm thinking of some words you quoted just now. You'd have done better, Trent, not to come home.'

'What do you mean?'

'Look behind you!' Trent spun round. In the doorway of the communicating room stood Claire—and Inspector Verall . . .

Trent was quick. The revolver spoke just once—and found its mark. He fell forward across the table. The inspector sprang to his side, as Dermot stared at Claire in a dream.

Thoughts flashed through his brain disjointedly. His uncle—their quarrel—the colossal misunderstanding—the divorce laws of England which would never free Claire from an insane husband—'we must all pity her'—the plot between her and Sir Alington which the cunning of Trent had seen through—her cry to him, 'Ugly—ugly—ugly!' Yes, but now—

The inspector straightened up again.

'Dead,' he said vexedly.

'Yes,' Dermot heard himself saying, 'he was always a good shot . . .'

# THE DRESSMAKER'S DOLL

The doll lay in the big velvet-covered chair. There was not much light in the room; the London skies were dark. In the gentle, greyish-green gloom, the sage-green coverings and the curtains and the rugs all blended with each other. The doll blended, too. She lay long and limp and sprawled in her green-velvet clothes and her velvet cap and the painted mask of her face. She was not a doll as children understand dolls. She was the Puppet Doll, the whim of Rich Women, the doll who lolls beside the telephone, or among the cushions of the divan. She sprawled there, eternally limp and yet strangely alive. She looked a decadent product of the twentieth century.

Sybil Fox, hurrying in with some patterns and a sketch, looked at the doll with a faint feeling of surprise and bewilderment. She wondered—but whatever she wondered did not get to the front of her mind. Instead, she thought to herself, 'Now, what's happened to the pattern of the blue velvet? Wherever have I put it? I'm sure I had it here just now.' She went out on the landing and called up to the workroom.

'Elspeth, Elspeth, have you the blue pattern up there? Mrs Fellows-Brown will be here any minute now.'

She went in again, switching on the lights. Again she glanced at the doll. 'Now where on earth—ah, there it is.' She picked the pattern up from where it had fallen from her hand. There was the usual creak outside on the landing

as the elevator came to a halt and in a minute or two Mrs
Fellows-Brown, accompanied by her Pekinese, came puffing
into the room rather like a fussy local train arriving at a
wayside station.

'It's going to pour,' she said, 'simply *pour*!'

She threw off her gloves and a fur. Alicia Coombe came
in. She didn't always come in nowadays, only when special
customers arrived, and Mrs Fellows-Brown was such a
customer.

Elspeth, the forewoman of the workroom, came down
with the frock and Sybil pulled it over Mrs Fellows-Brown's
head.

'There,' she said. 'It really does suit you. It's a lovely
colour, isn't it?'

Alicia Coombe sat back a little in her chair, studying it.

'Yes,' she said, 'I think it's good. Yes, it's definitely a
success.'

Mrs Fellows-Brown turned sideways and looked in the
mirror.

'I must say,' she said, 'your clothes do *do* something to
my behind.'

'You're much thinner than you were three months ago,'
Sybil assured her.

'I'm really not,' said Mrs Fellows-Brown, 'though I must
say I *look* it in this. There's something about the way you
cut, it really does minimize my behind. I almost look as
though I hadn't got one—I mean only the usual kind that
most people have.' She sighed and gingerly smoothed the
troublesome portion of her anatomy. 'It's always been a bit
of a trial to me,' she said. 'Of course, for years I could pull
it in, you know, by sticking out my front. Well, I can't do
that any longer because I've got a stomach now as well as
a behind. And I mean—well, you can't pull it in both ways,
can you?'

Alicia Coombe said, 'You should see some of my customers!'

Mrs Fellows-Brown experimented to and fro.

'A stomach is worse than a behind,' she said. 'It shows

more. Or perhaps you think it does, because, I mean, when you're talking to people you're facing them and that's the moment they can't see your behind but they can notice your stomach. Anyway, I've made it a rule to pull in my stomach and let my behind look after itself.' She craned her neck round still farther, then said suddenly, 'Oh, that doll of yours! She gives me the creeps. How long have you had her?'

Sybil glanced uncertainly at Alicia Coombe, who looked puzzled but vaguely distressed.

'I don't know exactly . . . some time I think—I never *can* remember things. It's awful nowadays—I simply *cannot* remember. Sybil, how long have we had her?'

Sybil said shortly, 'I don't know.'

'Well,' said Mrs Fellows-Brown, 'she gives *me* the creeps. Uncanny! She looks, you know, as though she was watching us all, and perhaps laughing in that velvet sleeve of hers. I'd get rid of her if I were you.' She gave a little shiver, then she plunged once more into dress-making details. Should she or should she not have the sleeves an inch shorter? And what about the length? When all these important points were settled satisfactorily, Mrs Fellows-Brown resumed her own garments and prepared to leave. As she passed the doll, she turned her head again.

'No,' she said, 'I *don't* like that doll. She looks too much as though she *belonged* here. It isn't healthy.'

'Now what did she mean by that?' demanded Sybil, as Mrs Fellows-Brown departed down the stairs.

Before Alicia Coombe could answer, Mrs Fellows-Brown returned, poking her head round the door.

'Good gracious, I forgot all about Fou-Ling. Where are you, ducksie? Well, I never!'

She stared and the other two women stared, too. The Pekinese was sitting by the green-velvet chair, staring up at the limp doll sprawled on it. There was no expression, either of pleasure or resentment, on his small, pop-eyed face. He was merely looking.

'Come along, mum's darling,' said Mrs Fellows-Brown.
Mum's darling paid no attention whatever.

'He gets more disobedient every day,' said Mrs Fellows-Brown, with the air of one cataloguing a virtue. 'Come *on*, Fou-Ling. Dindins. Luffly liver.'

Fou-Ling turned his head about an inch and a half towards his mistress, then with disdain resumed his appraisal of the doll.

'She's certainly made an impression on him,' said Mrs Fellows-Brown. 'I don't think he's ever noticed her before. *I* haven't either. Was she here last time I came?'

The other two women looked at each other. Sybil now had a frown on her face, and Alicia Coombe said, wrinkling up her forehead, 'I told you—I simply can't remember anything nowadays. How long *have* we had her, Sybil?'

'Where did she come from?' demanded Mrs Fellows-Brown. 'Did you buy her?'

'Oh no.' Somehow Alicia Coombe was shocked at the idea. 'Oh *no*. I suppose—I suppose someone gave her to me.' She shook her head. 'Maddening!' she exclaimed. 'Absolutely maddening, when everything goes out of your head the very moment after it's happened.'

'Now don't be stupid, Fou-Ling,' said Mrs Fellows-Brown sharply. 'Come on. I'll have to pick you up.'

She picked him up. Fou-Ling uttered a short bark of agonized protest. They went out of the room with Fou-Ling's pop-eyed face turned over his fluffy shoulder, still staring with enormous attention at the doll on the chair . . .

'That there doll,' said Mrs Groves, 'fair gives me the creeps, it does.'

Mrs Groves was the cleaner. She had just finished a crab-like progress backwards along the floor. Now she was standing up and working slowly round the room with a duster.

'Funny thing,' said Mrs Groves, 'never noticed it really until yesterday. And then it hit me all of a sudden, as you might say.'

'You don't like it?' asked Sybil.

'I tell you, Mrs Fox, it gives me the creeps,' said the cleaning woman. 'It ain't natural, if you know what I mean. All those long hanging legs and the way she's slouched down there and the cunning look she has in her eye. It doesn't look healthy, that's what I say.'

'You've never said anything about her before,' said Sybil.

'I tell you, I never noticed her—not till this morning . . . Of course I know she's been here some time but—' She stopped and a puzzled expression flitted across her face. 'Sort of thing you might dream of at night,' she said, and gathering up various cleaning implements she departed from the fitting-room and walked across the landing to the room on the other side.

Sybil stared at the relaxed doll. An expression of bewilderment was growing on her face. Alicia Coombe entered and Sybil turned sharply.

'Miss Coombe, how long *have* you had this creature?'

'What, the doll? My dear, you know I can't remember things. Yesterday—why, it's too silly!—I was going out to that lecture and I hadn't gone halfway down the street when I suddenly found I couldn't remember where I was going. I thought and I thought. Finally I told myself it *must* be Fortnums. I knew there was something I wanted to get at Fortnums. Well, you won't believe me, it wasn't till I actually got home and was having some tea that I remembered about the lecture. Of course, I've always heard that people go gaga as they get on in life, but it's happening to me much too fast. I've forgotten now where I've put my handbag—and my spectacles, too. Where did I put those spectacles? I had them just now—I was reading something in *The Times*.'

'The spectacles are on the mantelpiece here,' said Sybil, handing them to her. 'How did you get the doll? Who gave her to you?'

'That's a blank, too,' said Alicia Coombe. '*Somebody* gave her to me or sent her to me, I suppose . . . However, she does seem to match the room very well, doesn't she?'

'Rather too well, I think,' said Sybil. 'Funny thing is, *I* can't remember when I first noticed her here.'

'Now don't you get the same way as I am,' Alicia Coombe admonished her. 'After all, you're young still.'

'But really, Miss Coombe, I don't remember. I mean, I looked at her yesterday and thought there was something— well, Mrs Groves is quite right—something creepy about her. And then I thought I'd already thought so, and then I tried to remember when I first thought so, and—well, I just couldn't remember anything! In a way, it was as if I'd never seen her before—only it didn't feel like that. It felt as though she'd been here a long time but I'd only just noticed her.'

'Perhaps she flew in through the window one day on a broomstick,' said Alicia Coombe. 'Anyway, she belongs here now all right.' She looked round. 'You could hardly imagine the room without her, could you?'

'No,' said Sybil, with a slight shiver, 'but I rather wish I could.'

'Could what?'

'Imagine the room without her.'

'Are we all going barmy about this doll?' demanded Alicia Coombe impatiently. 'What's wrong with the poor thing? Looks like a decayed cabbage to me, but perhaps,' she added, 'that's because I haven't got spectacles on.' She put them on her nose and looked firmly at the doll. 'Yes,' she said, 'I see what you mean. She *is* a little creepy . . . Sad-looking but— well, sly and rather determined, too.'

'Funny,' said Sybil, 'Mrs Fellows-Brown taking such a violent dislike to her.'

'She's one who never minds speaking her mind,' said Alicia Coombe.

'But it's odd,' persisted Sybil, 'that this doll should make such an impression on her.'

'Well, people do take dislikes very suddenly sometimes.'

'Perhaps,' said Sybil with a little laugh, 'that doll never *was* here until yesterday . . . Perhaps she just—flew in through the window, as you say, and settled herself here.'

'No,' said Alicia Coombe, 'I'm sure she's been here some time. Perhaps she only became visible yesterday.'

'That's what I feel, too,' said Sybil, 'that she's been here some time . . . but all the same I *don't* remember really seeing her till yesterday.'

'Now, dear,' said Alicia Coombe briskly, 'do stop it. You're making me feel quite peculiar with shivers running up and down my spine. You're not going to work up a great deal of supernatural hoo-hah about that creature, are you?' She picked up the doll, shook it out, rearranged its shoulders, and sat it down again on another chair. Immediately the doll flopped slightly and relaxed.

'It's not a bit lifelike,' said Alicia Coombe, staring at the doll. 'And yet, in a funny way, she does seem alive, doesn't she?'

'Oo, it did give me a turn,' said Mrs Groves, as she went round the showroom, dusting. 'Such a turn as I hardly like to go into the fitting-room any more.'

'What's given you a turn?' demanded Miss Coombe who was sitting at a writing-table in the corner, busy with various accounts. 'This woman,' she added more for her own benefit than that of Mrs Groves, 'thinks she can have two evening dresses, three cocktail dresses, and a suit every year without ever paying me a penny for them! Really, some people!'

'It's that doll,' said Mrs Groves.

'What, our doll again?'

'Yes, sitting up there at the desk, like a human. Oo, it didn't half give me a turn!'

'What are you talking about?'

Alicia Coombe got up, strode across the room, across the landing outside, and into the room opposite—the fitting-room. There was a small Sheraton desk in one corner of it, and there, sitting in a chair drawn up to it, her long floppy arms on the desk, sat the doll.

'Somebody seems to have been having fun,' said Alicia Coombe. 'Fancy sitting her up like that. Really, she looks quite natural.'

Sybil Fox came down the stairs at this moment, carrying a dress that was to be tried on that morning.

'Come here, Sybil. Look at our doll sitting at my private desk and writing letters now.'

The two women looked.

'Really,' said Alicia Coombe, 'it's too ridiculous! I wonder who propped her up there. Did you?'

'No, I didn't,' said Sybil. 'It must have been one of the girls from upstairs.'

'A silly sort of joke, really,' said Alicia Coombe. She picked up the doll from the desk and threw her back on the sofa.

Sybil laid the dress over a chair carefully, then she went out and up the stairs to the workroom.

'You know the doll,' she said, 'the velvet doll in Miss Coombe's room downstairs—in the fitting room?'

The forewoman and three of the girls looked up.

'Yes, miss, of course we know.'

'Who sat her up at the desk this morning for a joke?'

The three girls looked at her, then Elspeth, the forewoman, said, 'Sat her up at the desk? *I* didn't.'

'Nor did I,' said one of the girls. 'Did you, Marlene?' Marlene shook her head.

'This your bit of fun, Elspeth?'

'No, indeed,' said Elspeth, a stern woman who looked as though her mouth should always be filled with pins. 'I've more to do than going about playing with dolls and sitting them up at desks.'

'Look here,' said Sybil, and to her surprise her voice shook slightly. 'It was—it was quite a good joke, only I'd just like to know who did it.'

The three girls bristled.

'We've told you, Mrs Fox. None of us did it, did we, Marlene?'

'I didn't,' said Marlene, 'and if Nellie and Margaret say they didn't, well then, none of us did.'

'You've heard what *I* had to say,' said Elspeth. 'What's this all about anyway, Mrs Fox?'

'Perhaps it was Mrs Groves?' said Marlene.

Sybil shook her head. 'It wouldn't be Mrs Groves. It gave *her* quite a turn.'

'I'll come down and see for myself,' said Elspeth.

'She's not there now,' said Sybil. 'Miss Coombe took her away from the desk and threw her back on the sofa. Well—' she paused—'what I mean is, someone must have stuck her up there in the chair at the writing-desk—thinking it was funny. I suppose. And—and I don't see why they won't say so.'

'I've told you twice, Mrs Fox,' said Margaret. 'I don't see why you should go on accusing us of telling lies. None of us would do a silly thing like that.'

'I'm sorry,' said Sybil, 'I didn't mean to upset you. But— but who else could possibly have done it?'

'Perhaps she got up and walked there herself,' said Marlene, and giggled.

For some reason Sybil didn't like the suggestion.

'Oh, it's all a lot of nonsense, anyway,' she said, and went down the stairs again.

Alicia Coombe was humming quite cheerfully. She looked round the room.

'I've lost my spectacles again,' she said, 'but it doesn't really matter. I don't want to see anything this moment. The trouble is, of course, when you're as blind as I am, that when you have lost your spectacles, unless you've got another pair to put on and find them with, well, then you can't find them because you can't see to find them.'

'I'll look round for you,' said Sybil. 'You had them just now.'

'I went into the other room when you went upstairs. I expect I took them back in there.'

She went across to the other room.

'It's such a bother,' said Alicia Coombe. 'I want to get on with these accounts. How can I if I haven't my spectacles?'

'I'll go up and get your second pair from the bedroom,' said Sybil.

'I haven't got a second pair at present,' said Alicia Coombe.
'Why, what's happened to them?'

'Well, I think I left them yesterday when I was out at lunch. I've rung up there, and I've rung up the two shops I went into, too.'

'Oh, dear,' said Sybil, 'you'll have to get *three* pairs, I suppose.'

'If I had three pairs of spectacles,' said Alicia Coombe, 'I should spend my whole life looking for one or the other of them. I really think it's best to have only *one*. Then you've *got* to look till you find it.'

'Well, they must be somewhere,' said Sybil. 'You haven't been out of these two rooms. They're certainly not here, so you must have laid them down in the fitting-room.'

She went back, walking round, looking quite closely. Finally, as a last idea, she took up the doll from the sofa.

'I've got them,' she called.

'Oh, where were they, Sybil?'

'Under our precious doll. I suppose you must have thrown them down when you put her back on the sofa.'

'I didn't. I'm sure I didn't.'

'Oh,' said Sybil with exasperation. 'Then I suppose the doll took them and was hiding them from you!'

'Really, you know,' said Alicia, looking thoughtfully at the doll, 'I wouldn't put it past her. She looks very intelligent, don't you think, Sybil?'

'I don't think I like her face,' said Sybil. 'She looks as though she knew something that we didn't.'

'You don't think she looks sort of sad and sweet?' said Alicia Coombe pleadingly, but without conviction.

'I don't think she's in the least sweet,' said Sybil.

'No . . . perhaps you're right . . . Oh, well, let's get on with things. Lady Lee will be here in another ten minutes. I just want to get these invoices done and posted.'

'Mrs Fox. Mrs Fox?'

'Yes, Margaret?' said Sybil. 'What is it?'

Sybil was busy leaning over a table, cutting a piece of satin material.

'Oh, Mrs Fox, it's that doll again. I took down the brown dress like you said, and there's that doll sitting up at the desk again. And it wasn't me—it wasn't any of us. Please, Mrs Fox, we really wouldn't do such a thing.'

Sybil's scissors slid a little.

'There,' she said angrily, 'look what you've made me do. Oh, well, it'll be all right, I suppose. Now, what's this about the doll?'

'She's sitting at the desk again.'

Sybil went down and walked into the fitting-room. The doll was sitting at the desk exactly as she had sat there before.

'You're very determined, aren't you?' said Sybil, speaking to the doll.

She picked her up unceremoniously and put her back on the sofa.

'That's your place, my girl,' she said. 'You stay there.'

She walked across to the other room.

'Miss Coombe.'

'Yes, Sybil?'

'Somebody *is* having a game with us, you know. That doll was sitting at the desk again.'

'Who do you think it is?'

'It must be one of those three upstairs,' said Sybil. 'Thinks it's funny, I suppose. Of course they all swear to high heaven it wasn't them.'

'Who do you think it is—Margaret?'

'No, I don't think it's Margaret. She looked quite queer when she came in and told me. I expect it's that giggling Marlene.'

'Anyway, it's a very silly thing to do.'

'Of course it is—idiotic,' said Sybil. 'However,' she added grimly, 'I'm going to put a stop to it.'

'What are you going to do?'

'You'll see,' said Sybil.

That night when she left, she locked the fitting-room from the outside.

'I'm locking this door,' she said, 'and I'm taking the key with me.'

'Oh, I see,' said Alicia Coombe, with a faint air of amusement. 'You're beginning to think it's me, are you? You think I'm so absent-minded that I go in there and think I'll write at the desk, but instead I pick the doll up and put her there to write for me. Is that the idea? And then I forget all about it?'

'Well, it's a possibility,' Sybil admitted. 'Anyway, I'm going to be quite sure that no silly practical joke is played tonight.'

The following morning, her lips set grimly, the first thing Sybil did on arrival was to unlock the door of the fitting-room and march in. Mrs Groves, with an aggrieved expression and mop and duster in hand, had been waiting on the landing.

'Now we'll see!' said Sybil.

Then she drew back with a slight gasp.

The doll was sitting at the desk.

'Coo!' said Mrs Groves behind her. 'It's uncanny! That's what it is. Oh, there, Mrs Fox, you look quite pale, as though you've come over queer. You need a little drop of something. Has Miss Coombe got a drop upstairs, do you know?'

'I'm quite all right,' said Sybil.

She walked over to the doll, lifted her carefully, and crossed the room with her.

'Somebody's been playing a trick on you again,' said Mrs Groves.

'I don't see how they could have played a trick on me this time,' said Sybil slowly. 'I locked that door last night. You know yourself that no one could get in.'

'Somebody's got another key, maybe,' said Mrs Groves helpfully.

'I don't think so,' said Sybil. 'We've never bothered to lock this door before. It's one of those old-fashioned keys and there's only one of them.'

'Perhaps the other key fits it—the one to the door opposite.'

In due course they tried all the keys in the shop, but none fitted the door of the fitting-room.

'It *is* odd, Miss Coombe,' said Sybil later, as they were having lunch together.

Alicia Coombe was looking rather pleased.

'My dear,' she said. 'I think it's simply extraordinary. I think we ought to write to the psychical research people about it. You know, they might send an investigator—a medium or someone—to see if there's anything peculiar about the room.'

'You don't seem to mind at all,' said Sybil.

'Well, I rather enjoy it in a way,' said Alicia Coombe. 'I mean, at my age, it's rather fun when things happen! All the same—no,' she added thoughtfully. 'I don't think I do quite like it. I mean, that doll's getting rather above herself, isn't she?'

On that evening Sybil and Alicia Coombe locked the door once more on the outside.

'I still think,' said Sybil, 'that somebody might be playing a practical joke, though, really, I don't see why . . .'

'Do you think she'll be at the desk again tomorrow morning?' demanded Alicia.

'Yes,' said Sybil, 'I do.'

But they were wrong. The doll was not at the desk. Instead, she was on the window sill, looking out into the street. And again there was an extraordinary naturalness about her position.

'It's all frightfully silly, isn't it?' said Alicia Coombe, as they were snatching a quick cup of tea that afternoon. By common consent they were not having it in the fitting-room, as they usually did, but in Alicia Coombe's own room opposite.

'Silly in what way?'

'Well, I mean, there's nothing you can get hold of. Just a doll that's always in a different place.'

As day followed day it seemed a more and more apt

observation. It was not only at night that the doll now moved. At any moment when they came into the fitting-room, after they had been absent even a few minutes, they might find the doll in a different place. They could have left her on the sofa and find her on a chair. Then she'd be on a different chair. Sometimes she'd be in the window seat, sometimes at the desk again.

'She just moves about as she likes,' said Alicia Coombe. 'And I think, Sybil, I *think* it's amusing her.'

The two women stood looking down at the inert sprawling figure in its limp, soft velvet, with its painted silk face.

'Some old bits of velvet and silk and a lick of paint, that's all it is,' said Alicia Coombe. Her voice was strained. 'I suppose, you know, we could—er—we could dispose of her.'

'What do you mean, dispose of her?' asked Sybil. Her voice sounded almost shocked.

'Well,' said Alicia Coombe, 'we could put her in the fire, if there was a fire. Burn her, I mean, like a witch . . . Or of course,' she added matter-of-factly, 'we could just put her in the dustbin.'

'I don't think that would do,' said Sybil. 'Somebody would probably take her out of the dustbin and bring her back to us.'

'Or we could send her somewhere,' said Alicia Coombe. 'You know, to one of those societies who are always writing and asking for something—for a sale or a bazaar. I think that's the best idea.'

'I don't know . . .' said Sybil. 'I'd be almost afraid to do that.'

'Afraid?'

'Well, I think she'd come back,' said Sybil.

'You mean, she'd come back *here*?'

'Yes.'

'Like a homing pigeon?'

'Yes, that's what I mean.'

'I suppose we're not going off our heads, are we?' said Alicia Coombe. 'Perhaps I've really gone gaga and perhaps you're just humouring me, is that it?'

'No,' said Sybil. 'But I've got a nasty frightening feeling—a horrid feeling that she's too strong for us.'

'What? That mess of rags?'

'Yes, that horrible limp mess of rags. Because, you see, she's so determined.'

'Determined?'

'To have her own way! I mean, this is *her* room now!'

'Yes,' said Alicia Coombe, looking round, 'it is, isn't it? Of course, it always was, when you come to think of it—the colours and everything . . . I thought she fitted in here, but it's the room that fits her. I must say,' added the dressmaker, with a touch of briskness in her voice, 'it's rather absurd when a doll comes and takes possession of things like this. You know, Mrs Groves won't come in here any longer and clean.'

'Does she say she's frightened of the doll?'

'No. She just makes excuses of some kind or other.' Then Alicia added with a hint of panic, 'What are we going to do, Sybil? It's getting me down, you know. I haven't been able to design anything for weeks.'

'I can't keep my mind on cutting out properly,' Sybil confessed. 'I make all sorts of silly mistakes. Perhaps,' she said uncertainly, 'your idea of writing to the psychical research people might do some good.'

'Just make us look like a couple of fools,' said Alicia Coombe. 'I didn't seriously mean it. No, I suppose we'll just have to go on until—'

'Until what?'

'Oh, I don't know,' said Alicia, and she laughed uncertainly.

On the following day Sybil, when she arrived, found the door of the fitting-room locked.

'Miss Coombe, have you got the key? Did you lock this last night?'

'Yes,' said Alicia Coombe, 'I locked it and it's going to stay locked.'

'What do you mean?'

'I just mean I've given up the room. The doll can have it. We don't need two rooms. We can fit in here.'

'But it's your own private sitting-room.'

'Well, I don't want it any more. I've got a very nice bedroom. I can make a bed-sitting room out of that, can't I?'

'Do you mean you're really not going into that fitting-room ever again?' said Sybil incredulously.

'That's exactly what I mean.'

'But—what about cleaning? It'll get in a terrible state.'

'Let it!' said Alicia Coombe. 'If this place is suffering from some kind of possession by a doll, all right—let her keep possession. And clean the room herself.' And she added, 'She hates us, you know.'

'What do you mean?' said Sybil. 'The doll *hates* us?'

'Yes,' said Alicia. 'Didn't you know? You must have known. You must have seen it when you looked at her.'

'Yes,' said Sybil thoughtfully, 'I suppose I did. I suppose I felt that all along—that she hated us and wanted to get us out of there.'

'She's a malicious little thing,' said Alicia Coombe. 'Anyway, she ought to be satisfied now.'

Things went on rather more peacefully after that. Alicia Coombe announced to her staff that she was giving up the use of the fitting-room for the present—it made too many rooms to dust and clean, she explained.

But it hardly helped her to overhear one of the work girls saying to another on the evening of the same day, 'She really is batty, Miss Coombe is now. I always thought she was a bit queer—the way she lost things and forgot things. But it's really beyond anything now, isn't it? She's got a sort of thing about that doll downstairs.'

'Ooo, you don't think she'll go really bats, do you?' said the other girl. 'That she might knife us or something?'

They passed, chattering, and Alicia sat up indignantly in her chair. Going bats indeed! Then she added ruefully, to herself, 'I suppose, if it wasn't for Sybil, I should think myself that I was going bats. But with me and Sybil and Mrs Groves too, well, it does look as though there was *something* in it. But what I don't see is, how is it going to end?'

Three weeks later, Sybil said to Alicia Coombe, 'We've got to go into that room *sometimes*.'

'Why?'

'Well, I mean, it must be in a filthy state. Moths will be getting into things, and all that. We ought just to dust and sweep it and then lock it up again.'

'I'd much rather keep it shut up and not go back in there,' said Alicia Coombe.

Sybil said, 'Really, you know, you're even more superstitious than I am.'

'I suppose I am,' said Alicia Coombe. 'I was much more ready to believe in all this than you were, but to begin with, you know—I—well, I found it exciting in an odd sort of way. I don't know. I'm just scared, and I'd rather not go into that room again.'

'Well, I want to,' said Sybil, 'and I'm going to.'

'You know what's the matter with you?' said Alicia Coombe. 'You're simply curious, that's all.'

'All right, then I'm curious. I want to see what the doll's done.'

'I still think it's much better to leave her alone,' said Alicia. 'Now we've got out of that room, she's satisfied. You'd better leave her satisfied.' She gave an exasperated sigh. 'What nonsense we are talking!'

'Yes. I know we're talking nonsense, but if you tell me of any way of *not* talking nonsense—come on, now, give me the key.'

'All right, all right.'

'I believe you're afraid I'll let her out or something. I should think she was the kind that could pass through doors or windows.'

Sybil unlocked the door and went in.

'How terribly odd,' she said.

'What's odd?' said Alicia Coombe, peering over her shoulder.

'The room hardly seems dusty at all, does it? You'd think, after being shut up all this time—'

'Yes, it is odd.'

'There she is,' said Sybil.

The doll was on the sofa. She was not lying in her usual limp position. She was sitting upright, a cushion behind her back. She had the air of the mistress of the house, waiting to receive people.

'Well,' said Alicia Coombe, 'she seems at home all right, doesn't she? I almost feel I ought to apologize for coming in.'

'Let's go,' said Sybil.

She backed out, pulling the door to, and locked it again.

The two women gazed at each other.

'I wish I knew,' said Alicia Coombe, 'why it scares us so much . . .'

'My goodness, who wouldn't be scared?'

'Well, I mean, what *happens*, after all? It's nothing really—just a kind of puppet that gets moved around the room. I expect it isn't the puppet itself—it's a poltergeist.'

'Now that *is* a good idea.'

'Yes, but I don't really believe it. I think it's—it's that doll.'

'Are you *sure* you don't know where she really came from?'

'I haven't the faintest idea,' said Alicia. 'And the more I think of it the more I'm perfectly certain that I didn't buy her, and that nobody gave her to me. I think she—well, she just came.'

'Do you think she'll—ever go?'

'Really,' said Alicia, 'I don't see why she should . . . She's got all she wants.'

But it seemed that the doll had not got all she wanted. The next day, when Sybil went into the showroom, she drew in her breath with a sudden gasp. Then she called up the stairs.

'Miss Coombe, Miss Coombe, come down here.'

'What's the matter?'

Alicia Coombe, who had got up late, came down the stairs, hobbling a little precariously for she had rheumatism in her right knee.

'What is the matter with you, Sybil?'

'Look. Look what's happened now.'

They stood in the doorway of the showroom. Sitting on a sofa, sprawled easily over the arm of it, was the doll.

'She's got out,' said Sybil, '*She's got out of that room!* She wants this room as well.'

Alicia Coombe sat down by the door. 'In the end,' she said, 'I suppose she'll want the whole shop.'

'She might,' said Sybil.

'You nasty, sly, malicious brute,' said Alicia, addressing the doll. 'Why do you want to come and pester us so? We don't want you.'

It seemed to her, and to Sybil too, that the doll moved very slightly. It was as though its limbs relaxed still further. A long limp arm was lying on the arm of the sofa and the half-hidden face looked as if it were peering from under the arm. And it was a sly, malicious look.

'Horrible creature,' said Alicia. 'I can't bear it! I can't bear it any longer.'

Suddenly, taking Sybil completely by surprise, she dashed across the room, picked up the doll, ran to the window, opened it, and flung the doll out into the street. There was a gasp and a half cry of fear from Sybil.

'Oh, Alicia, you shouldn't have done that! I'm sure you shouldn't have done that!'

'I had to do something,' said Alicia Coombe. 'I just couldn't stand it any more.'

Sybil joined her at the window. Down below on the pavement the doll lay, loose-limbed, face down.

'You've *killed* her,' said Sybil.

'Don't be absurd . . . How can I kill something that's made of velvet and silk, bits and pieces? It's not real.'

'It's horribly real,' said Sybil.

Alicia caught her breath.

'Good heavens. That child—'

A small ragged girl was standing over the doll on the pavement. She looked up and down the street—a street that

was not unduly crowded at this time of the morning though
there was some automobile traffic; then, as though satisfied,
the child bent, picked up the doll, and ran across the street.

'Stop, stop!' called Alicia.

She turned to Sybil.

'That child mustn't take the doll. She *mustn't*! That doll
is dangerous—it's evil. We've got to stop her.'

It was not they who stopped her. It was the traffic. At
that moment three taxis came down one way and two
tradesmen's vans in the other direction. The child was
marooned on an island in the middle of the road. Sybil
rushed down the stairs, Alicia Coombe following her.
Dodging between a tradesman's van and a private car, Sybil,
with Alicia Coombe directly behind her, arrived on the island
before the child could get through the traffic on the opposite
side.

'You can't take that doll,' said Alicia Coombe. 'Give her
back to me.'

The child looked at her. She was a skinny little girl about
eight years old, with a slight squint. Her face was defiant.

'Why should I give 'er to you?' she said. 'Pitched her out
of the window, you did—I saw you. If you pushed her out of
the window you don't want her, so now she's mine.'

'I'll buy you another doll,' said Alicia frantically. 'We'll go
to a toy shop—anywhere you like—and I'll buy you the best
doll we can find. But give me back this one.'

'Shan't,' said the child.

Her arms went protectingly round the velvet doll.

'You *must* give her back,' said Sybil. 'She isn't yours.'

She stretched out to take the doll from the child and at
that moment the child stamped her foot, turned, and screamed
at them.

'Shan't! Shan't! Shan't! She's my very own. I love her.
*You* don't love her. You hate her. If you didn't hate her you
wouldn't have pushed her out of the window. I love her, I
tell you, and that's what she wants. She *wants* to be loved.'

And then like an eel, sliding through the vehicles, the

child ran across the street, down an alleyway, and out of sight before the two older women could decide to dodge the cars and follow.

'She's gone,' said Alicia.

'She said the doll wanted to be loved,' said Sybil.

'Perhaps,' said Alicia, 'perhaps that's what she wanted all along . . . to be loved . . .'

In the middle of the London traffic the two frightened women stared at each other.

# THE HOUND OF DEATH

It was from William P. Ryan, American newspaper corre-
spondent, that I first heard of the affair. I was dining with
him in London on the eve of his return to New York and
happened to mention that on the morrow I was going down
to Folbridge.

He looked up and said sharply: 'Folbridge, Cornwall?'

Now only about one person in a thousand knows that
there is a Folbridge in Cornwall. They always take it for
granted that the Folbridge, Hampshire, is meant. So Ryan's
knowledge aroused my curiosity.

'Yes,' I said. 'Do you know it?'

He merely replied that he was darned. He then asked if
I happened to know a house called Trearne down there.

My interest increased.

'Very well indeed. In fact, it's to Trearne I'm going. It's
my sister's house.'

'Well,' said William P. Ryan. 'If that doesn't beat the band!'

I suggested that he should cease making cryptic remarks
and explain himself.

'Well,' he said. 'To do that I shall have to go back to an
experience of mine at the beginning of the war.'

I sighed. The events which I am relating took place in
1921. To be reminded of the war was the last thing any man
wanted. We were, thank God, beginning to forget . . .
Besides, William P. Ryan on his war experiences was apt, as
I knew, to be unbelievably long-winded.

But there was no stopping him now.

'At the start of the war, as I dare say you know, I was in Belgium for my paper—moving about some. Well, there's a little village—I'll call it X. A one horse place if there ever was one, but there's quite a big convent there. Nuns in white what do you call 'em—I don't know the name of the order. Anyway, it doesn't matter. Well, this little burgh was right in the way of the German advance. The Uhlans arrived—'

I shifted uneasily. William P. Ryan lifted a hand reassuringly.

'It's all right,' he said. 'This isn't a German atrocity story. It might have been, perhaps, but it isn't. As a matter of fact, the boot's on the other leg. The Huns made for that convent— they got there and the whole thing blew up.'

'Oh!' I said, rather startled.

'Odd business, wasn't it? Of course, off hand, I should say the Huns had been celebrating and had monkeyed round with their own explosives. But it seems they hadn't anything of that kind with them. They weren't the high explosive johnnies. Well, then, I ask you, what should a pack of nuns know about high explosive? Some nuns, I should say!'

'It is odd,' I agreed.

'I was interested in hearing the peasants' account of the matter. They'd got it all cut and dried. According to them it was a slap-up one hundred per cent efficient first-class modern miracle. It seems one of the nuns had got something of a reputation—a budding saint—went into trances and saw visions. And according to them she worked the stunt. She called down the lightning to blast the impious Hun—and it blasted him all right—and everything else within range. A pretty efficient miracle, that!

'I never really got at the truth of the matter—hadn't time. But miracles were all the rage just then—angels at Mons and all that. I wrote up the thing, put in a bit of sob stuff, and pulled the religious stop out well, and sent it to my paper. It went down very well in the States. They were liking that kind of thing just then.

'But (I don't know if you'll understand this) in writing, I got kinder interested. I felt I'd like to know what really had happened. There was nothing to see at the spot itself. Two walls still left standing, and on one of them was a black powder mark that was the exact shape of a great hound. The peasants round about were scared to death of that mark. They called it the Hound of Death and they wouldn't pass that way after dark.

'Superstition's always interesting. I felt I'd like to see the lady who worked the stunt. She hadn't perished, it seemed. She'd gone to England with a batch of other refugees. I took the trouble to trace her. I found she'd been sent to Trearne, Folbridge, Cornwall.'

I nodded.

'My sister took in a lot of Belgian refugees the beginning of the war. About twenty.'

'Well, I always meant, if I had time, to look up the lady. I wanted to hear her own account of the disaster. Then, what with being busy and one thing and another, it slipped my memory. Cornwall's a bit out of the way anyhow. In fact, I'd forgotten the whole thing till your mentioning Folbridge just now brought it back.'

'I must ask my sister,' I said. 'She may have heard something about it. Of course, the Belgians have all been repatriated long ago.'

'Naturally. All the same, in case your sister does know anything I'll be glad if you'd pass it on to me.'

'Of course I will,' I said heartily.

And that was that.

It was the second day after my arrival at Trearne that the story recurred to me. My sister and I were having tea on the terrace.

'Kitty,' I said, 'didn't you have a nun among your Belgians?'

'You don't mean Sister Marie Angelique, do you?'

'Possibly I do,' I said cautiously. 'Tell me about her.'

'Oh! my dear, she was the most uncanny creature. She's still here, you know.'

'What? In the house?'

'No, no, in the village. Dr Rose—you remember Dr Rose?'

I shook my head.

'I remember an old man of about eighty-three.'

'Dr Laird. Oh! he died. Dr Rose has only been here a few years. He's quite young and very keen on new ideas. He took the most enormous interest in Sister Marie Angelique. She has hallucinations and things, you know, and apparently is most frightfully interesting from a medical point of view. Poor thing, she'd nowhere to go—and really was in my opinion quite potty—only impressive, if you know what I mean—well, as I say, she'd nowhere to go, and Dr Rose very kindly fixed her up in the village. I believe he's writing a monograph or whatever it is that doctors write, about her.'

She paused and then said:

'But what do you know about her?'

'I heard a rather curious story.'

I passed on the story as I had received it from Ryan. Kitty was very much interested.

'She looks the sort of person who could blast you—if you know what I mean,' she said.

'I really think,' I said, my curiosity heightened, 'that I must see this young woman.'

'Do. I'd like to know what you think of her. Go and see Dr Rose first. Why not walk down to the village after tea?'

I accepted the suggestion.

I found Dr Rose at home and introduced myself. He seemed a pleasant young man, yet there was something about his personality that rather repelled me. It was too forceful to be altogether agreeable.

The moment I mentioned Sister Marie Angelique he stiffened to attention. He was evidently keenly interested. I gave him Ryan's account of the matter.

'Ah!' he said thoughtfully. 'That explains a great deal.'

He looked up quickly at me and went on.

'The case is really an extraordinarily interesting one. The woman arrived here having evidently suffered some severe mental shock. She was in a state of great mental excitement also. She was given to hallucinations of a most startling character. Her personality is most unusual. Perhaps you would like to come with me and call upon her. She is really well worth seeing.'

I agreed readily.

We set out together. Our objective was a small cottage on the outskirts of the village. Folbridge is a most picturesque place. It lies at the mouth of the river Fol mostly on the east bank, the west bank is too precipitous for building, though a few cottages do cling to the cliffside there. The doctor's own cottage was perched on the extreme edge of the cliff on the west side. From it you looked down on the big waves lashing against the black rocks.

The little cottage to which we were now proceeding lay inland out of sight of the sea.

'The district nurse lives here,' explained Dr Rose. 'I have arranged for Sister Marie Angelique to board with her. It is just as well that she should be under skilled supervision.'

'Is she quite normal in her manner?' I asked curiously.

'You can judge for yourself in a minute,' he replied, smiling.

The district nurse, a dumpy pleasant little body, was just setting out on her bicycle when we arrived.

'Good evening, nurse, how's your patient?' called out the doctor.

'She's much as usual, doctor. Just sitting there with her hands folded and her mind far away. Often enough she'll not answer when I speak to her, though for the matter of that it's little enough English she understands even now.'

Rose nodded, and as the nurse bicycled away, he went up to the cottage door, rapped sharply and entered.

Sister Marie Angelique was lying in a long chair near the window. She turned her head as we entered.

It was a strange face—pale, transparent looking, with enormous eyes. There seemed to be an infinitude of tragedy in those eyes.

'Good evening, my sister,' said the doctor in French.

'Good evening, M. le docteur.'

'Permit me to introduce a friend, Mr Anstruther.'

I bowed and she inclined her head with a faint smile.

'And how are you today?' inquired the doctor, sitting down beside her.

'I am much the same as usual.' She paused and then went on. 'Nothing seems real to me. Are they days that pass—or months—or years? I hardly know. Only my dreams seem real to me.'

'You still dream a lot, then?'

'Always—always—and, you understand?—the dreams seem more real than life.'

'You dream of your own country—of Belgium?'

She shook her head.

'No. I dream of a country that never existed—never. But you know this, M. le docteur. I have told you many times.' She stopped and then said abruptly: 'But perhaps this gentleman is also a doctor—a doctor perhaps for the diseases of the brain?'

'No, no.' Rose said reassuring, but as he smiled I noticed how extraordinarily pointed his canine teeth were, and it occurred to me that there was something wolf-like about the man. He went on:

'I thought you might be interested to meet Mr Anstruther. He knows something of Belgium. He has lately been hearing news of your convent.'

Her eyes turned to me. A faint flush crept into her cheeks.

'It's nothing, really,' I hastened to explain. 'But I was dining the other evening with a friend who was describing the ruined walls of the convent to me.'

'So it was ruined!'

It was a soft exclamation, uttered more to herself than to us. Then looking at me once more she asked hesitatingly:

'Tell me, Monsieur, did your friend say how—in what way—it was ruined?'

'It was blown up,' I said, and added: 'The peasants are afraid to pass that way at night.'

'Why are they afraid?'

'Because of a black mark on a ruined wall. They have a superstitious fear of it.'

She leaned forward.

'Tell me, Monsieur—quick—quick—tell me! What is that mark like?'

'It has the shape of a huge hound,' I answered. 'The peasants call it the Hound of Death.'

'Ah!'

A shrill cry burst from her lips.

'It is true then—it is true. All that I remember is true. It is not some black nightmare. It happened! It happened!'

'What happened, my sister?' asked the doctor in a low voice.

She turned to him eagerly.

'*I remembered*. There on the steps, I remembered. I remembered the way of it. I used the power as we used to use it. I stood on the altar steps and I bade them to come no farther. I told them to depart in peace. They would not listen, they came on although I warned them. And so—' She leaned forward and made a curious gesture. 'And so I loosed the Hound of Death on them . . .'

She lay back on her chair shivering all over, her eyes closed.

The doctor rose, fetched a glass from a cupboard, half-filled it with water, added a drop or two from a little bottle which he produced from his pocket, then took the glass to her.

'Drink this,' he said authoritatively.

She obeyed—mechanically as it seemed. Her eyes looked far away as though they contemplated some inner vision of her own.

'But then it is all true,' she said. 'Everything. The City of the Circles, the People of the Crystal—everything. It is all true.'

'It would seem so,' said Rose.

His voice was low and soothing, clearly designed to encourage and not to disturb her train of thought.

'Tell me about the City,' he said. 'The City of Circles, I think you said?'

She answered absently and mechanically.

'Yes—there were three circles. The first circle for the chosen, the second for the priestesses and the outer circle for the priests.'

'And in the centre?'

She drew her breath sharply and her voice sank to a tone of indescribable awe.

'The House of the Crystal . . .'

As she breathed the words, her right hand went to her forehead and her finger traced some figure there.

Her figure seemed to grow more rigid, her eyes closed, she swayed a little—then suddenly she sat upright with a jerk, as though she had suddenly awakened.

'What is it?' she said confusedly. 'What have I been saying?'

'It is nothing,' said Rose. 'You are tired. You want to rest. We will leave you.'

She seemed a little dazed as we took our departure.

'Well,' said Rose when we were outside. 'What do you think of it?'

He shot a sharp glance sideways at me.

'I suppose her mind must be totally unhinged,' I said slowly.

'It struck you like that?'

'No—as a matter of fact, she was—well, curiously convincing. When listening to her I had the impression that she actually had done what she claimed to do—worked a kind of gigantic miracle. Her belief that she did so seems genuine enough. That is why—'

'That is why you say her mind must be unhinged. Quite

so. But now approach the matter from another angle. Supposing that she did actually work that miracle—supposing that she did, personally, destroy a building and several hundred human beings.'

'By the mere exercise of will?' I said with a smile.

'I should not put it quite like that. You will agree that one person could destroy a multitude by touching a switch which controlled a system of mines.'

'Yes, but that is mechanical.'

'True, that is mechanical, but it is, in essence, the harnessing and controlling of natural forces. The thunder-storm and the power house are, fundamentally, the same thing.'

'Yes, but to control the thunderstorm we have to use mechanical means.'

Rose smiled.

'I am going off at a tangent now. There is a substance called wintergreen. It occurs in nature in vegetable form. It can also be built up by man synthetically and chemically in the laboratory.'

'Well?'

'My point is that there are often two ways of arriving at the same result. Ours is, admittedly, the synthetic way. There might be another. The extraordinary results arrived at by Indian fakirs for instance, cannot be explained away in any easy fashion. The things we call supernatural are not necessarily supernatural at all. An electric flashlight would be supernatural to a savage. The supernatural is only the natural of which the laws are not yet understood.'

'You mean?' I asked, fascinated.

'That I cannot entirely dismiss the possibility that a human being *might* be able to tap some vast destructive force and use it to further his or her ends. The means by which this was accomplished might seem to us supernatural—but would not be so in reality.'

I stared at him.

He laughed.

'It's a speculation, that's all,' he said lightly. 'Tell me, did you notice a gesture she made when she mentioned the House of the Crystal?'

'She put her hand to her forehead.'

'Exactly. And traced a circle there. Very much as a Catholic makes the sign of the cross. Now, I will tell you something rather interesting, Mr Anstruther. The word crystal having occurred so often in my patient's rambling, I tried an experiment. I borrowed a crystal from someone and produced it unexpectedly one day to test my patient's reaction to it.'

'Well?'

'Well, the result was very curious and suggestive. Her whole body stiffened. She stared at it as though unable to believe her eyes. Then she slid to her knees in front of it, murmured a few words—and fainted.'

'What were the few words?'

'Very curious ones. She said: "*The Crystal! Then the Faith still lives!*"'

'Extraordinary!'

'Suggestive, is it not? Now the next curious thing. When she came round from her faint she had forgotten the whole thing. I showed her the crystal and asked her if she knew what it was. She replied that she supposed it was a crystal such as fortune tellers used. I asked her if she had ever seen one before? She replied: "Never, M. le docteur." But I saw a puzzled look in her eyes. "What troubles you, my sister?" I asked. She replied: "Because it is so strange. I have never seen a crystal before and yet—it seems to me that I know it well. There is something—if only I could remember . . ." The effort at memory was obviously so distressing to her that I forbade her to think any more. That was two weeks ago. I have purposely been biding my time. Tomorrow, I shall proceed to a further experiment.'

'With the crystal?'

'With the crystal. I shall get her to gaze into it. I think the result ought to be interesting.'

'What do you expect to get hold of?' I asked curiously.

The words were idle ones but they had an unlooked-for

result. Rose stiffened, flushed, and his manner when he spoke changed insensibly. It was more formal, more professional.

'Light on certain mental disorders imperfectly understood. Sister Marie Angelique is a most interesting study.'

So Rose's interest was purely professional? I wondered.

'Do you mind if I come along too?' I asked.

It may have been my fancy, but I thought he hesitated before he replied. I had a sudden intuition that he did not want me.

'Certainly. I can see no objection.'

He added: 'I suppose you're not going to be down here very long?'

'Only till the day after tomorrow.'

I fancied that the answer pleased him. His brow cleared and he began talking of some recent experiments carried out on guinea pigs.

I met the doctor by appointment the following afternoon, and we went together to Sister Marie Angelique. Today, the doctor was all geniality. He was anxious, I thought, to efface the impression he had made the day before.

'You must not take what I said too seriously,' he observed, laughing. 'I shouldn't like you to believe me a dabbler in occult sciences. The worst of me is I have an infernal weakness for making out a case.'

'Really?'

'Yes, and the more fantastic it is, the better I like it.'

He laughed as a man laughs at an amusing weakness.

When we arrived at the cottage, the district nurse had something she wanted to consult Rose about, so I was left with Sister Marie Angelique.

I saw her scrutinizing me closely. Presently she spoke.

'The good nurse here, she tells me that you are the brother of the kind lady at the big house where I was brought when I came from Belgium?'

'Yes,' I said.

'She was very kind to me. She is good.'

She was silent, as though following out some train of thought. Then she said:

'M. le docteur, he too is a good man?'

I was a little embarrassed.

'Why, yes. I mean—I think so.'

'Ah!' She paused and then said: 'Certainly he has been very kind to me.'

'I'm sure he has.'

She looked up at me sharply.

'Monsieur—you—you who speak to me now—do you believe that I am mad?'

'Why, my sister, such an idea never—'

She shook her head slowly—interrupting my protest.

'Am I mad? I do not know—the things I remember—the things I forget . . .'

She sighed, and at that moment Rose entered the room.

He greeted her cheerily and explained what he wanted her to do.

'Certain people, you see, have a gift for seeing things in a crystal. I fancy you might have such a gift, my sister.'

She looked distressed.

'No, no, I cannot do that. To try to read the future—that is sinful.'

Rose was taken aback. It was the nun's point of view for which he had not allowed. He changed his ground cleverly.

'One should not look into the future. You are quite right. But to look into the past—that is different.'

'The past?'

'Yes—there are many strange things in the past. Flashes come back to one—they are seen for a moment—then gone again. Do not seek to see anything in the crystal since that is not allowed you. Just take it in your hands—so. Look into it—look deep. Yes—deeper—deeper still. You remember, do you not? You remember. You hear me speaking to you. You can answer my questions. Can you not hear me?'

Sister Marie Angelique had taken the crystal as bidden, handling it with a curious reverence. Then, as she gazed into it, her eyes became blank and unseeing, her head drooped. She seemed to sleep.

Gently the doctor took the crystal from her and put it on the table. He raised the corner of her eyelid. Then he came and sat by me.

'We must wait till she wakes. It won't be long, I fancy.'

He was right. At the end of five minutes, Sister Marie Angelique stirred. Her eyes opened dreamily.

'Where am I?'

'You are here—at home. You have had a little sleep. You have dreamt, have you not?'

She nodded.

'Yes, I have dreamt.'

'You have dreamt of the Crystal?'

'Yes.'

'Tell us about it.'

'You will think me mad, M. le docteur. For see you, in my dream, the Crystal was a holy emblem. I even figured to myself a second Christ, a Teacher of the Crystal who died for his faith, his followers hunted down—persecuted . . . But the faith endured.

'The faith endured?'

'Yes—for fifteen thousand full moons—I mean, for fifteen thousand years.'

'How long was a full moon?'

'Thirteen ordinary moons. Yes, it was in the fifteen thousandth full moon—of course, I was a Priestess of the Fifth Sign in the House of the Crystal. It was in the first days of the coming of the Sixth Sign . . .'

Her brows drew together, a look of fear passed over her face.

'Too soon,' she murmured. 'Too soon. A mistake . . . Ah! yes, I remember! The Sixth Sign!'

She half sprang to her feet, then dropped back, passing her hand over her face and murmuring:

'But what am I saying? I am raving. These things never happened.'

'Now don't distress yourself.'

But she was looking at him in anguished perplexity.

'M. le docteur, I do not understand. Why should I have these dreams—these fancies? I was only sixteen when I entered the religious life. I have never travelled. Yet I dream of cities, of strange people, of strange customs. Why?' She pressed both hands to her head.

'Have you ever been hypnotized, my sister? Or been in a state of trance?'

'I have never been hypnotized, M. le docteur. For the other, when at prayer in the chapel, my spirit has often been caught up from my body, and I have been as one dead for many hours. It was undoubtedly a blessed state, the Reverend Mother said—a state of grace. Ah! yes,' she caught her breath. '*I remember, we too called it a state of grace.*'

'I would like to try an experiment, my sister.' Rose spoke in a matter-of-fact voice. 'It may dispel those painful half-recollections. I will ask you to gaze once more in the crystal. I will then say a certain word to you. You will answer with another. We will continue in this way until you become tired. Concentrate your thoughts on the crystal, not upon the words.'

As I once more unwrapped the crystal and gave it into Sister Marie Angelique's hands, I noticed the reverent way her hands touched it. Reposing on the black velvet, it lay between her slim palms. Her wonderful deep eyes gazed into it. There was a short silence, and then the doctor said: '*Hound.*'

Immediately Sister Marie Angelique answered '*Death.*'

I do not propose to give a full account of the experiment. Many unimportant and meaningless words were purposely introduced by the doctor. Other words he repeated several times, sometimes getting the same answer to them, sometimes a different one.

That evening in the doctor's little cottage on the cliffs we discussed the result of the experiment.

He cleared his throat, and drew his note-book closer to him.

'These results are very interesting—very curious. In answer to the words "Sixth Sign", we get variously *Destruction*, *Purple*, *Hound*, *Power*, then again *Destruction*, and finally *Power*. Later, as you may have noticed, I reversed the method, with the following results. In answer to *Destruction*, I get *Hound*; to *Purple*, *Power*; to *Hound*, *Death*, again, and to *Power*, *Hound*. That all holds together, but on a second repetition of *Destruction*, I get *Sea*, which appears utterly irrelevant. To the words "Fifth Sign", I get *Blue*, *Thoughts*, *Bird*, *Blue* again, and finally the rather suggestive phrase *Opening of mind to mind*. From the fact that "Fourth Sign" elicits the word *Yellow*, and later *Light*, and that "First Sign" is answered by *Blood*, I deduce that each Sign had a particular colour, and possibly a particular symbol, that of the Fifth Sign being a *bird*, and that of the Sixth a *hound*. However, I surmise that the Fifth Sign represented what is familiarly known as telepathy—the opening of mind to mind. The Sixth Sign undoubtedly stands for the Power of Destruction.'

'What is the meaning of *Sea*?'

'That I confess I cannot explain. I introduced the word later and got the ordinary answer of *Boat*. To Seventh Sign I got first *Life*, the second time *Love*. To Eighth Sign, I got the answer *None*. I take it therefore that Seven was the sum and number of the signs.'

'But the Seventh was not achieved,' I said on a sudden inspiration. 'Since through the Sixth came *Destruction*!'

'Ah! You think so? But we are taking these—mad ramblings very seriously. They are really only interesting from a medical point of view.'

'Surely they will attract the attention of psychic investigators?'

The doctor's eyes narrowed. 'My dear sir, I have no intention of making them public.'

'Then your interest?'

'Is purely personal. I shall make notes on the case, of course.'

'I see.' But for the first time I felt, like the blind man, that I didn't see at all. I rose to my feet.

'Well, I'll wish you good night, doctor. I'm off to town again tomorrow.'

'Ah!' I fancied there was satisfaction, relief perhaps, behind the exclamation.

'I wish you good luck with your investigations,' I continued lightly. 'Don't loose the Hound of Death on me next time we meet!'

His hand was in mine as I spoke, and I felt the start it gave. He recovered himself quickly. His lips drew back from his long pointed teeth in a smile.

'For a man who loved power, what a power that would be!' he said. 'To hold every human being's life in the hollow of your hand!'

And his smile broadened.

That was the end of my direct connection with the affair.

Later, the doctor's note-book and diary came into my hands. I will reproduce the few scanty entries in it here, though you will understand that it did not really come into my possession until some time afterwards.

> Aug. 5th. Have discovered that by 'the Chosen', Sister M.A. means those who reproduced the race. Apparently they were held in the highest honour, and exalted above the Priesthood. Contrast this with early Christians.

> Aug. 7th. Persuaded Sister M.A. to let me hypnotise her. Succeeded in inducing hypnoptic sleep and trance, but no rapport established.

> Aug. 9th. Have there been civilizations in the past to which ours is as nothing? Strange if it should be so, and I the only man with the clue to it . . .

> Aug. 12th. Sister M.A. not at all amenable to suggestion when hypnotized. Yet state of trance easily induced. Cannot understand it.

> Aug. 13th. Sister M.A. mentioned today that in 'state of grace' the 'gate must be closed, lest another should command the body'. Interesting—but baffling.

*Aug. 18th. So the First Sign is none other than . . . (words erased here) . . . then how many centuries will it take to reach the Sixth? But if there should be a short-cut to Power . . .*

*Aug. 20th. Have arranged for M.A. to come here with Nurse. Have told her it is necessary to keep patient under morphia. Am I mad? Or shall I be the Superman, with the Power of Death in my hands?*

(Here the entries cease.)

It was, I think, on August 29th that I received the letter. It was directed to me, care of my sister-in-law, in a sloping foreign handwriting. I opened it with some curiosity. It ran as follows:

*Cher Monsieur,—I have seen you but twice, but I have felt I could trust you. Whether my dreams are real or not, they have grown clearer of late . . . And, Monsieur, one thing at all events, the Hound of Death is no dream . . . In the days I told you of (whether they are real or not, I do not know) He Who was Guardian of the Crystal revealed the Sixth Sign to the people too soon . . . Evil entered into their hearts. They had the power to slay at will—and they slew without justice— in anger. They were drunk with the lust of Power. When we saw this, We who were yet pure, we knew that once again we should not complete the Circle and come to the Sign of Everlasting Life. He who would have been the next Guardian of the Crystal was bidden to act. That the old might die, and the new, after endless ages, might come again, he loosed the Hound of Death upon the sea (being careful not to close the circle), and the sea rose up in the shape of a Hound and swallowed the land utterly . . .*

*Once before I remembered this— on the altar steps in Belgium . . .*

*The Dr Rose, he is of the Brotherhood. He knows the First Sign, and the form of the Second, though its meaning is hidden to all save a chosen few. He would learn of me the Sixth. I have withstood him so far—but I grow weak. Monsieur, it*

*is not well that a man should come to power before his time.*
*Many centuries must go by ere the world is ready to have the*
*power of death delivered into its hand . . . I beseech of you,*
*Monsieur, you who love goodness and truth, to help me . . .*
*before it is too late.*
    *Your sister in Christ,*
    *Marie Angelique*

I let the paper fall. The solid earth beneath me seemed a
little less solid than usual. Then I began to rally. The poor
woman's belief, genuine enough, had almost affected *me*!
One thing was clear. Dr Rose, in his zeal for a case, was
grossly abusing his professional standing. I would run down
and—

Suddenly I noticed a letter from Kitty amongst my other
correspondence. I tore it open.

*'Such an awful thing has happened,'* I read. *'You remember*
*Dr Rose's little cottage on the cliff? It was swept away by a*
*landslide last night, the doctor and that poor nun, Sister Marie*
*Angelique, were killed. The* debris *on the beach is too awful—*
*all piled up in a fantastic mass—from a distance it looks like*
*a great* hound *. . .'*

The letter dropped from my hand.

The other facts may be coincidence. A Mr Rose, whom I
discovered to be a wealthy relative of the doctor's, died
suddenly that same night—it was said struck by lightning.
As far as was known no thunderstorm had occurred in the
neighbourhood, but one or two people declared they had
heard one peal of thunder. He had an electric burn on him
'of a curious shape'. His will left everything to his nephew,
Dr Rose.

Now, supposing that Dr Rose succeeded in obtaining the
secret of the Sixth Sign from Sister Marie Angelique. I had
always felt him to be an unscrupulous man—he would not
shrink at taking his uncle's life if he were sure it could not

be brought home to him. But one sentence of Sister Marie Angelique's letter rings in my brain . . . 'being careful not to close the Circle . . .' Dr Rose did not exercise that care—was perhaps unaware of the steps to take, or even of the need for them. So the Force he employed returned, completing its circuit . . .

But of course it is all nonsense! Everything can be accounted for quite naturally. That the doctor believed in Sister Marie Angelique's hallucinations merely proves that *his* mind, too, was slightly unbalanced.

Yet sometimes I dream of a continent under the seas where men once lived and attained to a degree of civilization far ahead of ours . . .

Or did Sister Marie Angelique remember *backwards*—as some say is possible—and is this City of the Circles in the future and not in the past?

Nonsense—of course the whole thing was mere hallucination!

# BIBLIOGRAPHY

Agatha Christie's short stories typically (but not always) appeared first in magazines and then in her short story books, which tended to be different collections in the UK and the US. This list attempts to catalogue the first publication of each, and gives alternative story titles when used.

THE LAST SÉANCE
First published in the US as 'The Woman Who Stole a Ghost' in the November 1926 issue of *Ghost Stories,* and in the UK as 'The Stolen Ghost' in issue 87 of *The Sovereign Magazine* in March 1927. Reprinted in *The Hound of Death and Other Stories* (UK, 1933) and *Double Sin and Other Stories* (US, 1961).

IN A GLASS DARKLY
First published in the UK in the December 1934 issue of *Woman's Journal.* Reprinted in *The Regatta Mystery and Other Stories* (US, 1939) and *Miss Marple's Final Cases and Two Other Stories* (UK, 1979).

S.O.S.
First published in the UK in issue 252 of *The Grand Magazine* in February 1926, and in the US in *Ellery Queen's Mystery Magazine* Vol. 10, No. 49, in December 1947. Reprinted in *The Hound of Death and Other Stories* (UK, 1933) and *The Witness for the Prosecution and Other Stories* (US, 1948).

## THE ADVENTURE OF THE EGYPTIAN TOMB
First published in the UK in *The Sketch* Number 1600 on 26 September 1923, and in the US as 'The Egyptian Adventure' in *Blue Book Magazine* Vol. 39, No. 4, in August 1924. Reprinted in *Poirot Investigates* (UK, 1924; US 1925).

## THE FOURTH MAN
First published in the UK in issue 250 of *The Grand Magazine* in December 1925, and in the US in *Ellery Queen's Mystery Magazine* Vol. 10, No. 47, in October 1947. Reprinted in *The Hound of Death and Other Stories* (UK, 1933) and *The Witness for the Prosecution and Other Stories* (US, 1948).

## THE IDOL HOUSE OF ASTARTE
First published in the UK in *Royal Magazine* No. 351 in January 1928, and in the US as 'The Solving Six and the Evil Hour' in *Detective Story Magazine*, Vol. 101, No. 6, on 9 June 1928. Reprinted in *The Thirteen Problems* (UK, 1932) aka *The Tuesday Club Murders* (US, 1933).

## THE GIPSY
First published in *The Hound of Death and Other Stories* (UK, 1933) and *The Golden Ball and Other Stories* (US, 1971).

## PHILOMEL COTTAGE
First published in the UK in issue 237 of *The Grand Magazine* in November 1924. Reprinted in *The Listerdale Mystery and Other Stories* (UK, 1934) and *The Witness for the Prosecution and Other Stories* (US, 1948).

## THE LAMP
First published in *The Hound of Death and Other Stories* (UK, 1933) and *The Golden Ball and Other Stories* (US, 1971).

## THE DREAM
First published in the UK in *Strand Magazine* No. 566 in February 1938, and in the US in *The Saturday Evening Post*

Vol. 210, No. 17, on 23 October 1937. Reprinted in *The Regatta Mystery and Other Stories* (US, 1939) and *The Adventure of the Christmas Pudding and a Selection of Entrées* (UK, 1960).

WIRELESS
First published in the UK in the *Sunday Chronicle Annual* in autumn 1926, and in the US in *Mystery Magazine* on 1 March 1926. Reprinted in *The Hound of Death and Other Stories* (UK, 1933) and as 'Where There's a Will' in *The Witness for the Prosecution and Other Stories* (US, 1948).

THE WIFE OF THE KENITE
First published in Australia in *The Home* magazine in September 1922. Reprinted in *Bodies from the Library* (ed. Tony Medawar, UK, 2018).

THE MYSTERY OF THE BLUE JAR
First published in the UK in issue 233 of *The Grand Magazine* in July 1924 and in the US in *Metropolitan Magazine* the same year. Reprinted in *The Hound of Death and Other Stories* (UK, 1933) and *The Witness for the Prosecution and Other Stories* (US, 1948).

THE STRANGE CASE OF SIR ARTHUR CARMICHAEL
First published as 'The Strange Case of Sir Andrew Carmichael' in *The Hound of Death and Other Stories* (UK, 1933) and *The Golden Ball and Other Stories* (US, 1971).

THE BLUE GERANIUM
First published in the UK in issue 272 of *The Royal Magazine* in December 1929 and in the US in *Pictorial Review* Vol. 31, No. 5 in February 1930. Reprinted in *The Thirteen Problems* (UK, 1932) aka *The Tuesday Club Murders* (US, 1933).

THE CALL OF WINGS
First published in *The Hound of Death and Other Stories* (UK, 1933) and *The Golden Ball and Other Stories* (US, 1971).

## THE FLOCK OF GERYON
First published in the UK in *Strand Magazine* No. 596 in August 1940, and in the US as 'Weird Monster' in *This Week* on 26 May 1940. Reprinted in *The Labours of Hercules* (UK, 1947) aka *The Labors of Hercules* (US, 1947).

## THE RED SIGNAL
First published in issue 232 of *The Grand Magazine* in June 1924 and in the US in *Ellery Queen's Mystery Magazine* Vol. 9, N. 43, in June 1947. Reprinted in *The Hound of Death and Other Stories* (UK, 1933) and *The Witness for the Prosecution and Other Stories* (US, 1948).

## THE DRESSMAKER'S DOLL
First published in Canada in the *Star Weekly* magazine on 25 October 1958, then in the UK in the December 1958 issue of *Woman's Journal*, and in the US in *Ellery Queen's Mystery Magazine* Vol. 33, No. 6, in June 1959. Reprinted in *Double Sin and Other Stories* (US, 1961) and *Miss Marple's Final Cases and Two Other Stories* (UK, 1979).

## THE HOUND OF DEATH
First published in *The Hound of Death and Other Stories* (UK, 1933) and *The Golden Ball and Other Stories* (US, 1971).